BATTLETECH:

KELL HOUNDS ASCENDANT

BY MICHAEL A. STACKPOLE

BATTLETECH: KELL HOUNDS ASCENDANT
Cover art by Florian Mellies
Design by Matt Heerdt & David Kerber

Published by Catalyst Game Labs,
an imprint of InMediaRes Productions, LLC
7108 S. Pheasant Ridge Drive • Spokane, WA 99224

CONTENTS

**NOT THE WAY THE SMART
MONEY BETS**

CHAPTER ONE

Morgan Kell paused at the head of the gangway leading from the *Leopard*-Class DropShip's side to the spaceport's ferrocrete pad. He opened his arms, expanding his chest, smiling as he breathed in. His eyes closed for a moment, then he nodded. "Smell that, Patrick?"

His brother, not quite as tall or wide, but possessed of the same good looks, black hair, and dark brown eyes, cocked an eyebrow. "Am I sure I want to?"

Morgan hooked an arm around his younger brother's neck. "It's the future."

"Smells like a 'Mech overheated and boiled out two heat sinks."

"Yeah, that too."

Patrick hesitated, and Morgan looked to the gangway's foot. A slender, well-dressed man waited there. He smiled politely, but his foot tapped impatiently.

Morgan smiled. "Wonder what we have here?"

"Trouble." Patrick gave his twenty-four-year-old brother a little shove. "I told you to wait to send messages until we made landfall."

"And waste the week it took getting in from the JumpPoint? No, thank you." Morgan, tall and wolfishly lean, bounded down the ramp. He let the childish joy at doing so light his face, all the while watching the man waiting for them. The man's expression soured, but only slightly and in a pained way that vanished beneath a reluctant smile.

This reaction inclined Morgan to give him a chance. He took one last large step off the gangway, then thrust his hand toward the man. "Morgan Kell, late of the Tenth Skye Rangers."

The man, though much smaller, met his grip solidly and didn't flinch from pressure or eye contact. "Gordon Franck, Colonel Kell. I'm with the Lyran office of Mercenary Relations."

"Must keep you busy if you meet all the mercenaries arriving on Galatea." Morgan pumped his hand three times, then let it go. "Or are we special?"

Franck's smile broadened. "Oh, you're special. Not only are you the Archon's cousin..."

"...By marriage."

"Regardless, we take notice of that. After all, your family owns the Eire BattleMech Company on Arc-Royal, which is rather important to the defense of the nation." Franck pushed his glasses up on his nose and glanced at a small noteputer. "The messages you've been sending while incoming have attracted a lot of attention."

"As we intended."

"Not the attention you want, I'm afraid." Franck stowed the device in his pocket, then offered his hand to Patrick, who had just joined them. "You'd be Lieutenant Colonel Kell. Gordon Franck."

Patrick looked at him for a second, then shook his hand. "Something we can do for you?"

"He's here to see we don't cause trouble, Patrick."

Franck sighed. "Actually, I'm here to take you to see General Volmer."

"'Viper' Volmer?" Patrick glanced at his brother. "Did you know he was here?"

Morgan shrugged. "I think it slipped my mind."

Patrick punched his arm. "You should have told me."

"I'm sure he's forgotten all about that, Patrick." Morgan smiled, and rubbed at his arm. "So, are we walking, Mr. Franck?"

"No, the General sent transport."

Patrick jerked a thumb back at the DropShip. "I'll get our kits and haul them to the hotel, you think? You won't be needing me, will you?"

Franck hesitated, then nodded. "I'll tell the general you had a rough entry. He will want to talk to you, I'm sure; but he was quite insistent about seeing your brother."

Patrick smiled. "Thank you, Mr. Franck."

"You're welcome, but a word. Don't call him Viper out loud...anywhere. Many ears here report back to him."

Patrick nodded, putting a finger to his lips, then headed to the terminal as Morgan followed Franck to the executive VTOL waiting near the DropShip's nose.

The two men climbed into the rear, and the door sealed behind them. The pilot—little more than a pair of eyes in the rearview—eased the craft up and headed away from both the spaceport and the center of Galatean City. They rose above the local vegetation, which grew lush and thick in a circle around the gray city—a monumental feat on so hot and dry a world.

Franck closed the partition between the passenger and pilot's compartments. "I meant what I told your brother. Antagonizing the General is not a good idea."

"But your being here means I already have."

The smaller man nodded. "Galatea is the mercenary world. Every guy who's got a 'Mech that can twitch a myomer fiber comes here hoping he'll get a job. If he's lucky his unit will have the techs who can put his 'Mech back together, and his employer will have enough ammo that he survives his next battle. If he's really lucky, he takes out an enemy 'Mech, salvages parts and uses them, or sells them on the open market. Most mercs would make better money using their 'Mechs to pull a plow, but they won't give up the romance and drama and excitement."

Morgan tugged on the black sleeves of his uniform jacket. "I'm a MechWarrior, Mr. Franck. I've long known the thrill of piloting a 'Mech, and the fear of losing one. I've no desire to be Dispossessed, and I can feel for those who are."

"Yes, but you have no fear of it." Franck held his hands up. "Meaning no disrespect, but you're from a very privileged family. You and your brother both graduated from the Nagelring with stunning marks. You've had your choice of assignments and were even allowed to resign to form this mercenary unit of yours. But what you understand as life isn't what the people you'll be dealing with understand as life."

Morgan's brown eyes tightened. "I beg your pardon. Are you assigning virtue to being poor, or vice to someone who's been lucky enough not to have missed many a meal? If so, this conversation is over."

"That's not what I meant."

"Well, then, let's get to that point."

Franck nodded. "I'll break it down simply for you, Colonel. There are two Galateas. You're staying at the Nova Royale. Nice place. That's where all the big mercenary companies officials stay when they come here to negotiate contracts. Hansen's Roughriders, Twelfth Vegan Rangers, everybody. Even these Wolf's Dragoons we've been hearing about lately have sent a rep. It's a nice choice because it makes your unit look as legitimate as theirs. And I'm not saying that it won't be."

"What are you saying, Mr. Franck?"

"That's the platinum level of Galatea, Colonel. Elegant. Refined, the stuff of holo-dramas and diplomacy. I meant it when I said it's a good choice because all the liaisons you want to speak with will be there. You'll wine and dine them, they'll give you a contract."

Franck turned and pointed to a darker part of the city. Instead of tall towers that were brightly lit, this was a warren of crumbling and dusty warehouses. Here and there, the harsh glare of a welding torch broke the shadows. A 'Mech or two wandered through the city, but only half-armored and limping.

Morgan's guts tightened. They looked like the starving dogs that whimpered and cringed at the fringes of battlefields. It wasn't hard to imagine that the pilots in those machines were just that slender, that wasted away, and that their metal shells reflected both their physical and mental condition.

"So then, you're saying there is this other Galatea. What would you be styling it? Tin Galatea?"

"Rust Galatea." Franck shook his head. "The place has a delicate economy. Sometimes wealth trickles down. A MechWarrior gets lucky and catches a berth in one of the big units. Mostly, as I said before, guys just get by. But your recruiting offers are incredible. You've spawned more dreams than a new dancer at a strip club. There are dozens of mercenaries already painting their 'Mechs black and red. The streets already have bootleg shirts, black torsos, red sleeves with your logo on the chest, and folks are buying them so they'll look right when you interview them."

Morgan blinked. "Now that I hadn't expected."

"I didn't think so. You're not a stupid man, Colonel, but you come in here with money and celebrity and there are lots of people pinning their hopes on joining your unit. A unit that isn't even a one or zero in a database yet. And you can say it's not your fault if their expectations are unreasonable, but letting them down is the least of your problems."

The young mercenary cocked his head. "Meaning?"

Franck sighed heavily. "It's a delicate economy here. Any idea what an arm actuator costs?"

Morgan shrugged. "Depending, fifty to a hundred c-bills per ton of 'Mech."

"It's a quarter to half again as much here, depending if you want salvage or factory new. Salvage will sell to brokers here at ninety percent of what you quoted, so they'll make thirty-five percent if they flip it immediately."

Morgan frowned. He'd seen black market prices fluctuate, and had hoped having a line to a factory would be a way to keep costs down. For the MechWarriors living in the shadows below, the high prices—and they had to be artificially high—meant they'd never get their 'Mechs fixed. And that would only happens if someone was profiting from their remaining here.

"There's another mine to step on, isn't there, Mr. Franck?"

"Haskell Blizzard. Forty-five years ago he came to Galatea, borrowed money from a loan shark, had his 'Mech repossessed for lack of payments. He went to work for the shark, cut him out, cut him up and replaced him. Then he diversified quickly, taking on bookmaking and deftly manipulating the black market, especially in 'Mech parts. While there are other loan sharking and criminal operation on Galatea, they exist with his sufferance and because governments back them. Mister B likes having people in his debt, and he doesn't like loans being paid off. You are making folks believe they can have him out of their lives. It's also an odds-on bet that you won't pay him for the privilege of doing business on his world."

"'His world.'" Morgan laughed aloud. "And what does the General have to say about that?"

"I wouldn't know. If the two of them discuss it, it would be when they get together for family celebrations. The General's son Thomas has married Blizzard's grand-daughter."

"Oh, now that's an ugly thought." Morgan ran a hand over his jaw. "And our offering those contracts is going to make your life tougher, since the General will be grinding on you to grind on us, is that it?"

Franck closed his eyes and nodded. "I know you've come here to realize your dream of owning a mercenary company..."

"No. Let me stop you there."

Franck looked up and adjusted his glasses. "Are you trying to tell me it's not your dream?"

"Mr. Franck, I know it's a common dream. I grew up driving 'Mechs. Rank hath its privileges and all that. I know. I accept that. And being a pilot and fighting and winning glory, yes, I dreamed of that growing up. My brother, too. Just like every single one of the misery-sacks you've described as being out there. But their dreams haven't gone too well. It's because they're too small."

Morgan pressed his hands together and hunched forward. "My cousin was the Archon's husband. I got to see things through his eyes. You don't fight for glory. At the end of the day, killing some-one else isn't glorious. It's brutal. Reducing someone else to ground meat reduces you, too. Sure, we sanitize it because we're destroy-ing their 'Mech, and we like it when a pilot punches out. Fact is, war is nasty. Nothing clean about it, and while 'Mech battles make for great holo-footage, you don't see much about the buildings blown up when someone misses a target, or the little boys who cut through a minefield because they want to go fishing. No glory at all.

"But Arthur had vision. He said there was only one thing worth fighting for: freedom. Seems so simple, but so many miss it. It's out there. Our heroes: Robin Hood, King Arthur, Aleksandr Kerensky, they all fought for freedom. Other people, they fight to deny freedom, to control people. But there's a need for a strong force to be in place to oppose that sort of thing, and the Kell Hounds will be just such a force."

Morgan tapped a knuckle against the window. "We didn't come here to make the dreams of down-on-their-luck mercenaries come true. We're here to build a unit that can make dreams of freedom come true for whole planets, and whole swathes of planets. And mark me, there's going to be wars coming that will prove the need for the Kell Hounds, and a hundred units like them."

Morgan sat back, weariness washing over him. The VTOL banked and a landing light flicked on. He retightened his restraining straps.

Gordon Franck nodded slowly as he did the same. "I understand your vision. I like it. Hell, it's the most sensible thing I've heard suggested since I've been on this rock. You hiring administrators?"

Morgan smiled. "Not quite yet, but I'd always be looking at a friend for such a position. There's an opening for that right now, and so far you're meeting the qualifications."

"I'll be happy to be your friend. I'll do what I can to help you out." Franck shook his head again. "Most folks think you're insane. Half want to rob you, a quarter don't trust you, and the rest figure you need killing just because. Anyone looking to you for salvation will become your enemy when you reject them; and some folks are so sure of rejection, they'll be out to hurt you to postpone the inevitable."

"So, it would be a nest of vipers, then?"

"Sure, and the king viper controls his own militia regiment on world, has a spy network, a police force, and underworld informants and enforcers to help him out."

Morgan let a sly grin steal across his features. "So the smart money is betting against the boys from Arc-Royal?"

"Absolutely." Franck opened his hands as the VTOL settled to the roof of General Volmer's Headquarters. "Your only chance is to get in, operating in total stealth mode, and get out before they realize just how much you've accomplished. Calming the general down would go a long way to getting that done."

"Would it now?"

"It would."

Morgan threw him a wink. "Well then, let's see what happens when I call him Viper to his face, kick him in his dangly bits, and dance a step to whatever tune he happens to moan."

CHAPTER 2

GALAPORT
GALAPORT CITY, GALATEA
LYRAN COMMONWWEALTH
3 OCTOBER 3010

Patrick Kell watched his brother head off, torn between relief and desire to back Morgan up. It wasn't that he didn't believe his brother would be able to handle himself with Viper Volmer or anyone else. That's what always amazed Patrick. No matter the challenge, Morgan rose to it and always managed to do pretty well.

Though there are times... Patrick winced and headed toward the spaceport proper. Morgan did have a propensity for charging in where others might have exercised more caution. It wasn't because Morgan was stupid, either; but that he saw things from a different perspective. Still, his willingness to be confrontational did sometimes make things more difficult than they had to be.

Patrick found their bags and wrestled them outside to where he summoned a hovercab. "Nova Royale, please."

The driver, a smaller man in his mid-thirties, nodded and set the meter. "Red body, black sleeves, nice logo. Don't recognize the uniform, Colonel."

"It's new." Patrick smiled in spite of himself. "The Kell Hounds." It felt really good to say it.

"Then you're the younger brother?" The driver smiled, narrowing the eyes in the mirror. "Lot of excitement around your coming."

"Is that so?" Patrick stared out the window as they drove. The cab merged with traffic heading into the heart of the city. Tall buildings rose up around them, with heavy VTOL traffic flitting between rooftops as if there were people who might never deign to set foot on the ground. It made for an entertaining view. The part of Arc-Royal where Patrick had grown up had been hillier, so buildings never rose as tall as they did here.

"Lots of 'Mech jocks're hoping for a position with you."

Patrick idly held up his noteputer. "Had to buy more memory just to hold all the applications sent up." He glanced at the license hologram hovering over the driver's headrest. "You got one in here, Walter?"

"Not me. ComStar was charging a premium to send the messages to you fast. Anyone foolish enough to waste money with them like as not isn't a candidate for your unit."

"You could be right."

Walter snorted as he turned into the valet station of the Nova Royale. "I've listened to enough discussions to know that some people understand what you're doing. You're both young bucks, full of ideas, and that's good. You want seasoned warriors, but no one so old as to be afraid or stuck in his ways. That's also good. What most folks here don't understand is that you're not looking for the first guy, you're looking for the best guy."

Patrick smiled. "Sure you're not applying for a position?"

The driver smiled. "If I was applying, there'd be no mistaking it, Colonel."

The hovercraft drifted to a halt, then touched down lightly. Liveried porters quickly opened doors and hustled luggage onto a rack. Patrick handed the driver a twenty C-bill note. "Keep the change."

"Thank you, but no." Walter handed him back a ten.

Patrick refused to take it. "Consider yourself a talent scout. If you see any of the 'best men,' send them along."

Walter considered for a moment, then nodded and handed Patrick a card. "If you need a driver, let me know."

"Will do." They shook hands, then Patrick turned and studied the hotel. "Oh, Morgan, what have you gotten us into?"

The Nova Royale was too much, kind of the way maiden aunts are when they make themselves up, or marinate in cologne. The form is right, but it's all overwhelming. Porters swarmed over vehicles. A pair of doormen welcomed him, even though the doors opened automatically. On the other side, where the lobby opened up for twenty floors, another pair of greeters smiled and bid him welcome. Beyond them, even more porters were already scanning luggage tags and loading their gear into an elevator.

"Excuse me. Do I have the pleasure of addressing Colonel Kell?"

Patrick turned, his shiver at the man's formality covered by the motion. "I'm Patrick Kell."

A flicker of disappointment escaped the man's eyes, but he offered his hand nonetheless. "I am Hector Damiceau. I represent various interests here on Galatea."

"Various interests?"

Damiceau smiled cautiously. "Please, if you have a moment..."

"Well, I just arrived and—"

"Colonel, I assure you, it will be time well spent." Damiceau took his left arm by the elbow and guided him toward the lobby bar. "I have been told they stock an excellent assortment of your Irish whiskeys."

Someone's read a file on my brother. Patrick really wanted nothing more than to hit his room and relax. It would have been easy for him to shift his elbow up and drop the guy, and another time, that strategy would have worked for him. The fact that the man had been waiting, however, and wanted to talk with him, provided an excellent opportunity for gathering intelligence.

A gram of good intel is worth a kiloton of firepower.

Patrick settled into a chair opposite the man whose thinning blond hair let light reflect brightly off his scalp. "You have my attention, Mr. Damiceau."

A cute blonde waitress appeared at their table. "What will it be?"

"Two of your finest Irish whiskeys, please." Damiceau ordered with a crispness that implied authority.

She nodded.

Patrick held up a finger. "Do you have Wolf's Paw?"

The girl hesitated. "We do, but he said—"

"I heard him. Wolf's Paw will do. Price doesn't always determine quality."

The girl looked at Damiceau.

The small man opened his hands. "This is a good occasion. We shall have both, try them side-by-side. Money is not a concern."

Patrick nodded. "You're most kind."

"And generous. I can be more so." Damiceau leaned forward and lowered his voice. "I shall be frank with you, Colonel, you and your brother have attracted a great deal of notice here."

"So I've been told."

"A mercenary regiment, a new one, with hints of new equipment and leadership—leadership with ties to the Lyran Commonwealth's throne—this is special. There are those who look forward to it...and those who fear it."

"And your interests would fall where in that range?"

The man smiled and said nothing as the girl delivered the whiskey. The Wolf's Paw was on the darker side of amber, while the expensive stuff was nearly clear. They both lifted the tumblers of Wolf's Paw, clinked glasses and drank.

Damiceau tossed the whiskey back in one swallow, but Patrick merely sipped. Wolf's Paw, which was aged about as long as it took to get it from the distilling coil to the bottle, worked on the throat like molten sandpaper. It wasn't the whiskey Patrick would drink for pleasure, but it reminded him of the dangers of doing business. He let his pool on his tongue for a moment, then swallowed fast.

Damiceau had reddened, but hadn't coughed nor complained. He swallowed hard a second time, then forced a smile. "Memorable."

"Comfortable." Patrick set his glass down. "A shot of that in some warm lemonade and a sore throat will go away. Never really minded getting colds as a child because of it."

"I shall remember that, too." Damiceau's eyes tightened. "To answer your question, my interests fall on both ends. A unit such as you plan on building would be a powerful tool in the right hands. Employed against them, it would be a cause for concern."

That comment narrowed down Damiceau's backers. While the Draconis Combine and Capellan Confederation shared borders with the Lyran Commonwealth, a mercenary unit wouldn't be that much of a concern for them. It would just be one more enemy formation to deal with. The Free Worlds League, on the other hand, had a long border with the Lyran Commonwealth and had enough internal strife among the various member states that a powerful mercenary unit could seriously upset the balance of power. Working for the Commonwealth, or any of the smaller states, it could wreak havoc.

"Can't fault your analysis." Patrick sipped whiskey. "There is an obvious solution."

"There are a number of them, Colonel." Damiceau sampled the expensive whiskey and smiled. "One suggests itself immediately. My employers would pay you and your brother not to form the unit."

"What?"

"Come now, this concept is not foreign to you. You and your brother will profit well beyond anything you will see as mercenaries." Damiceau opened his hands. "I have seen your offers. We have run the numbers. You and your brother will be significantly out of pocket raising this unit. Were you to function for thirty years—five times the average lifespan of a mercenary unit—you will never recoup your money, much less profit. Given the estimated expense of dealing with the threat your unit would constitute, paying you not to fight is the most economical solution to the Kell Hound problem."

Patrick frowned. "I'm not sure how you're doing the math there. If you hire us, you force your enemies to spend the money you thought you'd have to."

"Well, yes, of course. Hiring you would be a solution, but then there is the trust factor."

"Trust factor?"

Damiceau smiled coldly. "Mercenaries can be fickle."

"There's not a ruling House in the Inner Sphere that doesn't hire mercenaries, sir, so I have to ask myself. Are you impugning mercenaries across the board, or just my brother and me because of our ties to the Archon? You're thinking we'd be spies for the LCAF?"

"It has been suggested, Colonel Kell, that this entire ruse of your forming a unit is, in fact, an end-around by Katrina Steiner to form her own personal bodyguard unit, in contravention of the Commonwealth constitution and the wishes of the Estates General."

Patrick stood. "I think the moment's past for our chat."

Damiceau did not look up. "Sit down, Colonel Kell."

"I don't think—"

The small man raised a hand and snapped his fingers. Four large men who had been seated around the bar shifted their chairs around. A fifth, a strongly-built black man with a shaved head, likewise betrayed awareness of the situation.

"Sit down, Colonel. I shall not invite you to do so again."

Patrick sat slowly. "Another solution: kill Morgan and me?"

"It has been discussed, but as a last resort." Damiceau's blue eyes glittered coldly. "Entertaining you as a guest and hoping that your brother would see reason in our previous offer is preferential. We would hate to cause the Archon to mourn again."

"If you think my brother will submit to this sort of action, you are sorely mistaken."

"Then I hope you had a chance to bid him a fond farewell." Damiceau pointed to the whiskey. "Drink it. It will be the last you enjoy for a long time."

"Colonel Kell, I'm sorry for being late. Walter de Mesnil, we'd spoken previously, if you recall."

Patrick's head came up as the cab driver, Walter, bounded up the steps and into the bar. He reached their side in a flash. He offered Patrick his right hand while pressing a slender silver tube to Damiceau's neck with his left. "Yes, it's a needle-stick. Yes, it's loaded. Yes, I know who you are. You can shout any other questions from the curb."

Patrick looked the driver in the eyes. "This would be you applying for a job?"

"I told you that you'd know when I did."

Damiceau twisted away from the needler and stood, tossed off his other whiskey, and straightened his collar. "It would appear our conversation will have to be concluded another time. And there will be another time."

"Best you understand one thing, then. You already know the answers to some of your offers." Patrick gave the man a hard stare. "The Kell Hounds will exist. Fear us, love us, it doesn't matter. You buy our service, you get our service. Everything will be in the contract, and the contract will be honored."

"And the contracts you have with others? The unwritten contracts?"

Patrick smiled. "If you go looking for things that don't exist, you're never going to be satisfied."

"But we will never be taken unawares." Damiceau gave him a curt nod. "Until we meet again." He turned and the quartet of men followed him from the hotel.

Patrick raked fingers back through his hair. "How did you happen to come back?"

"Damiceau is well known here as a bad tipper. The League has him and his office of mercenary procurement on such a tight leash that they use aircabs for travel. I called in after I dropped you off, and the guys who brought that crew here bitched about the cheap fares. Told me to leave them. I figured there might be trouble, so I came back."

"With a needle-stick."

Walter slipped the silver cylinder from his sleeve. "They don't let cabbies carry full-sized needlers, so we improvise."

"Could have blown up in your hand."

"Would have killed him all the same." The driver made the makeshift weapon disappear again. "And just so you know, sir, I do drive a 'Mech. *Blackjack*. Right arm needs some work, and I have the best Tech on the planet working on it. I'm a couple C-bills shy of an actuator, but everything else is tip-top."

"How much is a couple?"

Walter shrugged. "Five, five and a half thousand. I'm saving up, not borrowing like others do. Not getting snowed-under, if you know what I mean."

"I don't, I'm afraid."

"Haskell Blizzard is the local loan shark. Specializes in high interest loans on 'Mechs. You can work it off fighting in a arena or two he has."

"Puts on more damage, so more loans."

"Snowed-under, sir."

"Snowed-under. Got it." Patrick scratched at the back of his neck. "A lot to learn."

"You'll get it, sir." Walter smiled and offered Patrick a memory chip. "Now, about my application."

"You're hired."

"Would there be a signing bonus, sir?"

Patrick laughed. "Yes, we'll get your *Blackjack* back in action for you."

"That's kind of you, sir, but that wasn't what I meant." He nodded toward the table. "There seems to be this whiskey sitting here, sir, and it would be a shame to waste it."

"You're welcome to it, Mr. de Mesnil." Patrick smiled broadly as the man tossed off the expensive drink. "If we drink hard and fight harder, Damiceau and his ilk will be right to fear us. And that's just fine with me."

CHAPTER 3

A leutnant who didn't look much older than Morgan met them at the head of the stairwell. He neither saluted nor offered his hand, instead affecting a sneer that suggested a sense of superiority. Morgan had seen his type before: Teutonic stock and proud of it. That did count for a lot in the Lyran Commonwealth, but growing up in the District of Donegal had put those of Irish extraction on even footing.

"The General expected you sooner. He's not in his office."

Morgan shrugged. "Off to the hotel, then, I'm thinking."

The junior officer cleared his throat. "He's waiting for you in the 'Mechbay. Follow me."

Franck started, but Morgan held him back. The leutnant half-descended the stairs, then stopped and turned when he heard no footfalls on the metal steps. He looked back annoyed. "I said, follow me."

"I heard you, son."

"And?"

"Why exactly am I taking orders from the likes of you?"

The man's expression said what he'd never put into words: *You're just mercenary scum.*

Morgan stepped forward, towering over him. "Let's understand something here. I just left the Tenth Skye Rangers, resigning from a battalion command, so I outranked you, and that was in a line unit, not fetching tea for an officer who couldn't find his feet if you started him looking inside his socks. On top of that, son, the least of the warriors that will be under my command could snap you in two without breaking a sweat. Now, you may never decide to respect us because of that little fact of life, but you better show respect for our abilities, courage, and the fact that long before you ever need to fire a weapon in anger, the enemy will have had to fight through us to get to your pitiful ass."

The man's face froze. "The General is waiting. Please follow me, sir."

Morgan accepted the attitude, knowing it would have to be surgically removed. He followed, staying close, looming over his guide. He glanced over his shoulder, reading a mixture of bemusement and anxiety on Franck's face. He laughed. *I'm going to sorely test your friendship, Mr. Franck, but it will be worth it.*

Their journey to the 'Mechbay was fairly direct, but did lead them past the unit's "I love me" wall of awards and photographs. A portrait of General Volmer appeared central to it all. He stood proudly, his shaved head a contrast to the bushy walrus-like mustache of grey riding his upper lip. A host of medals decorated the breast of his dress uniform and doubtless impressed civilians. To a trained eye, however, the lack of combat awards told the story of a career bureaucrat whose only victories were in political skirmishes.

Which makes him just as dangerous an enemy.

Part of Morgan really wanted to follow Franck's advice. Getting in and out quietly would be good. He could recruit some good warriors, pull them off-planet, and do it quickly before he upset too many people. While he didn't want to play on his connection with the Archon, he could use it to keep Volmer off his back, provided he showed the man some respect and offered him a chance to save face during the Kells' time on the planet.

The problem was that playing it safe would be playing into Volmer's hands. He had a lot of power because he had a combined-arms militia regiment on Galatea, which included a rump battalion of assorted BattleMechs. The planet was, in effect, his own fiefdom. If he dared, he could even have the Kells murdered, pin it on someone, and while the Archon would not be pleased, he'd insulate himself from any serious repercussions.

As Franck had explained, the very act of hiring the mercenaries would upset the planet's economy and very directly affect Volmer's personal economy. This meant, regardless of approach, the Kells were going to be a thorn in Volmer's side. And if Patrick's stories about the general's son were an indicator of the father's temperament, the subtle approach would just cause more problems, because Volmer would see it as weakness. He'd then grind on the Kells just to reinforce their weakness, and Morgan had never had patience for such nonsense.

Still, caution shouldn't be abandoned capriciously. Morgan smiled to himself. *I'll give him a chance, then.*

Meeting the General in the 'Mechbay gave that chance about a minute of extra life. Two rows of giant war machines, ten meters tall, filled the hangar. Most were humanoid, yet with their arms sagging and faceplates dark and empty, their threat seemed diminished. Without a pilot, their lethal potential remained unfulfilled. Massive and terrible, they silently waited to be called to duty.

Technicians moved between them along catwalks and up ladders. Cranes and winches lifted ammo reloads, spare parts, and sheets of armor. Crews on scaffolds spread coats of light blue paint over repairs, while more skilled artists did the fine work, all wearing masks against the fumes.

Volmer's 'Mech lurked in the first bay. A JM6 model, the *Jagermech* had a very distinctive profile. A domed-cockpit capped the torso, while the 'Mech's shoulders rose above it. It had always seemed to Morgan that the 'Mech was cringing. While its array of autocannons and lasers made analysts tout it as a good fire support 'Mech, it couldn't deliver overwhelming destruction at range. Doing that was key to Morgan's conception of 'Mech warfare, so the *Jagermech* was an inferior 'Mech—implying that those who drove them were inferior MechWarriors.

In the hands of a skilled warrior, though, it can put up a bit of a fight. I doubt he's that skilled.

And Volmer, without saying a word, confirmed Morgan's assessment. He'd climbed up onto the scaffolding to supervise the tech painting his name, rank insignia, and kill-markers on the side of the cockpit. Aside from vanity, there was no need for kill-markers. Putting rank insignia on a 'Mech just made it a target; but having those things were a popular conception of how things were supposed to be done in a 'Mech Regiment.

Who does he think he's kidding? Volmer certainly did some live-fire training each year, but the rest of the time it would be pure simulator battles. He hadn't seen combat, so the kills were all virtual. And if you have to count those as victories, well...

Most important of all, Volmer had staged the whole encounter. The man was dressed in his cooling vest, shorts, and boots, as if he'd just brought his 'Mech in from a training run. Wet paint put a lie to that. Volmer didn't even have the presence of mind to look about and note Morgan's presence with surprise. He just glanced down, then stalked his way down the gantry stairs as if he was an avatar of Ares.

He stopped two paces back, so he'd not have to look up at Morgan. "Colonel Kell, welcome to Galatea. Forgive the informality of my dress."

"Nonsense. I've greeted many wearing as much or less."

"I am certain." Volmer opened his arms and turned to take in the 'Mechbay. "I'm very proud of our unit here. We have excellent facilities. If you feel the need for a training run, please let me schedule it. I'd be happy to make a run with you."

Morgan shook his head. "A most kind offer, General, but my brother and me, we didn't bring our 'Mechs." Morgan tossed in the hint of the Donegal accent, and let his grammar slip on purpose.

Volmer cocked an eyebrow. "You came without 'Mechs? I'd hardly have thought vaunted warriors such as the Kell brothers would allow themselves to be Dispossessed."

"Well, General, it's not like a cockpit is a womb now, is it? If a warrior needs to constantly prove he's a hot hand in a 'Mech, he's compensating for something, don't you think?"

"So the common wisdom would lead one to believe, but warriors like us, we know the truth, eh?"

"Often times, sir, it's common wisdom because it's wise, and it's true about people who are common." Morgan waited a half-second, then smiled. "But, you're right. MechWarriors know the truth. Nothing like being tested in battle to tell you the right way of things."

"Quite so." Volmer turned and waved Morgan to walk with him deeper into the 'MechBay. "Come with me. Mr. Franck, Leutnant Saxinger, you'll wait here. This is a conversation between warriors."

Morgan fell into step with Volmer, then shortened his strides to maintain the pace. "Mr. Franck painted me a picture of the situation here, General."

"Did he?"

"The delicate balance, sir."

"Good." Volmer's eyes tightened. "Colonel, for you to be successful here, there are accommodations you need to make. You do realize you're far from Tharkad, yes? The Archon's patronage, while impressive, will avail you little here."

Morgan smiled. "It's a good thing I understand you, General, because if I didn't, I could construe that comment as a threat."

"Not a threat, just an explanation of the realities here. While I would love to be of aid to you and, by extension, the Archon; my primary duty is to the people of Galatea. My job is to maintain order and stability. Anything or anyone which threatens either will be firmly dealt with."

"Got that loud and clear, sir."

"Good." Volmer paused and turned toward Morgan. "So this is how things will work. You can conduct your interviews, draw up lists of your candidates, then submit them to me through Mr. Franck. I'll have my staff review them, and you'll be told who you can take and who you can't take."

"I'm not sure I understand."

"It's that delicate balance, Colonel. Some people perform a valuable function here and we can't do without them. Others, quite frankly, have racked up a rather significant debt and are just looking for an opportunity to run out on it. This will not be permitted."

Morgan frowned. "Begging your pardon, sir, but wouldn't that be a matter between the warriors and the lender, to be dealt with through civil courts?"

Volmer forced a laugh and kept walking. "I thought you said Mr. Franck explained things to you. He might have missed this. Haskell Blizzard is a friend of Galatea, and a supporter of the government. He is rather kind-hearted, and it would be poor repayment to him to let unscrupulous mercenaries take advantage of him. Why should he enrich lawyers collecting what's due him?"

"You have a point, sir."

"I'm glad you agree." Volmer waved a hand at the 'Mechs. "Do you know why I have sleepless nights, Colonel?"

"I couldn't hazard a guess, sir."

"I have a great deal of responsibility here. The entire planet's safety is mine to preserve. I fear the day when strife will visit Galatea. I look at these machines, I see the faces of those who will fight in them and perhaps die in them. My choices will determine if they live or die."

Volmer glanced over at him. "You and I are alike in that, Colonel. We both assume a great deal of responsibility for the people we know and love. My venue is a bit more vast than yours, and yours encompassed within mine. I am trusting you to maintain order so I don't have to."

"So I should keep my people in line and avoid trouble."

"Exactly." Volmer smiled. "I think we understand each other."

Oh, I understand you perfectly, General. Morgan flashed a smile back. "Would you be having any specific ideas on what I could do to ensure we don't have any friction?"

"Follow the guidelines I've laid out. Maintain the balance." Volmer nodded. "Oh, and there is one more thing, on a personal level, that you could do."

"And that is?"

Volmer again stopped and a razor slid into his voice. "There is the matter of my son and your brother."

A chill ran down Morgan's spine. "And how would we resolve that?"

"Rather simply, I think. Your Kell Hounds will need permanent representation on Galatea. You'll make my son a major and give him that position. He will, of course, remain here to attend to business, at a customary salary and expenses."

"I see."

"And your brother will issue a public apology. I'm sure Mr. Franck knows the proper media outlets to facilitate that."

Morgan nodded slowly. "I see."

"But you don't agree, Colonel?"

"I'm just taking an accounting here, General." Morgan ticked points off on his fingers. "I run all my personnel choices past you and, by implication, Haskell Blizzard. I hire your son to stay here and suck money from my unit. I have my brother offer an apology on worldwide media, knowing it will be distributed by ComStar far and wide. And I'm to do all this because while the Archon is a relative and friend, she's not close enough to be helpful in protecting me. Do I have the read of this situation right?"

"I believe we have an understanding."

Morgan dropped the accent. "Let me disabuse you of a misapprehension, General. We could have had an understanding. I could have dealt with running choices by you. I could have hired your son. But asking my brother to lie? No. And knuckling under to your pressure because you think I'd do nothing without Katrina Steiner standing over my shoulder? If that were true, if I even dreamed it was true, I wouldn't be here."

Volmer's expression closed. "Do not thwart me, Colonel Kell. You won't like it."

Morgan stepped closer, dwarfing the garrison commander. "It's men like you that always have an 'or else' tacked on to things, but you don't have the stones to say what 'or else' is. But I know. It's a bluff."

"Think that, and you'll regret it."

"Ha! There you go again." Morgan looked the man in the eye and laughed. "I've got the lay of the land here, General. Haskell Blizzard is the power here. You're just a puppet. You have all these 'Mechs but you don't do anything with them. You're all bark, no bite because your pilots will gladly shoot the Dracs, but they're not turning their guns on the citizens here. And you'd never give that order anyway, since you couldn't paper over things and escape repercussions."

Volmer snarled, revealing yellowed teeth. "You can't speak to me that way."

"But I am, and will do further." Morgan jabbed a finger against Volmer's thick cooling vest. "Here's our understanding. You'll keep your nose out of my affairs. You'll keep your son away from my brother. You'll let us do what we want to do, do it quickly and we'll be out of your way."

Volmer's dark eyes narrowed. "Or else what?"

"Or else I'll bring your command down so quickly that you'll be forgotten before the paint dries on your *Jagermech*. See, no idle threat, unless you don't think I can do it. Fact is, I can, and I will."

"You're making a big mistake."

"Nope, just a little one." Morgan turned and started back toward Franck. "Don't make it into a big one, General. It might hurt me. It will kill you."

Morgan waved Franck along with him, as Saxinger scurried off to attend the sputtering general.

Franck hurried to keep up. "I didn't see you kick him."

"Didn't call him Viper, either, but as good as." Morgan reached out and knocked the general's portrait a centimeter out of plumb as they walked past. "He's going to be trouble because he's too stupid to realize he doesn't need to be. I'll need your help to fix that."

Franck nodded. "Whatever you need."

"Information. It should be easy to get." Morgan smiled. "I want the paint requisition orders for the regiment."

"Paint?"

Morgan merely shrugged, but something glinted in his eyes. "Once I have those," he said, "Viper Volmer loses his fangs and a whole lot more."

CHAPTER 4

NOVA ROYALE HOTEL
GALATEAN CITY, GALATEA
LYRAN COMMONWEALTH
3 OCTOBER 3010

Morgan poured himself another two fingers of Tyrone Rain whiskey, then turned to study the view from the hotel's penthouse. The city stretched out below, becoming canyons flowing with neon light as the night deepened. Energy. Life. He sniffed the whiskey, filling his head with warm vapors, then tasted.

He turned, facing the three men in the suite's sunken living room. His brother sat deep in an overstuffed chair, while Walter de Mesnil and Gordon Franck shared the white leather couch. He offered the bottle. Franck covered his glass, Walter shook his head, and Patrick just sipped slowly, to be polite, as ever.

"Now that we're all up to speed on each others' adventures, it's clear we're going to have to be cautious. Gordon, what threat does Damiceau present? Realistic, or not something we have to worry about?"

Franck frowned. "Realistic, but nothing I'd lose too much sleep over. I'll send a report up the chain—bypassing Volmer's office—and someone on the diplomatic side of things will get his chain yanked. Might take a week or two, but I don't think he'll try anything again."

"Are you sure?" Patrick sat up in the blocky chair. "He sounded like he meant what he said."

"I'm sure he did, but after your brother's meeting with the General, the Kell Hounds are a problem that Haskell Blizzard will deal with. Damiceau doesn't need to spend a kroner to get results. He'll sit back and watch."

Morgan ran a hand over his chin. "How will Blizzard make an approach?"

"He'll watch, he'll wait, he'll pick his time and come in soft. Rebuff him, he can get nasty."

"Begging the Colonel's pardon, there's a solution to both problems." Walter drained his glass and stood. "I'm not the only man who has no love for Blizzard, or stays wary of him. You've got some allies who could help you with security."

"Bodyguards?"

"Something like that." Walter crossed to the sidebar and splashed water into his glass. "I know a guy. He's got some radical ideas that might fit with your unit. I'll send him 'round. Even if you don't bring him in, he and his boys could pull security duty while you're here."

"We'll take a look. Can you get him here tomorrow?"

"Consider it done." Walter headed back to his seat. As he moved past, Patrick smiled and Morgan shot him a nod. *Nice hire.*

Morgan rubbed his eyes. "So the both of you know, Patrick and I do have a strategy. We'll be talking to MechWarriors because, without them, we don't have a unit. But Napoleon said an army marches on its stomach. A 'Mech unit doesn't march unless the tech staff can do its work. We're going to target techs and astechs, getting the best we can as fast as we can. We can offer them a chance to work with great parts, straight from the factory. Getting them in place will make us look better to anyone else we want to bring in. That's where we'll concentrate first. Referrals there will be appreciated."

Franck nodded. "Target or avoid techs with ties to Blizzard?"

"What do you think, Patrick?"

"We going to get out without destroying Blizzard?"

"If we can."

"But you don't think that's possible."

Morgan shook his head. "You really didn't need to ask, did you?"

His brother smiled. "Just wanted to know how committed you were to keeping the peace. If we can't avoid a fight, we might as well get the first punch in, and make it low. Pull his techs, and the 'Mech games operation goes into remission."

"True. And really no reason to delay the inevitable, is there?" Morgan looked over at Franck. "Blizzard have any action tonight?"

"No."

Walter laughed. "None you'd know of, Mr. Franck. He's got some small 'Mech skirmishing going on. Demolition derby out on the north side."

"Will Blizzard be there?"

"Usually is."

"Get us in?"

"Sure."

"Then let's go meet Mr. Blizzard."

Patrick finished his whiskey in a gulp. "Count me out."

Morgan arched an eyebrow. "Gonna get shut-eye?"

"Relax first, then sleep."

Walter smiled. *"Cherchez la femme?"*

The younger Kell stretched. "Could be. I'm getting a shower. See you in the morning—unless you need bail or ransom."

Morgan changed from his uniform to a dark suit, white shirt, black ascot, and an emerald stickpin. In some ways it felt wrong to be out of uniform, since he'd seldom worn civilian clothes in the last decade. Well, except for the time with the Red Corsair. Military life, from the academy on forward, had afforded him the right to wear a uniform. The respect that came with it had been an added benefit, but it would not be so in this situation.

Blizzard was a man of wealth and power who had once been a MechWarrior. He clearly found running a criminal cartel to be superior to that life. Having General Volmer as his personal soldier suggested a certain amount of contempt for warriors—especially those who would stand on principle, citing honor and duty as justifications for what they were doing.

Laughable, especially on a mercenary world where honor and duty were for sale.

If Blizzard was going to take him seriously, Morgan would have to present himself as a businessman, which he really was. A mercenary unit was a business, and those which went bust were the ones that had never been run as a business. It's fine to like what you do for a living, but if the "like" part distracts you from the "making a living" part, you lose it all.

Walter drove and got Morgan and Franck into the venue, which consisted of a huge, rectangular factory with catwalks fifteen meters off the floor. Clear ballistic polymer sheeting shielded the walkways and the seating. Three sides featured triple rows of bench seating, while the fourth had been broken up into a half-dozen private boxes. Concession stands offered food, drink, and souvenirs, with private waitstaff serving the boxes.

The clientele's appearance surprised Morgan for a minute. He'd actually expected to have dressed well above the average, but he fit right in. The audience had been drawn from that platinum level of Galatean society, with impossibly slender women in gowns dripping with jewels draping themselves on the arms of sharply-dressed men. Trophy-wives and boy-toys abounded, as well as a few celebrities. The only people who had eschewed evening dress were the few mercenaries who'd worn their uniforms. The others regarded them much as they might a vagabond peeing in a champagne fountain, making Morgan happy about his choice of attire.

The reason they'd come out became obvious the second the combatants entered the arena from opposite corners. Morgan recognized both humanoid 'Mechs by form alone: a *Commando* and a *Panther*. He'd seen both in combat, and destroyed a couple of each, but these looked unlike any he'd ever faced. The *Panther* had been painted up to look like a tiger, though every manner of corporate logo dotted it, and the number 16 had been painted front, back, on both shoulders and both hips. The *Commando*'s paint job more closely represented a nutcracker, and Morgan found that more disturbing than the tiger-stripes.

The *Commando* surrendered ten tons to its opponent—or would have in the real world—but these two machines had been configured for close-up combat. Ferro-ceramic armor had been replaced with fiberglass. Lasers and particle projection cannons had been powered down, missiles were glorified bottle-rockets and cannons shot vulcanized rubber bullets that could shred fiberglass armor, but never shatter the ballistic shielding.

Which is why we can sit so close. The boom of weapons, the flash of light and the rattle of fiberglass armor against the shielding terrified some and excited others. The battle became a thrill-park ride—combat made theatre. *Which means they will never understand the reality of it.*

The *Commando*, despite being more lightly armored, darted toward the center of the factory floor. Its feet struck sparks from the ferrocrete, scratching long white scars on it. The 'Mech brought both arms up, launching missiles from the right and firing a medium laser with the left. A second flight of missiles, jetting from over its heart, linked the two 'Mechs.

The missiles scattered damage over the *Panther*. Each exploded like a gaudy firework, looking more spectacular than the harm caused. Shards of fiberglass flew, scouring the shielding and glittering on the floor. The laser's incarnadine beam slashed across the *Panther*'s chest, cutting the number sixteen in half.

The *Panther*'s pilot returned fire. The PPC underslung on its right forearm swept an azure beam out, but missed wide. The SRMs shooting from its chest hit hard, chipping armor from the *Commando*'s chest and right flank. Its number nine became a seven as a result of the assault, but neither 'Mech's armor had been breached yet.

Down below odds were shouted, bets were taken. Society doyens studied the combatants with a fascination bordering on the vulgar. Men joked and shouted, women cheered. Spectators hid their faces behind their hands or bumped chests when their champion did well.

The *Panther* circled, stalking, moving more cautiously than Morgan might have were he piloting that 'Mech. The jumpjets that gave it mobility were useless in the arena, but, even without them, the Combine 'Mech kicked thirty percent more damage than its smaller foe.

If the pilot hits.

But he couldn't. The PPC flashed over the crowd like a spotlight. Morgan shied from its harsh light, feeling a fraction of the nova-like heat it would generate on the battlefield. Around him, women tittered at his reaction and men sneered. It didn't matter that they shied from the explosions of errant missiles, this was their element. They made the rules and enforced them.

The *Commando* pilot was as hot as his enemy was cold. SRMs pounded the tiger-striped 'Mech, taking armor off arms and legs and blasting away all but the last of it over the 'Mech's heart. The medium laser's red energy lance boiled away the final layer. A secondary explosion lit the *Panther*'s interior, followed quickly by a keening wail Morgan knew well.

"Gyro hit."

The massive gyroscope that translated the pilot's sense of balance to the BattleMech was the only thing that allowed the behemoths to stay upright. Bits and pieces of high-speed metal sprayed out of the Panther's chest. The larger 'Mech staggered, but the pilot wrestled it upright and prepared to return fire.

"Something's not right with that *Panther* pilot." Franck nodded. "No luck tonight."

Morgan shook his head. "It's something else. He didn't go down, so he's good. Not hitting at point-blank range, that's just wrong."

The *Panther*'s SRMs again flew awry, filling the arena with brilliant colors and fiery blossoms. The PPC did finally track its target. The blue beam slashed up along the *Commando*'s left leg, melting armor from ankle to hip. The beam's hot caress denuded the leg and roasted the skeleton, but failed to cripple the 'Mech.

It really didn't matter. The *Commando*'s pilot again proved his skill by tracking the laser over the other 'Mech's left arm, melting away most of that armor. More SRMs powdered armor elsewhere, but it was the two missiles that corkscrewed into the Panther's chest that finished it. Another scream heralded the last gyro's destruction. The *Panther* slammed to the ground, armor shattering, shaking the entire building.

Morgan grunted. "Targeting fairy."

"What?"

He turned to his companion. "Little module that can compensate for a pilot's natural tendencies. If you shoot low, it raises your guns. Guys cheat with them to get certified to fight."

"Wouldn't that be useful in combat, though, automatically correcting your shots?"

"Sure, if you could remain as calm as you are in training." Morgan shook his head. "Here it was slapped on the *Panther*, making him miss. Pilot probably didn't even know it was there."

The *Commando* stood over the downed 'Mech, then slowly raised its fists in triumph. The fighter's supporters aped the motion. People began chanting "*Titan, Titan, Titan,*" which Morgan took to be the pilot's name. Money exchanged hands and servants scurried to fill celebratory drink orders.

Morgan studied the *Commando* as it turned in the center of the arena, soaking in the accolades. Already repair vehicles buzzed around its feet. A hulking *Hunchback* emerged from the   shadows with chains welded to its body. Crews hooked the battered *Panther* to it, and the larger 'Mech dragged the vanquished war machine away.

Morgan shivered. Fiberglass armor, aluminum alloy internal structures, under-strength myomer fibers and—if he had to guess—seriously undersized engines came together to make what looked like a war machine, but wouldn't have lasted for a single salvo on a battlefield. A construction or AgroMech with minor modifications would be of more use. These were gladiators as compared to Legionnaires—similar in form, but utterly inferior. They were actors playing at battle.

It wasn't the fraud of the machines that bothered Morgan as the way the battle had gone. It was possible that the *Commando* pilot was vastly superior to his counterpart, but the *Panther*'s marksmanship was bad. Improbably bad. Bad luck was one thing, but the larger 'Mech should have been able to weather enough damage to put the *Commando* down.

The fight had been fixed. No doubt about it. The whole thing was theatre. The *Panther*, which was favored by the Draconis Combine, had to go down. Whoever Titan was, it was a sure bet that he was a loyal son of the Commonwealth. The *Panther*'s pilot likely hailed from the Combine as well. His defeat could be seen as a metaphor for any Combine invasion, which made the audience feel secure, both in their property and superiority.

And Blizzard gets to laugh all at them, while they pay him for the privilege of doing so.

The *Commando* walked from the arena, but before new combatants could appear, a heavy-set man in a dark suit eclipsed Morgan's view. "Colonel Kell?"

Morgan nodded.

"If you please, Colonel." The man waved a hand at the central box on the arena's far side. "Mr. Blizzard sends his compliments, and wonders if you'd be so kind as to join him in his box."

CHAPTER 5

Patrick Kell still felt a little disgusted with himself. He could have easily blamed his failure on being tired from the trip to Galatea, but that was no excuse. Damiceau had set him up, and Patrick should have seen it. The man had picked the time and place for battle, giving him all the advantages.

And I know better than that. He just hadn't expected that sort of tactical planning from someone like Damiceau. Making a general assumption based on nothing was the sort of error that would get him into trouble again and again, so he resolved to be more careful.

Up to a point. The most cautious thing he could do would be to stay in the hotel, but he couldn't for a couple of reasons. It might seem foolhardy to head out into Galatean City, but the hotel's security was illusory. Damiceau had been prepared to strike there without much fear, and if what Morgan had reported about Blizzard was at all true, he'd have even fewer qualms about violence at the hotel. So staying put at a known location was just inviting trouble.

More importantly, Galatea was a warrior world, and warriors love nothing more than gossip. Morgan's going to one of Blizzard's fights would circulate, as would tales of his facing down Volmer. If Patrick remained in hiding, that would be bruited about as well, and it wouldn't look good for the unit. He had to show that they couldn't be cowed, wouldn't take unnecessary risks, but were brave enough to deal with nasty situations.

On top of all that, however, if he didn't get out, he was going to come out of his skin. Morgan reveled in details and just seemed to handle it all so easily. Sure, there were a couple of instructors at the Nagelring who thought Patrick was sharper than his brother, but Patrick had worked harder than Morgan ever had. What came easily to the elder Kell had taken Patrick a lot of studying.

The trip down had been like cramming for finals for days on end, with limited physical activity available just because of the finite space on a *Leopard*. He'd always used exercise to bleed off stress and provide him some perspective. Not only had he been sedentary on the ride down, but he was constantly dealing with Morgan's ideas, incoming files and bunches of other data that filled his skull to bursting.

He needed to get out, and Walter had been close to guessing what he wanted. When growing up on Arc-Royal, Patrick's mother had insisted that all her children learn the social skills necessary to survive in polite company. This included, among other things, dancing lessons. While Morgan had done the requisite set and no more, Patrick had gotten to like dancing.

What isn't to like? He smiled as he wandered the streets of the city, heading west from the hotel. Dancing was a great physical release, you got to dance with women, it took place in a social atmosphere, didn't cost much and, if you were good at it, could be a lot of fun. And Patrick was good at a variety of dances, having sought local clubs or taken classes when available at school and his last duty station.

He'd not asked the hotel's concierge for any recommendations about a place to go dancing simply because he didn't want the man to be able to offer someone like Damiceau a list of spots he could be found. Instead he stopped in a café, used a public computer terminal to search for clubs that offered lessons, and picked one nearby. He wandered past it, turned the corner, waited and watched for anyone following him, then returned and entered.

He paid the modest cover and got to the rectangular dance floor just as things started. The club itself was well appointed, with flowing white draperies, dark slate tiles and blond wooden flooring all combining for a sense of elegance. Tables and chairs, rapidly emptying, surrounded the dance floor and when the lights were lowered, each would be lit by glowing candles.

The instructor stood in the middle of the floor and began teaching the basic footwork for the lesson. He was teaching Skye-swing, which was pretty much like swing elsewhere, save for the tendency to launch into brief Polka runs during breaks in the music. It wasn't his favorite brand of swing, but folks did enjoy it, which was, after all, the purpose of the exercise.

Patrick knew the basic and really didn't need the lesson, but the brush-up didn't hurt and since everyone rotated partners, during the hour he met a succession of twenty women. Half of them were in their thirties and older—just getting over a divorce, heading into one, or widowed. The rest were roughly his age, out to enjoy themselves. Experienced dancers were sprinkled through all ages, breaking things into two groups: partners who danced well, and those that drove like a balky *Jenner* in an earthquake.

It was after two matronly sisters had stepped on his feet in succession that a slender woman with long black hair rotated around to him.

"Hi, I'm Patrick."

"Tisha."

"Pleased to meet you, Tisha." He deliberately repeated her name so he'd not forget it. "You've done this before?"

"Sure. You?"

"First time here."

Her smile slackened slightly, but she refrained from rolling her hazel eyes. She stiffened slightly as Patrick took her in his arms and slipped his hand under her hair. They both faced in toward the instructor, watched the new move—an outside turn—then prepared to try it. Though the instructor suggested the first pass be without footwork, Patrick instinctively led her through the move including it, and by the time she'd completed the spin, Tisha's smile had returned.

"I thought you said this was your first lesson."

"I just said it was my first time here."

"Don't let it be your last." She thanked him and rotated on.

The lesson, which boiled down to the endless repetition of three simple moves, let Patrick work up a bit of a sweat. He shared laughs with a number of women, got appreciative nods from several, and just felt the tension melting away. And when he wasn't distracted, he was one of the better dancers taking the lesson.

He did get distracted a couple of times, however. He'd not let his guard down entirely and had taken a position on the floor that let him watch the door. He was pretty sure he didn't recognize anyone, save maybe the large black man from the hotel lobby earlier that day. While there were a number of folks who were mercenaries out to enjoy leave, most everyone else looked normal. If there was a threat out there, he didn't see it.

The lesson ended in applause for the partners and the instructor. He doubled as the DJ. He bounded from the floor, the lights dimmed and music started pounding—a bluesy number about being Dispossessed. Patrick started back off the floor, but a hand caught his wrist.

"You can't go anywhere." Tisha tugged him to the center of the floor. "This is my favorite song, so we're dancing."

Patrick nodded and danced. She moved easy and followed perfectly. She even continued through with turns and sequences he'd only led halfway. Better yet, she kept in sync with him, encouraged him to get caught up with the song's beat, and never tried to lead him. She made it easy for him to lose himself in the music and her presence.

And to have some fun.

The music ended abruptly, so he missed the chance to dip her. Tisha smiled. "Thank you."

"Thanks for asking." Patrick was about ask for another dance, but a large man offered her his hand, and she accepted with a laugh. As she spun away, he retreated to the bar and ordered a lager. He pressed the cold bottle to the side of his neck, then drank slowly.

People whirled and swirled, some self-conscious, others totally abandoning any sense of self-criticism. It didn't matter who they were or what they did, they'd all gathered together to enjoy a shared passion. Sure, some of them were there simply to get laid, but the folks having fun were the ones who were dancing. Skill and enjoyment were enough of an introduction that one could dance as much or as little as desired. Only the very foolish turned down an invitation to dance, and usually only because they'd promised a dance to someone else.

This was how life was supposed to be. It was normal. A lecturer at the Nagelring had once commented that, at our most basic level, human beings are tribal. While they ascribe to principles and nationalities, identifying themselves along those lines, they can only really know and love a finite number of people. They gravitate to small groups, feeling comfortable there, and welcome those who prove worthy of inclusion in their particular tribe.

The Kell Hounds would be like that. They'd be a tribe and a family. They'd be united, and through their abilities, they'd protect other tribes. The scene on the dance floor could have been taking place in millions of cities across the Inner Sphere, regardless of nationalities and conflicts on a state level. Protecting these people, allowing them to thrive and explore what made them happy was what Patrick hoped the Kell Hounds would be able to do.

Several women asked Patrick to dance, and he obliged them happily. He sank into the music, moving with it, letting his body handle the dancing. His mind flew elsewhere, watching the people, the door, the bar where he'd left his beer. Again he sensed no threat, saw nothing that made him wary, but he couldn't wholly relax. If his partners noticed that he wasn't focused on them, they said nothing and even extracted promises of other dances later.

After a half-hour of constant motion, he returned to the bar. He set his beer aside and ordered a new one. Though he'd watched as carefully as he could, he couldn't be certain that someone hadn't put something in his drink.

Tisha appeared at his side, blowing a lank lock from her face. "Afraid someone was going to drug you and take advantage of you?"

"It was warm."

"Nice cover." Tisha ordered a beer, then took a handful of napkins to mop her face dry. "What unit you with?"

"Haven't found one yet." He drank. "You?"

"Galatean native child. I watch you lot come and go." Her eyes glittered as she watched the dancers. "You have a ride?"

"I was kind of hoping..."

"Good luck on that." Tisha turned to him and smiled. "Whatever you do, don't get hooked up driving one of Blizzard's toys. It sounds like easy money, and you'll be promised it will enhance your reputation, but forget it. Quality unit like the Eridani Light Horse wouldn't touch one of Blizzard's guys."

"Thanks for the advice. Who should I look for?"

She studied his face for a moment, then drank. "I'm going to tell you this even though it probably means you'll get hired off this rock and we'll never dance again. Don't go out there looking for who's hiring. Merc units are always hiring. You look at their rosters and they've all got thirty percent more people than their unit strength requires. And they're not paying them, they just have them sign a conditional contract. See those two guys over there—beer-gut and khaki?"

"Sure."

"They're signed up with a dozen and a half units between them. Someone gets a contract, they could be heading out or not. Depends on the mission and if they will enhance the profile."

Patrick nodded. "So what do I look for, then?"

"You don't look for units that are hiring, you look for units that are getting hired. They're the ones that don't maintain a headquarters here, but have representatives on-world to negotiate contracts. They'll have the money to supply you with a 'Mech." She bumped him with her shoulder. "Sorry about asking you to dance to that song about being Dispossessed."

"It's okay." Patrick gave her a sidelong glance. "Besides, you'd sized me up as a MechWarrior and wanted to see how I'd react to the song. Did I pass?"

She blushed. "Yeah, and you just got extra credit."

"Good. Does that earn me another dance?"

Without waiting for her answer, he led her back onto the floor. They spun and laughed their way through a medley of steps—elegant ones and completely-blown moves. Her eyes flashed brightly, and her smile mirrored his. They flew apart and closed again with fluid ease as if they'd danced together for ages.

Finally the music ended, and they returned to their drinks. At the bar they faced each other, their body language warning others not to disturb them. Neither drank from their beers, he for a reason, she seemingly to indulge him.

Tisha smiled. "I'll give you one other piece of advice. There's a new unit—barely virtual—that's making a lot of noise down here. The Kell Hounds. Can't get taken in by the hype, though. They're heading for a lot of trouble."

"Really?"

"Really. They've got money, so every down-on-his-luck merce-nary is going to hit them for money to patch up their 'Mechs, draw a paycheck and wait for the unit to collapse. Most don't make it past a year anyway, and these guys are going to lay out a lot of C-bills to build a regiment, but they don't have a contract and no one will hire a green regiment. It's insanity. Even if it did get you a ride, when the unit goes down, lawyers will take it back away from you."

"Wow. Here I was thinking that looked like a good prospect."

Tisha leaned in and lowered her voice. "As I said, life-long Galatean. I've watched units come and go—mostly go. If I had a C-bill for every silver-tongued devil who spun a tale of a rosy future, the Archon herself would be hitting me for pocket change to balance the budget. They aren't the first to come in with a grand scheme, they won't be the last. If they make it a year, I'll be surprised."

Patrick smiled. "I think you're just afraid they'll snap me up and take me away from you and all this dancing."

"A little of that might be true."

"So I'll make you a wager. If they hire me on and they last a year, I'll come back, you'll hire this place out, hire in any band you name, and we'll have a private party with as many folks as you want to invite."

Her eyes narrowed warily. "And if you lose?"

"Same deal, but I foot the bill."

"But you'll be unemployed."

He laughed. "Maybe I'll teach dance lessons and save up."

Tisha offered him her hand. "It's a bet. And think hard about of-fering lessons. You're that good."

"Thanks."

They shook, but she didn't release his hand. "And just so you know, odds for making a fortune teaching dance are much better than your making a single pfenning in the cockpit of a 'Mech."

CHAPTER 6

GASLIGHT FACTORY
GALATEAN CITY, GALATEA
LYRAN COMMONWEALTH
3 OCTOBER 3010

Many interested gazes tracked Morgan Kell as he walked three-quarters of the way around the arena. Roman emperors had paraded their vanquished foes around in a similar manner. Even the next pair of 'Mechs awaiting combat lurked in the shadows so everyone would watch Morgan.

At least Blizzard is not so vulgar as to put my image up on the holotrons.

It really didn't matter. Since the seating was so close to the arena, everyone got a good look at him. Morgan made that easy, marching along in an easy step, his head held high and smile broad. Anyone looking for a sign of fear would be hard pressed to find one.

They passed out a door and along a corridor, entering the sky-box through a rear door. Blizzard's guests all studied Morgan as he entered, many through veiled glances. They didn't care if Morgan noticed their interest. They feigned disinterest for the benefit of their host—and because they feared his reaction if appearing too interested.

Only two people watched him openly. A woman, tall, slender, with cascades of golden hair and icy blue eyes raked him up and down with her gaze. She wore a blue gown, sleeveless, sparkling with sequins and teardrop beads. A sapphire set in platinum rode the hollow of her throat, with flawless twins dangling from her ears. Her gaze remained neutral until her eyes met his, then it took on a predatory nature.

It was nothing, however, in comparison to that of Haskell Blizzard. The man was unremarkable, being somewhat short, decidedly stout, and despite his fine clothes, unkempt in appearance. He'd shaved his head because he was balding, but had not shaved it within the last day. A wooden toothpick hung from his lower lip, and his fingertips were cracked and bloody from where he chewed his nails.

He would have been easy to dismiss save for the ravenous hunger in his eyes. Flat and gray, but always moving, they betrayed the restless mind behind them. Though the man's face remained impassive for the most part, micro-expressions of disgust tightened the lines around his eyes and mouth.

Blizzard did not offer Morgan his hand. Instead, he sketched a tiny, mocking salute. "Welcome, Colonel Kell."

His voice threw Morgan for a second. It was far softer than he had expected, and the accent more cultured. *Is he playing with me as I did Volmer?* Morgan doubted it, as it was much easier to play dumb than smart.

"A pleasure." Morgan looked out into the battlefield. "I'd been told you run the best action here."

Blizzard snorted and left the seats as the battle began. He crossed to the bar at the back of the luxury box. "A drink? Not sure I have anything you like, and a little late to send out for it. Next time, perhaps."

Morgan suppressed a smile. Blizzard was playing with him. He made an offer, then immediately discouraged it. Any of the people in the box—perhaps save the blonde—would have run through a firefight to fetch anything Morgan wanted, had Blizzard even suggested it. And there would be no next time, the both of them knew that.

Morgan approached him, under pretext of studying the liquor selection. "You're most kind. At least you have the good grace to offer courtesy."

The loan shark half-grinned. "Yeah, the Viper isn't much of one for social amenities. He met you in the 'Mechbay. That wows the tourists, but not you?"

"Frankly, your operation impresses me more. Scaled back fights here, so the rich can get up close and, I assume, larger venues with actual BattleMechs blazing away for the weekend battles."

"Never assume."

"How many do you get on the weekends?"

"Enough. I make my money off merchandising and concessions. Admission pays for purses and some salaries." Haskell glanced toward the front of the box. Heads snapped around to watch the fight. "You have stones coming here."

"Stones? Not a lack of sense?"

Haskell set his drink down. "A lack of sense would have been coming in uniform representing a mercenary unit that doesn't exist. Now, coming like this, you're trying to tell me you're a businessman. We should do business."

Morgan clasped his hands at the small of his back. "General Volmer outlined how I'd have to do business here. I made it clear to him that his ideas weren't going to work. Was what he told me coming straight from you, or was he cutting himself in where he didn't belong?"

"Direct, good, I like that." Blizzard nodded. "Sure you won't have a drink?"

"Maybe next time."

Blizzard pressed his hands together. "I'm not going to give you my history. You have it, or will have it, and probably will get a lot of different versions of it. Whatever you hear, when you say to yourself, 'he can't be that bad,' stop. I can be. I am. Underestimate me, and it will be the last thing you ever do."

The man smiled and tapped his temple. "Oh, yes, I hear you don't like idle threats. Let me clarify. When I say 'last thing you do,' it's not idle. I'll take you and your brother, cut you up into little pieces, and scatter them across the desert belt. The sun will never set on you, and no one will ever find all the pieces. That specific enough for you?"

Morgan nodded. "I get it."

"Good." He opened his hands. "That being said, you and I both understand that my killing you is really counterproductive. If you die, your unit dies. It stops making money, which is not good for you. It would also not be good for me."

"Because you'll profit if I profit?"

"No, Colonel Kell. I will profit regardless. You do business on my world, I expect to be paid. It's pretty simple." Blizzard smiled easily. "Now, all the list-checking that General Volmer wanted to do, forget that. Bureaucrats and quartermasters, they like the paperwork. What I'll do is simple. I'll send you a menu of pilots. If you hire them, there will be a number attached. That's what you'll pay me for their services. It's what they owe me, plus a reasonable return on my investment. It's fair."

"And their 'Mechs?"

"I'm certain we can reach an accommodation there, too. I can be a reasonable man."

Morgan arched an eyebrow. "And if the amount is in dispute?"

"I'll address that. I can be charitable, too. I once was a warrior like you, and I have a soft spot for the Dispossessed. This is why I try to help so many of them."

The mercenary nodded. "It's agree to this, or there will be open warfare between us?"

"A war you will lose, I assure you." The man's eyes narrowed. "Ah, you doubt me, don't you? You're thinking you can win a battle between us. That you can goad me into fighting."

"Seems to me, Mr. Blizzard, you're the one intent on fighting."

"No, Colonel, that is where you are wrong." Blizzard's voice grew softer but sharper. "This is my world. I am the power here. Every so often, however, someone comes to challenge me. It just happens to be your turn. A fight is not productive, but you're unconvinced of my power. You require a demonstration."

Morgan shook his head. "Actually, I don't."

"In fact, you do." Blizzard pulled a small communicator from his pocket. "I'm going to have to hurt someone you know. It's your choice. Gordon Franck or your brother?"

"Don't do this."

"An implied threat if I do?"

Morgan folded his arms over his chest. "I don't need a demonstration."

"Too late for that. These people here, they know you defied me by defying Volmer. I have to make some sort of demonstration, otherwise your challenge to my power has been tolerated."

He snapped his fingers and Morgan's guide approached. "Get the man he came in with. Break his arm and throw him out. Now."

The man spun on his heel and left.

Blizzard faced Morgan. "What will you do? Chase my man down, stop him? You know that if you do that, I'll just order your brother hurt. You can't possibly stop me from doing that. You can't hurt me here, physically, because I will still come after you. Murder me? You'd be on trial for murder. You are trapped, Morgan Kell, because this is *my* world."

Morgan's expression hardened. "Call your man off."

"Incentivize me."

"The deal you offered. I buy out debt. I buy 'Mechs."

"Very good. A young dog learning a new trick." Blizzard keyed the communicator. "Baker, stand down. Dolan, mark your man."

Morgan's eyes widened with surprise. "What?"

"Just a demonstration, otherwise you still won't believe my power." Blizzard pocketed the communicator again. "Your brother is out dancing at a club tonight. I have a man on him. My man will mark his jacket. A minor thing. You can look for it when he returns to the hotel. It'll be a reminder that this is my world."

Morgan nodded. "You have your deal."

"One more thing." Blizzard smiled as the suite's door opened. In walked a young man wearing a 'Mech cooling vest, boots and shorts. He carried a lot of muscle, which wasn't uncommon for Assault 'Mech pilots, but had to have been put on for show. His forehead had two red patches where the NeuroHelmet he'd used pressed against his flesh, but his blond hair was clean and dry; and his cooling vest dry and pristine.

Blizzard's assembled guests applauded, chanting *"Titan"* over and over again.

"Come, Colonel, you have to meet our champion, Titan." Blizzard took his elbow and steered him toward the pilot. "Titan, someone for you to meet."

The muscled man looked him over expectantly. "I'm Titan, and you are?"

"Morgan Kell."

The man's face slackened, then purpled. "You're Patrick Kell's brother."

Something clicked in the back of Morgan's head. "And you're the son of the Viper."

Titan hauled back with a fist, but Blizzard got between the two men. "Now Titan, you'll not want to be hitting your new employer. You're going to be a Lieutenant Colonel in the Kell Hounds. Liaison officer for them here on Galatea. Won't that be splendid?"

Morgan shook his head. "We have a Lieutenant Colonel."

Blizzard smiled. "There's always room for two, unless you want there to be just one."

The mercenary stared at the small man. He'd purposely provoked Tommy Volmer. He'd willingly ambushed him. There seemed no doubt that the remark about lieutenant colonels could cut either way, too. Blizzard would kill his own grandson-in-law as quickly and remorselessly as he would Patrick. He'd probably even justify it as the cost of doing business, and think nothing more of it.

But that would be a lie. Blizzard would do something like that simply because he could. He was the most dangerous of men; one who had vast amounts of power and despised those who sought his. Blizzard could look out into the arena and know that he could kill anyone with impunity. There simply was no way, short of murdering him, to stop him.

Blizzard shoved Titan toward his adoring fans. "Now you understand, Colonel Kell. The only way to beat me is to go lower than I will. I assure you that you cannot. You hold to some silly moral code. Religious, perhaps, or just that faux-chivalry in which MechWarriors are the shining knights of yore reborn. But you see, there is no God to render judgment. Knights never shined back then; and their counterparts today have feet of clay.

"And the pity is that you, a warrior, should know the truth. You may, and just refuse to acknowledge it." Blizzard pressed his hands to his own broad chest. "There is only self. Everything else may well be an illusion. I do what I want because I am the only important person in the world. Your life, your goals, your ideals—they mean nothing to me. I cannot be shamed, I fear no enemy, and I allow no slight to go unpunished. You are defeated before you raise a hand."

Morgan smiled. "You're wrong, you know."

"Pray, do enlighten me."

Morgan lowered his voice and leaned in. "You figure you're safe because I won't go as low as you will. But what if you motivate me to do so? What if you give me reason to see that you're right, then it's just you and me. You think you'll get out of that alive?"

Blizzard's face brightened. "So you will oppose me after all."

"No, I won't." Morgan's face became a grim mask. "I have larger battles to fight. You're an annoyance. An inconvenience. I may not like doing business with you, but mercenaries seldom have any affection for their employers and partners. Our bargain has been struck. I'll uphold my end."

"I trust you will." Blizzard nodded solemnly. "You'll just have to see if I do mine."

"Oh, you will. You will because you understand something about me."

"And that is?"

Morgan nodded toward the loan shark's guests. "They could never get lower than you. They wouldn't know where to start trying. I might not get lower than you, but you surely won't like the damage I'd do in my attempt."

CHAPTER 7

Even though the expression of worry melted quickly into one of relief on Morgan's face, it shocked Patrick. *He looks so like our father.* Patrick closed the suite door behind him and slung his jacket on a chair. "What's wrong? You okay?"

"I'm better now." Morgan got out of his chair and picked up Patrick's jacket. He studied it closely, taking it near a lamp. "You have fun? Nothing weird happen?"

"Morgan, just give it to me straight. What are you looking for?"

His older brother shook his head, then tossed the jacket down. "I met with Blizzard. He threatened you. Said he had a man watching you. He ordered the man to mark your jacket."

Patrick closed his eyes for the moment. "I was out dancing. I took my jacket off. Anyone could have marked it. I never would have noticed. Aside from the normal bumping on the floor, nothing odd." He held up a hand. "And, yes, I exercised caution. I made sure no one put anything in my drink. I'm okay. Nothing weird."

Morgan nodded solemnly. "On the Amaris scale of sociopaths, Blizzard is right off the charts. He makes Takashi Kurita look like a teddy bear. To teach me a lesson, he asked me to choose between you and Franck as to who he should hurt. I refused to choose, and bought him off by agreeing that we'd pay off the debts of any pilots we want to take away with us."

Patrick's stomach roiled. "It's that bad? He'll rape us, you know. Do you think you really bought him off?"

"No, what I think I bought is time. Time for him to consider just how much he can get from us, and time for him to figure out how to hurt us the most." The elder brother shook his head. "The deal will last until he finds something better for himself."

"So we get in and out before he knows we're leaving?"

"That's our best bet." Morgan frowned. "Our original plan of hiring techs and support personnel still works. We get them in place, and others will have to come. If we don't have them, we can offer nothing but money."

Something Tisha had said flashed through Patrick's mind. "A woman I met cautioned me against joining merc units that were hiring, but said I should look for those that are being hired. That might be something else we can offer."

Morgan laughed. "Good idea, but even Katrina won't hire a unit that doesn't exist yet."

"You're forgetting Damiceau, Morgan." Patrick stretched, the muscles in his back already tightening from dancing and fatigue. "He was afraid of us enough to want to buy us off. And both he and Volmer are pretty sure we've got some sort of a backdoor deal with the Archon."

"Go on."

"So remember the story from Sun-Tzu about the general who bluffed an enemy into thinking an open city was a trap? It worked because his enemy was already thinking that this general was so good, he had to have something up his sleeve. Folks already assume we do, so we trade on that. Damiceau and his counterparts will assume they have to beat any deal we've got, so they'll start negotiating. Once they do that, we will be fielding offers, legitimately."

Morgan slowly smiled. "Now I remember why I don't play poker with you."

Patrick's cheeks reddened. "You would have gotten there."

"A little trial and error first." Morgan smiled. "You know, you have everyone else fooled into thinking I'm the brains of this outfit."

"You are, Morgan."

Morgan rested both hands on his brother's shoulders. "You don't have me fooled. I stand out because I can't always keep my mouth shut. You, on the other hand, well, it's like our mother used to say: 'Beware the man with his eyes half-shut—he ain't sleeping.'"

"She never said 'ain't.'"

"The point is—"

"I get it." Patrick chewed his lower lip for a second. "If we are going to do this, we're going to have to accelerate our schedule. We'd figured two months. How long?"

"If we're out of here by All Saint's Day, we'll be good."

A month. Patrick thought, then nodded. "We'll have to hustle."

"Agreed." Morgan's head came up. "There is one other thing, one last detail."

"I'm not going to like it, am I?"

"I ran into Thomas Volmer. He goes by the name Titan, and fought in one of the battles. Tin-toy 'Mechs pounding each other, and the fix was in. He's not bad, but short of having a total incompetent in the other 'Mech, he shouldn't have won."

"And the bad part of this is what?" Patrick smiled. "You only broke his jaw in two places?"

"I agreed to hiring him as a Lieutenant Colonel to be our local liaison."

The younger Kell's stomach collapsed in on itself. "We share the same rank?"

"And you'll do all the hard work, and he'll get paid. It was agree or you'd get badly hurt."

"He doesn't go off-world with us?"

"Nope."

"And no public apology?"

"Nope."

"As long as he stays here, he won't get any of us killed. I can live with it, provided you promise me one thing."

Morgan arched a dark eyebrow. "That being?"

"When we fire him, I get to do it."

Morgan laughed. "Agreed. Now we both better get some sleep. It'll be a long day tomorrow. I'll fill you in on details and you can tell me about this woman you met. Deal?"

"Deal. Sleep well." Patrick slapped his brother on the back. "And, Morgan, thanks for waiting up."

Morning came all too quickly, but not because Patrick hadn't managed to sleep. He had, far more peacefully and solidly than he would have expected. Morning arrived too early because it cut short a dream he was having about dancing with Tisha.

He woke with a sigh. She was pretty, and danced like a dream. She held her own in a conversation, too, and hadn't resorted to the old standby questions that amounted to an interrogation. She felt like a friend he'd not seen in a while, and she intrigued him. He'd have liked to get to know her better.

Fact was, however, it wasn't going to happen. She was a native, and he was going to be going away. There wasn't a chance of any sort of lasting relationship. Even if they'd fallen in love at first sight, she wouldn't follow him off-world unless they were married, and maybe not even then, and he wasn't ready to get married. While enjoying her company on a more intimate basis would have been fun, it would have also stressed the futility of their situation.

Anyone else, his brother included, really wouldn't have sweated that last part. Morgan would be content to let be what was, living more for the moment than worrying about the future. Patrick was cursed with seeing the longer picture—and it was that focus that sometimes prevented him from seeing shorter-term problems, like Damiceau's goons waiting to ambush him in the hotel lobby.

He pushed away all those considerations, showered, and got some breakfast before tackling terabytes of data. Morgan appeared from his room about an hour later and told him Walter had set up several meetings. Morgan would handle those interviews, leaving some urgent requests by Mechwarriors to Patrick. They agreed he'd do no hiring immediately, but he'd take data and follow-up. The most desperate likely weren't the best candidates, but finding a grain of wheat amidst the chaff couldn't be discounted.

Typical of the cases he handled was a bedraggled MechWarrior who was ushered into the suite of offices the hotel had given the Kells. Medium height and build, the man had nicked himself a couple of places shaving, and had the sallow skin of someone who avoided the sun and compensated by drinking. His uniform was clean, and his thin hair had been combed, but the wind had blown a few locks astray. He'd have come hat-in-hand, but Patrick was pretty sure he'd long since pawned any hat he owned.

"Confident Guinn, of Guinn's Gunnes. You can call me Con."

Patrick shook his hand. The man's grip was stronger than he expected. "Patrick Kell. Please, sit. How can I help you?"

Guinn tried to relax in the chair, but just made himself look more awkward. "I'll be straight with you. I have a 'Mech company, a light company. We were never big time. We've subbed out garrison duty for some larger units, like the 12th Vegan Rangers and the Light Horses. We do okay. No atrocities, no disturbances, no problems."

Patrick punched up a company history on a computer tied to the ComStar Review Board. Guinn wasn't dressing his history up by much, save for the last incident. "A year ago you got mauled in a fight with some Capellans."

"House Ijori. One of the Warrior Houses. Master Yadi needed to prove a point to Pavel Ridzik. We got banged up, but delayed them enough that reinforcements were able to drive them off." Guinn shrugged. "There's no gilding a turd. Our employer had ignored signs that something was up. Someone had to take the blame, and we got it."

Patrick read a bit closer in the file. The Gunnes had deployed in a standard formation and invited a strike by a much stronger force. It was totally by the book, with the Gunnes counting on fortifications to make the odds against success deter the enemy.

What he missed, however, is that the Capellans hadn't come for turf. They'd come for combat experience, and the Gunnes had provided a nice training scenario.

He tapped the computer screen. "I see by this—"

"You can't go by that." Guinn gripped the edge of Patrick's desk. "I've got good people, top people. They're loyal and hard working and disciplined. We thought folks would understand, and we'd get off this rock but... Everyone knows we got mauled, but it wasn't our fault. We had a mission, we did it."

Patrick raised a hand. "I'm not looking to place blame."

"You're just looking for a reason to say no, just like everyone else." Guinn stood. "Look, it was probably a mistake for me to come here like this. You know, I thought maybe I could get you to hire us *en masse*. That probably doesn't fit with your plans. Please, just tell me that you won't hold being a Gunne against any of my people."

With an attitude like that, no wonder no one's hiring. Patrick almost blurted a comment to that effect, but a chill ran down his spine. Though Guinn was giving off vibes like he was done with combat and had lost confidence in himself, he still had the spine to come and try to cut a deal for his people. His loyalty to them had to be a reflection of their loyalty to him. Having the guts to make the appeal impressed Patrick.

If I'm ever in his position, I hope I have the same courage.

He motioned the man to sit again. "Your people know you're here?"

Guinn looked down at his hands. "No. I floated the idea. They discouraged me. I got a lot of young kids in the unit. They figured you'd cherry-pick the best and leave the rest—me included—for the vultures here."

"How deeply snowed-under are your people?"

Guinn's head came up. "You've learned fast. The best aren't. They earned their way clear fighting for him. The others, they get by."

Patrick thought for a moment. He'd have to study the Gunnes' roster more, but bringing a light company in wholesale would shorten their process considerably. The Gunnes would be broken into three scout lances and encouraged to use speed to their advantage, instead of trying to slug it out with heavier 'Mechs.

"Here's the deal, Captain. I'll look things over and talk to my brother. No promises, but no instant rejection."

The man blinked, then swallowed hard. "Really?"

"No promises. Just remember, no promises."

Guinn nodded, then stood and saluted. "Thank you, sir."

Patrick rose, returned the salute, then shook the man's hand. "We keep this just between us. I will get back to you quickly."

"Just between us, yes, sir." Guinn smiled. "And thank you again."

Guinn squeezed past Walter in the doorway. "Colonel, your brother isn't in his office."

Patrick glanced at the time on his computer. "You set him up for a meeting in a half-hour. He's gone."

"Must have missed him as I was coming up in the lift." Walter jerked a thumb at the suite's reception room. "I got Lattie, my tech, to come over. I hoped to introduce the Colonel. You want to handle this?"

"Sure." Patrick saved the information about the Gunnes for later study as Walter guided his guest into the office.

The man beamed. "Colonel Kell, this is Lattie Hamilton, the best 'Mech tech on this mudball."

The Tech stared at him. "Patrick?" Patrick's jaw dropped. "Tisha?"

Walter stared at the woman. "Tisha?"

She glared at him. "Laeticia. You only ever heard my father's nickname for me. He wanted a son."

A smile blossomed on Patrick's face. "Please, come in. Sit down."

Tisha folded her arms. "No thanks. You lied to me."

"What?"

"You didn't tell me you were one of the Kell brothers. You lied."

"You never asked."

"No, and you were content to let me make a fool of myself." She turned and waved at Walter to clear the doorway. "As for you, you'll be walking for a long time."

"Tisha, please, wait. Let me explain."

She glanced back over her shoulder at him. "You really think you can?"

He held up a pair of fingers. "Two things. First, last night, I just wanted to dance. I was really happy being anonymous. Walter can tell you, I'd had a rough day being Patrick Kell. In fact, half the folks who already knew who I was here wanted me dead."

"It's true, Lattie."

Tisha arched single eyebrow. "And that gave you leave to let me make an idiot of myself?"

"You didn't. You were the first person here to give me a realistic and unbiased look at how Morgan and I were being seen. We're all wrapped up in what we want to do, but nobody wants to give that any weight. It's easier to figure folks are motivated by selfish reasons than to believe in selfless ones. Believing we're foolish or greedy comes naturally. Figuring we're after something more is harder."

She frowned. "What are you after?"

"Please, sit." Patrick waited for her to take the seat Guinn had just quitted. "You're skilled at patching up 'Mechs. You know it's a game of entropy. Ever since the collapse of the Star League, our ability to replace 'Mechs is outstripped by our capacity for destroying them. Technological know-how has been lost, and if the factories break down or are destroyed, we can't replace them. Another century of this, and even the tin 'Mechs Blizzard plays with will be a memory."

"And you're forming a mercenary unit that will continue to pound big 'Mechs into little pieces." Tisha shook her head. "And you're going to profit by it."

"No. You were right last night when you said chances were better that I could make a profit teaching dance faster than I can as a mercenary. That's not what we're out to do. We want to create an elite unit, with good equipment and maintenance, that will be so feared that no one will want to fight against us."

"How do you profit from that?"

Patrick smiled. "We profit because peace is profitable."

"War is more so."

"But profiting from war is immoral." Patrick sighed. "If profit was taken out of war, we wouldn't have any wars. By making a unit that's so good it can beat all comers, we raise the cost of war to the point where there is no profit in it."

Tisha's brows remained knotted. "Is he telling the truth, Walter?"

De Mesnil smiled. "I've signed on."

"So you believe this?"

"I believe if anyone can make this plan work, it's these two boys."

Her expression eased a little.

Patrick smiled. "Interested in coming aboard? Top pay, the best equipment available, and a chance to see the rest of the Inner Sphere."

"I don't know. I think I'll take some more convincing."

"Like what?"

Tisha smiled. "That'll be up to you to figure out. Tonight. Over dinner, between dances. Make me believe you're as good a leader in combat as you are dancing, and we might have a deal."

CHAPTER 8

Morgan spotted her the moment he stepped off the lift. She'd been sitting in the lobby, casually reading a small noteputer. She'd looked up expectantly, but didn't react with surprise. Instead, she finished the paragraph she was reading, turned the device off, and tucked it into a soft leather briefcase.

She waited for him to approach before standing. Despite having her golden hair up and wearing a business suit, she was no less ravishing than she had been the night before in Blizzard's suite. In some ways she was more alluring. Not dressed for display, her intelligence shined more brightly.

"You needn't have waited."

She smiled carefully. "You presume I was waiting for you."

"Am I wrong?"

"Partly. It's true, I was waiting." She hitched up her bag's shoulder strap. "I was waiting while trying to decide if you are the most foolish man on the planet or the most intelligent. Not an easy puzzle to solve."

"Perhaps there is another choice."

"No, I don't think so."

Morgan smiled. "Then I must be the most foolish."

"Because you think your brother is smarter than you?"

"Not think. That I know." He extended his hand. "Foolish because I still don't know your name."

She laughed lightly, and his stomach fluttered. "Charming, too, but not so practiced at it that it bores you. Good. Veronica Matova. You want to walk with me."

Morgan glanced at his chronometer. "I was actually on the way to a meeting."

"You really want to delay it." Her blue eyes flashed cautiously. "Trust me, Colonel, it will be more than worth your while, fool or genius."

He nodded and produced his communicator. "Walter, can you call your man and postpone our meeting for two hours? Have him come here. Something's come up, something important. Thank you." He snapped it shut. "I'm all yours."

"Come." She slipped her hand inside his elbow and guided him from the Nova Royale. They crossed the street and entered a dimly lit restaurant. Bypassing the maitre'd, they headed for a shadowed booth in the bar. She slid into the booth on the right, and Morgan took the red leather seat opposite her.

"Okay, I'm trusting you. Justify my trust."

"A fair request, given where you first saw me." Veronica watched his face for a reaction. "I am this world's highest-paid courtesan. I have business interests that include a number of agencies that provide entertainment and companionship for visitors and society's elite. This would include Haskell Blizzard, General Volmer, and Titan. No comment?"

Morgan shook his head. "You're expecting moral outrage, perhaps?"

"That's often the reaction, especially among mercenaries who will hire one of my girls at midnight, and pretend not to know her on the street next morning."

"Irony." Morgan nodded. "I get paid to kill. You get paid for making love. No difference, right?"

"For the moment, I'll pretend I agree." She slipped her noteputer from the bag. "I have to know. Did you just get lucky, or were you really thinking a move ahead of Blizzard?"

"I'm not sure I follow."

Again she watched him. "If you're lying, you're very good. The fact is that after you left the box, Blizzard decided you still needed to be taught a lesson. He called his man and told him to hurt your brother."

Goosebumps puckered Morgan's flesh. "That was fast."

"In part it was to distract Titan. Mostly it was just Blizzard."

"So what's the lucky part?"

"You really don't know, do you?"

He shook his head.

She turned the noteputer around so he could see the screen, then she started holo-footage playing. It had been shot by a security camera outside a place called Club Manning. Patrick exited and headed away from the camera. A second man emerged five seconds later, then a third on the heels of the first. The second man stretched his stride to catch Patrick. The third remained only a step behind the second, then when they reached the mouth of an alley, the third man shoved the second into the shadows. They disappeared.

Ahead of them, Patrick never even turned around to see what was going on.

Morgan shrugged. "I owe someone some thanks."

"You want me to believe that wasn't your man?"

"I'm gathering it doesn't matter, since Blizzard must believe it was."

"Oh, he does. His man landed in the hospital. Three broken ribs, broken arm, lacerated liver, ruptured spleen. Lost a handful of teeth as well." Veronica shut the noteputer off. "Quite the guardian angel your brother has."

"It's good he has someone looking out for him." Morgan frowned. "Now why are you looking out for me?"

She sat back languidly, betraying no urgency nor emotion. "Unlike yours, my business thrives on stability. You are upsetting Haskell Blizzard, either by accident or on purpose. This creates an atmosphere of chaos. People get worried when that happens. They shrink from adventure and enjoyment. I suffer, my people suffer."

"By coming here and warning me that Blizzard thinks I've out-thought him, you guarantee chaos. Now I'm on my guard. Without your warning, he could have just taken me out. Your peace would be restored."

"I wish." She inspected a perfectly sculpted nail. "Power is the most corrosive thing in existence. Unchecked power means there are no challenges left. Blizzard amuses himself by putting people in situations they don't want to be in and watching them get out. And he's not stupid in shaping his traps. Over the years they've become more and more cruel. He's descending into nihilism, and when he melts down, everything goes with him."

Morgan pressed his hands flat to the table. "I can see that everything you've said is true, but I have to wonder once again why you're warning me? You have an agenda, or did Blizzard pay you to come here and distract me while he moves against us?"

Veronica laughed, more heartily this time, but it didn't warm Morgan. "There it is, your moral outrage. You pretend you don't mind that I sleep with people for money, but the moment I could be paid to betray you, this is when I become apostate? Or is it that you entertain some fantasy that he might pay me to seduce you, so you get to have me and then get betrayed?"

Color appeared on Morgan's cheeks. *"Touché."*

"More than a touch, Colonel, that goes straight to your soul." Her eyes hardened. "We are exactly the same, Colonel. We both kill. You do it directly. I'm more subtle. For money, I give the illusion of pleasure. I'm paid to make my partners think, for the time we're together, that they are the most desirable person in the world. But they know it's all an illusion. The session will end. The money will run out. Another patron will supersede them. And that's when they see themselves for what they truly are, and they slowly die inside.

"My agenda is simple. Either you are smart and strong enough to oppose Blizzard." She tapped a nail against the table. "You can put him down, or you can't. I need to know which it is because I have to make some decisions. I have people depending on me. I want to keep them safe. Do you understand?"

Morgan snatched her hand up in his. "We're exactly alike, Veronica, and not for the reasons you cited. I, too, have people I care about. I have people I want to protect. My brother is first and foremost. Then there are those who are trusting us to be good leaders. And then there are all the people who will be able to live peacefully under the umbrella of the Kell Hounds. I made agreements with Blizzard last night to protect all of them, and I'll stand by those agreements. You can tell him that."

"I'm not a messenger."

"And I'm not an assassin." He looked her straight in the eye. "What's your connection with Blizzard?"

"Strictly business. I pay him protection money. I give him and his friends pick of my seasoned girls and the new hires. I provide women for Volmer and Titan."

"Blizzard pays for his grandson-in-laws' mistresses?"

"Would you want your granddaughter sleeping with him?"

"I guess not." Morgan frowned. "He's a nasty customer, isn't he? His physique. He's still using steroids."

She nodded. "He has these rages."

Morgan released her, then scrubbed his hands over his face. "So, after last night, Blizzard thinks I ordered my man to take his out. That makes me dangerous, treacherous, and a threat. He'll smile, we'll talk, and he'll try to destroy me."

She nodded.

"And all you want is stability."

"That's all." She grinned impishly. "Just because a dragon needs slaying, Colonel, doesn't mean I'm a damsel in distress."

She slid from the booth and leaned forward. "And to answer your unspoken question, no, I'd not sleep with you for all the money in the world."

Then she kissed him, full on the mouth, her fingers slipping into his dark hair.

Morgan had been kissed before, and had done his fair share of kissing, but it had been nothing like this. He remembered every nanosecond of it, the warmth, the pressure of her lips on his, the moistness of the kiss, and even the surprised thrill thrumming through his belly. The kiss promised everything and withheld nothing.

And then it was broken.

She straightened up. "Thank you for your time, Colonel. I hope you find it was well spent." She turned and walked away.

He turned to slide from the booth, but stopped and just watched her walk. He couldn't tell if she expected him to follow or not, but he knew if he did, she'd be disappointed. So he sat back and licked his lips, tasting her again.

"A sociopath wants to kill you. A courtesan wants to...well, I have no idea what she wants to do. The garrison commander hates you, and every mother's-son who ever sat in a 'Mech cockpit thinks you're the BattleMech fairy come to fix his ride..."

He sighed heavily, then smiled. "Not bad work, all in all, for your first day on the planet."

Morgan returned to his office and occupied himself with financial matters until Walter brought a thickly-built man with an aquiline nose and buzz-cut into the office. Morgan judged the guy to be about ten years his senior, and spotted enough little scars on his face and the backs of his hands to mark the man as a combat veteran. The man returned the scrutiny, his restless brown eyes taking in the office as well as the man in it.

"Richard O'Cieran."

"Morgan Kell. Please, sit."

The man jerked a thumb back toward the door Walter had just closed. "Walt tells me you have a security problem."

"Blizzard."

Richard laughed. "You've been on planet a whole day and you have him angry with you?"

"Yeah."

"Good God in Heaven, you're slow. It only took me four hours."

Morgan couldn't help but smile. "On top of Blizzard being angry, and thinking I have a man who crippled one of his, we have Mr. Damiceau who tried to kidnap my brother and has threatened both of us. We need some protection. Want the job?"

Richard pursed his lips. "What I want is you to hear me out. You've probably read a file about my Crashers. Jump Infantry. We do spec ops, in/out fast and clean. We hire for big jobs and small, with a lot of small ones in a string. Thing is, we don't mind the work, but it's not using us to our full potential."

Morgan nodded. "Keep going."

"I can do your security. I can tell you the ins and outs of this place and any other you care to name. I have guys you'll never see who can cover you. Fact is, couple of my guys picked up on your brother last night as a lark."

"Did one of them take down Blizzard's man?"

"Wish I could claim credit, but I can't. They were out dancing, too, and weren't carrying." Richard smiled. "Whoever got him has a place with the Crashers whenever he wants. My point is that if we come aboard, you're going to be set for everything this side of a full blown regimental 'Mech assault. You sweat-box jocks can handle things then."

"That's good. You're hired."

"I didn't say I was signing on yet." Richard leaned forward. "Walter's high on you guys. Says you have some ideas. Let me give you another one. You 'Mech jocks, you figure yourselves the Queens of the Battlefield. Infantry, we're the Pawns. You rip things up, we hold them. Fair assessment?"

"Sure."

"Well, the way I see it, you're forgetting that Pawns that advance far enough can become Queens, too. My people, we're that advanced. Other 'Mech companies will see you coming. They'll never know we're there. Recon. Support. Attack. We can do it all. If you're really willing to embrace the future, you're going to want the Crashers for more than just making sure a snowball doesn't hit you in the ass."

Morgan couldn't help but like the man's attitude. He was right—'Mechs might win territory, but they couldn't hold it. And the simple fact was that if the Kell Hounds were going to become as feared a unit as their owners hoped, having more tactics available to them than just direct 'Mech assaults would be important.

Morgan and Richard spent the next hour deep in discussion. Morgan started by positing scenarios. Richard explained how he'd deal with them, then started challenging Morgan. Rather quickly, Morgan found himself tactically outmaneuvered in exercise after exercise.

Finally, he raised his hands. "Okay, I surrender. You win."

"No, sir. Together, *we* win." The infantry leader nodded. "I'll have my security guys covering you inside a half-hour."

"How wired into the city are you?"

Richard shrugged. "Many of my people work personal security. A bunch are bouncers for clubs. No one works for Blizzard. No one has been snowed."

"Good." Morgan half-closed his eyes. "What do you know of Veronica Matova?"

Richard whistled. "I hear tell her girls are worth it. She pays off Blizzard, but so does everyone else. You need a date, there's some that's more economical."

"No, thanks." Morgan sighed. "What's her reputation? Personally, I mean?"

"Cold, aloof, but a good whore. Stays bought until the money's gone." The man shrugged. "Same as a good mercenary, I figure."

"Would you trust her?"

"As far as I'd be inclined to trust anyone here." Richard smiled carefully. "That isn't far, Colonel, and that's a big part of the reason I'm still alive."

CHAPTER 9

NOVA ROYALE
GALATEAN CITY, GALATEA
LYRAN COMMONWEALTH
4 OCTOBER 3010

Patrick hung in the doorway of his brother's office. "I tried to get in here earlier, but you were busy. Did you have a chance to look at the file on Guinn's Gunnes?"

Morgan smiled. "They look good. One of them, Erin Finney, was at the Nagelring when I was, but washed-out halfway through. Your idea is that we bring them in, split them up?"

"I think it will work."

"What do we do with Guinn?"

"Bring him with?"

"Or?"

Patrick smiled. "He may not be the greatest leader in the Inner Sphere, but he does have an eye for talent. We could use him here as a recruiter."

Morgan hooked a hand over the back of his neck, and he suddenly looked very tired. "That's also a plan, though leaving anyone behind here is going to be tough."

"Why?"

"Blizzard has decided to repudiate the deal we struck last night."

"That's fast." Patrick decided he didn't like the weariness in Morgan's voice. "How did that happen?"

"He tried to hurt you last night. He sent a man after you, not to mark your coat as I thought, but to hurt you." Morgan stood and came around in front of his desk. "I saw some holo from a security camera. Someone followed your stalker and gave him an old-fashioned beating."

A chill ran down Patrick's spine. "I don't like the sound of that, but I'm glad he was on our side."

"Thing is we don't know if he was or not. But Blizzard thinks he was. He thinks I'm one step ahead of him. He cannot afford to let that impression grow. If he appears weak..."

"...Others will defy him, and his house of cards collapses." Patrick nodded. "Okay, I'll be super careful tonight when I go out."

"I'd prefer if you didn't."

Patrick smiled. "You want the best tech on the planet on our side?"

The elder brother's eyes narrowed. "Walter's Tech, Lattie something?"

"Laeticia Hamilton. She was the woman I met dancing."

"So this isn't all business."

Color flooded Patrick's cheeks. "Well, she dances real easy."

"Barely twenty-four hours here and you're romancing someone. What would the good fathers at Saint Bridget's think?"

"That I'm a lousy candidate for life in a monastery."

"You and me, both." Morgan shook his head. "You'll have a security detail on you."

"Okay. What about you? You're not staying in, are you?"

"No. I need to talk to several governments. There's a reception at the Combine embassy."

Patrick raised an eyebrow. "And you've been invited?"

"Not yet, but I'm sure I'll be able to get in." Morgan leaned back against his desk. "I want to make sure you understand that Blizzard is insane. If absolute power corrupts, this guy has carried it beyond anything we've imagined. He can kill with impunity, and only holds back because dead men can't pay him anything."

"I get that."

"I'm not sure you do."

Patrick rolled his eyes. "I do, Morgan, I really do. Look, he profits off this teeter-totter of hope and despair. You and I haven't been Dispossessed, but good folks who come here, looking for work, are on that knife's-edge. They have this BattleMech that's been handed down from parent to child for generations. Some since before the Star League collapsed. They come here and find that Blizzard controls the black market, so repairs and prices are high. He lends money at usurious rates. When they can't pay, he threatens to possess their 'Mechs, or he lets them work debt off. Heck, he even lets some folks—chosen at random nearly as I can tell—get hired on with merc units. He gives some recommendations for that hiring. He is the wellspring of hope here.

"And then we come along. We're offering hope, too, not just of getting off this rock, but having a future. Sign up with us and you might afford to produce that next generation to pass your 'Mech on to. Blizzard has to hate us, and has to destroy us. Just by our being here, we threaten him. It's all or nothing as far as he's concerned."

Morgan nodded. "And he'll resort to anything to win."

"But, Morgan, he washed out as a warrior." Patrick ran fingers back along his scalp. "You say he's willing to wage a war, but he doesn't know what war is. He's ready to wage a fight, but tactics and strategy? Please. He has people he can manipulate, like Volmer, but does he trust any of them enough to delegate? He can't, because the moment he shows weakness, someone supplants him just as they did the guy he took down."

Morgan chuckled. "By God, you are the smartest guy on the planet."

"Where did that come from?" Patrick smiled, feeling a little giddy. The heartfelt sentiment running through his brother's voice sparked some hope.

"Someone I met recently said it, but what you said is more important. It's us against him. He is at the heart of his organization, and can only handle so much. He has a lot of enemies, and we can make use of them. Yes, yes, that will work." Morgan smiled. "Gordon Franck gave me some information that will be helpful there, but, yes, if we overwhelm him with things, he'll break down."

"Okay, what do you need me to do?"

"For right now, just be careful. Get me your tech, and the best of the rest. Hire them away from Blizzard if you can, and get them working on the Gunnes 'Mechs. We bring the Gunnes in, we keep looking for others. Let the techs tell us who drives easy and who drives hard."

"And whose 'Mech won't be too expensive to get operational?"

"Exactly." Morgan frowned. "Our timetable just got crunched badly. We stay flexible, move fast, we can do this."

"We will do it."

Morgan smiled. "You're right. Enjoy yourself, but not too much. We have a lot of work to do tomorrow."

When Tisha walked into the restaurant, heads turned and Patrick smiled broadly in spite of his attempt to be very debonair and collected. She wore a wrap-around dress that would be perfect for dancing, and high heels that would not, but showed her legs off to great advantage. Walking with her head held high, she looked at no one but him; yet her smile suggested she knew all eyes were on her.

"Sorry I'm late. Were you waiting long?"

Patrick, standing, shook her hand, then came around and pulled the chair out for her. "Just long enough to be confused by the menu. I thought a place called Maison d'Avalon would have dishes I had a chance of recognizing but..."

She laughed and sat. "Yeah, this is some weird Liao-Davion fusion cuisine. Artichoke-Rhubarb dip, sweet-and-sour fried cheese, it is a bit daunting."

"I picked it because it was close to Club Manning." Patrick checked himself. "Actually, the hotel's concierge suggested it."

Tisha brightened. "Oh, this is the place to be seen, which is probably what she figured. A lot of mercenary leaders come here, local celebrities, the works. I've had a drink in the bar before."

"Well, dinner is on the Hounds. I just hope I can find meat here."

A waiter arrived and they ordered drinks. They each had a glass of wine. She said she didn't drink much, and Patrick didn't feel like drinking, so they were well matched. To start they split a salad and shared the artichoke-rhubarb dip which, on toasted chips of flat bread, wasn't that bad. Just enough chili powder had been tossed in to give it an edge. Their entrees—blackened redfish for her and a mango-chili marinated filet for him—were far better than he'd expected.

Tisha toyed with a flake of fish. "What convinced you and your brother that forming a mercenary unit would be good? You've said peace is profitable, but there must have been something that catalyzed your thinking."

"I don't know what it was for my brother, or for Arthur, our cousin, who bequeathed us the money to create the Kell Hounds." Patrick wiped the corner of his mouth with a napkin. "For me, there was this time at the Nagelring, when we were out on exercises. Just a tactical thing, and folks from the town came out, set up picnic lunches, and watched. One guy even drove an aircar out there, the trunk full of ice and bottles of water. Another clown—literally a clown—was making balloon animals for kids."

He leaned forward. "Look, I get the fascination for 'Mechs. When I was a kid, I'd go down to the factory whenever I could and watch them putting them together; but turning an exercise into a spectator sport, that was just not right. And I recalled that back on Terra, over a millennia ago, folks came out to a battle at a place named Gettysburg and had picnics while soldiers fought and died. And you had your gladiators and bread and circuses of Imperial Rome..."

"Like the Solaris VII games today, and the things Blizzard puts on."

"Sure, but those were sport, and you know they're sport. But there is this ghoulish fascination with war and destruction that's just wrong." Patrick frowned. "If you do a computer search on warholo, you'll find more than you could watch in a lifetime. I've seen infrared gun camera holo in which a man on foot is this glowing green figure. You hear radio chatter about a target being acquired, and all of a sudden there is this glowing splatter and pieces of him are everywhere. And you look at that and it's easy to say, 'Wow, those weapons are powerful.' But not enough people stop to think, 'Hey, that was someone's son that just got wasted.'"

"What if he was a bad guy?"

"I'm assuming he was, but that doesn't make things better. Is there anyone so evil that death is the only solution to his being a problem?"

Tisha raised an eyebrow. "But you're a Mechwarrior. Killing bad guys is what you do."

"No, it's not." He opened his hands. "Von Clauswitz suggested that war is just politics carried on by other means. What is politics? It's the process through which individuals project and manipulate their personal power. So, if we follow that back, my job as a Mechwarrior is to project and curb the projection of power. I can do that by killing someone, or I can do it by outmaneuvering him and letting him realize he'll die if he fights. Both techniques are effective, and one keeps the odds of casualties very low.

"And here's the thing. Diplomacy would work in *all* these situations. Economic trade or embargos would also work. Its just that some folks get impatient and play the war card really fast. Then others are forced to respond. But when a guy has a war card you don't want to see played, then you are more likely to agree to diplomatic solutions."

Tisha looked at him, then glanced down. "I have to confess, Patrick, that I expected you to give me this speech about glory and honor and being part of something special. I expected bands playing martial tunes and patriotism to be invoked. You're sounding fairly pacifistic here."

"Since when is pacifism unpatriotic? Realistically, isn't wanting to avoid having your fellow citizens killed patriotic?" He smiled. "When you're the guy who's going to be catching the bullets, you'd just as soon not have them flying in the first place. That doesn't mean you won't do your job. If someone else forces me to kill him, I will. What I won't be forced into doing is reveling in it. And, to get back to my original point, too many people do. Armchair generals, folks who've never been in uniform, much less commanded troops. Neither they nor their children are in the military, so they can cheer for war without fear."

Patrick sighed. "Think about it this way. I'm a warrior, and I've trained for war, the same way a surgeon trains for surgery. Do you think there is any surgeon that wants to see someone come into his operating theatre after wrapping an aircar around a tree?"

"No."

"Exactly right, but that doctor will do his job. Same thing with me. And here's the pitch, Tisha: join us and you do get to be part of something great. You'll be making sure that our people are safe, and that they can do their jobs. My brother and I will do all we can to make sure you never need to do more than routine maintenance on the 'Mechs. You'll see the Inner Sphere, you'll make good money, and you'll actually make a difference in the grand scheme of things."

She smiled and gave him a nod. Then her gaze flicked past his shoulder. The look of horror tightening her features was his only warning.

Instinctively he kicked his chair back, landing at the feet of the man who had come at him from behind. The crystal platter he'd been carrying shattered against the table. A heavy chocolate cake exploded, spattering the man's suit, Tisha, and the nearby tables. A heavy dollop of black frosting splashed his left cheek.

He never let surprise stop him. He continued back, his feet coiled, then kicked out. He caught his assailant just below the breastbone, lifting him off his feet. As that man flew back, landing on a table and collapsing it, Patrick finished his somersault and spun, fists cocked.

Thomas Volmer rose from the ruins of the table, but remained somewhat hunched over, struggling for breath. He brandished a steak knife.

Patrick laughed. "You can't honestly believe I'm afraid of you?"

"You should be."

"Really? Why's that? Because your drug use got you kicked out of the Nagelring and I wouldn't cover it up? Because your daddy controls the planet garrison? Because your wife's grandfather fixes fights so you can pretend you're a champion?" Patrick snorted. "If you had the balls God gave a...oh, wait, you're using steroids. You don't have any balls."

Volmer's eyes widened as his pupils shrank. He looked to the left and right, the knife revolving as he twitched his hand. "You think I have no balls? I can still kill you, Kell."

"In one of the toy 'Mechs you drive? I could take you with that steak knife." Patrick retrieved his napkin and wiped his face clean. "You want to challenge me to a real fight, it can be done. Right here, on Galatea. Everyone here is a witness. You can be a coward here, or in an arena. Your choice."

Some murmuring began among the patrons.

Patrick tossed the soiled napkin at Thomas' feet. "Pick it up, if you dare."

Thomas hesitated. Someone laughed.

He grabbed it. "Arastavos Arena. Real 'Mechs. To the death."

"If that's how you want to go out, your call."

Patrick turned. Tisha was standing, and another woman was helping her clean cake from her dress. Beyond her, the maitre'd was looking stricken.

Patrick made a circle with his finger. "All these dinners are on my account at the hotel. If anyone cares to bring their soiled clothes, they'll be washed. I'm sorry for disturbing your dinner."

He offered Tisha his arm. "Shall we?"

She looked at him, then nodded. "I'm not sure we're dressed for dancing still."

"Getting food stains out is better than blood." He patted her hand. "We can find new clothes and, then, I'm sure, we'll find music and a dance floor."

CHAPTER 10

Morgan had arrived at the consulate without much of a plan. Intellectually he understood that people crashed the gates at events all the time. His family's gatherings always had one or two people who managed to get in through inexplicable means. It was as if they had some sort of carte blanche which enabled them to enter.

Because the event was billed as a charity reception for some hero of the Combine, Morgan assumed he could just buy his way in. He'd had Walter try to scare up a ticket, but to no avail. Charity event tickets weren't high on the list for scalpers.

Despite not having a ticket, we went anyway. He rented a very nice tuxedo, with a ruby vest and bow tie. It was a little bolder than he liked, but he wanted to stand out. He wanted representatives seeing him speak with others of their kind, priming the pump along Patrick's suggestion.

Walter dropped him off, at his request, a block from the Consulate. He walked toward it as if he owned the place. No one at the gate even gave him a second glance, so he mingled, then moved toward the door, where some rather large ISF agents flanked a bureaucrat with a noteputer. He was scanning the invitations.

For just a half a second, Morgan's confidence failed him, and he was lost. He patted his chest as if looking for his invitation, and one of the ISF agents noticed him. About that same time Morgan figured out that the patting-your-chest routine had to be a warning sign that a gate-crasher was close, so his chances of getting in had just shrunk to nothing.

Then he felt a hand on his elbow. "I'm sorry I'm late, Colonel. Traffic was horrible."

Morgan turned and blinked. "You're right on time, Miss Matova. And quite transformed."

Veronica had opted for traditional Japanese garb, which half the people attending had chose, but none wore as well as she did. The kimono was mostly black, with red sleeves and white blossoms, so the color scheme very closely matched his tuxedo. Her cosmetics had been applied in a traditional manner, accentuating her beauty and hiding her behind the demure mask of a geisha. She shortened her gait and lowered her head. Even her hair had been bound up tightly, being woven around jeweled platinum sticks.

"You are so kind." She extended her invitation to the clerk.

He scanned it and waved them in. Morgan smiled, which did not decrease the glare the one ISF agent gave him. Once inside, he drew Veronica to a corner.

"Were you having me watched, or is this serendipity?"

"Perhaps it's both, Colonel. At the very least, it is convenient." She smiled. "You needed entry, and it would not have done for me to come alone."

Morgan looked back outside. "So someone will be waiting for you there."

"I'll make it up to him." She gave his arm a tug. "The reception line, then we can mingle."

Morgan moved with her and greeted a succession of officials up to the guest of honor. He was an officer with the feared Second Sword of Light, and his name had been emblazoned boldly on broad banner streaming down behind him. To Morgan's eye, the man seemed pained and a little bored with the reception, yet he enjoyed being the center of attention. Perhaps just a bit too much.

Morgan bowed his head, waiting for a functionary to whisper his name into the Combine officer's ear. "A pleasure to meet you, Kurita Yorinaga-*san*."

The Combine officer returned the bow. "And you, Mister Kell."

"Colonel Kell."

Yorinaga looked at him curiously. "Of which unit, please?"

"Late of the Tenth Skye Rangers. My brother and I are forming a mercenary unit. The Kell Hounds."

"I am sure you shall know great success." Yorinaga nodded kindly. "And this is your lovely wife?"

Veronica shook her head. "Good heavens, no. His wife is back home with their half-dozen children. It is a half-dozen, isn't it, dear, or has she finally delivered those twins?"

Her question gave Morgan enough time to gather his wits, otherwise he would have been stunned to silence. "Triplets, darling, and she's being induced as we speak."

Yorinaga's face became blank. Either he did not understand the conversation, or chose to feign ignorance to cover his surprise. "Good fortune to you both. Thank you for coming."

They moved on, suppressed laughter shaking both of them. Morgan steered her toward a table and took a champagne flute for both of them. "To surprises. May they all be good."

"May they all be survivable." She drank, then nodded. "You passed the first test."

"Only because you gave me a chance."

"Last time for that."

"Understood." Morgan sipped. "Whom do we terrorize next?"

"You'll have to decide that yourself." Veronica studied the room. "We see things differently here, I'm sure. I see lovers, clients, jealous partners, hopeful-nevers, and people I will have to acknowledge though I would rather gouge an eye out."

"Theirs?"

"Preferably." She smiled. "You, on the other hand, are seeing employers, enemies, and innocent bystanders. Speaking of the former: How are you, Mr. Damiceau? Do you know Colonel Kell, Morgan Kell?"

The small agent of the Free Worlds League looked rather comical attired as a samurai, but at least he had eschewed the topknot. "I believe I made the acquaintance of your brother the other day."

"You bought him a drink."

"I made him a business offer. It still stands."

Morgan sipped champagne for a second. "Which offer was that? Buy us off, or kill us off?"

"Your brother must have misunderstood."

"It's possible." Morgan smiled. "I'm willing to allow as how you and Patrick got off on the wrong foot. You ought to know, however, that I've taken out some insurance. If my brother or I are killed, maimed, or even inconvenienced, there will be a bounty on your head. Before our bodies have been claimed, you'll be on a slab in the morgue beside us. Is that clear?"

"As clear as it is rash and imprudent." Damiceau snorted haughtily. "I am not going to be the one who will visit harm upon you."

"Blizzard will. I know."

"So shift your assassins to him."

"Just easier to employ another assassin." Morgan patted the man on the shoulder, leaving his hand heavy there. "I think you understand now that we have a vested interest, you and I, in keeping my brother and me alive. I think that unity of interest is a good basis for negotiations, don't you?"

The little man quaked. "You're being unreasonable."

"No, that will come when we negotiate terms. For now, though, the idea that we won't form the unit is off the table. You might be able to purchase a contract codicil that bars us from attacking certain areas for a certain amount of time. Perhaps we should talk about that, tomorrow, in my office? The afternoon? I'll have whiskey available."

Damiceau's face knotted up, then he nodded. "Tomorrow, then."

Morgan offered the man his hand. Damiceau took it, then Morgan pulled him into a backslapping hug. "Glad to do business with you."

The Marik agent retreated and many watched him go. Veronica nodded appreciatively at Morgan. "So young and so skilled."

"When your family controls the output of a 'Mech factory, lots of people come and make promises. My uncle Seamus had the gift. He could charm birds out of trees, C-bills out of budgets, and yet turn around and cut the heart out of someone who had betrayed him. That was good for starters, however."

"Shall I leave you to it?"

"Not too long. How long had you planned to stay?"

She laughed mildly. "I've come, I've been seen. I can leave any time at all."

"And catch up with your companion for the evening?"

Her eyes narrowed, becoming cold and feline. "You are my chosen companion, this evening, Colonel Kell. For reasons of my own. Reasons I will not discuss with you. If this does not suit you, we can terminate our alliance right now."

"I beg your pardon." He stepped close to her, close enough to catch a hint of the cherry-blossom perfume she wore. "That was ill-mannered of me and uncalled for."

"Forgiven, this once." Her smile returned, radiant. "I will find you."

Morgan watched her go. The crowd parted around her quickly, but crushed in at her wake even more so. Everyone gawked and hands hid whispers behind her back. Men confided to their buddies that they'd had her. Women discussed rumors—about her, about her clients, about how the Inner Sphere had so declined that someone like her could enter polite company.

"She is quite exquisite, isn't she?" An older woman approached Morgan from the left. "Amanda Heartsthorne, Federated Suns. You'd be Morgan Kell."

"I am, and she is."

"Your unit must already be doing well if you can afford..."

"We can always do better. You could use a regiment on the Combine border." Morgan nodded at the guest of honor. "You know you're going to see him and the Second Sword on the border soon enough. Mara. Klathandu IV, either of those could be targets."

"Some of our people predict Mallory's World."

"That would be a miserable place to fight."

"Agreed, Colonel, to both points. We could use someone."

"Kell Hounds will be the answer to your prayers."

"The problem with that idea, Colonel, is that prayers require God, and God requires faith. While I might have faith in God, I have no faith in a mercenary unit that has, at last count, three pilots and an infantry unit doing security work. Hardly a regiment."

"We've only been on planet for a day and a half."

"And not likely to last another day." Heartsthorne accepted a glass of champagne from a passing waiter. "I won't enumerate the difficulties you have with Blizzard. You are being watched, however, on how you deal with him. There is more than one unit which has seen its bargaining power hurt by how they dealt with him."

Morgan arched an eyebrow. "Is that because they're beholden to him, so you know you can chisel them down, or is dealing with a crime boss supposed to be a test of one's mettle?"

"You forgot the other two choices. Am I in his employ?" She shook her head before continuing. "Or could it be that we judge sagacity by one's ability to work around him without major trouble?"

"Doubtless you think it's the latter." He set his glass on the table. "But avoiding a fight isn't the mark of wisdom. Knowing which fight to avoid is. And when you can't avoid it, you figure out how to win it. Strikes me, that's what you want in a mercenary leader."

"A good point." She looked into the depths of her champagne as if searching for inspiration. "If you survive this fight, we will have to speak further."

"I think you'll find, Ambassador Heartsthorne, that if we don't speak before then, the Kell Hounds will become very expensive afterward."

"Given the odds, that's a risk I will take."

She withdrew as well. Representatives from the Combine and Capellan Confederation came by to pay their respects—and it did seem like more of a funeral call than a legitimate overture for business. Still, they did come by.

General Volmer sauntered over. "We meet again."

"I'd have thought you had enough of me at our last meeting, General."

"I would like to think you've grown since then, Colonel, and have seen the error of your ways." Volmer smiled easily. "I only wanted my son to be made a major. Now he'll have the same rank as your brother."

Morgan folded his arms over his chest. "Let me ask you something, just between us. What do you see when you look at Haskell Blizzard? Really. In your heart of hearts. You hold him in contempt, don't you? He's something you ought to be scraping off your shoes, right?"

Volmer's expression became grim. "A gentleman doesn't—"

"No, of course not, but it's true." Morgan leaned in. "So how is it, then, that you can stand taking his money, his orders, and knowing your son looks up to him the way he should be looking up to you?"

The general's face burned crimson. "You, sir, are neither honorable nor a gentleman."

"You may be right on both of those counts, General, but I'm not the one suckling at a shylock's teat. Oh, yes, that's right, get your indignation up. Tell me that if you were a younger man you'd challenge me to a duel, or that I have more trouble brewing than I know how to handle." Morgan laughed loudly. "Go on, that was what you were going to do, wasn't it?"

Volmer's chin came up. "Perhaps, just perhaps, I was going to offer you an opportunity to make things right. You've lost that chance, Colonel, through your arrogance and insolence."

"Nice cover, General, but it doesn't wash. You can bark all you like, but it's your master's voice that's to be listened to. He wants this right, he can come to me."

Morgan dismissed Volmer with a wave, then found Veronica at his side. "Time to go already?"

"Quite. Our welcome is wearing thin."

"My fault or yours?"

Her eyes twinkled. "Theirs."

Arm in arm they slipped from the consulate, and once on the street, shared laughter. All the tension drained from Morgan. He'd made contact with people and even if some of the representatives were standoffish, Damiceau would come talk to him. That meant the others had to as well. Every day he'd be a step closer to putting the unit together and leaving Galatea.

Veronica leaned against him as she laughed, then slipped. He caught her in his arms, held her fast. Her head came up and their gazes locked. She reached up, brushing fingertips over his cheek, then he crushed her to him and they kissed.

Morgan had once heard it said that there was nothing as exciting as a first kiss. From that moment forward, it wasn't a statement he'd let go unchallenged. The first kiss had taken him by surprise, but this one he was prepared for. The hunger, the urgency, the warmth. This time he gave as good as he got, and then some. When it seemed their mouths would part, they kissed again and again, lost in each other.

Finally, with hands on his shoulders, Veronica pushed back. "You're not taking me home with you."

"You mean that as a statement, or an unfinished question?"

Her eyes half-closed. "Perhaps both. Doesn't matter. I'm not the kind of woman you want to take home."

Morgan released her and took a step back. "This noon we established there's no difference between us."

She nodded. "And you're probably the first man I've met from whom I believe that. But when I say I'm not the kind of woman you take home, I mean it in a different way. You don't trust me, Morgan."

An icy realization trickled through his guts. "You may be right."

"I am. No, I'm not offended. You really can't trust me. You know my connections to Blizzard, and we first met in his company. And even if our having a mutual enemy makes us allies, that's no reason for trust."

"Point well taken."

Her smile contracted into a grim grin. "And I suppose I don't trust you. You could still fail me. Chances are very good that you will."

"Veronica..."

She held a hand up as a black limousine pulled up at the curb. "No, Morgan, don't disappoint me. Don't tell me that a physical alliance could build trust. If you think sleeping with people is a good reason to trust them, you're more of a fool than I want to imagine. Good night, Morgan Kell, and sweet dreams."

CHAPTER 11

Even before Tisha and he left the dining room, Patrick knew they were in trouble. The two inside members of the security team sat very still at the bar, their empty hands pressed flat on the bar. Two larger gentlemen stood behind them, smiling, clearly prodding them with hidden needlers.

He shivered. The needle pistol shaved flechettes from a block of ballistic polymer and expelled them at high velocity. At long range the needles might stick in you like quills, but at point-blank range they'd snap bone, tear flesh and reduce internal organs to paté.

That shiver repeated itself when he felt something hard jammed to his spine.

A gruff voice whispered in his ear. "We're going out through the kitchen. Mr. Blizzard has transportation waiting. Don't do anything stupid, or she dies first."

He glanced at Tisha. She'd grown pale, but her expression was anything but hopeless. A man had his hand on the back of her neck, and if he could have seen the fire in her eyes, he'd have removed it no matter how well armed he was. She gave Patrick a little nod, which he returned.

Their captors shoved them through the kitchen door, into a world of clanging pots, stained white clothes, and utter chaos through which they passed unnoticed. In fact, the help studiously avoided looking at them. That didn't surprise Patrick—these people had to live in Blizzard's world. In their shoes...

He thought for a moment. In their shoes, he would get involved, but that was precisely why he wasn't in their shoes. He had the luxury of means that allowed him to look past issues of daily survival. He'd been brought up believing that it was his duty to serve others as best he could. While he wanted to hope that the staff would agree with that idea, at least in principle, he understood their reluctance to act.

Then one of them did.

Just past the ovens, a large black man was mopping the floor. With a twist of his wrist, he snapped ten centimeters of the mop handle off and stabbed Patrick's captor through the neck. Blood gushed hot against Patrick's scalp. The MechWarrior spun, shoving his dying assailant back as Tisha cut to her left.

The man who'd been holding her shot, missing both Trisha and their savior. His companion's body slammed into him, pitching him back against the ovens. He reached out to steady himself. Flesh sizzled, and he screamed.

The black man slapped the pistol away, then smashed the stick against the man's head. He started to fall, but their savior caught him, shoved his head into an open oven space, then kicked the door closed hard. Vertebrae snapped, and the stink of burning hair filled the room.

Patrick scooped up a needler and trained it on the door. He kicked the other one toward Tisha, but the black man intercepted it.

Patrick shook his head. "You've done enough. You don't need to get any deeper into this."

The man laughed, white teeth flashing. "What is it with you Kell boys? Always wanting to be the martyr."

"Excuse me?" The man looked vaguely familiar, then Patrick placed him. He'd been in the hotel lobby bar, and out dancing at Club Manning. "Who are you?"

"Cat Wilson. Know your brother. Tenth Skye."

"And he had you watching me?"

"He doesn't even know I'm here."

The ruckus had caught someone's attention. Both doors to the kitchen burst open. The man coming through the out door collided with a heavily laden waiter. His gun went one way, the waiter another, and both of them were buried by a clatter of serving-silver and steaming bisque.

That distracted his gun-toting partner for a nano-second, which it all it took for Patrick's first shot to shred most of the meat from his thigh. Cat's shot ripped up his shoulder and Patrick's second shot removed a chunk of scalp and drove bone fragments into the man's brain. He was dead before he sprawled on the floor.

The other man struggled to get up, but a whirling skillet slammed into the side of his head. Hair melted and flesh bubbled against the hot metal, but it was the dent in his skull that was his biggest problem. He went down hard and the skillet spun to a stop in a puddle of boiling soup.

Tisha blew on her hand and the burns from throwing the skillet.

Patrick went for the front of the house. *If transportation's out back...* Stepping over the man Tisha had brained, he went through the door low, knowing the bar would cover him from anyone in the dining room.

Both of O'Ciernan's men were down, but unhurt. One was digging for a compact needler in an ankle holster, while the other was on a communicator. Their faces brightened as he emerged.

Cat came behind him, then Tisha. She carried a needle pistol in her good hand and had a towel wrapped around the burn. Cat moved forward, covering the dining room, while Patrick moved the other way around the island bar. Tisha followed Cat and the security men focused on the kitchen.

In the dining room, two more of Blizzard's men flanked Volmer. They had their pistols out, but were exposed. The patrons had all hunkered down, leaving the three of them the only viable targets.

Pistol leveled and held in two hands, Patrick came around the edge of the wall. "We still have our date, Tommy. You two, guns down. Give them to that nice lady there. That's good."

Thomas Volmer sneered—which might have been fearsome save for the way frosting still darkened his pale eyebrows. "You have no clue how badly you've stepped in it, do you, Kell?"

"It isn't the stepping-in that's important, Tommy, it's the getting out and scraping off. Four of your boys need to be scraped off the inside of that kitchen. And everyone here's a witness to your accepting my challenge, and Blizzard not thinking you have the guts to meet me. There's only one way of getting out of that for you."

One of the security guys moved to the door. "We're clear to go, Colonel."

"Again, sorry for the disturbance, folks." Patrick waited for Tisha to get clear, then slipped through the door. Walter had pulled up in an aircar. Patrick dove in after Tisha, and Cat jammed himself into the front seat.

Walter gave him a look.

Patrick shrugged. "Like you, he knows how to submit a job application."

Walter laughed. "Back to the hotel?"

"Yes, we should be safe there." He turned to Tisha. "You can stay in the suite. Blizzard will figure out who you are and your place won't be safe. I'm sorry about that."

"Don't be. I'm a big girl. I knew the risks of getting involved." She handed him the needle pistol. "I just didn't..."

Patrick accepted the gun, then slipped an arm around her shoulder, pulling her close. She started trembling, so he held her tight. "It's going to be okay."

"This is what it's like in combat?"

"Yeah, years of boredom, hours of terror, seconds of action, and then it starts all over again." He kissed her forehead. "And now you know why we're working to hard to make that decades of boredom."

She clung to him, burying her face against his neck. She didn't sob, but tears did soak his shirt. He hung on, stroking her back. "We'll get your hand looked at, hot bath, warm brandy and bed. It will be okay."

"Do you think the guy I hit..."

"Colossal headache. It was the only thing you could have done."

"He didn't leave me any choice."

"Neither did Blizzard." Patrick stroked her hair. "And his will be the consequences to live with."

Patrick woke up only when Morgan sat on the couch at his feet and extended a cup of coffee toward him. "Busy night?"

Patrick pulled himself into a sitting position and accepted the coffee. "Not quite what I expected."

"O'Ciernan filled me in."

"You know this guy Cat Wilson?"

Morgan smiled. "Well enough to know he's AWOL from the Tenth Skye Rangers. They won't be happy about that. Cat knows that, too, which is why he took off before I got back. I'd like to have him in the unit, but we'll have to clear his status up first."

Patrick took a swallow of the coffee, then set the cup down. "You still make the world's worst coffee."

"You don't see me drinking it, do you?"

"Heh." Patrick pulled his blanket around him. "Did O'Ciernan tell you about my challenging Titan? It was kind of heat of the moment. Not proceeding in stealth mode but..."

"I've been thinking." His brother's face took on a quixotic expression that usually betokened some rather clever scheming. "This is going to work in our favor. You challenged Titan. Blizzard's lost face in having his kidnap attempt thwarted. Now if something happens to you or me, he's cheating because his champion is a coward. This actually buys us a bubble of safety. This can work."

The suite's door clicked, then swung open. Gordon Franck stepped in. "Sorry for doing this, but it's important. The messages you wanted sent got sent, Morgan. Coming back from ComStar, I ran into Haskell Blizzard in the lobby. He wants to talk to you. Now."

Morgan's smile ran from ear to ear. "Send him up."

"You gonna poison him with your coffee?"

"Nope, I have better plans."

"You know he'll manipulate things so we lose."

"I know." Morgan nodded toward Patrick's room. "Go get dressed. You don't need to say anything, but you'll want to see this."

Haskell Blizzard entered the suite accompanied by four bodyguards, but he dismissed them immediately. They slunk from the room like whipped puppies. Outside, in the hallway, they stood trapped between two rows of O'Ciernan's people.

The crime boss accepted a chair without its being offered and perched on the arm. "You put me in a very curious position, Colonel Kell. Do you actually believe that this public challenge between your brother and Titan will in any way affect things between us? I really don't feel hampered by it at all."

"I never would have assumed you did. Public opinion means nothing to the man with all the power, and you're that man." Morgan shrugged. "But, if you do something rash, you have two problems. First, the Archon may be a long way away, but she does have a certain affection for the two of us. You might be able to bribe officials like Volmer, but Loki agents are notoriously fanatical in their loyalty to the Archon. On top of that, there are members of the nobility who would crush you simply because you dared challenge someone from their class."

"I'm not concerned."

"Because that's not your big problem. Your big problem is that if you act rashly, someone in your organization is going to see that as a sign of weakness." Morgan moved to a desk in the far corner and turned a computer monitor around. "I've done some research. In the last two days you've lost five men, all of whom were attempting to hurt my brother. You've not lost that many in five years, save the ones you've had who have met with 'unfortunate accidents.'"

Blizzard chuckled coldly. "I have no fear of rebellion in the ranks."

"Nice cover. Of course you do. This is the reason you're moving as fast as you are. You know this is all or nothing for you."

Blizzard sat forward, his expression sharpening. "You presume too much."

"I presume to see a solution."

The crime boss's expression softened. "I'm listening."

"It's simple. Everything is decided by Patrick's fight with Titan."

"I would be foolish to risk everything on that fight."

"You have little choice; and if you think that way, you're missing what's most important." Morgan called up a spreadsheet. "You're fighting us because you see we could cut into your profit potential. We can take away people who will continue to pay you money for the rest of your life. But you're missing the fact that when you look at it, your gaming operations can prove far more profitable than your shylocking, especially if you get off-world distribution of the fights. Battles among mercenaries are far more serious than the glorified actors on Solaris VII. This fight has great aftermarket potential, not to mention what you'll make here off it."

Morgan opened his arms. "What's more important to you? That people hold you in high regard, or that they give you money?"

The older man's eyes narrowed. "I can see the profit potential, surely. What's in this for you?"

"Publicity." Morgan laughed. "We make this big. We make it huge. Pull out all the stops. You get General Volmer there in his 'Mech, with an Honor Guard for the playing of the Lyran anthem. You pack the arena with notables. I'll buy a suite. I'll host the Mercenary liaisons. After we're done, everyone on this rock will know of the Kell Hounds, and our fame will spread further."

His brother's voice dropped. "But that's not all. I'll guarantee you a minimum of ten million C-bills."

"And how will you do that?"

"I'll bet a lot of money on my brother. Everyone already knows Titan's fights are fixed, so the smart money will bet with me. Long odds against Titan. And then my brother will throw the fight."

"What!" Patrick's jaw dropped. "No! No goddamned way, Morgan, no way!"

Morgan pointed at him, but addressed Blizzard. "You thought I couldn't go lower than you? There, big step in that direction. It'll be a good fight, but Titan gets his reputation back, you clean up in the betting."

"But your brother looks bad."

"There is no such thing as bad publicity. Plus, I lose heavily on the fight, I get to plead poverty when negotiating with mercenaries to come aboard. I win, too. You'll give me five million in credit against monies owed to you, and we settle up on anyone else I take."

"Morgan, I am not throwing that fight!" Patrick slammed a fist against the wall.

Morgan's eyes blazed. "You will follow orders, Colonel, do you understand?"

The edge in his voice brought Patrick up short. He'd only heard Morgan speak like that a couple times, and it hadn't been good. "Yes, sir," he replied stiffly.

Blizzard stood slowly. "I may have underestimated you, Colonel Kell. I wondered if you were a worthy adversary."

"No more wondering. I make a better ally. We both get what we want, and other fools pay."

"And handsomely at that." He smiled at Patrick. "It will only sting for a moment."

Morgan nodded. "He'll learn. I'll have Mr. Franck draw up a press release about the battle and get it out to media outlets. Typical rhetoric. We'll get things going."

"Satisfactory. I'll send the standard contract around. Could be I'll enjoy doing business with you." Blizzard nodded. "For your sake, you better hope I do."

The crime boss left the suite and Patrick hands knotted into fists. "How can you even imagine I'd throw a fight?"

Morgan held a hand up, then went to the chair Blizzard had occupied. He flipped a cushion around, then pulled it away from the chair. Plucking a slender black filament from it, he dumped it into the half-empty bottle of Wolf's Paw on the sideboard.

"I can't and I don't. He knows that, too."

"So he knows you're scheming."

"Right. And he knows he'll have to sabotage the fight himself, to make sure Titan wins. Moreover, he'll do it in a way that disgraces us." Morgan smiled. "It'll be pretty disgusting."

"Then why..." Patrick closed his eyes and sighed. "He's going to be trying to figure out what you're doing, which is going to keep him distracted. We can do anything, even random things, and he'll be trying to make sense of them."

"Right, and random patterns make no sense, so he can't, but he'll keep trying." Morgan slipped an arm over his brother's shoulder. "As you said, he can wage a fight. We're waging war.

"His learning the difference will be a very costly lesson."

CHAPTER 12

NOVA ROYALE
GALATEAN CITY, GALATEA
LYRAN COMMONWEALTH
5 OCTOBER 3010

Morgan smiled as he opened the suite door for Veronica Matova. "You look radiant."

"And you look predatory." She caressed his cheek. "It's a good look for you."

He ushered her in past him with a hand on the small of her back. "I wasn't sure you'd come after last night."

"Why?" She turned her profile to him. "Did I judge you incorrectly?"

"Partly."

"Which part?"

Morgan glanced down. "I'll admit I wanted another kiss."

"And another and another?"

"Perhaps, at another time." He guided her to a chair. "Drink?"

"Too early for me, but you go ahead."

"Too early is right."

She looked up, smiling. "I don't believe you want just one kiss."

Morgan shook his head. She was, without question, one of the most beautiful women he'd ever met. Her poise and confidence attracted him. It marked her strength, yet suggested there was some weakness in there somewhere. And, until he learned what that was...

"What I want and what I wanted last night are two entirely different things. You were correct. I can't trust you because I don't know you. I know the person you project yourself to be. I can make judgments based off that, but to go any further, that's too risky."

"So, you don't want to sleep with me?"

"The tone of your question—you know the answer." He let a grin slowly reveal his teeth. "But that's really immaterial between us, isn't it, since it will never happen."

She laughed and sank back into the cushions. "Reverse psychology, Morgan?"

"Statement of fact, Veronica." His grin died. "You had it right when we first met. You know I would never buy you. You would never sell yourself to me. And since we can't trust each other, we're not going to share a bed. We hold ourselves in too great esteem to do that and, though we barely know each other, we do respect each other."

"So you don't think there is any attraction between us?"

Morgan's bass laughter filled the room. "Darling, if they could hook leads onto us, the attraction would charge a Kearny-Fuchida drive in 4.2 nanoseconds. There's attraction, and it's all the stronger because this lack of trust makes us forbidden. You know that. It's part of your stock in trade. You are forbidden, which makes you that much more desirable. Not that you need to be more desirable."

She cocked her head for a second. "I must be slipping. You shouldn't have been able to see through me that quickly."

"I'm only seeing through what you let me see through." He shrugged. "I know that. I accept it, just as I accept you'll never reveal to me any more than you want me to imagine. You could spin a fantasy for me, and I'd believe it. Again, part of your stock in trade."

Veronica sat forward again. "And this is the part of the story where I open myself to you. I tell you about my tale of woe, how my mother was widowed and how my stepfather abused me. I fled to the streets and a kindly madam uncovered my beauty. She taught me all I need to know, and I gradually surpassed her. I built my empire providing girls the same nurturing environment we all fled to find. I create fantasies for customers and appear hard and cold to be that much more alluring, but really I'm just a twelve-year-old girl inside who wants to be loved for being me. Will you be the one to love me, Morgan?"

As she spoke, his mind raced. The story she wove fit perfectly. It tugged at his heartstrings. She was a damsel in distress, and he was a white knight.

Except, she's not in distress.

Morgan applauded politely. "Nicely done."

"But you don't believe it?"

"It's believable. I could believe anything, but it really doesn't matter, does it? The past isn't real. All we have are memories, which are notoriously inaccurate. You could tell me that story with full conviction that it's true, and it might be a total fabrication that you've taught yourself to believe. Your whole being could be wrapped up in it, so you'll never open yourself to the truth. But the fact is that the person you are today is based on whatever core truth you choose to acknowledge."

"What's your core truth, Morgan?"

"You don't really want to know." He crossed his arms over his chest. "The only core truth that's important here is that you and I do share an enemy. You've heard about the fight. You know Blizzard is not going to let my brother win. That doesn't mean Blizzard won't be defeated or hurt. I need you to help me to hurt him. I want to hire you and your people to do that."

"What do you have in mind?"

Morgan smiled slowly. "I want to place a lot of money on my brother, to win. I'll bet some openly. I want to hire some of your people to place bets on my behalf. If it gets out that I'm financing their bets, that's fine. I'd also like the word spread that a bet on my brother is a sure thing. I don't know when Blizzard will get uncomfortable about the betting, but I don't want to have to use my money alone to get to that level."

Her eyes tightened. "How certain a bet is it?"

"A hundred percent lock."

"You say that as if you mean it." Veronica tapped a finger against her chin. "And if I said I'd put a million c-bills of my own on your brother, would that change your statement?"

He shook his head. "I'll indemnify you for that million."

"And in return?"

"When Patrick wins, you'll tell me your true story."

Surprise flickered over her face for a heartbeat, then the serene mask returned. "We have a bargain. And here is what I shall do for you, Morgan. You don't need to hire my people to place your bets. I'll let them know where my money is going. I'll have them place bets for you, and they will certainly let their clientele know. There are enough people here who want to take a piece out of Blizzard that money will flood in."

"Good. Know one thing. My brother will win." Morgan nodded. "I will, however, need to hire some of your people for the day of the fight. I will be entertaining, in a luxury box. I need..."

"Eye-candy?"

"It may be a bit more, depending. I'll have the Mercenary liaisons there."

"Oh, so delicate." She laughed. "I know them all. They're a yes, yes, no, maybe, and twins if I have them. I do. It will be tasteful and pleasing."

"And I would like you to be there, too."

"I might have a previous engagement."

"Break it."

"I'll be there as a hostess, or your companion, or your co-conspirator?"

"As a friend."

"Are we friends, really, Morgan, or just allies?"

He shrugged. "Depends on what story you want to make up about us, Veronica."

She nodded. "I'll work on the story, but I think it will include my being there. Maybe."

Morgan laughed, but before he could make a comment, a heavy fist pounded on the suite door. "Galatea Constabulary. We have a warrant!" The door clicked and a frightened housekeeper stood back as a half-dozen law officers flooded in. In their wake came General Volmer and a major wearing military police insignia.

Morgan forced a smile. "Good to see you, General. This saves me a trip out to your base."

"Turn him over now, Kell, and save yourself a lot of trouble."

"Who would that be?"

The major stepped forward as his minions searched the suite. He produced a noteputer and punched up surveillance holo from the restaurant. It showed Cat Wilson very plainly stabbing a man in the neck. The officer froze the image, zoomed in, then split the screen and brought up an order for the man's arrest on charges of being AWOL.

"Clarence Wilson. Do you know him, Colonel?"

Morgan shook his head. "I don't believe I do."

"Oh come on, Kell. Save the lies for something that might possibly be true." Volmer threw his hands into the air. "Wilson was in your company in the Tenth Skye Rangers. Of course you knew him."

"Do you remember everyone who was ever under your command, General?"

"This was two months ago. You resigned, he vanished."

"And you think I would form an acquaintance with someone who took his duty so lightly that he would desert?"

Volmer snarled. "The man saved your brother's life!"

The major nodded. "We believe he may have also been the man who mugged a citizen outside Club Manning two nights ago."

"He saved your brother twice, Kell, now where are you hiding him?"

"You have your warrant. You're doing your search. You won't find him here." Morgan spitted the major with a hard stare. "It's rather odd, though, that this man has, according to the General, 'saved my brother twice,' and yet I don't recall hearing about any arrests in either of the alleged incidents where my brother needed rescuing. Did you come here to arrest my brother for last night, too?"

The major suddenly looked stricken.

Volmer slapped the man on the shoulder. "Go supervise the search." He turned to Veronica. "You'll want to leave."

"She's my guest, General."

"Not a surprise." He snorted. "What I have to say to you, you won't want her hearing."

"That would be my choice, General."

Veronica stood. "No, Morgan, it's my choice. I will be leaving. Good to see you again, General. I hope your wife is well. She's the only person you'll be sleeping with for the next month."

Volmer didn't even have the good graces to blush. He ignored her, remaining silent until the door closed behind her. "You think you've got this all figured out, don't you? You and Blizzard have an arrangement. This fight is something you worked out."

Morgan chuckled. "And he's not let you in on it, has he? He's told you that you have to be there, yes? Honor Guard and all?"

"Yes."

"Did he tell you to bet heavily on your son?"

Volmer hesitated. "He said that would be a safe bet."

"But you know your own son. You know he couldn't beat my brother with an assault lance joining in."

"I'm not going to allow my son to be humiliated." The man shifted uneasily. "Your brother's hurt him enough."

"My brother did what had to be done. Your son couldn't control his rages. He was using steroids and drugs, he was taking his rages out in hazing on younger cadets. Patrick and others reached out to him, but Tommy rebuffed them. Patrick had no choice but to bring him up to an Honor Board. He's lucky he was just expelled, and not imprisoned."

"Mark me, Morgan Kell, my son will not be humiliated."

Morgan let his words roll out in a low, rumbling growl. "And understand me, General. I've only been here a short time, but I've collected some interesting files on you and how you run the garrison. Very interesting files. Now I've prepared some documents. I've distributed them to people. You interfere with me and this fight, and they're going to ComStar. They'll be on Tharkad in an eyeblink, with return messages paid for. Yes, that's expensive, but in this case, it will be well worth it."

Volmer stared at him, his eyes flickering as he imagined every little impropriety being spun into a disaster. Then his eyes narrowed. "You cannot threaten me."

"I just have."

"And you forget that this planet is under my command. You have no idea the resources I wield."

"No, General, this planet is under Blizzard's command. You can't squeak out a fart but he doesn't give you an order." Morgan smiled. "Well, your boss and I have reached an accommodation. Just your luck that you and your son are the fulcrum. So sorry if you get crushed, but that's the way it is when you annoy your betters."

"I'm warning you, Kell—"

"Sure, General. All bark, no bite. In this Blizzard and I agree. You're a joke. We both know it. Someday you'll see it, but I don't think you'll find it very funny."

Morgan pointed toward the door. "The constabulary has their warrant, so they must be here. You are no longer a guest. Wait in the hall. I'm sure they'll fetch you."

Volmer waited in the hall, alternately fuming and trembling with fear. The mercenary's insolence infuriated him. Kell had the audacity to confront him with his son's shortcomings, talk down to him, and threaten him with exposure.

The threats he could handle. Everyone threatened him, but with Blizzard at his back, none of those threats came to fruition. Blizzard supported him, and he supported Blizzard. It was a wonderfully symbiotic relationship, and one that benefited them both mightily.

But Kell had hinted at something dark, and that was where the fear came from. Volmer had always known that, some day, Blizzard would turn on him. He always had an escape clause, of course. He could resign his commission and head to any of the dozen worlds where he could retire. He should have done it years ago, though the allure of Matova's women, and Blizzard's willingness to foot the bill, had been one among many inducements that kept him around.

He'd even handed his son over to Blizzard to solidify their alliance. Volmer's stomach knotted as he thought about it. He loved his son, but couldn't control him. Blizzard could, or could control the circumstances that threatened his son. Both men knew Tommy was a hostage and might someday outlive his usefulness, but Blizzard's granddaughter seemed to have true affection for him.

Volmer wondered when that wouldn't be enough to save his son.

Could be that it's already gone... Volmer hugged his arms around himself. Kell and Blizzard had reached an agreement. Though the fix was supposed to be in so Tommy would win, Volmer couldn't help feel doom overshadowing his boy. Something wasn't right. Something odd was happening. He had to find out what it was.

His head came up as Major Choate and the constables left the suite. "Well?"

The major shook his head. "Nothing. No hair or fingerprints. If the man was here, there's no sign."

Volmer nodded. "Thank you, constables. Major, a moment." The civilian authorities took the lift down and the military officers waited for another.

Once inside the box Volmer looked at his subordinate. "There is something going on here. I'm issuing Order Maroon."

"Sir?"

"I have an understanding with Precentor Kinnock. We are delaying and embargoing some messages."

Choate exhaled slowly. "As ordered, sir. Subjects?"

"Anything having to do with the coming fight. Anything Morgan Kell is sending out. Any messages going out to Tharkad alleging impropriety on my part."

Choate made notes on his computer. "You will be reviewing these yourself?"

"Yes." Volmer nodded solemnly. "A disaster is brewing, Major, and it is my duty to stop it before it explodes."

CHAPTER 13

Haskell Blizzard studied the returns scrolling over his computer screen. His betting parlors were doing land-office business. Odds on Patrick Kell had become short, and long on Titan. Two days out from the fight and Morgan Kell's prediction of a ten million c-bill profit looked to be low by half.

Morgan Kell had even kept up his side of the bargain. He'd bet his own money. He'd used agents to bet even more. Haskell was uncertain if those efforts were meant to deceive him, or to weave a phantom conspiracy that others would join into. Intention really didn't matter, since the bets came flooding in.

Veronica Matova had also bet and bet heavily. She was a bit of a problem. A lovely bauble, to be sure, but she had a mind of her own. Blizzard had allowed her to grow powerful because she so often served his purposes. Here, however, she was standing up on her own hind feet. She needed to be taught a lesson, and it would be a painful one. Once he would have warned her about the fix, but not this time. Her arrogance would cost her dearly.

Still, the volume of betting was a problem, and it didn't matter that the fix was in. Morgan Kell had to know that he'd do anything he needed to do to cover his win, this side of murdering the Kells. There Morgan had been correct. That would have been seen as weakness, and Blizzard could not afford that, nor could he afford any scrutiny from Tharkad.

He fully assumed Morgan was prepared to double-cross him. Patrick Kell would win the fight and Blizzard would both be hit hard economically, as well as having his image trashed. The former would hurt more than the latter; and it was the former he'd have a hard time surviving.

At the current levels of betting, if Patrick Kell won, Blizzard's liability would be in excess of thirty million C-bills. The betting on Titan would not cover that gap. Aside from freezing all betting—which would be tantamount to running and hiding—Blizzard had only one alternative.

He had to lay off bets.

In essence, he had to take some of the money he'd collected and bet on Patrick Kell to win, too. If Kell did manage a miracle, Haskell's winnings would help him repay his losses. He couldn't, however, place those bets on Galatea, since someone would smell a rat. Others would stop taking his bets, while people would increase their betting on Patrick. It would be a disaster.

Fortunately, the fight had attracted some off-world interest, and since the oddsmakers there were basing their odds on information Blizzard had sent them, they were much more evenhanded in what they were offering. By sending five million off-world, he could easily cover his debts and make a more modest profit. If Kell lost, he'd still have his ten million.

This was nothing out of the ordinary, and Blizzard even enjoyed doing the calculations. He shaved things as finely as he could, then arranged for agents to place the bets through ComStar. With the fight two days off, he'd be covered no matter what happened.

Satisfied, he sat back in his chair and smiled. "So now you may do your worst, Morgan Kell. I guarantee you that it shall be nothing compared to how I shall repay you in kind."

HAMILTON ARMOR AND DENT, LTD.
GALATEAN CITY, GALATEA

Patrick Kell paused, crouched on the *Blackjack*'s shoulder. "Walter, are you sure about this?"

Walter, standing on the ground next to Tisha, gave him a salute. "Absolutely, sir. It's an honor to have my commanding officer check out my 'Mech. Been with the de Mesnils for the last two centuries." Walter scratched at his hair, parting locks that had been fused with red paint. "More of an honor when you kick Titan's sorry ass in this thing."

The humanoid 'Mech had no hands, since both arms ended in cannon muzzles. Twin medium lasers ran on the outside of each forearm, giving it considerable firepower for something considered only medium weight. Tisha had repaired the damaged actuator, then

Walter had spent all night repainting in Kell Hound colors: a red body, with black arms.

Patrick slipped in through the hatch and closed it behind him. The closeness of a cockpit unnerved some people, but felt like home to him. Walter had cleared out personal mementoes, but it had a lived-in feel that none of the factory fresh 'Mechs ever had. The centuries of history, though only visible in a scratch here, or a scuff on the command couch's leather, pressed in on him.

He slid into the command couch, reclining it just a little since he was taller than Walter. He fastened the restraining harnesses, then plugged the leads from this cooling vest into the chair. The 'Mech was fairly efficient, and would build heat up slowly, but the cooling vest would keep the pilot comfortable and prevent heat stroke.

Reaching up over his head, he pulled the neurohelmet from the shelf and settled it over his shoulders. While neither he nor Morgan had brought a 'Mech to Galatea, both had packed their neurohelmets. Because the helmet would translate the pilot's sense of balance and motion to the computer that regulated the gyroscopes, helmets became almost as prized as 'Mechs.

He adjusted it so it rested fully on the vest's padded shoulders, then tightened the chinstrap and clipped the tie-downs to the vest. Sensors pressed to his skull and though the faceplate made things a bit close, it just felt right. He plugged the communications leads into his helmet and smiled.

"As ready as I'll ever be."

He reached out and punched in the ignition sequence. Lights flickered. Monitors came to life, though no weapons came on line, nor did the fusion engine's thrumming purr begin.

"Pattern check: Patrick Kell."

The 'Mech's computer replied in a soft, feminine voice. *"Voiceprint match detected. Initiate confirmation sequence."*

"Kell Hounds unequaled and unbowed."

"Authorization sequence complete. Welcome aboard, Colonel Kell."

Below, in the 'Mech's broad breast, the fusion engine came to life. Power flooded through it, and the weapons monitors came to life. Moving the targeting sticks on each arm, Patrick selected and armed each system in turn. Since he'd only be doing some orientation, hitting a trigger would only fire targeting lasers that had been mounted on the muzzle of each weapon. The 'Mech's monitors would simulate heat build-up and even vent heat in from the engine to keep the simulation real. The heat monitors started in the cool blue range, but soon would spike green and yellow, on up to dangerously red territory.

Patrick keyed his microphone. "All systems are green and go."

Tisha's voice filled his helmet. "This is your weapon and targeting check. You'll get to run it later. I want to make sure the right arm actuator is tight enough."

"Roger, Tisha."

"You're clear to the turntable."

Patrick guided the 'Mech clear of the small bay and marched it to the center of Trisha's shop. Instead of a full-fledged arena, she'd invested in a turntable and holographic challenge display. He positioned the Blackjack's feet in the center, then clamps rose and locked down. Walter plugged cables into the heels of each foot, freezing them.

Patrick hit another button on the console. A two-hundred-twenty degree holographic display burned to life before him. It gave him a full three-hundred-sixty degrees of vision, with gold lines marking his forward firing arc. Twin red crosshairs floated in the display, moving beyond the gold bars when he spread the 'Mech's arms wide. He brought them back in, then moved them up and down.

As nearly as he could tell, they were responding perfectly. But the proof is in the score.

"I am go for targeting simulation."

"Package one, coming up."

A blue ball appeared at the display's center. Patrick covered it with a crosshairs. A dot in the center flashed red, so he stroked a trigger. The dot burst as if it was a balloon. Another one appeared, moving right to left, then another angled down. Each time he shot and destroyed a target, a new one materialized. They became smaller, moved faster and bounced off invisible obstacles.

Patrick tracked and fired, exploding each one in turn. Then they split when he hit them, becoming smaller and faster. He had to target with both arms independently, opting for quick shots from the autocannons over the medium laser's stabbing beams.

As fast as things came, he handled them. Though the *Blackjack* wasn't his, and he wasn't that familiar with it, it felt great to be back in a cockpit. Almost better than dancing with Tisha. The heat, the lights, the information flowing up over screens, the sounds, and watching targets explode; all of this was what he lived for. He'd trained hard, and he was good.

And loving every second of it.

Then the balloons stopped and a BattleMech materialized in their place. Barrel-chested, with an oversized cannon replacing the right forearm, the *Vindicator* strode boldly forward. The missile pod hatch on its left breast snapped open. Fire blossomed and a handful of missiles raced toward him.

Patrick jerked the *Blackjack* to the right. The turntable ground with the dodge, then swung back. Three of the long-range missiles pulverized armor, but did no serious damage. Then the simulator pumped blue lightning from the particle projection cannon. It slashed up over the *Blackjack*'s right thigh, consuming half the armor there. Another hit in that spot, and it would be eating into myomer muscle and support structures.

The *Vindicator*'s medium laser, mounted on the 'Mech's head, missed wide. Patrick's auxiliary monitor showed a momentary heat spike for the enemy, but the heat sinks brought it under control. The simulated pilot would feel nothing.

Patrick whipped his crosshairs over the 'Mech's outline and hit it with everything he had. All four medium lasers raked through armor on the *Vindicator*'s chest, left flank and arm. The autocannons hit over its heart and right breast, chewing away virtual armor plates. The monitors showed no internal damage, and a wave of heat poured up into the cockpit.

Another strike like that and I'll get sluggish controls. Despite that threat, Patrick had no choice but to hit again and hard. Though it was the same tonnage as his *Blackjack*, the *Vindicator* carried about five percent more armor. That gave it an edge in survivability, which went a long way toward determining which 'Mech would be standing after the battle.

And Titan Volmer would be driving a *Vindicator* in their fight.

Patrick pulled his 'Mech back and to the right, then brought the weapons up. He punched buttons and pulled all the slack from triggers. Lasers burned more armor from the left flank and center of the chest. They melted armor from the left arm and leg. The autocannons both hit as well, chipping away at the broad breast and left flank. They finished the armor on the left, sending hot metal ricocheting around in the chest, but doing no damage.

The *Vindicator* hit back. The LRMs overshot their target, but the medium laser and PPC didn't miss. The laser's ruby red beam burrowed through armor layers over the left shoulder. The PPC's hellish, jagged beam gnawed armor from the *Blackjack*'s chest. The damage monitor flashed red over the right leg, left arm and heart—another PPC strike there would be through the armor and doing serious damage.

Patrick abruptly reversed his motion and fought to bring his crosshairs to cover the enemy. Heat choked him as he fired, but the *Blackjack* didn't fail him. The lasers thoroughly denuded the 'Mech's chest of armor and drilled into the left flank. Gray-green coolant from a burst heat sink sprayed out of the wound, but the real damage was done in the *Vindicator*'s heart. Heat spiked as lasers carved away physical shielding from the reactor core.

The *Vindicator* fired back, blazing through armor on the *Blackjack*'s left leg with the PPC, and crushing armor where three LRMs hit. The medium laser missed wide, but it really didn't matter. The catastrophic damage already done to the *Vindicator* made it unstable. Try though

the simulated pilot might, he couldn't keep it upright. It sprawled before Patrick, then vanished in a cloud of disappearing pixels.

Sweat stung Patrick's eyes. His heart pounded in his ears.
Warning lights flashed on the monitors and slowly the heat bled off.
It had been a close fight, his edge being superior training and not a
small dose of luck.

He keyed his microphone. "What's the verdict, doc?"

Tisha came back sounding only slightly grim. "Groups on that
arm are not as tight as I would like, but within your guidelines for Kell
Hound equipment. We'll be revising that document, by the way."

"Any way you want." He smiled. "Want me to bring it back in so
you can make the adjustments?"

"No, I'll do that after you take it for a run. Things always loosen
up. But it will be ready for the fight. I promise."

"I'm glad you're taking care of me, Tisha."

"I'm taking care of a 'Mech, Patrick Kell." Her voice softened just
a touch. "But if you take care of you, I shall be a very happy woman."

GALATEA GARRISON HEADQUARTERS

General Volmer came around his desk and warmly greeted the slender, pinch-faced man Leutnant Saxinger ushered through the door.
"This is an unexpected pleasure, Precentor. To what do I owe the
honor?"

"Does an old friend need a reason, General?"

Volmer glanced at his subordinate. "That's all, Leutnant, thank
you."

The ComStar Precentor, resplendent in red robes, waited with his
hands in his sleeves for the door to close. He then pulled a noteputer
from a sleeve and laid it on the General's desk. "These are Maroon
notes. They are urgent, and I would like your permission to send them
on as quickly as I can."

Volmer rubbed his hands together. "I've got you, Morgan Kell."

"I'm afraid, General, these are not from any of the Kells nor their
agents."

"No?" Volmer sat and studied the messages, letting them scroll
past. They were short, terse, and very direct. *Bets being placed against
my son.* He looked at the amounts. Only one person on Galatea had
that sort of capital.

"These are all placed by Blizzard's agents?"

"Most of them are known to us, yes. A few are not, and might
be uninvolved in any schemes." The Precentor's grey eyes slitted. "I
know your ties to Mr. Blizzard, and I almost sent these on without

approval, but you do represent the legitimate authority on this world, so I chose to approach you. What do you wish me to do?"

He's betting against my son. Something is up. Volmer's mouth turned sour. *This is it. He's going to let Kell kill my son, make me look the fool, and profit from it.*

He looked up slowly. "Thank you, Precentor. This is, of course, a matter of national security. I need you to freeze these messages, escrow the money, and produce confirmations to go back to the agents that the messages have been sent."

The Precentor nodded. "If Patrick Kell does win, we are exposed to liability for Blizzard's losses."

"Not if he is involved in criminal activity, Precentor, and we both know he is. In fact, you have rather bravely acted to stop crime. Thank you."

"I hoped that would be the situation, General, thank you." Volmer smiled. "Will you be attending the fight?"

The Precentor blushed. "In fact, I've accepted an invitation to watch from the Kells' box. You understand."

"I do." Volmer handed him back the noteputer. "if anything else similar comes through..."

"We know what to do."

Volmer guided the man to the door and waved as he left the office. "Saxinger, here, now."

The Leutnant enter the office and closed the door. "Yes, sir?"

"I need to know what 'Mech Patrick Kell will be driving. I need to know where it is stored and how it will be getting to the fight. I need it immediately."

"Sir, yes, sir."

"And one other thing." Volmer smiled coyly. "I need a plan for making certain it never gets near that arena. We have to make certain by whatever means, that Patrick Kell cannot fight tonight."

CHAPTER 14

Veronica Matova found Morgan standing before the windows over-looking the arena floor. He had his hands on the glass, shoulder-height, almost as if surrendering. His forehead lay pressed to the window, and though the reflection was dark and indistinct, she thought his eyes were closed and his lips moving with silent words. In that instant, she felt as if she was intruding. She almost backed out, despite having been invited to meet him there.

Such a strong man, and yet so vulnerable. She wanted to reach out, but immediately smothered that impulse. It wasn't that she thought being sympathetic or maternal was wrong, she just couldn't afford to be either. A little voice mocked her. *That will be extra, won't it?*

But it wasn't about money. Morgan was a means to an end, and she couldn't afford to lose sight of that fact. Of Morgan Kell she'd come to understand one thing: he was easy to underestimate, and that doing so would be a gross mistake. No matter what Blizzard was setting up, she was confident that Morgan already had plans in play to outmaneuver him.

Still, he looked helpless. Was he betraying himself to her by acci-dent, or did he mean for her to discover him like this? Did he want her to assume that he was breaking down? What benefit would he reap from that? Did he expect she would report this to Blizzard, further confusing him?

That might not have been the case, but she had to assume it was. It fit with how Morgan had to be thinking. If she was betraying him to Blizzard, he had to give her disinformation. If she truly was his ally, it wouldn't hurt to see him being weak, since the information would stay between them.

She paused in the doorway and cleared her throat. "Morgan?"

He lightly slapped his hands against the glass and glanced back at her. "They've got it laid out for the fight. Lot of debris, obstacles made out of girders. It looks like an urban fight, but the best thing is that the debris will also take damage. Seeing a girder run like a crayon in the sun is pretty thrilling, even if you're seated too far back to catch much detail. This won't be a little arena and toy 'Mechs. Blood might flow."

Veronica joined him at the glass and looked down. "Your brother will win."

"I know." His words came as a tight whisper.

She studied his profile. "You can't be worried."

He turned and looked right through her. "This isn't a sport, Veronica. Either of the BattleMechs out there tomorrow could level a city block with a targeting error. Doesn't matter that the 'Mechs match up well on paper, or that Titan is untrained, undisciplined, and insane. One lucky shot and there won't be enough left of my brother to wipe away with a handkerchief. And that's if the fight is clean."

Again she stifled the impulse to reach out. "It will be okay, Morgan."

"It has to be, doesn't it?" He chuckled coldly. "Everyone's either counting on it or working against it."

"Have you figured out what Blizzard is going to do to give Titan the edge? He's not trusting that your brother will throw the fight." She shook her head. "That's a risk he can't take."

"Roger that." Morgan's head came up and fire returned to his eyes. He smiled, a predatory mask slipping into place. "There's a couple things he can do. I'm locking as many of those down as I can. Contingencies, you know."

"Don't worry, I won't ask."

He half-grinned. "Truth be told, I wish I could run things by you. Another pair of eyes, another sharp brain would be good."

"Don't trust me enough?"

"I don't trust Blizzard. If he thought I'd confided in you, he wouldn't hesitate to make you talk."

She caught a thread of genuine concern in his voice. "You could prevent that by just having me stay with you."

An eyebrow arched in surprise. "If you're not joking, you're just insane enough to be thinking the way I need someone thinking."

Was I joking? There was something about Morgan—an earnestness, and a belief in himself—that she hungered for. Her life was one of compromise. Morgan had said they were both mercenaries, but she imagined it would be far easier for him to make a stand on principle than it would be for her.

"Killing is serious enough that you have to draw lines," she replied. "I just weigh more handsome offers."

He laughed. "Good. A joke. You almost had me there."

She slipped a noteputer tablet from her bag. "Here are the people I've chosen for tomorrow. A few of the representatives are acquainted with some of them, but the others are new. I chose them for their ability to hold conversations. They've been being schooled in what they'll see in the fight, so their reactions will be informed and genuine."

Morgan tapped the screen and scrolled up through thumbnails. He tapped one or two of them, scanned the profiles, then handed the noteputer back to her. "Good choices, all. If any of the representatives want to indulge, I'll cover that."

"And bill it back to them later?"

He laughed. "Yeah, we have a category: Liaison services and training."

"Need to hire an officer in charge of it?"

His eyes twinkled. "You looking to leave this rock for a life of hardship and adventure?"

She'd offered her question as an idle quip, but his riposte surprised her. For a fraction of a second she saw herself in red and black, entertaining dignitaries. Using all the skills she possessed to overcome new challenges.

The biggest of them being Morgan.

Veronica glanced down, buying herself a moment of time, then nodded. "Are you making me an offer?"

He reached out, took her chin on fingertips and tilted her face up. "You would be miserable. Most of the time you would have little to do, and the billets we're likely to get would leave you entertaining more bugs than dignitaries. And those dignitaries who did visit us would make you think fondly of the bugs. Then, if we were attacked and overrun, things would likely not go so well for you."

"But you'd not let them hurt me, would you, Morgan?"

He stepped closer, the heat between them building. "I'd be dead before that happened."

She looked into his brown eyes and panic soared in her. She could lose herself in him, in his cause, in his dream. The future they'd create would wipe out her past and any past she could imagine.

Until that moment—when Veronica realized he could be her salvation—it had not even occurred to her that she wanted to be saved.

"You make it sound very attractive, Colonel Kell." She traced his lips with a finger. "Why don't you let me sleep on it?"

SNOWSQUALL ENTERPRISES

It didn't surprise Haskell Blizzard that Titan looked nervous when he entered the office. Tommy Volmer took after his father: an inflated sense of self-importance and a congenital lack of anything approaching a spine. The illusion of dignity would be preserved at all costs.

Blizzard despised Titan almost as much as he idolized his own granddaughter, Penelope. His princess could do no wrong, and she loved Tommy. It was a pure and innocent love on her part, all romance holo and friends cooing about her having found "the one." It would sour and, when it did, he'd take great delight in ridding himself of Tommy. Until then, however, he endured him—confident in the fact that Tommy was so terrified of him that he'd commit suicide before he ever hurt Penelope.

"You wanted to see me, sir?"

"Yes, son, please, sit down. A drink?" Blizzard poured himself some scotch, then stopped above an empty cut-glass tumbler. "Forgive me, you have a fight tomorrow. You won't be drinking."

"No, sir, I won't." The expectant expression melted slowly from his face. "What can I do for you?"

Blizzard sipped. "I'm a little concerned about the fight."

"Don't be, sir. I'm going to win." Tommy nodded confidently. "I mean, you want me to win, right?"

"Yes, Tommy, I want you to win." Blizzard held the glass in both hands, watching light play through the liquor. "The betting-line, however, suggests that your chances of winning are slender. Does this concern you?"

"Well, you know..." The 'Mechdriver opened his hands. "Being honest here, you know, you control the bookmaking, and there's a lot of money going against me. You profit if I win, but, I mean, if I don't..."

"Yes, this is a concern." Blizzard lowered his glass. "The fact is that Patrick Kell isn't just going to lay down and die. Your *Vindicator* has an edge over the *Blackjack* he'll be piloting. It's about an eight-point edge, between armor and heat to firepower ratio. Do you think that's enough?"

"I don't know. I mean, Kell was good at the Nagelring."

"Top two percent of his class—a class you were expelled from. His piloting scores, well, he is as efficient in a cockpit as you are when you are fighting for me." Blizzard smiled as Tommy flinched. "And to answer your correct and unspoken question, no, I do not think it is enough of an edge."

"Then what?"

Blizzard turned the computer monitor around to face his son-in-law. "I don't imagine you have ever read the contracts for any of your fights, have you?"

"N-no."

"Clause fifteen, usually called XV for the Roman numerals and 'extra vehicle.' 'If, in the mind of the promoter...blah blah blah...a suitable replacement 'Mech may be substituted on the card. Suitable replacement means the new 'Mech can't outweigh the opponent by too much, but up to a 50% difference in tonnage is acceptable."

Tommy nodded as if he understood.

Blizzard smiled. "Son, do you have any idea what sort of 'Mech I used to fight in?"

"No, sir."

Blizzard rotated the computer screen so it faced the ceiling, then engaged the holographic display function. A powerful-looking humanoid 'Mech without hands slowly twirled there. "It was a heavy. Seventy-five tons. An ON1-V *Orion*. I have had it completely refitted, and you'll be driving it."

Surprise widened Tommy's eyes. "But an Orion is more than fifty percent heavier than a Blackjack."

"Not after the LRM launcher racks and ammo have been removed. We also had to cut the autocannon's ammo in half to shave a ton and get it down to sixty-five tons. Not that you'll use it all. Two shots will rip off any limb or be internal on the torso. Lasers and short-range missiles will finish what the autocannon starts. You, on the other hand, have enough armor to withstand two full salvos anywhere without his scoring more than armor. If you lose it will be..." Blizzard shook his head. "Even you couldn't screw this up."

"But if Kell knows, he'll make a change, too."

"He won't learn of the change until right before the fight. I guarantee there will be no replacements available to him." Blizzard reached back for his scotch and took a swallow. He let it burn its way to his belly, then smiled. "Tomorrow Patrick Kell dies in a Blackjack, and then I'll find an even more interesting way to rid myself of his brother."

GALATEA GARRISON HEADQUARTERS

General Volmer couldn't believe his superior fortune. He stood outside the interrogation room, staring at the black man chained to the chair in its middle. A bruise on the man's head wept blood and one of his eyes was swelling shut.

"Have you started without me, Major?"

Chaoate blinked. "Sir?"

"Interrogating the prisoner. He's bleeding."

"That's from when we apprehended him. As per orders, we stopped the vehicle transporting a *Blackjack* to the Arastavos arena. We'd gone in heavy, and we noticed a vehicle that had been trailing the transport. When we stopped the transport, the vehicle tried to speed off. We stopped it, found Clarence Wilson in the vehicle. He refused to surrender, and had to be subdued."

Volmer smiled. This was perfect. Morgan Kell thought himself above the law. They now had Wilson, and connecting him to Kell was simple. Just the fact that he was trailing the other Kell's *Blackjack* was proof of conspiracy.

"Has he said anything about Kell yet?"

"No, sir." Choate glanced at his noteputer. "We've got him on desertion, sir. Procedure is to get him back to his unit as fast as possible and let them handle it."

"And let Morgan Kell get away with aiding and abetting?"

"Begging the General's pardon, but we've no evidence of any connection between them. It's all circumstantial."

"The man knew Morgan Kell. He twice committed violence to save Patrick Kell."

"But neither brother said they knew of his presence in advance."

Volmer shook his head. "Major, do you trust them?"

"Sir?"

"They are lying. They are mercenary scum. They have aided and abetted a deserter. That is tantamount treason."

Choate winced. "Sir, it could seem like that but—"

"But nothing." Volmer pointed at the window. "I want Morgan Kell implicated in a conspiracy, Major, and I want this man's confession so we can get a warrant. I want you to use any means necessary to obtain that confession. Do you understand me?"

Choate's head came up. "Perhaps the General would define 'any means necessary.'"

"You want to play games, Major, fine." Volmer's expression hardened. "I don't care if you take the man to pieces, just as long as one chunk can scream out a confession, and another chunk can sign it."

CHAPTER 15

'MECHBAY THIRTEEN
ARASTAVOS ARENA
GALATEAN CITY, GALATEA
LYRAN COMMONWEALTH
7 OCTOBER 3010

Patrick Kell slumped back against the wall. "I don't believe it."

Tisha shivered. "I thought they weren't letting me in to stop me from making final adjustments to the 'Mech, but..."

"There is no 'Mech." Patrick held his head in both hands and tried to think. It didn't help that one of the undercard fights, a four-on-four battle pitting a lance from Guinn's Gunnes against real BattleMechs Blizzard had somehow produced, was filling the hollow bay with thunderous echoes. "This is unbelievably bad. If I don't report within a half-hour of being called, I lose. Can we get a replacement 'Mech in time?"

Tisha shook her head, her lower lip trembling. "There's nothing available. Patrick, what are we going to do?"

He caressed her cheek. "It's going to be okay." He pulled a communicator from his pocket. "Morgan's got to have a plan."

KELL HOUNDS LUXURY SUITE
ARASTAVOS ARENA

Morgan Kell pointed to the battle raging below. "Pay attention to the Blue squad. They're a lance of light 'Mechs formerly of Guinn's Gunnes..."

Damiceau, his left hand covertly caressing the buttocks of the gorgeous blonde beside him, laughed. "The Gunnes have been old news for a long time, Colonel. I thought you were going to show us something new."

"What's new about the Gunnes is that we're breaking them up. Each of their lances will move to a separate company in the regiment." Morgan smiled confidently. "The Gunnes have been miscast and misused in the past. We will be employing them at their best. As you can see here, they know what they're doing, especially in a battle where speed and mobility are paramount."

The four 'Mechs—a *Jenner*, a *Firestarter*, a *Commando,* and a *Panther*—all moved well together. They coordinated fire, using short range missiles to pepper the closest of the Red Squad's 'Mechs, then let their energy weapons hold the others back and soften them up. As the Reds moved forward to provide cover for a stricken comrade, the Gunnes would withdraw, again isolating the closest Red 'Mechs while making themselves difficult for the others to hit.

"As impressive as this display is, Colonel, you're offering the services of a regiment." Amanda Heartsthorne clutched a champagne flute in her bony hands. "Do you wish us to judge your whole unit based on the action of a lance that you didn't train and are not now directing?"

"Absolutely." Morgan ticked points off on his fingers. "Right people, right equipment, right missions, and full coordination, which means they all know they're supported no matter what happens. All these things build a unit that will respond in a solid and decisive manner to any challenge put to it."

His communicator buzzed. "If you will excuse me." He stepped away from his guests. "Morgan. Go ahead."

"We have a problem. I have no 'Mech."

"That's not what I expected Blizzard to do."

"I know, you said he'd XV me. What do I do?"

Morgan looked up as two men stepped through the doorway. "Relax. I'll be with you shortly, Patrick."

General Volmer, still wearing his cooling vest, shorts, and boots from his part in the Honor Guard, strode directly to Morgan. "Was that your brother? The only way you're joining him is in prison. Major, do your duty."

Major Choate, in full uniform, stepped up beside the General. He hesitated as the representatives of the Inner Sphere governments crowded around, but then steeled himself. "Colonel Morgan Kell, you are under arrest for aiding and abetting the desertion of one Clarence Wilson."

"Am I?"

"Yes!" Volmer stabbed a finger into Morgan's chest. "You messed with the wrong man, Kell. I have no doubt the Archon will get these charges voided, but I am packing you up on a ship with your brother and Wilson, and you're headed back to the Tenth Skye for prosecution."

Morgan smiled and looked at Choate. "You're operating off a warrant issued on the thirtieth of last month?"

Choate tapped his noteputer. "Yes, sir."

Volmer fumed. "Don't sir him."

The mercenary carefully drew a sheet of paper from inside his jacket pocket. "I got this through ComStar three days ago. I had them provide a physical copy so the General couldn't claim I'd manipulated a data file."

Choate took it and read. He glanced at Volmer, then read again. "It's in order. Sergeant Wilson has been seconded to the Kell Hounds as a training officer, by order of the Archon. The warrant is old."

"No!" Volmer snatched the paper from his subordinate, crumpled it and tossed it to the floor. "That was a forgery. They're under arrest until you get confirmation from Tharkad yourself. Arrest him. That is an order, Major. Do your duty."

Morgan produced another sheet and handed it to the Major. "You'll want to read this, first."

Choate took it and stepped out of Volmer's reach. His jaw dropped open. He looked up at Morgan. "This is genuine as well?"

"Do your duty, Major."

Choate nodded. "General Volmer, I'm placing you under arrest for grand theft and misappropriation of government property."

"What?"

Morgan chuckled. "The first day you met me, it was in the 'Mechbay of garrison headquarters. The place stank of paint. You'd let Blizzard use garrison 'Mechs in his battles here, putting ammo and armor damage down to training exercises. All your records match up, so there was no way to trace things, save for one."

"Impossible!" Volmer had gone white as a sheet.

"Not impossible. Blizzard painted your 'Mechs in his house colors. You had to repaint 'Mechs back to regimental standard after the fights. You used far more paint than would have been required to cover the training damage. It's a trail of records that will have you court-martialed."

"You can't do this."

Choate held up the paper. "He can. Pending the arrival of a replacement for you, Colonel Kell has been given command of the garrison. Sir, surrender your sidearm."

Volmer, trembling, slid a pistol from his hip and handed it to Choate. "I'll remember this, Major."

Any reply Major Choate cared to make was eclipsed by a public address announcement. "We have a change in the final bout for this evening. Titan Volmer's *Vindicator* has suffered an equipment failure. A suitable replacement has been found. He will be piloting Haskell

Blizzard's personal 'Mech. The *Orion* has been modified to bring it down to sixty-five tons, making it legal for this fight. Within the hour, ladies and gentlemen, you'll see a battle you'll never forget."

Volmer threw his head back and laughed. "Oh, the irony. Blizzard fixes it so your brother will die in a *Blackjack*—something I should most like to see—and I made sure the Blackjack wouldn't be here. Your brother will still lose, not having a 'Mech, and you lose with him. You played this well, Kell, but I played much better."

Morgan clapped the man hard on his shoulders. "I'm glad you think that, General. Major, please indulge me and let the General remain here until after the fight."

He turned to his guests. "This wasn't exactly what I'd expected or intended, but that's fine. You want to judge a unit, judge it on how well it handles adverse situations. We've been boxed in, we have no resources, and the enemy is at the gates. If you'll excuse me, I'll now show you how the Kell Hounds will win no matter how dire the odds against us."

'MECHBAY THIRTEEN
ARASTAVOS ARENA

Patrick's head snapped around as the sound of running footsteps reached him. "Morgan, thank God."

Tisha jerked a thumb at the empty 'Mechbay. "We've got no 'Mech."

Morgan laughed, then shook his head. "Silly people."

Patrick studied his brother's face for a second. "Um, Morgan, this is serious."

"I know." He threw an arm around Patrick's shoulder. "In fact, I'm wondering what you're doing waiting here. Shouldn't you be in your 'Mech?"

Tisha darted ahead of them and turned around. "Colonel, there is no 'Mech."

"No, Miss Hamilton, there is no *Blackjack*."

Her expression did not lighten. "There's no *Vindicator* either. We've been XVed into fighting an *Orion*."

"I heard the announcement." Morgan blithely steered his brother to 'Mechbay twenty-seven. Two garrison guards looked up from a noteputer, then snapped to attention. "Colonel on deck."

"As you were, soldiers." Morgan waved a hand at the 'Mech standing there. "Fully loaded. Ready to go."

"You want me to drive *that*?" Patrick looked back at his brother. "General Volmer's *JagerMech*? You want me to take that out against Tommy?"

Morgan nodded. "I just saw the General. He mentioned something about irony. I'm pretty sure this is exactly what he had in mind."

CHAPTER 16

Patrick Kell murmured a prayer to Saint Jude of Lost Hopes as he waited to be introduced. While both BattleMechs were of equal weight, they were not evenly matched. The *Blackjack* he should have been driving had much better armor than his *JagerMech*—in some areas as much as fifty percent more. While the *JagerMech* could pump out a bit more damage, most of its weaponry was located in the arms, and they were the most lightly armored portion of the 'Mech.

The *JagerMech* is a fire support 'Mech, not designed to slug it out against another 'Mech.

Which meant he couldn't slug it out. The Orion doubtlessly had the LRMs removed to bring it down in weight. They would have been the least useful of the weapons in the arena anyway. One hit from the autocannon it carried would rip right though the *JagerMech*'s armor and could even tear an arm off. The twin medium lasers and dual SRM launchers would do more damage, so in one strike he could lose a limb or be through the armor on his torso.

And if he hits the cockpit...

Patrick did have a couple of advantages. While Titan might have learned a thing or two about piloting and shooting, at the Nagelring he'd been an indifferent pilot. His skills would have gotten him a billet in any garrison unit, but he wasn't line unit material.

Patrick, on the other hand, piloted and shot very well. And since his 'Mech was not built to go toe-to-toe with an enemy, he was forced to maneuver. That would make him harder to hit, which gave him a shot at winning.

His *JagerMech* was better at handling heat build-up than the *Orion*. A full strike by the *Orion* would exceed its heat handling capacity by fifty percent. It would be tougher to handle and balky in aiming. If Patrick could induce Titan to panic and start running around needlessly, he'd defeat himself.

Light splashed over the 'Mech's cockpit as the doors to the arena slid open. Spotlights played over the *JagerMech* as Patrick guided it forward. The debris strewn over the field would limit mobility a bit, but provide some cover, too. *It'll be tough to shoot my legs out from under me.*

Patrick resisted the urge to flip communications over to the arena announcer. Something about seeing a crowd clapping and cheering in utter silence confirmed the surreality of the situation. Patrick had trained for years to be a warrior, and people were treating it as entertainment. And yet, circumstances had forced him to become part of the circus.

He smiled. *If you have to be in the circus, it might as well be center ring.*

As Titan emerged at the arena's far side, banners unfurled in the crowd. Women begged him to father their children. Parents held kids aloft, the whole family attired in Titan gear. People held up dolls in Kell Hounds uniforms, stuck through with plastic knives.

All of which should have struck him as absurd, but the red light on his console went green, and the evening's grim entertainment began.

Titan fired a full salvo before either 'Mech had a chance to move very far. The autocannon on the right side of its chest lipped flame, but the storm of projectiles missed wide. Missiles speared out of the paired SRM launchers, and three scored armor on the right leg, left arm and over the center of the *JagerMech*'s chest. One of the two lasers also ablated armor off the 'Mech's left flank, leaving it vulnerable to punishing damage from the autocannon.

Patrick moved to the left, tracking the *Orion* and let loose with everything. His autocannons vomited fire, but only one hit, doing minimal damage to the 'Mech's breast. Both of the medium lasers missed as well. His weapons scattered their fire all over the place, and if he continued shooting that badly, the fight would be over well before Titan ever hit the ground.

What the heck is going on? He took a deep breath and let it out slowly. He didn't feel jittery, but he was shooting as if this was his first time in combat. *Settle down, or it's going to be your last time in combat.*

The Kell Hound brought his 'Mech up to a run. Titan's 'Mech turned to track him, but did so with a torso-twist. The autocannon chewed through the sand behind him, while the lasers lit up a tangle of steel girders. Short range missiles cratered the ground, though three did hit him again, nibbling away at armor on the opposite leg and arm as before, as well as shattering armor over his heart.

Patrick grumbled. "I wonder if Titan thinks his daddy is in here and really wants to kill him?"

He brought his weapons to bear. His autocannons missed entirely, as did one of his lasers. The other burned through armor over the Orion's left shoulder.

This is not happening. I'm better than this!

The damage wasn't much, but Patrick would take it because of two other factors. On the secondary monitor displaying the Orion's status, the heat index was climbing. Another full salvo and Titan's 'Mech could conceivably shut itself down. That limited his ability to shoot, and the heat would seriously affect his ability to target the *JagerMech*.

More importantly, Patrick had closed the gap between the two war machines. Moving rapidly, he ducked through a forest of debris, then popped into the open. The *Orion*, which could not continue to track through twisting its body, had just begun to turn when Patrick laid into it.

The heavier of the autocannons missed wide, but their smaller twins crushed armor plates on the right arm and leg. The only medium laser to hit stabbed its energy beam into the *Orion*'s right arm, melting a dark scar up to the shoulder. Less than half the armor had been taken off that limb, but it was the most serious damage done yet.

Sweat began to sting Patrick's eyes. His stomach knotted. Something wasn't right, but all the diagnostic were reporting everything was perfect. Even a garrison 'Mech shouldn't be this bad.

Titan fought back and hit hard. A medium laser slashed through armor on the *JagerMech*'s left flank, reducing it to tatters. Three more SRMs hit, popping armor off both flanks and the chest. If anything hit Patrick's left flank, it would be through, and the fight would be over.

Still, Titan's heat management strategy hadn't been fully thought out. His 'Mech remained dangerously hot. Patrick's heat had been creeping up as well. *I need to make a change, but can I risk not shooting?* Given that his choices were stand and cool off, thereby making himself a great target, or keep moving and become hard to hit while hitting back weakly, it wasn't an easy decision to make.

Then again, I'm not hitting hard because I'm not hitting. Concentrate, Patrick. He opened his hands for a second, flexing them, then closed them around the targeting sticks. "Time to do some damage."

The red crosshairs drifted over the Orion's strong outline. One of the heavier autocannons hammered armor into dust on the 'Mech's right arm. The first of the small ones chipped armor over the *Orion*'s right hip. The only laser and the other small autocannon hit the right flank, sending armor sheeting away to smoke on the ground.

The *Orion* retaliated, and did so in a devastating manner. The SRMs all missed, but the autocannon finally tracked true. A hail of depleted uranium shells pulverized the armor on Patrick's right flank.

Warning lights flashed in the cockpit. The armor was down to less than seven percent coverage. The crowd reacted with a eager rumble, knowing the fight was all but over.

Frustrated and worried, Patrick kicked out at the targeting computer console. Monitors flickered for a second, then a wire dangled down. "What the...?"

He hit his restraining strap release and felt up under the console. Where there shouldn't have been anything but a flat panel, he discovered a tiny square with a toggle switch.

"Son of a sea cook! A targeting fairy!" He toggled the switch off.

That better be the last surprise! Sweat stinging his eyes, Patrick targeted the Orion. I have to do it now.

He tightened up on his triggers, and finally hit with everything. His autocannons blasted armor from all over the 'Mech, from right leg to left flank. One of the heavier autocannons tracked across the *Orion*'s head, splintering armor. The medium lasers vaporized more armor off each flank. One more concentrated strike, and Patrick might get internal on the machine.

But Titan hadn't given up yet. He shot back, missing with the autocannon and one of the missile racks. The other sent projectiles spiraling out from the launch canister on the right arm. Two hit. One cratered armor over the center of the 'Mech's chest, but the other smashed through the armor on the right flank. Shrapnel ripped into the *JagerMech*'s chest, but miraculously did no further damage.

It didn't matter to Patrick. He smelled blood and circled his 'Mech. The targeting crosses flew up to spit the *Orion*. The dot at their hearts flashed to life, and Patrick fired again.

A wave of heat crested over him as his weapons scraped armor from the left arm, right leg, right arm and over the right flank. One of the smaller autocannons missed, as did one of the lasers, but the *Orion*'s armor was already tattered. The door to Patrick's winning had opened.

Titan panicked. He cut loose with everything he had, spiking his heat. As strategies went, it was a good one. Any combination of hits would be devastating and could put the *JagerMech* down. That required him to hit, however, and panic did little to steady his hands on the joysticks. The autocannon and both lasers missed, bracketing the smaller 'Mech and devastating the cinderblock ruins behind him. SRMs did hit, shattering armor on the *JagerMech*'s left arm and leg. One even exploded against the cockpit, shaking Patrick, but coming nowhere close to breaching the armor.

The *JagerMech* stalked even closer. The autocannon fire plunged through armor, breaching the right flank. More autocannon shells finished the last of the armor on the right leg, then a coruscating red beam sizzled in to toast myomer muscles. The other laser melted more armor over the Orion's heart, leaving a black scar smoking from shoulder to hip.

Titan's panic went unabated. His autocannon swung toward the JagerMech, spitting flame. The shells narrowly missed their target. Neither laser shot, and launch ports of the two SRMs remained dark. His heat profile dulled, but he was still running too hot to fight effectively.

Patrick sent his *JagerMech* to the left, even as Tommy tried to withdraw. The *Orion*, which was handling none too smoothly, slammed into a small building. It rebounded and froze for a heartbeat.

Titan fired. His autocannon missed again, but SRMs chipped armor from the *JagerMech*'s right leg and the center of its chest.

Too little, too late.

The Kell Hound remorsefully settled his crosshairs on his enemy, and let loose with his entire arsenal. A laser and a heavy autocannon missed, but the others made up for it. A laser beam boiled myomer fibers in the right leg. One heavy autocannon stippled the armor over the 'Mech's chest, but the fire from the other two went straight through the right flank. Hot metal ricocheted around in the 'Mech's chest with catastrophic consequences.

A shell hit the magazine holding the autocannon's remaining rounds. This triggered a chain-reaction explosion. Fire geysered from the hole in the 'Mech's chest. The right arm whirled away. The 'Mech lurched left, stumbling drunkenly. It caught more debris with an ankle and went down hard, armor fragments sprayed glittering over the sand. Fires burned in its chest, smoke rising to the heavens as if a sacrifice to appease an ancient god.

Patrick slowed his 'Mech, watching and waiting. He moved around out of any firing arc, but kept his weapons trained on the *Orion*. He studied it, hoping to see a sign of life in the cockpit, but the smoke obscured his view.

So he looked up, hoping one of the arena cameras would have a better shot. The screen didn't show the cockpit. Instead, it had focused on the crowd, chanting, raising the fists.

And thrusting thumbs downward.

Patrick didn't need sound to know what they were chanting. *Kill him, kill him.*

He watched them for a second, then raised the JagerMech's arms fully vertical so he could shoot nothing. It didn't quiet the crowd, just shifted their chanting, and the nature of their gestures.

He didn't care. It's easy to be bloodthirsty when guns aren't aimed at you. Anger flashed through him. He despised those people and yet, he realized, through his victory he'd guaranteed that he and his brother would be able to lay their own lives on the line to protect them.

CHAPTER 17

When the *Orion* finally hit the ground, Morgan bowed his head and covered his eyes with a hand. His lungs burned. He'd been holding his breath.

So close, so foolishly close. Never again will I put him in jeopardy when I'm not at his side.

Veronica came close, slipping her arms around him. She kissed him on the cheek, then whispered into his ear. "Hold me. Return my kiss. Compose yourself for your guests."

He encircled her with his arms and kissed her cheek. He watched the arena through the veil of her gold hair. Rescue crews flooded the ground. Men in silver suits climbed onto the *Orion*, filling the burning cavity with foam. Another group worked on the cockpit and pried the faceplate open. Morgan couldn't see in, but one worker turned and gave a thumb's-up. That coaxed a sob of relief from General Volmer.

Morgan gave Veronica another squeeze, then brought his head up. With his arm drifting down around her waist, he smiled at his guests.

"Courage. Tenacity. Skill and daring, strategy, tactics and a commitment to getting the job done. That's the Kell Hounds. You can bet every man and woman we bring into the unit will be held to very exacting standards. We've already hired the best tech on planet, and are actively recruiting the rest. Our people will have the best of everything, from training and leadership to 'Mechs that are in top condition."

Amanda Heartsthorne smiled slyly. "I shall look forward to seeing your final roster. If what I saw today is truly exemplar of your performance, the Federated Suns might well have a place for you. When do you expect to be operational? Six months?"

"Six weeks at most." Veronica shivered against him, but he gave no sign he'd noticed. "We're picking the best, and we're looking at more than a list of kills or gunnery scores."

The Federated Suns representative frowned. "Colonel, the paint will hardly be dry on your 'Mechs in six weeks. How could you possibly imagine any of us would hire you?"

"Well now, if it's dry paint you're wanting, I'll leave the 'Mechs out in the sun." He moved away from Veronica. "I'd like you to think about this. My brother and I have been here a total of four days. Now putting together a unit might have taken six months in the past. In that past people would have been dealing with Blizzard, playing the game here, taking too much time, spending too much money, and not seeing a return on it. You'd have to say that those units were complacent, and complacency in warfare is third to timidity and bad intelligence for a way to get people killed."

He pointed to the arena. "You can't judge warriors by years in grade and throw-weight of metal. If you could, my brother would be dead. If you could, Guinn's Gunnes would no longer exist. But battles aren't fought through simulations. They're fought where shrapnel fills the air, and screams, and the scent of melting hair and boiling blood.

"And they're fought in the mind." He tapped a finger against his temple. "My brother won because he couldn't conceive of losing. Titan couldn't conceive of winning without the fix being in. That's how wars get won, too, by getting into your enemy's head, out-thinking him, forcing him to think too much, and then presenting him with a situation where he can't win. Once he knows he can't, he won't."

Morgan opened his hands. "You'll all have to make some decisions. They might even need to be made above your pay grade. That's fine. It's actually good. I just urge all of you to get those decisions made fast. You might all doubt right now, but one of you will doubt a little less. That'll be the one we go to work for, and the rest of you will have to remember that we know how to win."

SNOWSQUALL ENTERPRISES LUXURY SUITE

Haskell Blizzard looked down into the arena and suppressed the desire to weep. He didn't care if Tommy Volmer crawled from the *Orion* or not. He hoped he would, but only because that would save him the cost of cleaning blood and brains from the cockpit interior.

The *Orion* lay broken. It had been damaged worse than ever before in this fight. Two centuries of service in the Federated Suns, dozens of campaigns, countless battles, and it had never fallen, unable to rise. Even when its right leg had been badly damaged while he drove it, Blizzard had limped it off the battlefield. And only after the enemy had been vanquished.

He thought back to that time, that distant time, when he had been idealistic. He'd bought into the family legend, the idea of service to House Davion. He'd been as optimistic and enthusiastic as either of the Kells combined. In that time, he would have been proud to know them. *I would have been first in line to join their little mercenary band.*

The course of his disillusionment really didn't matter. He'd grown jaded, that much he acknowledged freely. People under pressure, especially financial pressure, reacted the same way. Stupidly and predictably. He'd used his recognition of this fact to build his empire.

And he'd used his empire to break men like Morgan Kell time and time again.

He turned from the window and settled himself at the desk in the corner. The one expense he'd not calculated was the cost of repairing the *Orion.* He had never imagined defeat, much less the damage. Of course, he'd counted on Kell driving a *Blackjack.* But that would have given Titan even more of a fight.

He flicked on his computer and brought up his accounting program. Instinctively he glanced at the balance. Something was woefully wrong. It was off, and off seriously. By an order of magnitude. The numbers adjusted themselves. By two orders.

He scrolled down. Even though it was too early for ComStar to have transferred his winning from the off-planet betting to his accounts, their preliminary calculations would have been reflected in his total.

The ComStar reckoning showed a zero in yellow. He clicked on it. A note popped up explaining, very simply, that for reasons of national security, the messages with those bets in them had not been transmitted. His lay-off bets had never gone through.

His account total continued to atrophy. People who owed him money were using their winnings to pay off huge chunks of their debt to him. The weekly estimates of his income declined faster than the *Orion* had hit the ground, and his wealth evaporated as if everyone leaving the building was doing so with a duffle bag full of money.

Blizzard flicked the computer screen off and stared at the Kell Hound suite across the way. Somehow Kell had turned Volmer against him. The double-cross had been simple. Blocking the lay-off bets was meant to ruin him, and it had been quite a blow.

"But, it wasn't low enough, Morgan Kell, not nearly low enough." Blizzard sat back, his eyes narrowing to slits. "I'm not dead, and that fact is one you will rue sooner than you could possibly imagine."

'MECHBAY TWENTY-SEVEN

Patrick Kell descended the gantry steps, then nearly toppled over when Tisha all but tackled him. She hugged him up snug and planted a big kiss on his mouth. He gasped, then kissed her back, holding on to her tightly. She felt so small and light in his embrace.

Finally she broke the kiss and slipped around under his arm. "Oh God, Patrick, I must have died a dozen times during that fight."

"You're saying you were worried?"

"Well, only because I hadn't checked that 'Mech out. For a while there, I wasn't sure you were going to be able to hit anything."

"I almost wasn't." He handed her the module he'd pulled from beneath the targeting computer. "Volmer had a target fairy wired into his controls to give him good scores. My aim points were being boosted past where I thought they were. Once I shut that thing down, I had control."

"So a Volmer almost killed you anyway?"

"Almost." Patrick pulled her to him and kissed the top of her head. "But I wasn't going to let that happen."

"Why's that?"

"Cuz the hottest Tech on the planet promised we could celebrate my win by going dancing." He smiled as they headed from the Mechbay.

"I hope you brought your dancing shoes, darling, because we're going to celebrate like this is the last day of the universe, and we're the ones who get to turn the lights out when we're done."

A TINY SPOT OF REBELLION

CHAPTER 1

Patrick Kell paused at the entrance to the Powder Keg. "I'm telling you, Morgan, I really think you want to take a more subtle approach."

His brother, tall, with black hair and glittering brown eyes, rested both hands on Patrick's shoulders. "I heard you. Subtle. Got it. Trust me."

"Morgan, your idea of subtle is using a .50 caliber bullet instead of a 20 millimeter shell."

Morgan spread his hands wide. "And see, I'm not even armed. C'mon, it won't be that bad."

Sighing, Patrick followed his brother into the tavern. Two steps in, he almost backed out again. The dominant feature was rust, and that wasn't in terms of some fru-fru color an interior designer had chosen. Jagged metal edges just loaded with tetanus lurked everywhere. The bar, which had probably been a small repair shop once, had been gutted—by fire or a 'Mech assault—and never really cleaned up. In fact, Patrick guessed it had been a 'Mech assault, since a lot of the decorations were BattleMech parts nailed to most free surfaces.

The whole sharp-edged theme extended to the patrons. The Powder Keg was the place MechWarriors came to be seen. *Sure. Survive an hour in here, and there's no bug in the Inner Sphere that could kill you.* The patrons wore uniforms from dozens of mercenary units, more than half of them no longer in existence, and most mixed and matched from several. They all looked hungry, lean, and mean—and not necessarily in that order.

Morgan, by contrast, looked very smart in his uniform. The Kell Hounds' black-bodied tunic with red sleeves really stood out, and that didn't make Patrick any less anxious. Men eyed Morgan. They laughed at his rank insignia. He was all of twenty-four years old and a colonel.

Patrick, for his own part, blushed as they read his rank as Lieutenant Colonel.

If Morgan noticed their scrutiny, he gave no sign. He marched straight through the tangle of tables toward the back, where a heavy-set man lounged in the shadows. The man looked Morgan up and down once, then smiled easily, running a hand over his unshaven jaw.

Morgan nodded. "Mr. Garlett?"

"Yeah, kid?" The man answered slowly, bringing his booted feet up to rest on the table.

Morgan pulled a sheet of paper from his back pocket. "You applied to join the Kell Hounds. Your log book said you served with the Fifteenth Lyran Guards on Hesperus II. Your commanding officer was Katrina Steiner."

The mention of the Archon's name made a few more people take notice of the exchange. Garlett pursed his lips and nodded. "That's right, boy."

The elder Kell shrugged. "She says you're a liar."

Garlett's eyes widened with shock. He'd been found out. He'd been bragging that he'd join the Kell Hounds, get his 'Mech refitted, draw pay for a while and take off. He'd faked hunks of his log, never expecting the Kells to check and, somehow, foolishly, never expected his comments to get back to them.

And Morgan had called him a liar in front of his peers.

Garlett swung his legs from the table and came up, fists cocked. It really didn't matter how ready he thought he was. It wasn't enough.

Morgan's fist arced in a roundhouse right too fast to follow. Garlett's jaw cracked audibly. The man flew back into the wall, rebounded and collapsed his table.

Two yellowed teeth with bloody roots bounced off Morgan's boots.

Morgan crumpled the paper and tossed it on Garlett's twitching body. His head came up. Steel entered his voice. "Listen up, you 'Mech lice. My brother and I are hiring *warriors*, not chiseling vagrants who figure the Kell Hounds to be a paid vacation and a pit stop. You can join up and be part of something great, or you can sit here and tell others you could have been a Kell Hound."

Most of the patrons looked from Morgan to Garlett, grunted, and went back to drinking. One man, wearing a Hsien Hotheads jacket similar to the one Garlett had on, uncoiled himself from a table. As big as Garlett had been, this guy was bigger, with a broken nose, scarred knuckles, and half an ear missing.

"And why would I join a unit with a leader stupid enough to come in here alone and jack a pal of mine?"

"Morgan, subtle..."

Morgan snorted. "Thanks for sending your application. Rejected."

Which was when a third guy in a Hotheads jacket slipped an arm around Patrick's throat.

Without thinking, Patrick drove his head backward into the man's face, then stomped down on the man's right foot. His heel crushed bones. Blood from a broken nose splashed against the back of his neck. Reaching up, he grabbed the man's thumb, snapped it back and spun, turning the arm with him. Patrick came around behind the man, locking his arm against his spine, then grabbed a handful of greasy hair and dropped, driving the man face first into the floor.

Adrenaline surging through him, Patrick rose above his unconscious foe and opened his arms. His breath came heavy and fast. He slowly spun, facing everyone down. "Who's next?"

Morgan's eyebrow rose. "What about subtle?"

"I don't think they get subtle, Morgan."

The giant took a step forward, but a red laser dot appeared on his forehead. He stopped.

Patrick turned. A long, lean, unkempt man with tired eyes held a pistol in one steady hand. *Not a needler, an old slug-thrower.* "Sit on down, Boris."

"You saw what they did, Frost."

"Garlett had it coming. You know it."

"But—"

"Butt. Yours. In that chair."

The giant sat.

Morgan turned, smiling, and stepped toward the man.

The laser dot shifted to the center of his chest.

Morgan's hands rose. "Just wanted to thank you."

The beam didn't waver. "No need. Just wanted some quiet."

Patrick smiled, his hands raised. "Are you a MechWarrior? Looking for work?"

The man's eyes half closed. "Not a driver. Mudbug."

"We have an infantry company attached and—"

Frost shook his head. "O'Cieran's company."

Morgan nodded. "Right."

"Used to work for him. We parted over religious differences."

Patrick frowned. In the last two weeks he'd spent a fair amount of time with Richard O'Cieran, and hadn't noticed the man being religious at all. He glanced at Morgan.

His brother shrugged. "Thank you anyway. If you do want work..."

"Nova Royale. I know." Frost holstered his pistol and picked up a noteputer. The screen backlit a gaunt, lined face above a brown beard with hints of grey.

Morgan turned, nodded toward the door. Patrick preceded him. He didn't say anything until they'd left the alley and were back on a main street.

"We could have handled that better."

Morgan sucked on a knuckle. "It went fine. Message delivered. How's your head?"

Patrick reached back. He found a lump, but no open wounds. "Ice and drugs, I'll be fine."

"Colonel Kell."

The brothers stopped. A kid came running down the street toward them. He wore an old Eridani Light Horse jacket, but it was two sizes too big for him. He couldn't have been more than sixteen. His white shirt and dark slacks looked clean and even recently pressed. His bright blue eyes shone and his blond hair had been cut close to his scalp.

"I was in there. The Powder Keg."

Morgan frowned. "I don't recall you..."

The kid smiled infectiously. "In the back, washing dishes. They let me. Name's Jimmy Stanton. I want to join up."

Morgan blinked. "I really don't think..."

"No, please, listen, okay?" Jimmy swallowed hard. "My dad, he was a 'MechWarrior. Marcellus Stanton. Maybe you heard of him? Well, okay, no, but see he was here and had to get his 'Mech fixed. And Mr. Blizzard loaned him money. And my dad was fighting for him to pay it off."

Patrick nodded slowly. Haskell Blizzard had been an underworld boss on Galatea until recently. He had manipulated the black market so it became impossible for mercenaries to repair their 'Mechs, loaned them money to make the attempt, and ran a series of arenas where fighters could work off some of their debt. Patrick had won an arena duel with Thomas Volmer, and Blizzard had been financially crushed in paying off the bets on the fight.

"But my dad, see, he died. And we got a message saying his 'Mech would be sold for his debts if we didn't claim it. So I came east from Peterstown. The 'Mech's been in his family for a hundred-fifty years. And now it's almost paid off, and I want to be a mercenary like my dad, but no one will give me a chance."

Morgan folded his arms over his chest. "Jimmy, this isn't going to be like in the holovids."

"I know that. But I have obligations. My mom. My brothers and sisters. Geez, Liza's not even a year old. My dad never saw her except in holo." The boy held out a datacard. "I did some fighting for Blizzard. I did good. And I'm checked out in the 'Mech. It's a *Centurion*."

Patrick stepped up and took the datacard.

"Patrick, don't."

"He just wants a chance, Morgan." Patrick studied the kid. "I'll look at this, Jimmy. No promises. No real hope, okay? But I'll look."

"Thank you. God bless you." The boy's face brightened. "You'll see. It'll be okay. Thank you. I'll remember you in my prayers."

He started to back away, then came to attention and snapped a salute. The Kells returned it, then Jimmy turned and ran, holding back a loud "Wahooo!" until he'd disappeared back into the alley.

"Patrick..."

"Morgan, I know." Patrick tucked the datacard inside his jacket pocket. "I know we can't put him under arms. The idea is immoral and repugnant, but we have to do something because someone else *will* use him. If the kid's got any promise at all, maybe we can call in a favor or two and get him an appointment to the Nagelring. That would keep him out of trouble and get him training that will keep him alive."

Morgan looped an arm over his brother's shoulders. "Okay, it's a plan, but it's one you have to stick with. We're not keeping him around as a unit mascot, even for a little while. What we want to do means we might take in people with rough edges, but we can't bring a kid, a totally green kid, into that sort of environment."

"Ah, Morgan, technically I'd be one of those 'totally green kids.'"

"Sure, who graduated at the top of his class at the Nagelring, and who's been driving a 'Mech since before you mastered a bicycle."

Patrick laughed. He actually had more scars from bicycle riding than anything to do with 'Mechs. "Okay, point made. Now do you think we're going to get any of the guys from the Powder Keg?"

Morgan glanced back, then shrugged. "We should. With Blizzard's organization falling apart, we've snapped up the best techs on the planet. That has to make us look good to a lot of folks. Many pilots won money betting on you, but buying repairs for 'Mechs doesn't come any easier, since all that money is chasing a handful of parts. With our access to a factory, we also have the parts they need."

"But, do we need them?"

"That's the big question." Morgan sighed. "It's a balancing act. We want experience, but we don't want so much of it that someone gets inflexible. We want independent thinkers, but we also want folks to take and follow orders. We're looking for an elite bunch. As much as they were an unsavory lot, there probably were a handful who have what we need."

Patrick sidestepped an unconscious pilot snoring away in a pool of vomit. "What about that Frost guy?"

"Don't know. Really old eyes."

"Not terribly sociable."

"At least he wasn't trigger-happy." Morgan scratched the back of his head. "You know that's the odd thing about warriors and how we make them. Take a kid like Jimmy. For him, it's a tradition. I'm sure there's romantic notions all mixed up in there. Chances are, if he gets some training, he'll be brave, he'll serve with honor, and he'll pass the tradition on to his own children. But that training, that's the weird thing. That's where we prepare for the worst, and break down that last taboo. We put young people into a position where we tell them it's okay to kill their fellow human beings."

"But we have to, Morgan."

"I know. I've killed. You've killed. It's changed us in ways we can't even imagine. All the training in the world can't prepare you for that. It can't direct your reaction."

Patrick frowned. "But wouldn't our background determine how we react?"

"Sure, more than likely that's the end of it. You and I have had a solid foundation. Good education, religious training, we have a framework for understanding what we've done and the consequences of it. Sounds like Jimmy has that going for him, too. But, you know, there's one reaction I don't think any foundation can prepare you for."

"What's that?"

Morgan's expression tightened. "When you find out you like it."

Patrick slowly nodded. There were times it happened to almost any warrior. They called it Blood Fever. You got into combat and all you wanted were kills. You became the hunter, merciless, invincible, and just went out there and destroyed things. If you were lucky, the battle ended before you ran out of ammo or were killed yourself. Then you calmed down and after the battle you rationalized things. You were out there protecting your friends. You thought about those you were avenging.

That rationalization allowed you to sleep at night.

But some warriors never came down from it. They were always the hunters, never able to turn it off. They liked killing. They hungered for it. Sometimes Patrick wondered if that sort of bloodlust had been the source for legends about vampires and other creatures that survived on blood.

"I'm glad I've not been there." Patrick looked over at his brother. "Have you? I mean, you've never really talked about the time you were away with Katrina and Arthur."

A smile lit up Morgan's face. "Don't worry about me, Patrick. I'm fine. I've not been there either, but you have to wonder. What would you do if you looked into the future and only saw blood?"

"That's what our future is likely to be, isn't it?"

"Not if we do our jobs right. We pick the right people, the right equipment, the right battlefields, and we'll be able to beat people without having to fire a shot." He nodded. "When war costs too much, folks will stop waging it."

"I agree." Patrick slapped his brother's back. "So we'll pick the best recruits, put an end to all war, and retire undefeated."

"Amen, brother, amen."

CHAPTER 2

GOVERNOR'S MANSION
GALATEAN CITY, GALATEA
LYRAN COMMONWEALTH
16 OCTOBER 3010

Morgan Kell had never liked wearing the uniform of the Galatea Garrison, but while he'd been in temporary command of it, he'd had little choice in the matter. His assuming command of the garrison had been critical in ousting General Volmer, the former commander. That, in turn, had contributed to the downfall of Haskell Blizzard, without which the Kells would not have had any success in recruiting mercenaries to their unit. The arrival of the new governor called for a reception being held in his honor. The fact that the man brought an officer to replace Morgan meant Morgan could return to the Kell Hound colors.

The Governor's Mansion, which had been designed in a very Mediterranean style, with stucco and tile in most places, marble, mosaics and fountains in others, struck the right note on a dry world like Galatea. It was a welcome contrast to the scrap-metal décor of many places in Galatean City—remnants of failed industrial efforts, or reactions to the elegance of new buildings like the mansion. Morgan found himself envying the governor's living quarters, even though the Nova Royale hotel was equally opulent.

Not so much envy as begrudge. Baron Lawrence Bonham had been incoming to take command of the world even as General Volmer was being brought low. Bonham had gotten the position as a sop to Alessandro Steiner, the former Archon, who retained a great deal of power on the Isle of Skye. Alessandro had been a despot whom Katrina Steiner supplanted. Morgan, Arthur Luvon, and Katrina had even fled the Lyran Commonwealth for a time to elude Alessandro's assassins, so Morgan wasted little love on him or his agents.

Even so, he stopped himself from bristling as the Governor approached bearing two glasses of wine. The man moved easily—the gait of someone who had never labored or been achy in his entire life. Painfully slender and taller even than Morgan, Bonham's thinning brown hair had been raked across his scalp to cover, but not with the precision that would have marked extreme vanity. The man's brown eyes were lively and wide, which set Morgan a bit at ease.

Morgan's replacement trailed in his wake. Colonel Sarah Thorndyke's blonde hair showed a few streaks of gray, but she seemed otherwise ageless. Morgan knew little about her. She appeared uneasy enough at the reception that he decided to like her. Volmer would have felt quite at home, whereas *fighting* warriors seldom did.

Bonham extended a glass to Morgan. "It's not poisoned, as Colonel Thorndyke can attest."

"It isn't?" Morgan accepted the glass. "If you can't poison a cup of wine, I can't imagine why Alessandro ever would have chosen you for this position."

Bonham laughed easily. "You wound me, sir. I was hoping you and I could get off on the right foot, Colonel. I'm aware of the history—at least all that is public and much of what is not. An apology would fall on deaf ears, so I shan't make one. I will, however, suggest that I am not prone to making the same mistakes as others."

Morgan sniffed the wine, but did not drink. "That could be taken two ways, Baron."

"True, but I meant it only one. I don't feel assassination is a suitable political tool. I regret how often and carelessly it has been used." The Baron sipped his wine. "I would like a rapprochement with you. I've read many things about you and your brother. Accepting that what's been reported about your motives and goals are true, I find us allied in many things."

Morgan arched an eyebrow. "Really?"

"Absolutely. You don't see war as profitable. Neither do I. A well-balanced economy, in which the needs of the population are met, and excess goods can be shipped off in trade, is the best way to make a place prosper. You've actually helped me. Breaking Blizzard's power and redistributing his wealth is priming the pump for an economic revitalization of the world. When I succeed, we will still be the mercenary planet, but mercenaries will be a side-show."

Colonel Thorndyke nodded. "And one which will also be run economically, for the benefit of all."

Morgan half-smiled. "A strong economy will benefit Alessandro, funding his plans for the future—plans which will require mercenaries, I have no doubt."

Bonham smiled, then glanced down. "It might, but he is not my primary concern. May I ask you a question?"

"It's your party."

"You're most kind." The Governor's eyes tightened slightly. "Do you collect anything?"

"Scars."

"Of course. I collect coins. I like to collect them from the border worlds. Do you know why?"

Morgan shook his head, then sampled a bit of the wine.

Bonham dug in his pocket, then handed Morgan a silver coin. It had been overstamped with the profile of Archon Elizabeth Steiner, but *kanji* had been milled into the edge. The armored fist had been stamped on the back, but the original figure of a samurai with sword drawn could still be made out.

"It's a hundred and fifty years old, more or less, from Lyons. After we took the world from the Draconis Combine, we overstamped their coins with our dies. Same value to the coin as before the conquest, just a different picture on it."

Morgan handed the coin to Colonel Thorndyke. "Hardly rare, these coins."

"Correct, and this goes to my point," the Governor continued. "Alessandro, Katrina, Takashi Kurita, Janos Marik, it doesn't matter to the people whose face appears on their coins. All that matters is their coins still having value. They need to make a living, to have food for the table, and a good economy ensures that. I want to ensure that."

Bonham looked around the room. "When the settlers first came to Galatea, all they wanted to do was farm. They rejected technology for the most part, and struggled to make things work. But they did. Those original people are all clustered to the west, in the only really fertile zone on this world."

"I've heard it called Majistan by the locals." Colonel Thorndyke handed the coin back to Bonham.

"Quaint appellation." The Governor thumbed the edge of the coin. "Regardless, the farmers keep us alive with food shipments, but it requires technology to transport the amount of food we require here. Can you imagine if that would break down?"

"It wouldn't be good." Morgan thought for a moment. "Ten days?"

"Galatean City would be starving in a fortnight. Some of the smaller cities would last longer. There are towns that would vanish overnight." Bonham looked at the coin, then slipped it back into his pocket. "My goal is to make certain that this world can support itself, then make a contribution to the national economy. Peace and stability will do that. So, you see, we are allies."

"Or perhaps just men with a common enemy." Morgan drank more of the wine. "But I hear your message. I think we can keep out of each other's way. I'm sure Colonel Thorndyke can handle the garrison. Now that she's in place, I won't be a worry at all."

Colonel Thorndyke nodded. "Thanks for your stewardship, Colonel Kell. If you gentlemen will excuse me?"

Bonham drank as the garrison commander took her leave. "Contrary to what you might believe, you're not a worry. And, yes, I know that can be taken more than one way, too. You have integrity. Another man with your connections would have killed both Volmer and Blizzard, trusting that higher powers would absolve you of any wrongdoing."

Morgan shook his head. "The higher powers that concern me, Baron, do not condone murder."

From behind Morgan another voice, strong and loud enough to be overheard, broke into the conversation. "Those higher authorities also do not condone whoremongery."

Morgan wheeled. "I beg your pardon?"

An older man stood there, just slightly shorter than Morgan and with an average build. His close-cropped, kinky hair had silvered at the temples. The light brown hue of his skin and the almond shape of his eyes bespoke a mixed Asian and African heritage, while the beard lining his jaw hinted at the Amish culture still revered in Galatea's west. The man's suit, which was clean, was also worn.

"You, Colonel Kell, are a whoremonger." The man pointed a reedy finger at him. "Do not attempt to deny it."

Morgan killed the initial impulse to shatter the man's jaw as he had Addison Garlett's the night before. "And you base this judgment on?"

The man shifted his focus, pointed at a tall, slender woman standing over near Patrick Kell. Even from across the room her icy-blue eyes stood out, matching the gown she wore. "Everyone knows Veronica Matova is a whore, and you consort with her."

"And this is your business, why?"

"It is not my business, Colonel Kell, it is God's business! I am merely his vessel."

"Are you?"

Baron Bonham nodded, his wine glass having disappeared onto a side table. "Colonel Kell, this is Bishop Arlington Poore, of the Church of Jesus Majificent."

Morgan wasn't certain he heard correctly, since Bonham pronounced the word with a soft j and without an n, making it *ma-jif-i-sent*. Still, something rang a bell in the back of his head. An alarm bell. Danger. Though he knew he should back off, retreat was not in his nature.

"Let me ask you, Bishop Poore, how you define whoremongery?"

"Consorting with whores!"

"Does that mean sleeping with them, or *any* contact?"

Poore's expression sharpened. "I am no simpleton, Colonel. You're preparing to point out that our Lord Jesus is purported to have associated with whores and thieves, and to have told us to love the sinner but hate the sin. You may even profess your innocence of carnal contact. But you are not our Lord, and any contact you have with that woman does not concern the fate of her immortal soul. You would engage in a game of words, dicing for your salvation."

Morgan hid rising anger behind an impassive mask. "Then I would ask this: when is a whore forgiven her sins?"

"When she repents, accepts Jesus as her personal savior, and sins no more."

"And how do you know she hasn't already done that?"

Poore snorted and pointed again. "Look at her. She has put herself on display. Ostentation. Cosmetics. That raiment, the way she flirts. It is up to God to judge, but my place is to warn."

The Baron rested a hand on the Bishop's shoulder. "And we both appreciate that very much. The Bishop came all the way to Galatean City to ask me to intervene on behalf of General Volmer. His wife has long been a member of the Church."

That's it! Morgan remembered where he'd heard the church mentioned in passing. "And her son, Thomas, recently joined the church, yes?"

Poore nodded solemnly. "He came to us at Paradise Mountain and renounced his sinful ways. He no longer uses the drugs that made him a tool of the devil. He labors in the fields like the others. The bread you eat, the wine you drink, it is made with our hands."

"And we appreciate that, Bishop." Bonham turned to Morgan. "General Volmer was baptized into the Church *in absentia*. There has been a tradition of church courts disciplining their own members. The Bishop would like us to turn the general over to him."

Poore nodded, then fixed Morgan with a dark-eyed stare. "You will oppose this, of course."

Morgan shrugged. "Contrary to what you have chosen to assume about me, Bishop, I'm not opposed to religion. I'm all in favor of justice being meted out. The General misappropriated hundreds of thousands of C-bills in government property. What sort of punishment will that earn him?"

"He will be tried, and we will pray. God will choose his punishment." The man clutched his hands together at his belt. "God judges, I just—"

"You just warn."

"I watch and warn. And I pray." Poore again watched Morgan closely. "You consider yourself Catholic, yes?"

"Born, schooled, and raised."

"Ah." The Bishop nodded. "Then another warning: there is but one true God. Follow him. Renounce your ways. Save your soul."

"Will you introduce me to your friend, Morgan?" Veronica slipped her hand through the crook of Morgan's elbow, then extended a hand toward Poore. "I am Veronica Matova, but you already know that."

"You are *unclean*." Hysteria and outrage raised the man's voice to a shrill tone. "Get thee behind me, Satan."

"'Behind you' will cost *more*, Bishop."

"How *dare* you speak to me thus?" Poore's beard quivered. "I am a man of God!"

"You're just a man, Bishop, as full of self-importance as any other. You just feel it is righteous and deserved, since God smiles upon you—much in the same way that an imaginary friend's appreciation of a child's antics makes that child feel good. In fact, there's as much evidence for the existence of that imaginary friend as there is of God—yours or any other. And given the number of gods there are, the chances of yours being the *only* God are rather slender."

"You are a sinner!"

"Last time I checked, Pride was every bit as much a sin as Lust."

A vein pulsed in Poore's forehead. He turned on the Governor. "Ward well your soul, Baron, if these are the people with whom you associate. God will judge you by the company you keep. And you, Colonel, sever yourself from this witch. Her soul is forfeit, and I'll see she burns in hell."

Morgan twisted, pushing Veronica behind him, and thrust his face into Poore's. "Exactly how soon is it you want to meet your Creator, Bishop? Harm one hair on her head, and you'll be there."

"I would be a martyr."

"Yeah, you would, and you know what happens to most martyrs? They're forgotten. Dead men, it turns out, make lousy leaders."

Poore stepped back, then straightened his coat with a jerk. "I will be leaving Galatean City at noon, Baron. I expect to leave with General Volmer at my side. God will not be pleased if he is not with me."

"I'll bear that in mind, Bishop."

Poore, his nostrils still flared, nodded curtly and marched stiffly from the mansion. The crowd watched him go in silence. A few people crossed themselves, and few others nodded in Morgan's direction—though no nods came while the Bishop was still in the room.

The Baron sighed. "That will complicate things."

Veronica snorted dismissively. "Don't expect me to apologize."

"I don't." He shrugged. "Though I am afraid I'll have to order the Constabulary to raid one of your establishments. Could you gather together some troublesome employees, or some who want to be sent off world? Would tomorrow morning, around ten, be inconvenient?"

"In time for the Bishop to learn of the crackdown before he leaves?"

"Yes." Bonham recovered his wine and took a healthy gulp. "You see, he's bound to be disappointed. General Volmer is already headed to the jump point and back to Tharkad. He requested we not let his wife or his son know, given that they've fallen under Poore's sway. It will be a bit of a shock all the way around, so I was hoping for a bone to toss to him. It's that, or next week I make a pronouncement for Martyr's Day and give everyone a day off."

"You'll get a dozen. Eight will go off-world. Four will be released with suspended sentences, as it will be a first offense." Veronica's eyes narrowed. "You'll also pick up two customers who are with the Church. You'll want to seal the records on those arrests, for the Bishop's benefit, of course."

"Thank you, my dear."

"I'm not your *dear*, Baron. You owe me."

The man thought for a moment, then nodded. "And I shall repay my debt. If you will excuse me. Colonel. Miss Matova."

The only lingering indication of the confrontation came from a slight quiver of Veronica's lower lip. Morgan placed his hand over hers and squeezed. "You did good, Veronica."

"And you were very cute, protecting me that way." She leaned in and kissed the tip of his nose. "Fact is, you stopped me from strangling him."

"Next time, he's all yours." Morgan pulled her into a hug. "And I meant what I said. If he harms you, he's dead."

"But Morgan, you said that if anyone ever threatened me, it would be because he got through you first. How will you be able to kill him?"

Morgan pulled back and looked her straight in the eyes. "For him, I'd come back from the dead and pull him screaming down into Hell."

CHAPTER 3

HAMILTON ARMOR AND DENT, LTD.
GALATEAN CITY, GALATEA
LYRAN COMMONWEALTH
17 OCTOBER 3010

Patrick Kell looked up from the computer and smiled. "What's the good word?"

Tisha Hamilton wiped her face with a rag. She wore a sleeveless Kell Hounds' t-shirt—one she'd bought on the street—and a pair of stained overalls. Not the most appealing attire in the world, but with her long black hair braided and her hazel eyes sparkling, she fully fit his definition of beauty.

The fact that she was the best tech on the planet didn't hurt, either.

She shrugged. "For a *Centurion*, the Stanton machine's in pretty good shape. The left upper leg actuator is shot. We could fix it easily enough, but there will be bigger problems down the line. The right hip has stress fractures. Not uncommon when the pilot has been compensating for damage on the other side. That whole joint has to be replaced. You're looking at twenty-K to make the machine combat ready, thirty to bring it up to Kell Hound specs."

"What about just replacing the actuator to make it ambulatory?"

"Six, give or take. The kid can march it home and it can pull a plow."

"Pull a plow?"

"He's from the west, Patrick. Farming and running away are all they do there." She shook her head. "Sorry, I forget you're still new to Galatea."

Patrick shook his head. "But I'm learning. I was hoping that if he has a functional 'Mech, we can get him some work."

"A *Centurion* is kind of big for delivering pizzas."

"I know, but an operational *Centurion*, there are academies that will look more favorably on an application."

Tisha came over and gave him a kiss on the cheek. "It's wonderful you're helping this kid out."

"Thanks. I just hope I can help." He turned to the desk and pushed a button on a communications console. "Walter, Jimmy, the simulators are all set. Have at it."

Both pilots signaled their readiness. Streams of data cascaded down the screen. Patrick minimized the window showing a battlefield map. Walter de Mesnil, driving a *Blackjack*, would square off with the *Centurion*. The two 'Mechs were relatively evenly matched, but the outcome didn't really matter. Patrick wanted to see how Jimmy Stanton handled a 'Mech, especially under pressure. He had no intention of inviting him into the Kell Hounds—*well, maybe if he beats Walter significantly*—but his showing some talent would make his getting into the Nagelring much easier.

He glanced over at Tisha as she filled out a report form on the *Centurion*. "So at the reception last night, Morgan and Veronica had a run-in with some bishop from the Church of Jesus Magnificent."

Tisha turned in her chair. "Majificent, not magnificent."

"That's not a word."

"It is now, and one more reason to get Jimmy off this rock. This bishop, he was a tallish, skinny guy, dark, graying hair?"

"That was him. Loud, too. Said Morgan was a whoremonger."

"That was mild." Tisha shook her head. "Not a good man to get involved with. He's one of the most dangerous of clerics—he uses all the tricks of the mountebanks, but he actually *believes*."

"Tricks?"

"Classic one: the seed-corn message. All the preachers use it. The story always involves someone who had very little—the family is down to their last crust of bread, for example. Someone worse off than they are comes begging. They don't want to hand over their last crust of bread, but they know Christian charity demands it. And they believe that Jesus will provide for them if they offer their problems up to him. They do, and inside a couple of hours, a truck pulls up outside the house and gives them a metric ton of bread. Their prayers are answered.

"This is immediately followed by a call to the congregation to hand over money, even if they can barely afford to. They're told that God will repay them a hundred-fold, or a thousand-fold or a million-fold. The truly desperate—who are the same folks who buy lottery tickets—will give their last C-bill, waiting for God to pay them back."

Patrick raised an eyebrow. "You know a lot about this."

Tisha snorted. "When my dad ran the shop here we had an astech who was a Church member. He invited me to a service. The really sad thing is this: when God doesn't repay the debt, the preacher just defaults to the fact that the believer is *weak* in his faith, same way Moses was when God tested him in the desert. Buying a lottery ticket has a better chance of payoff."

He sat back. "And the bishop is one of those?"

"Poore does all that, but he truly believes. He doesn't keep the money he gets for himself—at least it doesn't seem that way—and helps the *plow herds* out in the west. He's not much on ostentation, but that's in keeping with the whole anti-technology tradition out there. The government has let him set up his own judiciary, so the west is pretty much a theocratic state. They don't cause much trouble, however, so he's been given his head."

"State within a state. Wow. That could be trouble."

Tisha nodded. "Every couple years someone comes out with a story about underage marriages, corporal punishment, and things we'd abandoned a millennia ago, but nothing ever comes of it."

"Interesting. Why 'majificent?'"

"Stress on 'maji.' Some mainstream Christian religions have de-emphasized the miracles in the Bible, concentrating on the philosophical side of Christianity. Poore is the backlash, embracing miracles. It works perfectly with folks who feel threatened by tech. They believe in miracles, and believe God is going to protect them. It's not quite gotten to the point where Poore proclaims himself to be the Second Coming, but I'm pretty sure it will."

"Sounds odd, but not dangerous. Why do you think Jimmy is best off away from there?"

Tisha shivered. "Rumors again. There's supposed to be a secret splinter group, called the Petrine Order, that focuses on Peter's cutting the ear off a slave to protect Jesus in the Garden. They're big on Old Testament law. You hear about stonings and other things. None of it proved, but too consistently raised to not start you wondering. Ten years ago the governor was almost murdered by an ex-Church member, and many folks figured it was at Poore's orders. The two of them did not get along."

I'm going to have to clue Morgan in.

The computer console beeped. Patrick turned and opened a window. Both 'Mechs appeared in it in profile. Using a joystick, Patrick brought the camera up and pulled back, giving him a top-down view of the fight. He hit a button and a scale grid appeared.

"What is that kid thinking?"

Tisha hit two keys on her console and the same windows appeared over there. "The *Centurion* is best at range. He should be holding back, not trying to close."

"Right, and Walter is trying to pull back, giving the kid an advantage. Dammit." Patrick shook his head. "The kid's totally blown."

"What do you mean?"

"He said he'd done some fighting for Blizzard. I checked. Twenty fights, as many wins as losses. I thought it was good experience." Patrick punched up another data window. "But look at the distribution of the wins. Completely random. Cross it with opponents he faced multiple times, and there's no sign of improvement. He's not learning and, worse yet, having fought in the tiny arenas, he's got a tiny-battlefield view of things. He's not matching tactics to terrain, range or foe."

Tisha frowned. "But that's something they can teach him at the Nagelring, right?"

"They could, but they won't." Patrick signed. "Most recruits have spent years in prep academies. That's where you learn past this sort of thing. The Nagelring won't teach it to him because they don't need to. They can just pick recruits who already know it."

"What about getting him into one of the preps?"

"No school for the last year. Indifferent marks before that. His age. That will be a really hard sell."

She smiled. "But you'll get him in somewhere."

"Yeah, I will. He'd have to wait until February to get an appointment, probably next August." Patrick groaned. It wasn't hard for him to see Jimmy's expectant expression collapse into disappointment. *Oh hell, if the kid cries...*

He watched the monitor hoping Jimmy would reverse course or reveal some previously hidden genius. Even the most slender glimmer of hope could be spun into something that would give the kid a chance. As it was, he wouldn't even look appealing to a fighting stable on Solaris, much less a military academy.

Hope did not glimmer. Not even dimly.

Jimmy's *Centurion* came on gamely and Walter pounded it. His small autocannons chipped away at armor. Lasers slashed molten black scars over the humanoid 'Mech's torso and legs. Patrick imagined that Walter wanted to immobilize the 'Mech so he could pull back and Jimmy could fight at his best range, but Jimmy just wasn't buying into that strategy.

The kid did have pluck, however. Long-range missiles sprinted across the narrowed gap between 'Mechs, hammering armor all over the barrel-chested *Blackjack's* torso and upper body. The heavy autocannon, the muzzle of which replaced the *Centurion's* right hand, vomited metal and fire. The shot blasted completely through the armor on the *Blackjack's* right arm. Sparks exploded and one of the lasers housed there died.

It was a good hit, but Jimmy made the mistake of believing a wounded animal was a dead one. Walter's experience came to the fore. He pulled his 'Mech back initially, encouraging Jimmy's advance. As Walter retreated he shifted around to present his left side to the *Centurion*, protecting his wound and still letting him fight hard.

Jimmy fired with everything he could bring to bear. A few of the missiles hit, but again did nothing more than shiver armor from the *Blackjack*. The autocannon carved deep into that left flank, but failed to open a hole into the 'Mech's chest. His laser's ruby lance blackened the other 'Mech's right thigh, but did no serious damage.

Walter's return strike, however, proved devastating. Two lasers finished the last of the armor over the *Centurion's* right thigh. Myomer muscle fibers smoked and snapped, spraying liquid tissue into the air. The *Centurion's* right leg failed to respond, catching the toe in the turf. For a half-second it looked as if Jimmy would keep the fifty-ton war machine upright. Then the knee sheered, and the 'Mech sprawled face first into the ground.

Patrick killed his monitor. "I guess that's that."

"Want me to go with you to deliver the bad news?"

"Thanks. Can you fix the actuator on the real *Centurion,* so he has something?"

"Sure, I'll get right on it."

He rose from his chair and paused to kiss her. "Thank you."

"You're welcome." She hung on to his sleeve, not letting him straighten up. "You tried, you know."

"Not much else to be done."

"Go tell him, and later we'll do some dancing, okay?"

"You got a date." He kissed her again, then made his way to the simulators. He wished Morgan was the one who would break the news to the kid. Morgan had a way of making folks feel happy, as if their failure wasn't a failure, but some other kind of success. *No, Jimmy is my problem.*

He arrived as Walter helped the young man from the simulator pod. The boy's neurohelmet hid his face, denying Patrick any sort of read on him. Then it came off and the boy wore a huge smile. That wasn't going to make it any easier to break his heart.

Jimmy set the neurohelmet just inside the pod, then offered Walter his hand—surprising Walter. "Lieutenant, thank you. I really learned a lot."

"You're welcome, Jimmy."

The boy turned to Patrick. "Colonel, I really appreciate this opportunity. I know I stunk out there."

"Jimmy, it wasn't that bad."

"You don't have to make me feel good, Colonel." The boy displayed no distress, only a serenity that seemed grossly out of place. Patrick had fought hundreds of simulator battles, and even the easiest of them left him breathless and exciting. Jimmy's reaction wasn't quite natural.

"Jimmy, I'm going to write up a recommendation for you. We'll try to get you into a prep academy and, down the line, we can bring you back to the Hounds."

"That's terribly nice of you, sir, but you needn't go to that trouble. You see, this morning, before I came here, I prayed. I was with a few others here at the Church dormitory and we all prayed. And I offered this exercise up. See, if Jesus wanted me to be a Kell Hound, I would have—no offense, Lieutenant—I would have been triumphant. He would have steadied my hand and guided me, just like he did the Emperor Constantine."

Walter's brows furrowed. "You have to understand, son, that fighting a 'Mech requires a lot of experience."

"I know that, sir, but who has more experience than Jesus?" Jimmy's smile broadened. "You know, when my family and I came here, it was for me to continue a tradition that I really didn't understand. I thought of it as a purpose, but I know there is a higher purpose. Bishop Poore has helped me see that."

Patrick blinked. "So you *are* a member of the Church of Jesus Majificent."

"Yes, Colonel. They offered solace to my mother, and help, too; after my father passed. They asked me to look into my soul and I felt an emptiness. Then I heard Jesus call me, so I accepted him as my Lord and Savior." He looked over his shoulder at the simulator. "This was the last vestige of that family tradition. I thank the Lord for indulging me. And you, too, gentlemen. I hope I didn't waste your time. The Lord moves in mysterious ways and I know he had a purpose for me being here today."

The younger Kell brother shivered. Jimmy's nature and the warnings about Poore seemed utterly at odds. He didn't doubt that an evil man could manage some good, but Jimmy's self-possession was something he'd not seen in, well, *anyone*. The boy was simply at peace with himself and his fate. Patrick found himself slightly envious.

"Jimmy, I don't know what to say."

"You don't need to say anything, sir. I can't thank you enough for your time and kindness."

Patrick took the boy's proffered hand and shook it. "Jimmy, I had the shop look at your *Centurion*. We're going to replace that damaged actuator. We're just going to do it. If you change your mind, I will work to make you a MechWarrior."

"Thank you, sir. That's very kind." Jimmy smiled and broke their grip. "But the Lord is my shepherd. I shall follow Him, do His will, and know the greatest rewards possible. I don't expect you to understand, sir, not now; but I hope you will very soon."

CHAPTER 4

Morgan, standing behind his desk, nodded to a thickly-built man with a crew-cut. "Thanks for filling me in, Richard."

The man nodded. "Look, I'd love to have Frost back in the unit. Technically he's never resigned, but he's a pain when we're fighting, and worse when we're not. Security work doesn't give him much to do. As I said, he's the best damned sniper I've ever seen."

"Right." Morgan ran a hand over his jaw. While he acknowledged that warfare was hardly a clean business, something inside him didn't like snipers. Not that using artillery to kill at range was really any different—but it seemed that way. A bombing run, or artillery, killed anonymously. A sniper took deliberate aim at a target. If there was a dividing line between killing and murder, sniping seemed on the murder side.

"You want me to reach out to him and bring him in?"

"I didn't think that would be possible. He said you parted over religious differences."

Richard laughed. "Most of my cast-offs say that. They usually follow with 'He thought he was God, and I disagreed.' Not Frost."

Morgan arched an eyebrow.

The infantry Major's eye tightened. "I like my soldiers to have a soul. I'm not sure Frost does anymore."

A shiver ran down Morgan's spine. "We can probably do without him, then."

"As ordered." Richard and Morgan exchanged salutes. As the Major departed, Walter de Mesnil appeared in the doorway. "A

Lieutenant David Donelly to see you. He's a walk-in. Says he's from Arc-Royal, knew your family?"

Morgan frowned. He didn't recognize the name, but something remained hauntingly familiar about it. "Show him in. Check with me in fifteen minutes."

"Yes, sir."

Walter showed a short, stocky man into the office. His thinning black hair had been cut short. Morgan couldn't actually judge his age, but guessed it was on the high side of forty. The left side of the man's face and neck showed the twisted, fluid scars of a burn, and he wore a black glove on his left hand. That made it easy to imagine his hand and arm likewise were scarred, though they moved easily enough.

Donelly stopped two paces into the room. "Look at you. I'm thinking it's been far too long. You're not remembering me, are you?"

"I'm afraid you have me at a disadvantage, Lieutenant." The man's voice had the lilting brogue of an Arc-Royal native, and Morgan's recognition of the sound was more than just being familiar with the accent. He had met the man before. "I don't recognize your unit. How do I know you?"

Donelly approached, sketched a salute, then took a chair. He sat forward, resting elbows on his knees. "The unit is—was—Killian's Red Raiders. The Dracs weren't liking our contesting of ownership of a world. Chewed us up smart. The cowards ran, the best died or are in some prison somewhere. Those who survived aren't worth your time, I'm thinking."

Morgan sat, wondering if the man realized his frank recitation had killed any chance of his being hired on with the Kell Hounds. "I appreciate that assessment, Lieutenant. I'll make a note. How can I help you?"

"It would be me helping you, I think." His brown eyes flashed. "Of course, I came to see you as part of a promise I made to your mother. How is May?"

May? Morgan's mother's name was Margaret Maybelle Kell. Most of her friends called her Margaret or some variation thereof. The only ones who referred to her as May had known her since childhood.

"My mother is doing very well, thank you."

"Good, always glad to hear. I think of her often, and fondly, too."

"I'll pass along your greetings." Morgan pressed his hands flat against the top of the desk. "Are you looking for a position with the Hounds, Lieutenant? What sort of a 'Mech do you pilot?"

The man sat back, the whole part of his face smiling broadly. "Well, of course, that's it. That's why you're not remembering me."

"Please, help me here." Morgan glanced at the door, hoping his fifteen minutes was up. "Who are you?"

Donelly laughed. "Well, you were a wee lad, when I last saw you. Couldn't have been more than six, I'm thinking. Last time I saw your mother, though, was the year you went missing. She was powerful sad then."

The man held his hands up. "You won't remember me as a Lieutenant, Colonel. I was introduced to you as *Father* Donelly."

"Oh my God." Morgan blinked. "Forgive me, Father."

"Nothing to forgive, lad." Donelly laughed. "Left matched right back then, you were a mite shorter and I was a wee bit taller."

"You know my father, too."

"Served in the same unit, we did. Him after the Academy, me after Seminary." Donelly leaned forward again. "So I'm here, Morgan, to ask you to make me the chaplain for your Hounds."

Morgan leaned back. "Chaplain? I hadn't..."

"I know, lad." The priest unbuttoned his black Raiders' jacket. "All the way in I've been hearing what you and your brother want to do. Not an easy path. Men of war hoping to make war go extinct. I'm thinking there's much bloodletting to be done before that happens. And I'm knowing you want the best for your men. You'll take care of their needs here in the physical realm. I'll be tending to their souls."

"I'm not sure they're all Catholic, Father. It would be in the files somewhere, but..."

"It doesn't really matter, Morgan." Mirth left Donelly's face. "I won't be hitting you with the old bromide that there are no atheists in a foxhole. You're in war, you're wonder what sort of a stupid god can allow that sort of thing to happen. Fact is, though, a warrior is asked to break that last taboo. Creation, life, that's God's province. Killing is usurping His authority. Now, there's fools what will tell you that if the other guy dies it's God's Will, but I'm thinking that's because the man is too stupid or too afraid to realize he's playing God right there."

Donelly pointed off toward Galaport. "The boys I came back with, I ministered to each and everyone. Now we had us a unit shrink and he did some good. But all he could do was put things in perspective of the warrior's life. But when you're making yourself a god, you open up bigger questions. Fell to me to show them answers. A shrink can get into your head, but being a god gets into your heart. Heads, when broken, are a lot easier to fix."

"Good point." Morgan's eyes tightened. "You know we're picking the best we can get. Young enough to be enthusiastic, experienced enough to be good. This won't be an easy post for a chaplain."

Donelly laughed. "Lad, the Church wouldn't be trusting me with a parish anywhere. Like your warriors, I take a drop now and again, and have even been known to curse—when playing poker. And while I don't indulge in pleasures of the flesh, nor am I the sort to go counseling those who don't ask for counsel."

Morgan blushed in spite of himself. *I've not even slept with Veronica and here I'm embarrassed being associated with her—because of her profession.* "You've heard my brother has a girlfriend?"

"Whiff of a rumor, which will go no further—whether or not you hire me." Donelly grinned impishly. "God made certain things pleasurable not, I'm thinking, to tell you that you shouldn't indulge. He wants you to take responsibility. If someone is wanting pointers on that, my door will always be open."

None of the Kell brothers' discussions had ever touched upon having a chaplain attached to the unit. They'd both wanted the Hounds to be like a family. They'd figured that if they chose the right people, that would just sort of happen. It occurred to Morgan that the dynamics of human chemistry might need some tinkering here and there. If people were constant and unchanging it wouldn't, but rigid and hide-bound people weren't going to find a place in the unit.

Moreover, and more importantly, having someone whose focus was beyond tactical and logistical would be a huge asset. Morgan hated the concept of "collateral damage," in which bystanders were assumed to be a statistical constant—albeit an unimportant one. It made war into a spectator sport where spectators could be killed. While no one in his right mind would tolerate that in any sport, in warfare civilian casualties became incidental information that seldom got a public accounting.

For too many warriors, *collateral damage* meant absolution from the consequences of being sloppy. A good officer could call artillery in on a position with a tight grid. A less than competent officer—or one for whom anyone who wasn't with him had to be against him—would use a larger grid that was guaranteed to kill enemy civilians. As long as there wasn't wholesale slaughter—like the Kentares Massacre—the incident would pass without notice.

But people would still be dead.

Morgan nodded. "If the Diocese agrees, you're a Hound. Do I have a lieutenant, or is a promotion in order?"

"Lieutenant is fine. If you make me a sergeant, someone will expect me to actually do something." The priest smiled. "And if I'm a captain, my advice becomes an order."

Walter appeared in the doorway. "Colonel."

"It's okay, Walter. *Father* Donelly is our new Chaplain."

Walter blinked, then smiled. "Glad to meet you. Colonel, there's a situation. Baron Bonham sent a car for you. He wants you at the mansion immediately."

"Really." The Galatea garrison unit had scrambled the previous day and headed out of Galatean City. Despite having been relieved of command, Morgan had been mildly curious about the move. *I guess I'll learn what happened.*

Morgan stood and shook Donelly's hand. "Welcome to the Hounds, Father. Glad to have you aboard."

Baron Bonham looked as if he'd been drinking heavily and nonstop since Morgan had last seen him. Had he not clearly been bathed and dressed in fresh clothing, Morgan would have found it easy to believe that was *all* the man had done. The Governor's haggard face and bloodshot eyes revealed more than the weary sigh and his inability to summon a smile.

"We have a situation, Colonel."

"Yes?"

The Baron waved him to a chair, then hit a button on a remote. The frozen face of General Volmer appeared above a holoprojector on the desk. "I met with Bishop Poore concerning General Volmer. I explained the General was on his way out of the system. Poore insisted on speaking with him, and I agreed that if the man asked to be returned to the Church, I'd have him sent back."

"That's a rather expensive proposition."

"I wasn't going to recall the DropShip. We were going to pack him into the backseat of an aerospace fighter and shoot him down the gravity well."

"Okay."

"ComStar set up a circuit. Poore was at Paradise Mountain, his retreat. I was here. I'll just play the event for you."

He thumbed the remote again, and Volmer's face became animated. A disembodied voice asked if Volmer understood the question before him. The general nodded, then began speaking in very precise and even clipped tones. It struck Morgan that Volmer normally didn't speak that way, but folks often got funny when distance created a delay in the circuit.

"Yes, I understand that Bishop Poore is offering me the chance to return to Galatea. I will be taken to the western provinces. The Church of Jesus Majificent will put me on trial. Whatever their punishment is, I will abide by it."

The General exhaled and seemed to deflate a little. "While I understand that the Bishop, my adoring wife, and my son, are all praying for me and my return, I cannot come back. I am an officer in the Lyran Commonwealth Armed Forces. I have duties and responsibilities. Moreover, I am innocent of the charges pressed against me. Only if I return to Tharkad to face courts martial will I be able to restore my good name. I appreciate the Bishop's intervention on my behalf, but I shall not return."

Aside from the artificial pace and tone of his words, Morgan detected nothing wrong.

Then it happened. Volmer's eyes grew wide. He lunged toward the camera. His florid face filled it. Spittle flecked it.

"Save me, save me, save me! They're in league with Satan! They made me swear blood oaths! They've stolen my soul! They are evil incarnate! Save me! I am lost! Save me!"

Morgan shivered. The man was mad.

Bonham froze the image again, foam at the corners of Volmer's mouth. "Poore broke contact immediately. The ship's captain reported Volmer was laughing at the trouble he'd caused. He despised his wife for joining the Church—she'd done so, apparently, in response to his taking so many mistresses. He wants nothing to do with Galatea, and has promised to fight extradition if we wanted to get him back here."

"You can still stuff him in an aerofighter."

"And risk a public trial with another outburst like that? No." Bonham killed the projector. "It took Poore less than an hour to proclaim a *fatwa*."

Morgan raised a finger. "Christianity doesn't have *fatwas*."

"I'm not an idiot, Colonel. It's what he called it, since he thinks 'Crusade' has a Catholic tinge to it. He announced that there would be no more shipments of food to the east. He'll starve the devil out of us." Bonham sighed. "So, I did the only thing I could."

Morgan shook his head. "You sent the garrison?"

"I had no choice. Twelve hours and they hit Ephaseus. They came in from the north and took the warehouse quarter. No food. Reports of crowds having swarmed over the warehouses and just packing it all away like an army of ants. So they started to go house to house."

Morgan's blood ran cold. "Do you have holo?"

"Do you really need it? Ephaseus is a city of fifteen thousand. Half the garrison are Churchers, so they defected. The rest of them pulled back and set up a headquarters on the edge of town. It's constant sniping, mortars, improvised explosives. Colonel Thorndyke doesn't believe she can extricate herself without help."

"No infantry?"

Bonham closed his eyes. "Majii all. They've gone over, and have taken their weapons with them. I sent detachments of Constabulary to restore order, but they were ambushed on the road in. AgroMechs with machine guns mounted on them. The survivors turned around and are incoming even now."

Morgan's head came up. "You want the Hounds to go pull the garrison out?"

"That would be more than enough to satisfy me."

Morgan looked closely at him. "You can't expect the Hounds to go in there and stop Poore."

"I don't." Bonham tossed Morgan a folded note. It bore a seal which ComStar had replicated with only the highest of authority. "Archon Katrina Steiner, on the other hand, does."

CHAPTER 5

Patrick Kell both relished and hated the tone of his brother's voice. It filled the hotel's auditorium easily, more because of the size of his voice than the size of the room. Morgan's words echoed full of sincerity and urgency, marking both the seriousness of the situation and his natural leadership skills.

"This operation is completely off the books, ladies and gentlemen. It's a training exercise for the Kell Hounds, nothing more. Mentioning it outside the unit will be grounds for dismissal, and the government will prosecute you for violations of a variety of secrecy acts. Sorry to lay it out that way. It's not because I don't trust you, but because the government can't afford to."

Morgan used a remote to bring up a holomap of the west. "The situation is dire on several levels. Bishop Arlington Poore of the Church of Jesus Majificent has declared a boycott of foodstuffs against anyone outside Majistan. His people grow the food, they warehouse it and they sell it. Galatean City has less than two weeks worth of food in warehouses. If word of the boycott gets out, prices will skyrocket, there will be food riots, it won't be pretty. That reality prompted the Governor to order the garrison in to Ephaseus to secure the warehouses there. What they found were stripped warehouses and an ambush. The garrison's infantry was largely made up of Majii, so they went over to the other side. At least a company of 'Mechs did as well. The rest are trapped in the warehouse district on the city's north side."

With the flick of a thumb he focused on Ephaseus, a small city built at the convergence of two rivers, either of which only ran as a trickle except in the rainy season. "Our primary mission is to pull them out. Ephaseus has a population of fifteen-thousand, seventy percent of whom are assumed to be Majii or Majii-sympathetic. This whole region has a long history of semi-independence, and even those who are not church members like their freedom."

Major O'Cieran shifted a toothpick from one corner of his mouth to the other. "So you're saying it's total bandit country."

"Completely hostile."

A grumbled mutter worked its way through the assembled pilots and infantry.

Morgan held his hands up. "Just wait, it gets worse. Rules of engagement are very specific. We must identify weapons and hostile intent before we are free to fire."

Erin Finney, a *Javelin* pilot late of Guinn's Gunnes, raised a hand. "You're saying we have to wait for an AgroMech sporting short-range missiles or machine guns to actually fire upon us before we can shoot at them?"

"I'm pretty sure that's what the Governor meant. I tend to be a bit more liberal in my definition of 'hostile intent.' You warn them off twice, if they keep coming, fire for effect."

The pilots in the room nodded and most made notes.

"The rules of engagement are intended to be a brake on collateral damage. These are our own people. I don't want to have to spill a single drop of blood. I imagine some will flow, but I don't want a drop more than is absolutely necessary. You shoot as if your family is downrange of your target, got it?"

O'Cieran looked at his troopers. "This goes double for you."

Morgan pointed back at the map. "We're going in hot and hard. We put down hostiles and we pull our people out. We will set up a firebase four kilometers north of the city. While we're there, the government will negotiate with Poore and try to talk some sense into him."

Patrick looked out at the warriors in the audience. They were already doing the math. An extraction raid was doable. It really was pretty much of a training exercise. A reasonable man would, in Poore's position, negotiate, win concessions and avoid further fighting.

But if it doesn't work...

Morgan brought an organizational chart up. "Here's where we stand. We have a full company of light 'Mechs, a full company of mixed 'Mechs and down here is my brother's command, a reinforced company of Ultralytes. Patrick, please explain."

He stood, taking a deep breath. "We're repairing 'Mechs as fast as we can, but we just don't have enough rides for as many pilots as we've got and need. What we've done is requisition the Ultralyte 'Mechs that used to fight in Blizzard's small arenas. We've got twenty of them broken into five lances. They're armed with lasers, missiles and cannons. The lasers and missiles have been brought up to full strength, but the cannons are really just machine guns. The armor is still crap, save for the cockpits, but these things are fast and run cool. They'll be an even match for industrial 'Mechs outfitted for battle."

"But the 'Lytes will get mangled if they face a real 'Mech."

Patrick couldn't see who'd made that comment, but he nodded. "I'm with the rest of you. I don't have a 'Mech here, so I'm riding in a 'Lyte *Commando*. Our mission is to use our speed to scout and work behind the lines to disrupt communication and supply."

Morgan nodded. "You've all figured it out. If Poore is unreasonable, we've got no choice but to take control of Majistan. If we don't, Galatea starves. The Majii aren't so worried about that because they have all the food *and* they all think we're demonspawn. What this means is that we'll have to take three cities, combined population of a hundred thousand, and maintain control until Tharkad can get some troops here. Minimum ETA on that would be two weeks."

One of the infantry raised his hand. "If we move on Poore's people, won't his worshippers over here react? You hear stories about this Petrine Order. They're crazy."

"We have an agreement with ComStar to shut down all news and information flowing from the west. That ought to cut down on their getting orders." Morgan shook his head. "I don't know how long that will last, but Poore precipitated things by cordoning off all ComStar offices with his religious police. Some news will get here from the west, certainly, but we'll have a window of opportunity to get things in hand before there can be a panic or uprising. We hope."

Con Guinn leaned forward, draping his arms over the seat in front of him. "What kind of intel do we have on the enemy?"

"Less than I want, but ComStar is supposed to be pulling together what it can. The garrison sent a medium company over, plus two battalions of infantry. They're green, but likely know which end of a rifle to point at us. They'll have conversions and maybe a few battle-ready 'Mechs, though we have no idea about their ammo supply. Ditto for supplies of small arms and explosives."

"Are the mediums at Ephaseus?"

"Don't know, but not likely. Seismic monitoring stations throughout the region reported data that reads like mediums heading to Thessalon."

"They'll use the same equipment to know we're coming."

"Which is why we'll have to fight better than they do."

Con nodded. "Much as I don't like the idea of taking war to our own, when do we go?"

Morgan smiled. "Inside two hours. The 'Lytes will move out first and fast. The rest of us will rendezvous with them just outside of Ephaseus. We'll bring the infantry in. We do our mission, we get out. Things go the way we hope. We're home in two days."

Morgan dismissed the troops and they hurried from the room. Some seemed excited. Others were nervous, but most had a grim, purposeful expression plastered on their faces.

Patrick felt a giddy flutter in his stomach. He'd seen combat before, but never in a tiny 'Mech with no armor to speak of. Moreover, he'd never fought against his own people.

He shivered. "I wish we were going against the Dracs."

Morgan landed a hand on his shoulder. "Just keep reminding yourself that they're bandits. They may dress this up as a fight for religious freedom or principle, but that's all just chaff. Letting others starve isn't a tenet of Christianity. It's the opposite of it, in fact, so the whole religious question is swept away in a pack of lies. This is a simple grab for power by a man who has messianic pretensions. People are going to starve so he can gorge his ego."

"I know, I know." Patrick sighed. "I'll keep a tight rein on the troops."

"I have faith, Patrick." Morgan smiled, then shifted his gaze. "Richard, did you reach Frost?"

"Yeah. Pulled in four more snipers, too. None as good as he is. Told him not to shave his beard off, told the others to start growing them. They'll need them if they're going to recon for us."

Patrick shook his head. "I wouldn't want to have their jobs. With that tight-knit of a community, the odd man will stand out."

"But we need the intel." Pain flashed over Morgan's face. "This isn't going to be good. If Katrina hadn't asked..."

"You know what's not true, Morgan." Patrick gave his older brother a frank stare. "You'd have done it because you can't stand people like Poore. He's just like Blizzard: someone using others for his own ends. And you don't like the idea of some child here going to sleep hungry when you've got the ability to bring him food."

"Do I, Patrick?" Morgan folded his arms over his chest. "It's one thing to go out there, smash an enemy force and even do some looting. But pacifying a whole fanatical population with a handful of men? I know everyone will do their best, but we're not trained for that. Garrison duty against a hostile populace is the fastest way to dull the edge on a fighting force."

"As you said, Morgan, this is a training exercise." Patrick clapped him on the shoulders. "The lessons we learn here will likely resonate for decades. Let's make sure they're the right lessons. I'll see you outside Ephaseus."

The trip west in the Ultralytes *Commando* gave Patrick a lot of time to consider what they were going to face. He deployed three of his lances in column, with the other two wide on the wings. The flanking units would take high ground that commanded the area through which they moved, then would drop down onto the road and catch up with the main body. The main body would deploy two lances to become the wings, and the progression would continue.

They didn't move as quickly as he might like, but part of that was just working out the chemistry of the unit. By and large the pilots were used to driving much larger machines. Their reaction to the "toys" varied from utter disdain to trepidation. They could be facing anything, and anything they faced was likely to be more powerful than they were.

It took eight hours for them to get into territory that the Majii controlled. The area around Galatean City had bloomed because of industrial efforts at irrigation and fertilization. Once the city had vanished on the horizon, Galatea went from green to a golden-brown of grasses that had flourished during spring rains, but had long since surrendered to the hot sun. The only blessing in that was a general lack of cover, save for where date-palm groves surrounded watering holes—and those were few and far between.

Majistan showed lots of green, the results of centuries of the farmers' hard work. The rolling hills had been terraced, creating more arable land, and a means for conserving water. At the top of a hill the Majii put in fish ponds. As those overflowed, they carried sediment and fish excrement down to fertilize the terraces below. There the Majii grew a variety of grains and vegetables. Down at the bottom of the hills, in massive wallows that caught the runoff from the terraces, they raised swine. The animals' waste, along with the night-soil of the Majii themselves, was used as yet more fertilizer. Chickens and other fowl wandered the hillsides, finishing off a mutually-supportive ecosystem that made the most of the resources available.

The Majii's homes sat atop the hills, for the most part. Many were of earthen construction, with thick walls that provided a great deal of insulation and cover. Windmills powered wells and probably generated electricity—though there was scant evidence of electric lights as they moved through at night. It struck Patrick as odd that people would choose to abandon the last millennium of technological advances, but the Majii seemed quite content to have done just that.

They passed through many homesteads and skirted villages. The villages themselves were centered in vast plains that were used for growing more grain. Here technology did play a part because the only efficient way to farm that much territory would be with AgroMechs. Patrick looked for the large sort of buildings that would house them, however, and found them to be fewer than he would have thought necessary. Instead of the people having banded together to buy as many machines as they could, it appeared they worked cooperatively to make the most of the machines they had.

And while some of the pilots joked about facing people armed with sticks and stones, Patrick took a different view of things. The

Majii clearly were people who liked their independence, and worked hard to maintain it. Even if they were reduced to fighting with sticks and stones, they'd keep coming until they were dead. They were fighting for life, liberty, and God—a powerful trio when it came to human motivation.

As they came in, the Kell Hounds kept an eye out for observers. They saw some here and there—mostly herders with flocks of horned beasts that passed for sheep. While the herders noticed them, they didn't seem particularly alarmed. Nor did they race off to warn anyone. In keeping with their distrust of technology, the Majii relied on telegraphs, which the Kell Hounds were prepared to take down as needed.

Despite the fact that the Majii in Ephaseus knew they were coming, they didn't set any ambushes. The Kell Hounds came in fast and unmolested, moving north and west toward both the city and their planned encampment. Patrick took a lance in toward Ephaseus on a scouting run, leaving the rest of the unit poised to cover their withdrawal.

There was no mistaking the signs of fighting in the warehouse district. A number of buildings had collapsed into smoking ruins. The garrison was clearly holed up in a large warehouse which benefited from traditional Majii construction methods. The others around it had been cleared, likely by the garrison, to create open lanes of fire. Still, there was enough cover that infantry sporting close range missile packs could get in, strike, and likely escape again.

And without infantry to chase them off, it's like a bear swatting at bees. The more you expose yourself, the more you get stung.

A couple machine guns opened up, but only briefly. The Hounds remained well outside their effective range. The shots did give away the machine gunners' locations, which prompted Patrick to believe they were totally green troops. Then again, a wily commander might have wasted a few shots to lure the Hounds in to punish them. Patrick found it hard to believe that the Majii wouldn't have some heavier weapons around to nail the garrison. If they didn't, the garrison could have escaped easily.

Patrick opened a satellite communication line and bounced a connection up to his brother. "Scout One to Hound Lead. We're on site."

"How is it?"

"Too quiet."

"Contact with the garrison?"

"I haven't tried." A chill ran down Patrick's spine. "Something just isn't right, Morgan. I need to take a closer look."

"Negative. Pull back to our rendezvous point, set a perimeter." His brother's voice remained grimly even despite some static. "We can't surprise them. We have to overwhelm them. Our ETA is five hours. When we get there, that's exactly what we'll do."

CHAPTER 6

EPHASEUS
MAJISTAN, GALATEA
LYRAN COMMONWEALTH
20 OCTOBER 3010

Morgan Kell opted against waiting for night to attack. Though his troops were tired, they were also anxious. The scout force only had interim contact with the garrison, and that contact could only be described as suspicious. While the communications officers trapped in the warehouse were competent enough to get a signal out, they lacked discipline, didn't use encryption, and what they reported just didn't pass the sniff test.

It was a trap. Morgan knew that with every fiber of his being. So did his troops. Normally that would have kept all of them back, but the fact that a trap had been set meant the garrison troops were gone. Even though the Kell Hounds hadn't known them, they did feel that bond that exists between all MechWarriors. If those men and women had fallen, someone had to recover their bodies.

More importantly, however, the Hounds had been sent to demonstrate power and resolve to Poore. Having figured out they were looking at a trap gave the Hounds a slight advantage. Speed, skill, and discipline would further help. Fighting in daylight would also reduce errors, and no matter what they found, Morgan was determined that this operation would be decidedly conservative in terms of damage inflicted.

Morgan arrayed his troops in a simple battle formation. He commanded the Fire Company in the center. His command lance consisted of medium-weight 'Mechs with serious long range missile delivery capability. Walter de Mesnil had a medium assault lance that used a lot of short range missiles and lasers. A lightweight lance of SRM platforms was poised to go in after Walter's lance, while Morgan's hung back to use the LRMs to their best effect.

The light company occupied the right wing and O'Cieran's infantry waited with them. Patrick and the Ultralytes made up the left wing. Realistically they should have been held back as reserves, but by putting them on the line, Morgan forced his counterpart to account for them. Most of the breakdown in combat came when a commander was forced to pull resources from one part of the battlefield to another, so by spreading his troops out, Morgan made the commander commit forces that he would later have to move.

If things go according to plan.

Morgan shifted the neurohelmet on his shoulders, redistributing the weight, then keyed his microphone. "Move in steady. Fire two and three, eyes on the warehouse. That's where the surprises are going to come from. One, you have your coordinates. Counter-battery fire on my order."

The *Centurion* Morgan was piloting had the smallest payload deliverable. The holographic display in the cockpit condensed a three-hundred-sixty degree view of the world into an arc roughly half that big, and gold bars delineated his forward firing arc. Morgan kept the display in visible light, but increased magnification and studied his target. He'd assigned himself the apartment building directly south of the one where the garrison waited. Its façade showed some scars from earlier fighting, though nothing more serious than the tracery of machine gun bullets. Most of the windows had been shot out, however, and gingham drapes fluttered through many shattered panes.

Radio chatter filled his helmet. "I've got two on the roof. Could be a SRM launcher. Sending data now."

A grainy image of two bearded men on a roof appeared on Morgan's secondary monitor. Robin Buckley, in the *Dervish* on Morgan's left, broke into the circuit. "They're on my building."

Distant sparks flashed from within another apartment building. Bullets sped out toward the incoming 'Mechs but fell short. Walter kept his people coming on steady, both aware of the range to the apartments, and the range to the warehouse. All of them had to assume the warehouse was packed with hostiles.

And the fact that no one from within is shooting at the machine gunners practically confirms it. The gunners would have been an easy kill for a medium laser from within the warehouse. Even the most disciplined troops wouldn't refrain from firing, especially when rescue was at hand.

It's just going to be a hornet's nest.

Morgan keyed his radio again. "Fire two and three, it's a nest. Scout lances, prepare your sweep. Fire one, light up your primaries and set your secondaries. Hit it now."

Morgan dropped his crosshairs on the apartment building and hit the trigger. The *Centurion* swayed left as ten missiles jetted from its right breast. They arced up over the warehouse and slammed into the building. The façade disappeared in a flash of fire, then slide down, with flaming curtains fluttering. The building's side collapsed, exposing the pigeon-hole apartments and the armed men scrambling to safety.

Fire started from the warehouse, sporadic and largely ineffective. A couple SRMs spiraled out from shoulder-mounted launchers, but hit nothing. Walter's people held their fire, moving in closer. They picked targets and hit them with their lasers. Stone melted, and the men hiding behind it burst into flames.

Morgan's lance shifted to the warehouse and launched a full salvo on it. Missiles exploded everywhere. It didn't really matter if they hit or missed because even those hitting the rubble around it scattered soldiers who'd been hiding there. A couple of missiles blasted the warehouse doors off their hinges, offering a frustratingly shadowed view of the interior. Even with his magnification on full the display revealed nothing more than silhouettes.

At least they're not moving. That was reassuring on one level, and thoroughly ominous on another.

"Keep going, Fire three. Tell us what we don't want to know."

Morgan's order to the scout lances set them free on mission that both excited and terrified Patrick. It had to be done, however, whether or not the warehouse was a trap. To avoid it would be to assume the enemy commander was an idiot, and that assumption lost a lot of battles.

Specifically, the Majii commander likely had troops in reserve held far back out of LRM range. Once the attack commenced, he'd have to bring them up to spring the trap. Those troops were either going to be former garrison 'Mechs or infantry armed with a variety of anti-Mech weapons. Given time to deploy them, the Majii could inflict some serious damage, and having that happen wasn't part of the Kell Hound battle plan.

Morgan's plan for dealing with them was simple: hit them quickly and hard. He needed a force that was fast and could be overwhelming. Within a city, the fighting would be up close, and the Ultralytes could get badly hurt. On the other hand, the city provided maximum cover, and they weren't going to be far from support.

Patrick set his *Commando* off at a run. No one in his unit had blanched at the plan, despite knowing they were a tripwire force that would draw a lot of fire. The chance to get in and mix it up outweighed that consideration. Moreover, the pilots liked Morgan's willingness to adapt strategy depending upon who he faced and the resources he had at hand.

The 'Lytes cut southeast for half a klick, then turned west and lined up on a broad boulevard called Ezekiel Way. The apartment houses were two blocks to the north, and the downtown, with its central cathedral square, lay eight blocks to the south. The district was mixed residential and commercial, with a modest shopping center at the far end. His pilots had joked about racing to a food court and catching the early-bird special at the buffet.

Thirty-feet high in the humanoid 'Mech's cockpit, Patrick had an odd view of the city. The buildings between which they ran showed no signs of fighting. Flowers bloomed in window boxes. Small children peered out from between curtains until pulled back by hidden parents. Laundry fluttered on lines between buildings.

And down below, irregular troops in trucks, horsecarts and on foot, surged north. Patrick had to characterize them as irregulars because they wore no discernable uniforms. They came in homespun suits of black, with white shirts buttoned high. Some wore broad-brimmed hats, but none showed any sign of decoration. No splashes of color until the SRMs he loosed exploded. Shrapnel ripped through the irregulars, speckling them with blood.

Some of them turned and fought. A couple shot SRMs from shoulder rigs. They shot from the crowded backs of trucks, their back-flash doing more damage to their own people than the missiles did to the 'Lytes. A couple even attacked with wooden pitchforks and axes, dying ignominiously as the *Commando's* broad feet smeared them along the pavement.

Patrick did his best to target vehicles. He told himself it was because that was the most effective way to slow the counterattack, but he knew it wasn't true. If he destroyed equipment, he could pretend he wasn't slaughtering defenseless men and women. *Defenseless men and women who aren't turning and running.*

Barely slowed by the opposition, the 'Lytes made it the length of Ezekiel losing a little armor and not a single one if their 'Mechs. They regrouped at the mall and turned around, ready to retrace their path up the blood-washed street. Though he didn't want to, Patrick was ready to issue that order.

Morgan called him off. They had the warehouse, and what they found inside made everyone who saw it question what they were doing in Ephaseus.

Morgan had dismounted before O'Cieran had declared the area safe simply because he couldn't believe what his cameras were showing him. The images, as horrible as they were, were sterile. Out of the

cockpit, with the stench of death filling his nostrils, the tableau became real. Disgustingly so.

The dozen-and-a-half garrison 'Mechs stood all around the warehouse interior, arrayed in a strong perimeter. Thorndyke had covered
all the lanes of fire. Taking the warehouse wasn't going to be easy.
With the emergency rations available in cockpit storage bins, her
command could have held out for at least a week.

All of the cockpits lay open, with computer equipment hanging
down on ribbon cables and tangled wires. It looked as if the 'Mechs
had vomited. Twisted metal showed evidence of axes, clubs and pry-
bars having been used to wreak havoc. Short of having the cockpits
completely refurbished, the 'Mechs weren't moving.

The pilots, seventeen of them, hung from the warehouse rafters.
They'd been bound by their wrists and left to hang. *Crucified.* Some
had bloodied faces, but most showed no signs of violence.

Which meant, because they'd been crucified, they'd smothered
to death. The weight of their own viscera pressing against their lungs
and diaphragm, making breathing impossible. *They just dangled and
died.*

Walter brought Morgan a memory card. "Got it from that *Catapult.*
Gun-camera holo. You'll want to look."

Morgan slipped the card into his noteputer. The datestamp put
the events on the eighteenth, the first night of the siege. Colonel
Thorndyke had gone out to meet a contingent of men flying a white
flag. As they spoke, more people came into the kill zone. They moved
through the rubble, searching and carrying off bodies.

Another group of people approached the warehouse. Women
mostly, and children. They bore baskets with food and jugs of water.
Colonel Thorndyke gestured toward them and tried to stem the tide,
but they kept coming. The men she was parlaying with made calming
gestures and Thorndyke's shoulders slumped.

Morgan shut off the holo and looked up at the hanging bodies.
"No Thorndyke."

Walter shook his head. "We'll keep looking."

"How could they? They came under a flag of truce."

Father Donelly appeared at Morgan's right hand. "It's the Book of
Judith, Morgan. From the Bible. Holofernes threatened her town with
a siege. She came to him, promising him her favors and information
about the enemy. She got him drunk, then took his head. That lifted
the siege."

Morgan shook his head. "The Bible can't justify this."

"Son, the Bible has been used to justify just about anything.
The misuse to which men set doesn't invalidate its values or veracity." Donelly lifted his gaze. "They mark them as bandits, hanging as
thieves hung beside our Lord."

Morgan snorted. "Terror tactic to scare our people off. The Petrine Order is mistaken if they think that will stop us."

"It wasn't for you, Colonel. It was for *them*. The common people." The priest pointed south. "Think about it, and not just the soldiers who were in here or in those apartments. You think about the men and women who so believe in what Poore tells them that they'd march their children across that kill zone. There was no hiding, no cover, no chance for survival if their mission failed. They drugged the water, let their own children drink to show it was safe, and the garrison fell. God's faith in them was proved beyond a shadow of a doubt."

Morgan covered his face with a hand. "We can demonstrate overwhelming force, and it won't matter to these people, will it?"

"They're a big rock, Morgan. Religion is the lever with which Poore motivates them. Volmer gave him the fulcrum."

Morgan closed his eyes. "Right. I can't destroy the big rock, though I can knock some edges off. The lever's a tough target, too. The fulcrum, gone. And if I take out Poore, I just make him a martyr."

The priest grunted. "I'll be treading close to heresy here, but I'm thinking that dealing with a martyr is better than a prophet. Dead men tell no tales, and they're crap at leading movements, in my experience."

"I recall mentioning that to Poore. He didn't listen." Morgan waved O'Cieran over. "Cut the bodies down. Booby-trap the 'Mechs."

The infantry commanded nodded. "I've got a perimeter set up. There are people out there going through the rubble. Rescue workers, it looks like."

Morgan shivered. *If they start coming like they did...* "Okay, we're moving out fast. Get the bodies, pull our people out. The rules of engagement we have are for a conventional war. This is anything but."

O'Cieran raised an eyebrow. "New rules?"

"We'll have to come up with something." Morgan sighed. "The enemy isn't playing by any rules at all."

CHAPTER 7

Morgan Kell stepped toward the berm surrounding the camp, night-vision binoculars in hand. He started to mount the bank, but a hissed voice stopped him.

"They're out there, Colonel. You don't want to do that."

Morgan turned, trying to cover his surprise. "Close enough to shoot me?"

Frost uncoiled himself from the shadows, but remained crouched, cradling a sniper rifle. "They may be backward, but mortars have been around for a long time. That's technology they can manage."

Morgan nodded at the rifle. "You can see them out there?"

"Little knots of 'em. Just watching." Frost smiled lazily. "Normally I'd use the IR laser to toast them a little, but they might be cheating and be able to spot it. I think they can't believe we got things together so quickly."

The Hounds had done a very good job of getting the camp set up. The heavier 'Mechs had gouged out a trough and heaped the dirt high, putting a four meter-tall wall around the camp. They'd clustered the missile-boat Mechs in the center, then stationed lances at the four cardinal points to cover all approaches. Tents had been erected, slit-trenches dug and everything prepared before night had fallen. Best of all, they'd built the camp around a well used for irrigation, so they had fresh water.

"Any thoughts on our situation, Captain Frost?"

"I don't get paid for opinions, sir. I get paid for knocking people down."

"No feelings about our enemy?"

Frost's eyes narrowed. "As I understand it, sir, you're wondering about the rules of engagement. We're not supposed to be shooting up anyone who isn't a threat; and how threatening is a man with a pitchfork to a 'Mech? They don't rise to the level of threat."

Morgan nodded. "And yet they used a white flag as a ruse to kill the garrison."

"Right. Their rules and ours don't match." Frost shrugged. "But think on back to why we're here. They want us to starve. That's a threat."

"They're our own people."

"Begging your pardon, sir, but what they did to the garrison shows they aren't. They're Poore's people." Frost jerked a thumb toward the city in the distance. "The Governor wants us to spot weapons, but that's not the threat here. Their minds are."

Morgan arched an eyebrow. "And a bullet through the brain takes care of that danger?"

"It does, sir." Frost's grin spread. "Think of it in public health terms. If that town there was full of diseased people who were out of their minds and infectious, we'd bottle them up and subject them to a cure, even if they didn't want it. And because their very existence was a threat to ours, we'd kill them all. Don't be kidding yourself, we would, and we'd count it as work well done."

"And that's how you see your job?"

"No, sir, but that's not really what you want to know, is it?"

"You tell me."

"You want to know how I justify splashing brains because all you 'Mechjocks got to hose your 'Mechs' feet off. You kill machines and the occasional pilot. I kill people. You think the way I justify it might help you deal."

"So, how do you justify it?"

Frost shook his head. "I don't. I just don't care. A Drac fighting for the Coordinator, some religious nutjob thinking Jesus will be his pal, it doesn't matter. Whacking 'em is just a job."

Morgan ran a hand over his unshaved jaw. "You're either crazier than everyone in Ephaseus, or the sanest man here."

"And we know which way the smart money is betting, don't we?"

"You'd be surprised." Morgan's eyes burned from a lack of sleep. "So, do we make this a free fire zone?"

"Just because they all need killing doesn't mean we have to oblige them." Frost shrugged. "Let us snipers take anyone carrying a weapon lethal beyond ten meters. If they come in a crowd, scatter them with LRMs. Having their friends die may not change their minds, but burying them will keep them out of trouble."

"I'll think on that."

Father Donelly came running over. "Colonel, the helicopter is ten minutes out. Your brother said you wanted me to go with you?"

"Absolutely, Father. We'll talk on the chopper." Morgan gave Frost a quick salute. "Thanks for your insights."

"Safe flight, sir." Frost disappeared into the shadows before the echo of his words had died.

Morgan strapped himself into the helicopter beside Father Donelly. They both donned crash helmets and plugged the commo gear into the nearest port. The pilot looked back and Morgan gave him a thumb's-up. He nodded and the craft rose into the air.

"I need you with me, Father, because we're going back to Galatean City. Bishop Poore is there and wants to meet with Governor Bonham to discuss terms."

The priest frowned. "I don't know why you need me to negotiate his surrender terms."

"Poore is there to accept *our* surrender." Morgan sighed. "I need you there as a brake on me. I'm having a hard time remembering he's a man of God."

"Of course, you are, son, but you're smarter than that." Donelly smiled. "You're just falling prey to one of the oldest problems of the human race. It was our salvation and our damnation."

"That being?"

"Our ability to make patterns. It's how we figured out cause and effect—very useful. Man became good at making patterns, but that doesn't mean every pattern we make is good." The priest's eyes flashed. "A millennium ago, back before we spread out through the stars and learned that as far as intelligent life went, Man was it, there was a form of mass hysteria where-by people believed in UFOs: unidentified flying objects. Flying Saucers. You've heard of them from old fairy stories."

Morgan nodded, confident there was a point in there somewhere.

"Well now, used to be that a witness who saw something would be described in terms of who he was, so as to determine his credibility. You might hear that a doctor, a prosperous man in his community, well respected, had seen a flying saucer clear as day. Now, the fact is, that being a doctor, being prosperous and being well respected has absolutely no bearing on your ability to figure out what something flying through the clear blue sky actually is. But, because people could say all these good things about the doctor, his credibility got extended to the story of what he'd seen.

"Now, you take the Bishop. He's a man of God, but let's stress *man* and let's remember that more than one man has warped the Word of God for his own purposes. And here's what's funny, Morgan. The Word of God doesn't do much changing, but the interpretations of it, I'm thinking, are all over the place."

Morgan nodded. "He's got people who believe him, and their belief makes them a potent force."

"And you have people who believe in you, Morgan. That's potent as well." The priest pursed his lips. "I don't mind telling you, what I saw yesterday made my blood run colder than ever. Everyone felt that way."

Excepting perhaps Frost.

"But, you know, Morgan, there wasn't a man jack or woman who didn't look to you for leadership. They found it. What you're showing them isn't false, and they know it. What Poore shows his people is false, and deep down, they know it, too. He won't see it, but you have to take confidence in it."

"Would that it is so easy."

"Easy isn't part of the game, Morgan. You do what it takes to win. You can't play his game."

GALATEA CITY

The chopper landed at the Governor's Mansion. Morgan and Father Donelly had a chance to shower, shave, and change into fresh clothes. Morgan's uniform had been sent over from the Nova Royale. Father Donelly made due with a suit from some minor functionary, and therefore wore nothing that indicated he was a Kell Hound or a priest.

Baron Bonham, looking unrested and ill at ease, led the two men to a huge conference room with tall windows through which streamed brilliant sunlight. The white marble floor and yellow walls retained the light, and crystal chandeliers split it into rainbows that slowly moved along with the sun.

The room's brilliance made Bishop Poore and his entourage seem even darker. The bishop had two large men behind him, and between them was a woman in grey homespun. Morgan looked hard, but until he'd closed to within four meters, he wasn't certain he recognized her.

Colonel Thorndyke.

She did not look up or acknowledge anyone.

Bonham started to introduce people, but the Bishop cut him off with a sharp gesture. "The time for manners would have been before you attacked my city of Ephaseus. You should have known how futile that would be. You cannot thwart God's Will."

The Baron opened his hands. "You requested this meeting, Bishop. We are here to listen to what you have to say."

The older man glanced skyward, then shook his head as if responding to an unheard request. "It is not what I have to say. It is God. You are godless. You have been judged and it is his judgment being visited upon you. When you chose to defy him and sent this woman as your agent, you angered God."

"I asked Colonel Thorndyke to execute an operation to guarantee the safety of the people of Galatea."

"And you're a fool." Poore reached back and dragged Thorndyke forward by the shoulder. "Tell them."

The woman trembled, dropping to one knee beside the bishop. "I have sinned against God. I must be punished. I beg forgiveness, if not in this life, in the next."

Morgan's stomach twisted slowly into a knot. This wasn't the woman he'd met less than a week previously. She'd been broken, and quickly. He wondered if her grey dress, which covered her from throat to wrists and ankles, also covered signs of physical abuse.

Morgan folded his arms across his chest. "What is it you want, Bishop?"

"Have you told him what you found in Ephaseus?"

"That your people approached the garrison under a flag of truce, betrayed that truce, and murdered them?" Morgan kept his voice even, and Colonel Thorndyke began to sob. "I've reported that. I have holo. Would you like to see it? Would you like to see holo of people being crushed beneath 'Mech feet because they followed your orders?"

The Bishop opened his hands and looked to Heaven. "I commend them to You, oh Lord."

"They violated a truce, Bishop."

The man fixed Morgan with an unwavering gaze. "They did as God directed. It's all in the Book of Judith."

"Funny thing about that, Bishop." Father Donelly gave him a quizzical look. "The Catholics and the Orthodox Church are accepting of the Book of Judith. Jews and Protestant sects are not. In fact, up until a year ago, you'd proclaimed belief in such documents to be heresy."

"And I have had a revelation."

"Or you've revised your feelings because that's what best suits your ends now."

"Do not argue theology with me, little man. You're hardly qualified."

Donelly's head came up. "I imagine my teachers at the seminary would disagree, but the fact is we can't argue theology. That would be the study of God and His wishes, whereas you're the master of little more than your own psychoses."

Poore shifted to Bonham. "You are doing yourself no credit here. A tool of the devil and a murdering whoremonger? You need better advice. You need to repent your sins. You need to do penance. You can be forgiven. I can absolve you, but it will not easy."

"What do you want, Bishop?"

"You will step down, and I will be appointed in your place. This world will no longer be known as Galatea, but as Galacia. Everyone here will join the Church and live in Christian fellowship as we do in the west, or they will leave."

Morgan's eyes became slits. "And if they don't leave?"

"They die."

The Kell Hound leader's chin came up. "Not terribly Christian of you."

"You have forgotten, Morgan Kell, that Jesus is one of three. This world is almost beyond redemption, like Sodom and Gomorrah. I am Lot, crying out for its salvation. Only some shall heed me. The rest will be destroyed, and it shall be by God's hand that they die. I can beg for mercy for you all, but unless you show contrition, God will show you no mercy."

Poore began to chuckle. It was that low, half-whispered laugh which, sometimes, betokens the kindly indulgence of a parent for the antics of a child. Or, as with the other time it is heard, it betokens madness, a narcissistic certainty of invulnerability. That's how Morgan heard it.

It made his flesh crawl.

"You have no choice, gentlemen. By now you know that food supplies are well hidden and defended. If you threaten them, or me, they will be destroyed. And you know that the Lyran Commonwealth does not possess sufficient shipping to replace that food. Harvests vary on each world, of course, but it would take months to set up a relay that could keep the east fed. By then everyone will have converted, left, or died."

Bonham scrubbed hands over his face. "I don't have the authority to grant what you're asking. You must be reasonable. The Archon, the Estates General, they will never allow this."

"It is God's Will, Baron Bonham. Do you wish to answer to *them* or to *Him*?" Poore looked at him as if the answer was obvious, and only madness could spawn further protest. "We will begin screening those who are suitable candidates for conversion. Once accepted, they will be fed and matriculated into their new families."

Morgan shook his head. "What are you talking about?"

"It's God's plan, Colonel Kell. The strong shall be enabled to be fruitful and multiply. The rest shall be banished from the garden."

Donelly gasped. "Faith. You want our women."

"Not all of them will be worthy." Poore looked at Morgan and snorted. "Your whore will be found wanting."

Morgan forced his hands open, and fought to keep them from closing around Poore's neck. He drew in a deep breath. He kept his voice low, both in tone and volume.

"I won't presume to know God's Will, Bishop, but I know mine and that of my troops. They are not going to allow you to starve the

rest of the planet, to rip apart families, to force people to choose between death and conversion. That's been tried in the past, and unless
you remember a different history than I do, it's never been terribly
successful.

"You've been generous in sharing your plan, so let me share
mine. I'm going to rip through the west. I'm going to take Ephaseus
away from you, and Acre and even Thessalon. I'm going to sweep up
all the little villages. I don't particularly care that you've told them to
destroy food stores, because they'll starve right along with us. And
then I'll be coming for you, Bishop and I guarantee you that I'll see
you in hell long before I ever join you."

For a heartbeat Poore's smug mask slipped. He took a step back
and his two bodyguards stepped forward. Colonel Thorndyke mewed
and clutched at his leg. Then he straightened up and tugged at his
sleeves.

"I believe this concludes our discussion, Baron. I shall take my
leave."

Morgan pointed at the Colonel. "She stays."

"Nonsense." Poore pulled her to her feet and put an arm around
her shoulder. "She is one of my wives now. One of the Majii. I cannot
abandon her."

Thorndyke, eyes wide with terror, huddled more tightly under his
arm.

"God's wrath is upon you!" Poore's voice echoed loudly through
the grand room. "Repent or the blood of millions is upon your hands."

He and his people swept from the room. Bonham grabbed
Morgan's left arm. "Can you do what your said? Can you take everything away from him?"

Morgan pulled his arm from the man's grasp. "I guess I'm going
to have to."

"I don't find that very reassuring. Tell me at least that you have a
plan."

"I do. Vague, but a plan." Morgan looked the man straight in the
eye. "Start praying, Baron, and hope God listens to you more than to
him."

CHAPTER 8

The sun rose, and with it came the heat of the day. Patrick Kell wore coveralls over his cooling vest and shorts, making him even hotter. He'd have loved for a breeze to come up, but that would only make things worse.

At the Nagelring, veteran instructors would comment that the military life was one of waiting quietly for those few moments where the universe visited all its violence on you. Most even characterized that waiting period as boredom, and Patrick often agreed, but not today. Granted, he'd not been in combat that often, but the waiting there outside Ephaseus was different.

Two things he couldn't get out of his mind. One was the blood and tissue he'd washed from his 'Mech's feet. As he was moving through the city, he was very well aware of how people were dying. He had no difficulty with shooting them up. They were heading forward to support the people who wanted to kill his brother. They meant to spring a trap on him and the other Hounds. For that reason alone, he had no regrets—if the Hounds hadn't sprung a trap of their own, his brother could have died.

By the same token, they shouldn't have been running toward the battle. Their rushing to fight against BattleMechs using rifles and shoulder-fired missiles and pitchforks was nothing short of insanity. A sand castle was more likely to damage a wave than those men were to hurt a 'Mech. That they didn't quail or run marked the devotion to their cause; and that sort of fanaticism made men capable of anything.

The scene from inside the warehouse had confirmed that. Seventeen people had been murdered. Patrick could have understood an angry mob attacking them out of rage and grief over their losses, but this was crime devoid of passion. They'd deliberately crucified the garrison force, then remained in place as those people died. They didn't even do what they'd have done for an animal and put them mercifully out of their misery.

Patrick wasn't alone in considering that sort of thing. Doubtless Poore intended the crucifixions to be a display that would weaken the resolve of those who learned about it. The problem for him is that he didn't understand warriors. They might not have known the garrison, but the Hounds considered them brothers and sisters. The desire for vengeance has a way of building resolution; likewise, the determination not to end up the way the garrison did.

Carrying an assault rifle, Major O'Cieran came jogging over to where Patrick huddled in the shadow of his 'Mech. "Just to give you a quick update. They're still out there. Small clusters, four or five men. They come out carrying burlap sacks so we can't identify what they're carrying. They know our rules of engagement."

Patrick frowned. "ComStar may have shut down information heading east, but not the other way around."

The infantry leader's expression soured. "Rules of engagement should have been secret."

"I'm sure they were. And just as sure that some functionary leaked them to some holo-anchor to get her into the sack."

"Amy Vandemeer, channel 127?"

"Oh yeah, her, too." Patrick shook his head, banishing images of the second hottest holovid newsie. "Secrets are a currency that has high value, and a quick expiration date. If Poore had half a brain, he would have had sleeper agents in Galatea City. They'd have tasks to perform; and they were triggered when they failed to get a call from the west telling them to stand down. ComStar's cooperation won't do anything to help in that situation. Low-tech insurgency becomes very difficult to stop."

"Only if you don't want to go through and shoot every silly son-of-a-bitch that buys into that crap."

"You ready to shoot children?"

"Of course not." O'Cieran jerked his head in the direction of Ephaseus. "I didn't like what I saw in that warehouse any more than anyone else, but I know children had nothing to do with that. Probably not most of the adults. Just a faction of them…"

"The Petrine Order."

"You learn fast. Not much I wouldn't put past them."

Patrick reached down and pulled a smooth round pebble from the earth. He let it roll around in the palm of his hand. "You figure the ones out there are Petrine Order?"

"Could be. Probably."

"They have to know we know they're out there. And if they're fil-tering out during the day, we posit an attack at night?" Patrick pitched the rock away. "So, mid-afternoon, I take a lance of the 'Lytes out and we sweep about a half a klick out. We draw fire, or we scatter them. You have a couple of squads ready to grab prisoners. If the start to light us up, we reach out with missiles."

"As plans go, it's workable." O'Cieran nodded. "You leading the lance?"

"Sure."

"Okay, means I have to stay back here since I'll be senior. Your brother gets back tonight?"

"Until I hear different, around midnight local."

"I'll be glad to have him back." The infantry officer held his hands up. "No offense intended, Colonel. I like your willingness to mix it up, but your brother's plan for the extraction was good. Showed some depth of thought. We're going to need that."

Patrick nodded. "I agree."

"The best way to spoil a fighting force is to make it into a garrison. The men and women we have, they'll take apart anything Poore tosses at us. What will wear them down is dealing with threats like those out in there. Mines. Snipers. Booby-traps. That's not what they're trained for. That's police work."

"If we're lucky, Poore has seen sense and Morgan will be bring-ing orders for our return." Patrick shrugged. "If not, we have to stop Poore's people fast."

"Hit hard. No mercy."

"I'm afraid you're right."

"Afraid because you don't want to do it?"

"No, Major, afraid because I'm far too ready to do it."

A sergeant came running over, saluted quickly, and pointed to-ward the front of the camp. "Begging your pardon, sirs, They're up to something. You're definitely going to want to see this."

Morgan couldn't help but smile when Veronica opened the door. He stood there for a moment, just drinking in her beauty. They'd been apart for less than a week, and yet, looking at her, it seemed far too long.

For a heartbeat, longing passed through her eyes, too. She turned away to invite him in, then hesitated for a second.

Morgan stepped forward, swept her into his arms, and carried her away from the door. He kissed her firmly, his eyes closing, pulling her tight against him. She stiffened for a second, then her body eased and her arms closed about him. They clung to each other, then broke the kiss, panting, foreheads touching.

"Four days."

"That's forever, Morgan." Veronica kissed him quickly, then slipped from his embrace. She closed the door, then took his hand and led him into her suite's living room. "Welcome to my home."

He smiled. He'd expected modern and spare furnishings, with a great deal of glass and steel and silver. The room was anything but. The furnishings had ornate scroll-work, and many were gilded. Most were antiques. Hand-woven rugs cover the floor and oil painting hung on the walls. Many of them were reproductions, but a few were originals and centuries old.

Morgan studied the room carefully, then nodded. "It is you."

"Old and overpainted?"

He pulled her to him and kissed her again. "Rich, beautiful, and very personal. It has a warmth. You're very much at home here. You don't have many visitors, do you?"

Her blue eyes flare slightly. "If you're asking if I bring customers..."

He pressed a finger to her lips. "No. You don't share this place, your sanctuary, with many people, do you? I'm honored."

"Good. I'm glad you came." She led him to a couch and bade him sit, then moved to a sideboard. "Drink? Tyrone Rain."

He nodded. "Thank you."

She poured three fingers of the Irish whisky into a tumbler and brought it to him. "I know you'll like that."

"You're not drinking?"

She took the glass back from him and sipped, then leaned forward and kissed him. His lips parted and he tasted the whisky from her lips. Veronica broke the kiss and returned the glass to him. "I'm not thirsty."

Morgan laughed, then took another sip. "Thanks. It's been a frustrating day."

"Meeting with Poore, and then with every Minister from Science to Transportation."

"Very good."

"It's my job. Your meetings canceled appointments they had with some of my people." Veronica smiled. "The war in the west is not going well?"

Morgan hitched, then glanced down into his glass. "How did you know?"

"The west produces more than just grain, Morgan. Fresh flowers and vegetables are trucked in every day, only the shipments have stopped. People notice. Prices rise. No panic yet, but there will be. Within two days the local holo-news will report that you're fighting against insurgents. They'll be blamed for stopping truck convoys. The meeting with Poore this morning will be seen as an attempt to enlist his help in stopping them."

"You know all that and how the news will spin the story?"

She laughed easily and he wanted to kiss her again. "I know the first half. You'll tell the Governor that's how he wants to spin the news. I know a lot more, which is why I've got a present for you."

She handed him a memory chip. "This is everything it's possible to learn about Poore, including a full analysis."

"Thanks, but the Governor loaded me down with...what?"

"Morgan, I know you're under pressure, but think for a moment. If the Governor had any clue about Poore, would things have gotten this far?"

Morgan grinned sheepishly. "I catch your point."

"Let me reinforce it." She tapped his glass with a finger. "Tyrone Rain. Your favorite. You've never ordered it in front of me. You've never mentioned it, but I have it. Coincidence?"

"I'm guessing not."

"You'd be right. My stock in trade is not sex, it's fantasy. If I have a client, I learn everything possible about him. Likes, dislikes, family names, background, triumphs, disappointments, passions, quirks and secrets. I know him better than he knows himself. He may not even know what will thrill him, but I learn it. I learn how to manipulate him within his own fantasy. I've gotten good at that."

Morgan nodded. "Just the way I want to know my enemy, know what he will do, know his 'Mech and his capabilities."

She leaned forward. "You have to understand something else, Morgan. This analysis of Poore isn't the work of the last four days. I've been tracking him for years. I expected trouble from him. The people who compiled the report for the governor did it in two days. Volmer had declared him to be benign, so the government didn't care."

Veronica got up and walked to the draped window. "Poore is utterly ruthless. He truly believes God speaks with him and blesses his every move. You wouldn't believe some of the things he has ordered done."

"He had seventeen pilots crucified, taking them under a flag of truce. He broke Colonel Thorndyke and made her one of his wives."

She nodded. "He's done both of those things before. He has one primary wife, and a host of secondary wives. They're really hostages against the loyalty of other leaders. He's taken daughters and sister, occasionally a wife someone wanted to get rid of. He's declared polygamy as a duty which God conveys on the most favored, and he's granted that right to bind certain people to him."

"But if he hold hostages, then there are some people who are hostile to him. The Governor's report didn't..."

"They wouldn't. They focused on his having consolidated power. The wives were seen as political alliances. When you're a politician, you read things for political content." She turned and shrugged. "When your business is fantasy, you learn what's inside."

"You think he's vulnerable?"

"Yes. You'll see some of that in the report. But you can't underestimate him. He might be from the west, but he's far from backward. He spent time off-world as an adult. His rise to power came through low level uses of technology. He would study trends from the east, from off-world, and would advise his people as to what they should grow. Their fortunes have increased. He's distributed sermons mixed with bulletins, getting Church Elders to listen to them, then share them with their communities. He even used some fairly sophisticated psychological techniques to get them to agree to outrageous ideas. His Churches here in the east get different messages, tailored to their circumstances, and to generate a lot of money for his Church."

An expression he couldn't identify passed over her face. He set his glass down and went to her. He took her in his arms and held her against his chest. "This is about a little bit more than his fighting the Hounds, isn't it?"

She nodded and sniffed, then looked up, wiping away tears. "I grew up in Acre. I ran away to the east. Not the first girl to do so, not the last. If I'd not run away, I'd have been married to a cousin, at Poore's direction. I'd have nine children. I would be a husk of myself. I'd be ignorant and incapable of thinking for myself. My life would be sheer hell, and yet I'd be thanking Poore for it with every breath I took."

Morgan kissed both of her cheeks, then held her at arm's length.

"Poore's offer to the Governor was a non-starter. It's going to be a fight. Very nasty. I won't let him win."

She caressed his cheek with a hand. "I believe you." Then Veronica glanced down. "You're a very interesting man, Morgan Kell. I'm drawn to you, and I don't want to be."

"Why not?"

She wouldn't meet his gaze. "I've spent a long time, since before I ran away even, becoming strong and independent; beholden to no one. And yet, in your company, I feel weak."

Morgan shook his head. "I don't see you as weak. Not at all."

"Which makes me feel weaker. You have a natural strength, Morgan. Blizzard missed it. He's gone. Poore hates it. I find it overwhelming and...and yet..."

"What?"

She shook her head then took his hands in hers. "I know you're going back tonight, but can you, do you have the time?" She glanced toward a darkened doorway which he assumed led to her bedroom. "Will you...?"

Before he could answer, his communicator buzzed. He fished it from his pocket and snapped it open. "Morgan Kell."

"The helicopter will be here for you in half an hour, Colonel." Bonham's voice just barely avoided hysteria. "There was an attack at the firebase. Your brother is one of the wounded."

CHAPTER 9

In the annals of warfare, the battle for Acre would not warrant even a footnote. Morgan was pretty certain that even if he ever got around to writing his memoirs, he wouldn't include it. Not that he wasn't proud of his people and how they acted. That one victory would do more to earn him work in the future than any other battle for a long time coming.

The task was not an easy one. Acre was a city of 20,000 souls located in the foothills of the Occident Mountains. The Blue River had once split the city, but the Blue Ridge dam had created Lake Steiner. The river's taming put an end to the floods that would periodically wash half the town away, and guaranteed an ample supply of water for both people and crops.

To take it and hold it, Morgan had approximately four hundred people, counting support personnel as well as his line troops. Acre could have had as much as two companies of garrison line 'Mechs, and three more of refitted AgroMechs—though he wouldn't know that until they arrayed themselves for battle.

The first job would be to cut down the number of 'Mechs available to Poore's forces. The information Veronica had given him made it quite clear that Poore, while eschewing technology as evil, had found a way to use it to his advantage. Morgan assumed Poore had a means for tapping the data from the area's seismic monitors just as the Hounds had done.

So, with the Governor's help, Morgan spoofed the sensors. The computers at the Planetary Tectonics Research Administration pulled the real data into one memory core and pumped fake data into the databases which the world used. They carefully split out data that corresponded to movements of Poore's troops and spliced that back in, while simultaneously shifting the Kell Hound data. While the Hounds pounded straight down south toward Acre, the data reports made it look as if they were hooking around west and north, to hit Thessalon from the west. The seismic track for any of Poore's troops checked with their actual movement, validating the Kell Hound data.

As they headed south, Majii seismic activity around and heading toward Thessalon increased. Poore, reading the data, was preparing a very warm welcome for the Kell Hounds in his home town. He clearly expected the big battle to be there.

Another problem for Poore came in terms of communication. Because ComStar wrapped their services up in mystical phraseology, the Majii viewed them as rivals, and perhaps even as being in league with the devil. ComStar had long since pulled out save from the biggest cities. To facilitate communications, and in keeping with their sense of proper decorum, the Majii relied on telegraphs and had wires slung from point to point.

The Kell Hounds found the telegraph wires to be painfully easy to tap. They'd hitched up a transmitter which pulled dots-and-dashes and sent it off to the Hounds. Computers decoded it and, through a brilliant bit of programming, preserved the cadence of each operator. Each operator had a unique way of tapping out messages, and the computer could mimic his "hand," so that when the Hounds wanted to send a message down a wire, recipients would believe it came from the operator who was supposed to be using that station. Thus reports of their own movements—the few that there were—disappeared from the wires and were replaced by messages that all was clear.

The appearance of two 'Mech companies on the plains northeast of Acre, therefore, did cause some consternation. Morgan arrayed them with his lance in the middle, the two other lances of his company on the right and the light 'Mech company stretched out to anchor the left flank against the dry riverbed of the Blue River. He angled his line toward the northwest, which would make it difficult for the Majii to come at him without being flanked. Moreover, the Majii were well aware of the 'Lytes, and had to assume Morgan was going to use them and their speed to spring a trap.

And they are so very right.

The Majii arrayed their defenses admirably, though it was with a sense of warfare that had last been useful when smooth-bore muskets had been the primary battlefield weapon. The citizens poured out of the city to dig and raise a bastion facing the Kell Hound middle. They failed to anchor it against the Blue River, which just made the line that much easier to turn. An irregular militia corps did file into the river bed, and used the bank as a breastwork, but they bore small arms, so presented very little threat to the Hounds.

They placed their converted AgroMechs behind the bastion, then arrayed their combat 'Mechs at the northwestern edge of the line. They had four lances of mixed medium and light 'Mechs, with three on the line and one held back in reserve. Presumably it would support the two lances in the middle, or the three on the left. It wasn't the battle line Morgan would have chosen, but it worked.

The Kell Hounds arrived at dusk, and watched the Majii prepare for battle throughout the night. Morgan used infrared sensors and picked up clusters of individuals located beyond the bastion, past the line of buildings on the outskirts of town. Mindful of Frost's caution about mortars around Ephaseus, he assumed they were staging artillery of some sort in those spots. If the Hounds got bogged down at the bastion, the artillery could hurt them.

Not an if *I'm going to entertain.*

Morgan opened a radio channel and broadcast a widebeam message to the 'Mechs on the other side of the line. "This is Colonel Morgan Kell of the Kell Hounds. This is an unlawful assembly. You are in revolt, and you are enemies of the state. Lay down your arms, and events here can be concluded peacefully."

The radio remained silent for about a minute, then it crackled with static. An older man's voice came through. "This is Patriarch Thaddeus Oltmann. We serve our Lord, and all must be on bended knee before him. He will deliver us from your threat and will smite thee mightily. We know no fear."

"I understand that, sir; but prayers don't stop bullets, nor do they staunch wounds."

"You do the Devil's work, Colonel."

"As does Bishop Poore, sir. No reason your blood should run for his cause."

That resulted in a moment of silence. Veronica's files had made very clear that the Acre region had long been the stronghold of the Oltmann family. Thaddeus had opposed Poore's rise to power, but Poore had attracted a base of support that threatened Oltmann's position. Oltmann agreed to a political union and offered Poore one of his granddaughters to seal the alliance. Despite that, the two men did not get along, providing Morgan an opportunity to sever that section of the rebels from the main body.

Thaddeus' voice returned, wary but resolute. "You cannot prevail, Colonel. We shall pray for the souls of your fallen."

"One last time, sir. Stand down. Save your people." Morgan, his head encased in the neurohelmet, sighed. "I will reduce your city if I must."

"We trust in our Lord, Colonel. May He forgive you your sins."

Morgan punched up a separate frequency. "Waterwitch One, report status."

Patrick's voice came back along the line, distant but strong. "In position. Waiting for a go."

"You are go. Luck."

"Skill back at you."

The Kell Hound boss then punched up his battle frequency. "By the numbers, people. Lieutenant King, begin your sweep. Fire lance, on my mark. Right flank, hold."

On Morgan's order, Lieutenant King took the light company, turned it south, then drove toward the dry riverbed. The infantry opened up, but the small arms fire might as well have been rain for all the good it did. One lance lit their jump jets and soared over the river, landing on the far side. Their jet exhaust scattered some of the infantry, and the enfilading fire dispersed the rest. They scattered headlong, with most retreating to the city in a panic.

The lance on the southern side turned west, facing the city and remained in place. The other two lances turned west as well, and pressed forward against the bastion's flank. As AgroMechs shifted toward that end of the line, Morgan and his missile boats launched. The fire of missile explosions completely hid the eastern end of the Majii line. The occasional piece of a 'Mech would spin high into the sky or clatter off a building's roof, but otherwise black clouds of smoke and dirt obscured that portion of the battlefield.

The Majii reserve moved to the bastion, and the other three lances tightened their lines up, all returning fire at the Kell Hounds. They hit and did some damage, but only scored armor. Morgan's *Centurion* weathered the assault easily. Under Walter de Mesnil's command, the right flank returned fire, targeting the 'Mech's with the longest range capabilities first, then working down. After four exchanges, the Majii had lost four of their 'Mechs on that flank and the Kell Hounds had to retire two.

King's light 'Mechs pressed their advantage and took the eastern end of the bastion. Ruby red laser light burned across the lines. An AgroMech hopped up onto the breastwork before two beams crossed and took its right leg off at the knee. It tumbled down, away from the city, splayed head first at the base of the bastion.

The Majii 'Mech commander finally made a decision he'd delayed for far too long. He'd held the western edge of the line for as long as he had, expecting the Ultralytes would do on the left what the Lights had done on the right. It left his troops too exposed, so he consolidated his position hastily.

He pushed his remaining combat 'Mechs into the bastion. The drive repulsed King's 'Mechs, but allowed Walter to bring his people around to cover the western flank. Morgan's lance continued to rain missiles down on the defensive works. Then the Majii mortars opened up, their fire falling short of Morgan's position, and landing with equally harmful effect to both sides on the western flank.

Slowly and steadily the Majii line contracted. The Lights returned and secured the eastern end of the bastion. Missile fire dropped two more 'Mechs, a *Jenner* and a *Panther*. The battle's outcome became inevitable

A light burned on Morgan's communications console. He punched the button. "Kell here."

"Colonel, this is Major Falkenthal. My people will lay down our weapons."

"You speaking just for the 'Mechs under your command, Major, or the whole city?"

"Just my 'Mechs, Colonel." The man's voice betrayed little. "We both know this was just a charade anyway. Two dozen 'Mechs can't subdue a city of 20,000."

"Surrender accepted. Power down your weapons, leave your 'Mechs, go back to your leader, Patriarch Oltmann. He has six hours to turn the city over to me."

"You know what his answer will be."

"Just tell him. Kell out."

Morgan punched up his command frequency and issued orders for a cease fire. His troops stopped shooting and the Majii did likewise after one more sporadic exchange. The mortars likewise stopped, but that was just so they could be relocated deeper in the city.

Morgan half-closed his eyes. Major Falkenthal had been right. Two dozen 'Mechs couldn't possibly pacify a city of 20,000. That had never been his intention. He just had to get their attention.

His brother had to bring the city to its knees.

Frost heard the order come through his radio's earpiece. He double-clicked the reply button, then moved forward with a camo-clad squad of soldiers. Fifty kilometers west of Acre, high in the Occidental mountains, they closed in on the guardhouse at the Blue Ridge Dam and Hydroelectric plant.

Two men, one wearing a uniform and the other clad in what the men had come to consider the Majii uniform of black suit and white shirt, paced back and forth. The guard looked tired, and the Majii expectant. The Majii clutched a rifle tight in his hands. The guard had a pistol and a radio.

Which was why Frost shot the Majii first. He'd advanced along the roadway, moving through the woods until he was fifteen meters away. The Majii was at the far end of his circuit and just turning to come back, presenting the broadest target. Frost came up, both hands on a silenced pistol.

The gun coughed twice. The Majii staggered. His rifle hit the ground, which was the first notice the guard had of any trouble.

He dropped a hand to his radio, which was why Frost didn't kill him instantly.

"Hands wide, down on the ground. Now."

The man looked over, his face slack with shock, as a dozen sol-diers appeared from the woodlands. He complied with orders, sliding his radio toward the gated fence and his pistol in the other direction.

"I can open the gate for you."

"No need." Frost snaked a hand between the gate's bars and picked up the radio. "Crawl somewhere. Find yourself cover."

The man stared at him blankly.

Frost keyed the radio. "It's the front gate. There's guys in the woods. Soldiers. Holy shit—" He smashed the radio on the roadway, then he and his companions pulled back into the woods to watch the fun.

Lights blazed all over the complex and sirens echoed from the tall white wall of concrete that was the dam. Over on the far side, massive doors scrolled up from built-in bunkers. Two armored per-sonnel carriers came racing out, followed by two companies of troop-ers, hastily pulling on body armor and helmets. The column strung itself across the top of the dam. Four kilometers below, at the base of the mountains, lights also went on in a garrison station, where men scrambled into their armored vehicles and began the long ascent up a winding road to the Dam.

The APCs slowed as they neared the gate. Once they were in position and began deploying their cargoes, Frost hit the radio. "Waterwitch One, you are a go."

The steel gate wasn't that much of a problem. Frost's men had explosives that could have blown it down and, in a pinch, that's what they'd planned to do if necessary. It wasn't necessary, however, because Patrick Kell came boiling down the road leading half the Ultralytes. A quick kick by one sent the gate flying.

One APC opened fire with a heavy machine gun. 'Lytes returned fire, slagging it with lasers. The other one tried to turn tail and run, but slammed into the half-melted hulk, then jerked forward and smashed into a retaining wall.

The soldiers, realizing how exposed they were, began to retreat, only to discover exactly how dangerous Major O'Cieran's troops really were. O'Cieran's men were trained as jump infantry. They'd deployed to the edge of Lake Steiner and used their jet-packs to race across the water and come up at the far end of the dam. One company secured the empty bunker while the other set up at that end of the dam. The Majii had a choice of being killed by 'Mechs or by infantry. With the exception of a few zealots, the infantry laid down their weapons.

And down below, the other half of the Ultralyte force ambushed the garrison troops racing up the mountain. The fight there was short and sharp. The Ultralytes destroyed the first and last vehicle in the column, trapping everyone else. They had to destroy two more APCs before those troops were convinced to surrender.

Less than a half-hour after killing the Majii at the gate, Frost joined Patrick Kell and Major O'Cieran in the dam's Operations Center. The managing director—an older, heavy-set man with thinning hair who was still wearing pajamas—sat at a console. Outrage and disbelief warred for control of his face.

"You're monsters."

Patrick Kell shook his head. "Hardly. I just want to make sure I have it right. This bank of controls shuts down the turbines. These lever here open the flood gates. This set controls the other outflows from the lake."

"Yes, yes, you have it right, but you can't touch those."

Patrick placed a hand on a floodgate control lever. "I think you're under the impression that I intend to jerk this all the way around. That would just send millions of gallons flooding through the river bed, wouldn't it?"

"Yes. It would flood the city."

"Really? Very good." Patrick smiled and keyed his radio. "Waterwitch One. We have our objective, Morgan. Everything works. You might want to ask Patriarch Oltmann if he's built himself an Ark. If not, tell him he's not got much time to waste before he needs it."

CHAPTER 10

Morgan gave a great deal of consideration for how he would meet Thaddeus Oltmann. He had three choices—the Goldilocks paradigm. He could force Oltmann to come to him. Morgan would remain clad as a warrior, surrounded by warriors, as if he was a Mongol Khan commanding a Han Mayor to turn over his town. The Kell Hounds, in capturing the Dam, had put Oltmann's balls in a vise, and that approach would have squeezed hard.

Morgan could approach Oltmann respectfully. He could dress himself as one of the Majii, attend one of their worship services, mouth all the right things about respect and religion. The problem there as that he'd be moving into the realm of theology, and a debate there would not be to his advantage. *If you're going to ask them to "render unto Caesar," you can't pretend you're not an agent of Caesar.*

The middle approach, and the one he chose, was to meet with Oltmann in the shattered redoubt, beneath the shadow of the 'Mechs that had once served the Majii. Morgan wore fatigues, but comfortably; and aside from a pistol at his hip and a knife hidden in a boot, he hardly appeared to be a soldier in a war zone.

Given the treachery of the Majii in Ephaseus, meeting with Oltmann in the open might not have seemed wise. Sniper teams had been recalled from the dam and had set up a perimeter. The unit's 'Mechs were arrayed in an offensive posture that would allow for a quick strike if anything untoward happened. Area-denial—mines, with their lethal cargo of high explosives and ball bearings—had been set up on the city side of the redoubt to reduce any human wave attacks to puddles of bone and blood.

Morgan reached the site first, bringing with him only Father Donelly. The priest wore a fatigue jumpsuit, but had it open to mid-chest to display the black collar and dickey that marked his office. He carried no weapons.

They said nothing while they waited. Morgan seated himself on the severed foot of an AgroMech. All the sharp bits had been lazed smooth. Splintered wood poked up through dirt and over there a 'Mech arm poked up, fingers clawing at the sky. The 'Mechs that had surrendered remained in place. Being this close made it easy to read the Bible verses that had decorated the 'Mechs before they went into battle.

Morgan smiled. "As much as we would like to get away from it or deny it, we're a superstitious creature."

Donelly toed a spent magazine from a rifle. "No surprise. Humans create patterns. We make errors in those patterns."

The warrior arched an eyebrow. "You're suggesting that it's an error to believe God will save you?"

"Oh, no, that's the truth." The priest pointed at one of the Majii 'Mechs. "It's a mistake to think He will protect you when you're not about his work."

"It strikes me, Father, that we have a fundamental disagreement, each side here, as to who is doing God's work." Morgan frowned. "Both sides can't be right."

"And it's tempting to suppose that since we're in the superior position here, we're right. That's not proven, however." Donelly smiled. "Could be God has us playing this all out for his own reasons."

A double-click in the earpiece Morgan wore alerted him to the arrival of his guest. He turned toward the city as the Patriarch, with a thick white beard and mane of white hair, threaded his way through the shattered trenches. He used a stick, which was his only concession to age and, had the terrain not been uneven, Morgan supposed he would have eschewed even that. He wore homespun, but not in black. He'd opted for brown, closely matching the earth, and his broad-brimmed hat shared that same hue.

Oltmann stopped at a flat spot that kept him a meter higher than Morgan. He looked the warrior up and down once, then rested both hands on his stick. A couple of younger men, both in black, paused behind him.

The old man set his powerful shoulders. "Thou wished to speak with me?"

"We have a situation I hope to conclude to the mutual benefit of our people."

"Thou hast denied us water."

"And you have denied food to the people of the east." Morgan waved a hand, inviting the Patriarch to descend and be seated. "Both of us would like to see our people well-fed and watered. Let's work toward that goal."

"You are of the devil, Morgan Kell."

Morgan held a hand up. "With all due respect, Patriarch, I'm not going to argue theology with you. You want that, talk to Father Donelly here, and you'll get all the fight you want. But it will be thirsty work."

The old man glowered.

Okay, let me get his attention. "Within the next twenty-four hours, one of two things is going to happen. You could decide that you want to wipe us out, so you arm everyone with a knife and keep them coming until we've run out of bullets or the will to slaughter the innocent. That will be a while. And if you do that, we will blow the dam. The wall of water that comes roaring down will wash this city away and everyone in it. Period. There will be no trace of Acre. And yet, Bishop Poore will remain, he will eulogize you, his people will be seen to weep, and he will consolidate further power. The Archon won't allow that and will crush him. Your people will die at the same time.

"We already know you've been a brake on his ambition in the past. With your loss, the Majii will be irredeemable this side of death.

"The other possibility is this: you will conclude, after hours of prayer and reflection, that Jesus never would have starved anyone. Bishop Poore has committed a heresy, or at least an error in judgment. You, having sought and received divine counsel, are withdrawing Acre from his union. You are declaring your neutrality, and resuming trade with the west. There are already trucks on the way to begin unloading warehouses."

Morgan folded his hands across his chest. "So, do I tell the trucks to turn back, or do you want time to pray?"

The Patriarch looked back at his aides and dismissed them with a wave. He descended to the level with Morgan, his steps a bit shaky, and seated himself on a flat slab of armor. "Thou *art* of the Devil."

Morgan killed his inclination to smile.

"I do not think thee cognizant enough of the political implications of what thou art asking me to do." The old man's blue eyes narrowed. "Thou knowest that I opposed Poore, but he hast reached my people. He enflamest their hearts. Were I to make the declaration thou demandeth, I would face a revolt. The people fear thee after Ephaseus. Poore hast told them of atrocities. He offers succor and comfort."

Morgan keyed his radio. "Bring the boy in."

Oltmann looked up. "What boy?"

"I don't know what you heard about Ephaseus. My brother was wounded in an action that was started when a pregnant woman and her four-year-old son were driven out of Ephaseus toward our lines. She was mistreated all the way out. Once she passed from Majii lines, we sent people to help her. Only it turned out she wasn't pregnant.

She had a bomb strapped to her belly. She killed two of my soldiers, wounded my brother, and would have killed her own son, save that my brother shielded the boy with his own body."

Frost arrived, leading the small boy by the hand. The youth's face brightened when he saw the Patriarch. With a shout of "Grandfather!" he raced to the old man and hugged him.

Oltmann hugged the boy back, then looked up, tears glistening. "Caleb's mother, Judith..."

Morgan nodded. "The granddaughter you gave to Poore. The boy is his son, yes?"

The Patriarch nodded, speechless, his tears spotting the back of the boy's jacket.

"I won't argue theology with you. This is not about theology. Poore was willing to sacrifice his own son, just as God sacrificed Jesus. Poore believes he is more than a messenger and servant of God, he believes he *is* God. He is idolatry and blasphemy on two legs, and is willing to kill your blood to advance his plans. And he would have told you that we killed her, or that she chose to glorify herself, manipulating you to hate us; but we've cut communications and isolated Acre."

The old man nodded slowly.

Morgan opened his arms. "My engineers have figured out how much water your city requires to meet human physical needs. We will give you two liters per person per day. No washing up, no cooking, no cleaning, but everyone will have enough to drink. While you are praying, I'll have the water turned on. In good faith. I won't test you as God tested Moses; but don't test me. It can be a trickle, or I can unleash destructive power the like of which hasn't been seen since Sodom and Gomorrah fell."

Morgan crossed and laid a hand on the old man's sagging shoulder. "And when you reject heresy and blasphemy and welcome us as liberators; then I shall join you to mourn Caleb's mother."

Oltmann looked up and swiped a hand under his nose. "I know what God is calling upon me to do. I will agree with thine plan in all things, save one."

"And that would be?"

Oltmann stood and Caleb hugged his thigh. "Bishop Poore is a test for me and my people. God does not call us to be neutral. What little force we can muster, we will go with you."

This I didn't expect. "I understand and appreciate your offer..."

"It is not an 'offer,' Morgan Kell, it is a fact." The old man clapped him on a shoulder. "We know this land better than thou ever will. God demands that each man work for his salvation. So we shall work now. I will go and pray. My answer will come in an hour; an announcement after that. Then I shall bathe and welcome thee into my home."

Frost stood in the shadow of a 'Mech's foot, his rifle resting across it. From time to time he'd look into the scope, staring at expectant faces, framed by windows. The Majii youth looked happy. Their elders, who never appeared for more than a moment or two, appeared worried, or oblivious to the 'Mechs. *Willing us to no longer exist.*

"You don't believe in the truce, Mr. Frost?"

The sniper looked over at the sky-pilot. "The dead don't betray the living."

"The dead can't change." Donelly looked toward Acre. "You don't trust the people's acceptance of us?"

"They hated us one moment, and love us the next? That's supposed to promote trust?"

"Circumstances, Mr. Frost, have changed. The Patriarch made his case. Many of the people in Acre knew his granddaughter. Half of them are related to her. Learning that one of us shed blood to save her son counts for a great deal. And the colonel's charity in giving them water, that appealed to many as well."

Frost leaned back against the 'Mech's foot. "Coercion I believe in, Father. But that's your stock in trade, isn't it? Be good or burn for eternity?"

"It's not coercion. It's a comfort knowing there is more to life than living, and that acts of charity and kindness will be rewarded in the next world." Donelly pointed toward the city. "You've been watching people. Don't you think the Patriarch's message has comforted them?"

"Sure, but break it down: he says that if they play nice, they'll have water to drink and their homes won't be washed halfway to Galaport. And do you imagine there aren't a bunch of werewolves in that city waiting for their chance?"

"Werewolves?"

"Shapechangers. They look like one thing on the outside, but they're something else on the inside. Sure, lots of folks might have had a change of heart because of the sob-story about the boy and his mother, but there's a bunch of them that think she wasn't forced to do this, that she went willingly and is being glorified in Heaven. And they'd love to be just like her. They lead miserable lives here, and this is the fast ticket to heavenly glory." Frost gramaced. "What the lot of them need is to get drunk, get laid, and smile once in a while. They're so depressed and repressed that blowing yourself up has got to seem like fun, especially when they think their big, invisible friend in the sky is urging them on to do it."

Donelly pulled back and gave Frost a curious look. "You would be an atheist, then?"

"Nice attempt to plug me into a box, padre, so you can dismiss me." Frost shook his head. "I'm a realist. No matter what someone says, the bottom line is that he will act in his own enlightened best-interest every time."

"Then how do you explain Patrick Kell saving the child? No, not with 20/20 hindsight, because he didn't know who the child was, or how effective saving him would be here in Acre. Patrick's enlightened self-interest would have him remaining behind cover."

Frost snorted. "Vanity. Kell knew it would look good for him to have saved the child."

"Or, perhaps he couldn't have lived himself if he hadn't acted, and the child had been harmed. His conscience motivated him to act."

"But conscience is not the sole province of theists."

The priest nodded. "No, but it may be one of a number of things, including religion, or love, or idiosyncrasies, that prompt people to act to save others."

"Heh, you're proving my point. If someone buys into delusions, his 'enlightenment' doesn't have to be rational. And face it, Father, the people who benefit from his actions are going to rationalize a wonderful explanation for what he did. After all, if a guy dies saving your life, it means you're valuable. You're worth two lives, and it's a lot easier to accept that than to realize some insane dope got himself scragged because you stupidly found yourself in a position where *you* probably should have died."

"Very interesting, Mr. Frost." The priest scratched at his chin. "You hold these beliefs very deeply. Do you know why you do?"

"I don't need psychoanalysis from you or anyone else, thanks." Frost thumbed a bullet from a magazine on his belt and held it up. "I don't know if men are created equal in God's eyes. They certainly aren't in each other's eyes. But there is a time when they *are* equal. When I pump a thirty-nine gram bullet traveling a kilometer a second through them, suddenly they're equal. Their motives, their fears, hopes, and desires mean nothing. I don't know if they see God in that last moment, or cry out for their mothers, I just know they die. Death is really all there is, Father. You can't escape it, and all the glory you wrap around yourself at the end doesn't bring you back."

"But your memory might inspire others."

"Yeah, inspire them to do more stupid stuff." Frost fed the bullet back into the magazine. "That's fine. I love my work."

CHAPTER 11

Peter finished his wordless prayer, Miriam's hands held tightly in his own. She still trembled. He squeezed her hands as reassuringly as he could. It would not do to let her know fear lingered in his heart as well.

He opened his eyes and smiled at her. "It is God's will, beloved."

She nodded, glancing down, not meeting his gaze. Her behavior was right and proper, but there was more to it than decorum. She hid her red-rimmed eyes from him, and he did not rebuke her. He did not want his last image of her to be a sad one.

Peter and Miriam had moved to Galaport a year previous, appearing to be refugees from the east. He'd always been good with his hands, and found work in a machine shop. Not only did it allow him to be useful, but gave him access to the tools he'd used to fashion the components for the bomb he would strap to himself.

Miriam took a position as a cook in a large cafeteria kitchen. Not only did she prepare food which they slopped into troughs so morbidly obese people could gorge themselves, but she worked on meals for some of the finer hotels and corporate headquarters.

These positions, or similar ones, had been mandated by Bishop Poore when he sent them in to the den of evil which was Galaport. He'd chosen Peter and Miriam for the Petrine Order because of their purity and their spiritual strength. Peter had never before seen Miriam, and was wed to her within an hour of the Bishop introducing them. They studied for a month as husband and wife, then fled to the big city to bide their time. The Bishop would call upon them, and they would do anything he asked.

Their positions were perfect. Not only did Peter have resources he could use, but his shop would be critical for maintaining 'Mechs that could be used against the Bishop. By manufacturing parts just a hair out of specification, he could sabotage the enemy, and make field repairs impossible. His work schedule would alert him to various goings on, and he would act accordingly.

Miriam's job not only informed her of places where many people—important people—would be gathered; but provided her a means of hurting them. A biological or chemical agent added to a tray of mashed potatoes could combine with another laced in a dessert to sicken or kill hundreds. Targets of opportunity came and went over the year, and while they waited, Peter and Miriam led perfectly quiet and ordinary lives.

Bishop Poore had set up a simple system for dealing with sleeper agents. They had been given a selection of pre-ordained targets and missions based on their positions. Daily messages—and the means of delivery varied depending on the date—prevented them from acting on any of these missions. Once they stopped getting these hold messages—something accomplished very easily through ComStar's embargo on messages from the west—they were free to act.

When Peter had accessed the plans Bishop Poore had drawn up for them, he marveled at the man's genius. Peter would machine up all the parts for his bombs. They consisted of a dozen metal cylinders packed with explosives and shrapnel. He would wear them, enter a building, and detonate the bomb, killing as many people as possible.

Miriam's part was two-fold. The target was chosen from the list of catering jobs on the appointed day. Peter was meticulous in looking that list over, then randomly selecting a target. There was no way anyone could have predicted his choice, but God had clearly had a hand in making it. His target was the smallest of the assignments: meals being provided to the juror pool in the case of a courtesan nabbed in a recent vice raid. The court room would be packed with supporters, and Peter could wipe them all out.

Miriam's second task became even more brilliant. She, at work, would hear about the blast and suggest that everyone pitch in and make food for the rescuers. This food she would poison, wiping out the very first-responders who would have otherwise safeguarded people from future attacks.

Peter reached over and lifted Miriam's chin. "Miriam, my wife, I have come to love thee almost as much as I love God."

The petite woman smiled despite the tears rolling down her cheeks. "Oh, Peter, I cannot bear losing you."

"God will not keep us apart long, darling." Peter pulled her into a hug and held on tightly. She felt so small in his arms. From the first he had wanted to protect her, then possess her. *And when we made love...* It had been glorious and wonderful—not the wanton animal act that whores like the woman on trial engaged in. They were married and committed to each other, united through their love of God. It had been right and proper, and they enjoyed it until...

He held her tighter, his cheeks burning. *Until we came to love it too much, and were tempted to forsake Him for the pleasure of the flesh.* They'd both come to realize their sin, and had held themselves apart from one another. They resisted Lust, keeping their love pure. *After all, lovemaking is for procreation and...*

The realization that they would never have children had wounded them both—Miriam more deeply than Peter. He recognized this. Miriam threw herself into other tasks. Like the bomb-vest she made, which was practical but also embroidered with little flowers in gay colors, reminding him of his home. It some how failed to strike Peter as odd that Miriam had sublimated her grief beneath a fervor to manufacture the garment he would wear to his death.

After all, it was God's will.

Peter let her slip from his arms. "I will always love thee, Miriam."

She reached up, pressing a finger to his lips. "No more. My heart will shatter."

"No, Miriam, God will keep thee whole and safe." He kissed her finger, then her forehead. "Now, beloved, help me into this vest and we shall be about God's work."

Veronica Matova loathed being late, and made no attempt to hide her ire from Angela Pring. The redhead had arrived at her work place out of her mind with a combination of worry, alcohol, and recreational drugs. Veronica's site manager had hustled her out to one of the safe apartments they maintained, then summoned Veronica. Veronica, in turn, had summoned two doctors and Angela's lawyer.

While the doctors worked on Angela, the lawyer did what she could to get the day's court proceeding put off. The government seemed anxious to press ahead with things, but the judge, in return for certain favors, saw fit to delay the opening of court until eleven. While Veronica knew the state wanted to push ahead to send a message to Bishop Poore, she revealed nothing to the lawyer about the government's motive.

Angela had gotten four hours of sleep, which was two more than Veronica, but still looked poorly. Veronica had tucked the girl into a spa, then had an army of experts work her over so she appeared young, innocent and intelligent—a façade that would last at least until Angela decided to vomit all over herself and learned counsel.

Veronica had firm hold of the redhead's arm as they marched toward the court building. "I have guaranteed you that you will not go to prison. I have guaranteed you that you'll never need to work another day in your life—provided you are willing to live modestly—if you follow the program and get through this. It really is very simple, Angela."

The girl shied from the remark and tried to pull away. "Please, can't they do this without me?"

"Unlikely." Veronica spun her around and shook her by the shoulders. "If you fail to show up, not only will there be an arrest warrant out for you, but when they find you, they'll slap you into a cell, they'll delouse you, hose you off, and dress you up in an orange jumpsuit. Not only is that *not* your color, but you will look as guilty as..." Veronica's voice trailed off.

"As guilty as?"

As that man over there.

A young man, utterly average save for his wearing a jacket over a vest on what promised to be a very hot day, paused on the sidewalk ahead of them. He looked around, trying to be inconspicuous, but that made him all the more noticeable. Moreover, the thickness of his chest contrasted too sharply with his slender thighs, hands, and angular face. Human physiology—especially of the male—Veronica knew very well, and people did not come naturally built the way he was.

But the vest cinched it for her. She only caught a flash of it, but the colorful embroidery gave it away. She'd decorated a vest just like that, the same flowers, the same colors, the same lines, for her father. It was a labor of love, and she'd not seen its like since arriving in Galaport.

"Angela, come!" Veronica yanked the girl toward the street.

"What's happening?"

"Quiet!"

The girl wailed louder and swung around to confront her. "Tell me what's happening."

Too late.

The man looked past Angela's back and locked eyes with Veronica. He knew.

His hand went to his pocket.

Veronica dove over a parked vehicle.

The bomb blast had been designed to have a sphere of lethality approximately seven meters in diameter. In the middle of a packed courtroom, hundreds would have been killed. Much as Angela was, they would have been reduced to a mist of blood, tissue and bone fragments as the shrapnel ripped through them. The fire and shockwave further disintegrated the larger chunks. Rather miraculously, one of Angela's red shoes landed forty meters away, straps still buckled, without the loss of so much as one rhinestone.

Of Peter, investigators would find little beyond stains and DNA samples. The same was not true of the bomb. Bomb experts are fond of noting that explosions don't destroy anything, they just break it down into really small parts. In the months that followed, they would reconstruct the bomb and trace it back to Peter's workplace. They'd even identify the lot from which the explosives had been stolen and would prosecute the construction engineer who'd sold them to Peter.

The one thing Peter had not counted on was detonating his bomb out of doors. Had he been inside, the compression factor afforded by an enclosed space would have magnified the effect from the shock-wave. Those who hadn't died in the initial blast could still take lethal damage as the shockwave passed through them. It could rupture organs and blood vessels, causing critical failures and strokes which would kill someone who had been otherwise untouched.

The blast shattered windows all around the square. Four people died when glass sliced them to bits, and dozens went to hospital with lacerations. Six drivers and passengers perished as shrapnel peppered their vehicles, and another two died in subsequent collisions. Heart attacks, strokes, and asthma attacks toted up more victims, putting Peter's total well above thirty killed and two hundred wounded.

In the most macabre death related to the blast, a man who'd heard the news, killed his wife, hid her body, then claimed she'd been in Judiciary Square. So convincing was his act, that he was inter-viewed by the media, got aid from multiple anonymous donors, and might have even avoided prosecution if he'd been wise enough to spend some of the money on his utility bill. When his power was cut off, the freezer into which he'd stuffed his late wife stopped working. As she thawed out, neighbors noticed an odd smell, and authorities arrested him.

All of this information would later fascinate Veronica, but meant little to her as she dove for cover. Nuts and ball-bearings hit her in the left leg and foot, that being the only bit of her anatomy exposed above the parked vehicle. Some bits of shrapnel did rip all the way through it and struck her in the face and body, but were so spent they only bruised and cut.

She landed hard, dazed, deafened by an intense ringing in her ears. The car, which had caught most of the blast rocked, then settled on flattened tires. The one further along, closer to where the man had stood, flipped in the air and crashed, then another vehicle slammed into it. Tires smoked as vehicles stopped sharply, some skidding, but all of them somehow avoiding her.

She rolled onto her back, refusing to surrender to the wave of nausea tightening her stomach. Angela dripped from the shattered windscreen of a parked car. Pain pulsed up her leg. She wanted to sit up and assess the damage, but she couldn't. She didn't want to know.

And, for the first time since she'd escaped the west, Veronica Matova began to pray.

CHAPTER 12

From the cockpit of his new Ultralyte—a *Javelin*—Patrick Kell surveyed Peterstown. He had to study the images hard because the heat shimmer rising off the dry plain all but erased the handful of mud huts marking the village's location. Most of it had been built underground, with windows and doors looking south and east into the canyon that curved around Peterstown.

Most of the population—and Patrick's information pegged it as between two hundred and three hundred individuals—had taken refuge underground. Just six faced the Kell Hounds' Ultralyte company. Five piloted modified AgroMechs.

The sixth, Jimmy Stanton, stepped his *Centurion* forward. Static crackled through the neurohelmet's earphones. "The people of Peterstown defy you and your Satanic Master."

Patrick closed his eyes for a second. Oltmann's people had come to Peterstown, as they had come to so many of the smaller settlements, and tried to enlist the locals in the counter-revolution. Many others had come over without a shot being fired. Peterstown, unfortunately, was home to one of Poore's wives and had benefited from limited patronage. They remained defiantly in Poore's camp and their possession of armed 'Mechs meant they couldn't be ignored.

Patrick keyed his radio. "Jimmy, you know this is foolishness."

"It is what God calls up on me to do."

"He doesn't want you to die."

"If I die, it is His will being done." The long-range missile port on the *Centurion*'s chest snapped open. "I am not afraid to die for Him."

The image of the boy he'd met in Galaport faded from Patrick's mind. He flipped his radio over to his unit's tactical frequency. "We do it as we laid it out. No heroics. We're faster than they are, and are an even match for the aggies. The *Centurion* is still lethal."

The Ultralytes split into two sections. Alpha, under the command of Jane Neary, drove east and a little south. They came around in an arc focused on the southern end of the Peterstown line. A modified harvester anchored it at the canyon. That was a good tactical choice, since it prevented anyone from flanking the formation, but the swarming Ultralytes had more than enough firepower to hammer that 'Mech.

Patrick's command headed in directly east, centering themselves on the *Centurion*. While the Ultralytes still sported light armor—each ton of it about twenty-percent as effective as the military grade alternative—their missile launchers shot military loads, and the lasers were fully powered. They could move very quickly and Patrick counted on their speed to win the engagement.

Patrick's *Javelin* pulled ahead, diving straight in at the *Centurion*. Short range missiles launched from the 'Mech's chest, spiraling in on flame-jets. Four hit, shattering armor on the *Centurion*'s broad chest. The massive 'Mech shied a bit—Jimmy clearly hadn't expected military loads on the missiles—but the 'Mech stepped back forward and let fly.

Long-range missiles arced from the 'Mech's chest, sowing fire along the plain. They hit nothing, though did smash an irrigation control gate. The autocannon in the 'Mech's right arm, vomited fire, tracing a line across Patrick's approach, but again didn't touch a single Kell Hound. The medium laser, however, caught a *Commando* on the right arm. The light armor evaporated in an eyeblink. The arm's bones glowed red, then came apart, dropping to the ground along with the smoking SRM launcher build into the forearm.

More short range missiles raced in at the *Centurion*, wreathing it in flame. Armor shards glittered on the ground. Lasers stabbed through the smoke and, in that brief moment when it cleared, a pox of blackened wounds dotted the previously pristine armor.

Again Jimmy Stanton let loose with every weapon in his arsenal. The LRMs sailed past Patrick's *Javelin*. The autocannon lipped flame, but the slugs again missed the Kell Hound. The medium laser, however, hit the *Javelin* in the right leg. It burned through the armor and started in on the internal structures. Alarm klaxons pulsed through the cockpit. The secondary monitor showed the leg's armor as red, then black, and colored the leg itself yellow.

Patrick put that out of his mind. He dropped his crosshairs on the *Centurion's* outline. The gold dot at their center flashed. Patrick tightened up on the triggers.

The *Javelin* launched a full dozen SRMs at the larger 'Mech. One missed. The rest pummeled the Majii 'Mech. The blasts stripped the last of the armor over the 'Mech's heart and left flank, leaving it open and vulnerable.

Fatally vulnerable.

The rest of the Ultralytes poured their fire into the *Centurion*. Missiles filled its chest with flames. One hit the LRM magazine, triggering a secondary explosion. White fire jetted up and out. The 'Mech's left arm went whirling away. The 'Mech staggered to the right and didn't go down—that being a miracle in and of itself.

More explosions shook the *Centurion*. An auxiliary monitor lit up as the 'Mech's heat profile shifted. Patrick stabbed a button to impose a data filter, but that just made the image brighter.

"Punch out, Jimmy, punch out!"

The Kell Hound missiles and the exploding magazine had combined to destroy the fusion reactor's magnetic containment bubble. The reaction, now unleashed, blossomed as a fiery djinn released from a bottle. It shot straight up, consuming everything in a roiling ball of golden flame. The fire collapsed in on itself, leaving a greasy black cloud rising above a 'Mech that now was nothing more than a pair of legs attached to a smoking torso.

Patrick looked up, hoping to catch a glimpse of a command couch that had somehow escaped the inferno. "Anyone see the pilot. Did he get out?"

"Negative, Colonel."

The *Centurion's* loss broke the Peterstown militia. One of the AgroMech's turned and ran right into the canyon. The 'Mech didn't survive, but somehow the pilot did. Two others had already been put down, leaving the two at the northern end of their line free to surrender. This they did, and Oltmann's envoys returned to quickly reach a doctrinal accommodation with the people of Peterstown.

Patrick didn't bother to look up as his brother slid a glass of whisky into the table. "Can't. There are regs against it."

Morgan shook his head. "It's medicinal. I'll have a medic write it up that way."

He looked at the glass. Considered it. The amber liquid would burn like hell going down. *That would be punishment, wouldn't it?*

The unit had moved past Peterstown and entered Arone. The town lay nestled in a deep and fertile valley which had always profited from trade with the east. A bit more modern than most of the western towns, it has facilities that made repairing and refitting the mercenaries' 'Mechs that much easier.

Oltmann's people had no trouble convincing the Aronians to join forces with them. Morgan and Patrick had been invited into the

Aronian Patriarch's home. Though the furnishing were rustic and of crude manufacture, they were sturdy. The home had a modest nature to it, and Patrick felt very welcome there.

The younger Kell shook his head. "No. And it's not just the regs, or the example we should be setting for the rest of the unit."

Morgan drew a wooden chair up. It creaked as he sat. "What is it?"

"If I drink that, I'm going to let myself forget. I don't want to do that."

Morgan nodded, but sipped his own glass regardless. "This isn't the first time you've killed."

"No, but the others were different. We were fighting enemies who had attacked us. That kid was just defending his home."

"And would have attacked us if we'd been foolish enough to by-pass Peterstown."

"I know. The difference is that I *knew* the kid."

"And you liked him. You helped him out." Morgan smiled. "You wanted to bring him into the family."

"Yeah, and now he's dead." Patrick looked up into his brother's eyes. "I've been going over all the intellectual arguments. He'd have killed me if he'd been successful with his shots. But that just goes to his youth and inexperience. We were a pack of wild dogs just tearing at him. He never had a chance. He never saw that, however, because his belief in God blinded him."

Morgan arched an eyebrow. "You going to be mad at God now?"

"No. Jimmy was believing in Poore, and I can lay the blame on him with no problem. And if bring up the fact that he was just defending his home, it gets met with the fact that we're here to prevent millions of people starving to death. I get that, too."

His brother nodded. "So you understand that Jimmy would have died whether you were there or not, whether or not it was the Kell Hounds who were shooting at him."

"I know all that, too."

Morgan frowned. "Then what's the root problem?"

Patrick rubbed a hand over his mouth. "There's a little piece of me that's glad he's dead. It wanted him dead. It was about revenge. Every one of us knows about the bombing in Galaport, the poisoning that followed. Anyone who could do that had to be insane. They're rabid. There's only one thing you can do with a rabid animal."

He looked up. "Have you heard any more from Veronica?"

Morgan shook his head. "No, which is good. She'll need rest. She got a bit more mangled than you did."

"Do you think they targeted her specifically? You know, to get at you?"

"I don't know." Morgan looked into the depths of his glass. "Poore's that vindictive, no question about it. I question the circumstances. Going after Veronica would have been easier if you hit her home or her business. Seems kind of random for her to be on the street."

"I think he did it to make things personal. You took Acre from him, he takes her from you."

"That's the way a novelist would write it up." Morgan grinned. "But there's the problem. Man is really good at making patterns—so go we see them where they aren't. There's probably a dozen people who lost friends in the blast who have figured their friend was the target. It gives meaning to a random action. It holds the cold and uncaring nature of the universe at bay. If there is a reason for things, then there is a way for us to avoid the bad things. So, perception of a pattern begets action, which reinforces patterns, and gets people marching inexorably toward a fate they never would have desired."

A chill ran down Patrick's spine. "You think God is just another of those 'reasons' made up to keep fear at bay?"

"Maybe not God, Patrick, but religion? There's no denying it's a means of social control." Morgan gestured back south toward Peterstown and Acre. "Religion as control got us into this mess. It's what has Oltmann's people marching straight north toward Thessalon."

"It's what had Jimmy and his friends waiting for us at Peterstown."

"True, but it might have been the solution there, too." Morgan set his glass down. "One of the biggest fears people have is of being wrong. We all know society and know the rules of the game. Or games, since there are so many being run out there. You think about it, there are tons of people who would be happy to visit Veronica at work, but nary a one of them will see her in hospital. Why? Because it's not proper—and we're not just talking married men who've been cheating. There's a whole class of perfectly ordinary, single men who would face criticism if they were to visit her—even just as a hospital volunteer. They could be completely innocent, yet their action would be taken as some covert means to get sex.

"So religion serves as a big referee. It lays down strictures, disciplines you if you screw up, and often forgives you and rehabilitates you. It doesn't want you going away. It wants you under control. And the big promise is that if you don't act morally, there's an eye in the sky that's watching you. You'll pay a price later, even if your crimes go undiscovered now."

Patrick scratched at the back of his neck. "I'm not sure which way you're arguing here, for or against."

"I guess I'm arguing both. Jimmy was out there because he didn't want to be wrong. He didn't want to be wrong with his people and his God. That was his choice, and he and his people were given ample choice in the matter. He could have even seen that you had him tactically outmaneuvered and could have surrendered. His death was neither inevitable nor a necessity unless he chose to make it so. You can't take responsibility for his decision."

"But he was a kid."

"You didn't see him as a kid when he wanted to join the unit. You were going to respect his choice then. You can't slice it both ways there."

"So, I was wrong initially? That doesn't get me off the hook for his death now."

Morgan's eyes narrowed. "But ask yourself, why do you want to be wrong now? Why are you in here, dwelling on his death?"

"My God, Morgan, this was a flesh and blood human being, and he's dead. He went in a horrible way."

"It's one thing, Patrick, to acknowledge and mourn his death. It's another thing to be dwelling on it to the point of haunting yourself. Now, sure, society says killing isn't a good thing. Most people are leery of it even when it's done in warfare. And you've killed more coldly and closely than with Jimmy, but you didn't dwell then."

Patrick nodded slowly. In the first week on Galatea he'd shot and killed men trying to kidnap him, and he'd not really thought on them until Morgan brought it up. Morgan had a point. Society said killing was wrong. Though Jimmy's death might be seen as a tragedy by many, no one else was going to blame him for what happened.

So why is it that I'm not letting myself free?

His flesh puckered with goosebumps. He reached for the glass of whisky but his hand never closed around it.

Morgan looked up. "What?"

"There is a difference, you're right." Patrick tapped a finger against the table. "I'm sticking with this because, if I don't, I'm afraid I'll become like Frost."

Morgan's expression hardened around the eyes. "That's a scary thought."

"The man has no soul."

"Oh, I think he has one." Morgan swirled his whisky and drained the glass in one go. "Something poisoned it a long time ago. He sees things differently than we do."

Patrick cocked his head. "Do you think, perhaps, he sees past the strictures and laws to a reality we're afraid to look at?"

"Maybe. Or maybe he's only got one tool in his kit: killing. It's the ultimate trump card. It wins every argument until that last one, when someone does it a bit better than you do." Morgan shook his head. "You're right in not wanting to become like Frost."

"What would you do if I did?"

"I'd weep for the brother I'd lost." All warmth drained from Morgan's expression. "Then I'd use you as I'll use him. There's a bit of an argument I need settled, and he's just the man to do the job."

CHAPTER 13

Morgan flipped his *Centurion's* sensor package from infrared to mag-res. The holographic display altered the image, outlining objects with blue lines when the computers could identify them, and leaving them yellow blobs of color when it could not. While the computers had no trouble picking out 'Mechs, its identification of other items could not be trusted. The results were only as good as the database backing them.

Morgan had come forward with a lance on a scouting run an hour past midnight. O'Cieran's scouts had already poured over the area thoroughly, and had teams in place to monitor enemy activity. The 'Mech patrols were really unnecessary, save that it gave the enemy something to think about. Reports were hastily being sent off to Bishop Poore, and their panicked tone told Morgan more about the situation inside Thessalon than anyone could have imagined.

Surveying the landscape revealed problems with the planned assault in the early morning. The city center occupied a raised plateau averaging thirty meters above the rest of the terrain on the south, and seventy to the northern side. Some housing existed on the plain itself, but the main roadway up to the plateau was narrow and switched-back before entering the city. While other roads existed, they couldn't handle 'Mechs, not even the Ultralytes. While many of those 'Mechs had jump jets and could reach the city, landing in an urban area and regrouping with any semblance of order would be tough.

The ground on either side of the main road had been sown with mines. Or so it appeared. O'Cieran's men had reported seeing work-crews out burying things, but those could have been dummy mines as easily as the real thing. Avoiding the minefields would channel the Kell Hounds straight north and bunch them up where artillery fire could do a great deal of damage. More importantly, with Thessalonian forces knowing safe routes through the minefields, they could speed through them and hit the Hounds in the flanks.

The Harvest River ran along the northern edge of the city and had carved a deep canyon behind Thessalon. It was deemed unassaultable even if Morgan wanted to loop his 'Mechs around and approach from that direction. Neither east nor west was much better since settlements had gone up along the river's edge. Any one of the houses could have been packed with explosives just waiting for a 'Mech to wander by.

O'Cieran's scouts had reported seeing a few 'Mechs within the city, but they'd not been able to clearly identify them. The party Oltmann sent in to negotiate had spotted a pair of *Victors*, which put no one at ease. Morgan wanted to take heart in the fact that those same men thought his *Centurion* was a *Victor*, but assuming the enemy is weak just because you don't want them to be strong is a wonderful way to lose a fight before the first shot is fired.

Morgan keyed his radio. "Hound lead to base. A few items that weren't here before. Roadside bombs, we have to assume."

"Roger that." His brother's voice remained neutral. "Still thinking we go in at the southeast?"

The most frustrating thing about the assault on Thessalon was the fact that the enemy wasn't showing itself, nor was it likely to emerge from the city. Morgan recognized the desperation in Poore's orders that Thessalon be held at all costs. He sent messages promising salvation for martyrs who perished in the fight. His messianic ego felt that if the city fell, the Thessalonians were not worthy of living. Moreover, if they failed, they'd not be around to point the finger at him. His failure would have no witnesses among his believers.

Thessalon's southeast quadrant was the older part of the city. Buildings were, in general, smaller and not suitable for hiding 'Mechs. That made the southeast marginally better than any other approach. The only real chance the Kell Hounds had was to push forward and hope that military discipline and training would prevail over half-trained troops with questionable equipment.

"That's the conclusion I'm forced to accept, isn't it?" Morgan's heavy neurohelmet prevented him from shaking his head. "And that's why I hate it. When you dance to the tune the enemy calls, you're opening yourself to a lot of hurt."

"Mine fields might be a bluff."

"Even if they're sowed with dummies, can we take that chance?"

"No, but remember, they're thinking that we think the minefields are as good as walls. We know where they want us to go. Our job is to pick another path."

"Agreed."

In scoping out the defenses, the southeast approach still had a minefield that had to be dealt with. The only expedient approach would be for the incoming 'Mechs to lay down pattern-fire with short-range missiles. That would detonate the mines, though the narrow corridor would still bunch the 'Mechs perilously closely.

There has to be another way.

Morgan smiled. "I think I have something. Can you make it to Arone and get back in a day? Ten Ultras?"

"We can do the trip in half that time."

"Perfect. Issue orders. Everyone stands down, gets sleep, gets maintenance, gets food. We're going on the 29th."

"Got it. Do we shut the lines to Paradise Mountain down?"

"Nope, keep them wide open." Morgan smiled. "We'll make a show of hesitating. That will amp Poore's rhetoric, and we'll use that against him when we need to."

"You're the boss."

"Just keep me honest. Oh, and send someone for the Patriarch. I have a new job for his Saints." Morgan nodded and turned his 'Mech around. "He wanted his people coming along? Well, now they'll have the chance to win the day."

PARADISE MOUNTAIN
MAJISTAN, GALATEA

Had Bishop Arlington Poore been rational, the latest message from Thessalon would not have filled him with joy and relief. Instead, he would have viewed it with suspicion. There simply was no reason for the Kell Hounds to slow their approach toward Thessalon. While many likened war to chess, stressing maneuvering, there was always a point in the game when pieces were exchanged, and often that was in a flurry that was neither pretty nor elegant, and denuded the board.

The thing about Poore was that he realized this about himself. He accepted that he wasn't rational in any societal sense of the word, but he didn't care. Society, with its rules and customs was a construct of the devil, meant to drag men away from God. Poore had a direct line to God, which allowed him to see that and much more.

It had not always been so. Though he had been born in the west, in a small town northwest of Thessalon, he had not always been a faithful member of the church. Like many a young man, the wonders of modern technology had seduced him. He'd fled from the family farm and went to Galaport. He briefly worked a series of menial jobs, and inside a month shipped out on a DropShip that bounced from world to world in the Lyran Commonwealth.

He'd earned the nickname Holo because of his fascination for the broadcast holovids on every world the ship visited. He had been content to let other crew members buy shore-leave time from him—what little there was with their schedule—and remained glued to local holovision entering and leaving star systems. While part of him knew holovids were blasphemous, he also recognized how powerful they were.

Being young, charismatic, and handsome, when he chose to leave the ship, it took him no time to find an internship with a broadcast company. He lived off his savings, made himself useful, and quickly earned a paying job. Within six months he was on-air, by nine months was a weekend anchor, and inside a year had switched companies and anchored an evening news program that topped the ratings.

Unfortunately, he began to believe all the things said about him. He lived and died with reviews and ratings reports. He turned to alcohol, drugs, and licentious behavior to celebrate his victories, and salve the wounds of his defeats. The roller-coaster of moods affected his work, and his career came crashing down.

Two years out from having left Galatea, Arlington Poore found himself in an alley, fighting a stray dog for a crust of bread. He smashed the animal in the head with his wine bottle, then used the jagged end to cut its throat. At that point he passed out, certain he was dying and would awaken in Hell.

Instead he woke up in a hospital charity ward, all clean and bright. He'd been bathed, salved and dog-bites had been bound up. He awoke to the voice of an angel reading to him from the Bible, and he began to weep. He confessed to the woman about all his horrible behavior. She calmed him, then invited him to her home and church.

That reconnection with God felt right. Though Poore seldom dwelled upon his time away—and nothing of it was said in his official biography—he did realize that psychologists and other men of science would rationalize his return to the Lord as a simple means of his refusing to take responsibility for the actions that landed him in the alley. All his misfortunes, of course, were laid on the Devil's shoulders, while his salvation was the province of the Lord.

Poore was willing to accept that because such deluded men of science refused to accept either the existence of the supernatural, or its profound influence in the world. The Devil had warped him. God had saved him. These things were his personal experiences, therefore he could never question the existence of either God or the Devil. If neither of them existed, he couldn't be in the position he was in. Since he was there, they must exist. It was obvious to even the most casual of observers.

Poore studied the most recent message from Thessalon. The Kell Hounds still had spotters in place watching the city, but the defenders were keeping their 'Mechs hidden. Work crews worked to fortify parts of the city. They created fortresses at strategic points that would allow them to stop the Kell Hounds. The mercenaries' only recourse would be to raze the city. This they would not do, since news of such an atrocity couldn't be kept quiet.

Though he never talked about his experience off-world—aside from suggesting that he had known "dark days" in the past—Poore did still understand the power of media. He had exploited it to build his empire, and would employ it to rebuild. Acre might have fallen, but that was a temporary setback. In fact, by sending forces north with the Kell Hounds, Oltmann had played into his hands rather nicely.

Poore would offer retroactive redemption for those who fell fighting against his people in Thessalon. Grieving relatives would quickly avail themselves of this expedient to purge their sense of guilt. Moreover, in hoping to see their kin in Heaven, they would be investing in Poore's vision and message. To leave him again would be to abandon their sanctified kin.

That they would never do.

It never occurred to him that his plan was overtly manipulative and evil. He knew he was playing with emotions and taking advantage of people in a time of weakness, but that was not evil. In weakness, they could find strength. In times of weakness, they needed God. They reached God through him. Since he was that portal, nothing he did could be evil, since he was saving their souls.

He sat down at his desk—a vast, ornate affair carved with a bas relief wood-cut crucifixion. Behind him, an arched window soared. The stained-glass showed a resurrected Jesus, his punctured hands spread wide, a pleased smile on his face. When someone entered the office, they would see the pained Jesus first, then look up to find Poore standing before a welcoming Jesus in his glory.

More than one man had wept at the vision.

Poore set pen to paper. He, himself, would later cable the message to Thessalon. It would be an inspiring message, warning them of treachery, but promising glory to the diligent and faithful. Selected words, positioned carefully, would alert his Petrine Order agents in the city to suggest the creation of suicide bombers. In the urban confines, their impact would be magnified.

Poore delighted in the scratch of pen on paper. In it he could hear the whispers of God. God chose his words for him. God dictated the message. The people would hear that, and they would act accordingly.

All would be good, and his Kingdom of God would continue to unfold on Galatea.

ARONE
MAJISTAN, GALATEA

Morgan Kell opened his arms. "The thing of it is, Patriarch, I'm not *asking*, I'm telling. You have to order your people to do what I need done."

"What thou wouldst have me do, have them do—it is blasphemy!" Oltmann pressed a liver-spotted hand to his chest. "We are a godly people. We are here helping thee because it is righteous that we join this battle. What you demand is wrong. The ends cannot justify the means."

Father Donelly shook his head. "This will save lives, Patriarch."

"At the cost of imperiling souls." The old man shook his head adamantly. "It cannot be done."

Morgan sighed. He wanted to say a million things, but as he ran each through his head, Oltmann's objections answered each. Even the most basic question, "What would Jesus do?" would bring an impassioned denial that Jesus would go along with Morgan's plan.

Donelly frowned. "I guess, Patriarch, I'm not understanding how it is that you see your people shedding blood as somehow of a lesser offense to God than doing what Colonel Kell requires."

The old man looked up wearily. "Art thou blind? They have been seduced by a false prophet. We came to them. We asked them to renounce their error and return to the fold. They have refused. Moreover, they present a threat to others whom they can seduce into their apostasy."

"But Colonel Kell's plan will leave them alive, so they can rejoin you, be forgiven, and known communion with God again."

Oltmann shook his head. "But the method he would have us employ will open the door to the dark one. You, Colonel Kell, entertain the notion that two wrongs will make a right. It is just not so."

Morgan's eyes narrowed. "With all due respect, Patriarch, you are forgetting one thing."

"And that is?"

The mercenary pointed off toward Thessalon. "Your scenario holds up provided only one thing: that your men only kill those who are apostate. In the coming battle, that won't happen. They'll kill innocents right along with blasphemers. God may want the apostates dead, but Jesus, he'd want the innocents to have another chance. And, while the ends may not justify the means, Jesus *will* forgive the little sin. Which will it be, sir? A minor sin requiring repentance, or the blood of children on your people's hands? Which do you think Jesus would prefer?"

Oltmann's eyes grew hard. "You are bound to Hell, you know."

Morgan nodded.

"Then I pity the Devil when you get there." The Patriarch's shoulders slumped. "I shall do as you desire. May God have mercy on my soul."

CHAPTER 14

The sun had not even traced a line on the horizon when Morgan keyed his radio. "We go in as planned. No heroics. We do it exactly as briefed. Sections report in."

Positive reports flooded back through the radio, making Morgan smile despite the anxiety knotting his guts. Warfare wasn't a game, but it wasn't always won by the guy with the biggest army. That was especially true here, and not only because Morgan had a smaller force than the one he was facing. The assault on Thessalon not only would make martyrs of everyone within the city, but had the potential to cause an uproar that could sweep the Archon from her throne.

The political considerations bothered Morgan less than the reality on the ground. Many of the Thessalonians were true believers who would follow Bishop Poore to the gates of Hell and beyond. Given their already-demonstrated willingness to commit acts of terrorism and self-sacrifice, the only obvious way to pacify them would be to kill them all. Aside from not having enough bullets to do the job, Morgan found that alternative morally repugnant and as something that would lower him to Poore's level.

He'd come up with another plan which, if successfully executed, would kill very few people and resolve the problem. While mindful of von Moltke's dictum that "no plan survives first contact with the enemy," Morgan had minimized the risks to his unit, and had also prepared for all-out disaster.

The Kell Hounds had come to the plains southeast of Thessalon after dusk, but they lit their 'Mechs up as they maneuvered. The Fire company and light companies set up on an axis running southwest to northeast, facing the city. The Ultralytes set up parallel to the north-south main road, but behind Morgan's Fire company. They prevented a flank attack. Two lances of AgroMechs stood behind the light and Ultralytes companies, and his infantry ranged to the rear. If things went completely disastrously, the 'Mechs would retreat, and O'Cieran would get to slow down pursuit.

In response to the Kell Hounds' appearance on the battlefield, Thessalon's defenders began to react. Shadowy 'Mechs moved within city precincts, reinforcing the southeast quadrant. They didn't light themselves up, but mag-res scans provided a fair amount of data.

One of the humanoid 'Mechs did, indeed, appear to be a *Victor*. The heavy autocannon built into its right arm would deliver a lethal payload of depleted uranium shells to any of Morgan's 'Mechs. The closeness of urban fighting would put that pilot at a decided advantage, since the *Victor*'s optimal range was perfect for that kind of battle.

The rest of the 'Mechs proved to be a nice mix of mediums and lights, with a fair number of conversions tossed in. Morgan took heart in the nature of the movement on the other side. It indicated the commander was shifting troops from strong point to strong point instead of bringing his reserves up. Either he didn't have any reserves or was extremely reluctant to use them—both being useful datapoints.

Then, at midnight, the Kell Hounds doused their lights. Using mag-res and vis-light scans, they shuffled their forces again, moving around to the southwest. The Ultralytes moved the least, just crossing the main road, while the lights went from 4 on a clock to 8. Inside an hour they were set up again, and turned their lights on.

As maneuvers went, it wasn't much of a one, and hardly a secret to anyone with vis-light or mag-res scans going; but the Thessalonians reacted as if the Kell Hounds had teleported from one side of the battlefield to the other. Very quickly 'Mechs shifted from the southeast to southwest. They accomplished this maneuver more quickly than the Kell Hounds had because of the smaller distance they had to travel.

So, at two in the morning, the Kell Hounds doused their lights again. The Ultralytes once more crossed the road. Fire company, led by Morgan's lance of missile boats, cut back east and the Light company quickly looped back around behind them. Everyone maneuvered quickly and crisply, getting into position far more swiftly than before, and all in complete darkness.

Morgan keyed his radio. "We go *now*!"

The missile lance and the Ultralytes laid down a pattern of long and short range missiles that swept over the southeast minefields. Brilliant explosions lit the night, followed by secondary explosions as mines detonated. Into that fiery hellstorm came the two lances of AgroMechs assembled in Arone, pushing rollers before them and dragging wide arrays of disc-harrows. They marched down the line of torn earth, letting their trailing wings catch mines, live and dummy alike. The live mines exploded, mangling the farm equipment, but too far away to harm the AgroMechs. More importantly, the AgroMechs cut a vast swath through the minefield, allowing the Ultralytes to dart in quickly.

The Thessalonians reacted immediately. 'Mechs moved across the city toward the southeast, but Morgan and his people had already seen the routes they'd taken when moving previously. The mercenaries had been able to plot ranges and block out buildings that would offer cover in their holographic displays. Walter de Mesnil's lance, which featured 'Mechs equipped with autocannons and lasers, filled the gaps with ruby lanced of coherent light and angry swarms of hot metal.

The damage done was minimal in a material sense, but psychologically it was devastating. Inexperienced pilots found themselves suddenly vulnerable. Lights flashed in cockpits as armor melted or disintegrated. The pilots slowed, assessing damage, and in turn caused other 'Mechs to slow.

Veteran pilots shifted, moving deeper into the city to get around the kill zones, or turning right to advance and return fire. The incoming Ultralytes offered a bounty of targets, though their speed made hitting any one of them difficult. Trying to track a target while shooting down an alley between two buildings made the task that much more challenging.

The *Victor* pilot just smashed his 'Mech through a building, tracked and fired. The muzzle flash strobed the battlefield into a sharp chiaroscuro, with long shadows arrowing back away from Thessalon. He didn't even bother to shoot at an Ultralyte, but rather wisely picked out an AgroMech. The line of dense metal projectiles sliced through the 'Mech's left flank, severing both arm and leg.

Being the biggest 'Mech on the battlefield does has its advantages. The *Victor* was heavily armored and had ample firepower, but it made itself a target. Morgan's lance launched eighty missiles, delivering seventy percent on target. Fire blossomed all over the *Victor.* Glittering shards of shattered ferro-ceramic armor scattered like stardust. The massive humanoid 'Mech staggered back beneath the sheer ferocity of the assault.

Two of the missiles pounded through armor gaps and detonated within the 'Mech's chest cavity. Each nailed one of the gyros that transferred the pilot's sense of balance to the war machine. Dented cases and metal shrapnel shredded the gyros. This had the impact on the 'Mech that a liter of chugged vodka would have had on the pilot. Rubble caught the assault 'Mech at the heels and it flopped over backward, crushing yet more armor.

The *Victor's* demise was more than Morgan had expected. He was quite happy to see it gone from the battlefield because that eliminated the biggest threat to his Ultralytes as they finished their run into the city's edge. With them in place, the leaders of Thessalon realized how vulnerable their city was.

Thessalon's defenders had correctly taken heart in holding the high ground. They'd even built their strong points a block or two deep in the city, so any defenders fighting their way up the slope would still face stiff opposition. Their position had been all but unassailable.

The Ultralytes reached the edge of the plateau and instead of trying to assault the sheer side, just waited there. The Thessalonian strongholds could not direct fire onto them, since the Ultralytes were a good twenty meters below the plateau's lip. And any 'Mechs marched forward to shoot down at the Ultralytes would face long range fire, as had the *Victor*. Any attempt to come around from the west or east to drive the Ultralytes away would be vulnerable to attack by the Kell Hounds' other 'Mechs *and* the Ultralytes. Their ability to deliver heavy payloads of short range missiles put them in a perfect position to support an assault on the city's main entry-point.

Morgan hit the radio. "Major O'Cieran, send in the Saints."

It took five minutes, but a simple, black, horse-drawn cart started down the main road toward Thessalon. The Kell Hounds used spotlights to illuminate it. Two men—Patriarch Oltmann and a driver—rode under a white flag of truce. The horse, head bowed, wearing blinders, plodded down the road, curiously placid as it traversed a battlefield.

Morgan waited. If Oltmann was received, things would work. If the Thessalonians treated the truce flag has had their brothers to the northeast, then the battle would be back on. Morgan would make it fast and sharp, but the cost would be incalculable.

He resisted the temptation to open a private channel to his brother. Patrick's Ultralyte *Javelin* waited there, holding the western edge of the Ultralyte line. If they had to continue, Patrick's people would provide covering fire for the main assault. The Thessalonians would be forced to sweep them away, and the resulting carnage would leave too many men wounded and dying, trapped in twisted metal cages.

The carriage mounted the switchback. It moved so incredibly slowly, creating a shadow-puppet against the plateau's edge. Men appeared from the city, blocking the road above. They spoke with Oltmann, then the carriage disappeared into the city.

So far, so good. Morgan glanced at the chronometer in the cockpit. 2:43. How long would be long enough. Or too long? Ten minutes? Fifteen?

The grisly vision of the carriage returning with two headless bodies rolled through his mind. He didn't want to think the Thessalonians capable of that level of barbarity, but he couldn't put the warehouse in Ephaseus out of his mind. How people could do such a thing, especially in the name of a God who preached peace, love and forgiveness, he couldn't understand. It made no sense, but the centuries had proved rationality to be the least valued human trait when it came to warfare or religion.

The Christian message rejected violence—at least in general terms. The Men who created Churches seemed to find lots of wiggle-room in the fine print. *Fine print* they *created.* Interpretations might deliver the message in a more culturally relevant form for believers, but they also served political considerations as well and, as with Bishop Poore, became tainted with evil in the process.

Jesus shed his blood to redeem Mankind. Morgan looked out at Thessalon. *Let's hope we don't have to shed ours to redeem Thessalon.*

Then, there, finally, twenty minutes after it had disappeared, the carriage appeared at the top of the switchback. Morgan punched magnification into his holographic display. Oltmann was at the reins, which was the signal. The old man even appeared to be smiling, which Morgan took as a very good sign.

He hit his radio. "We have an agreement in place. A lance at a time, Ultralytes pull out. Everyone be ready. This won't be another Ephaseus. Move it, now, back to our starting lines."

A light blinked on his communications console. Morgan punched it. "Report."

"Our teams are in place." O'Cieran sounded pleased. "If this works, Colonel..."

"It'll work, Major. There's more than one way to fight a war." Morgan sighed. "Thank God for true believers."

PARADISE MOUNTAINS
MAJISTAN, GALATEA

Dawn found Bishop Poore sitting in his office. He'd been up for an hour, fully dressed, waiting for news from Thessalon. The Kell Hounds' delay in assaulting the city had annoyed him. It cost him valuable time, but it was not time he had wasted. It was, in fact, time he'd used to make an important realization, and the massacre of Thessalon would allow him to fully demonstrate his power to all who dared question him.

He'd sought the reason for the Kell Hound delay and it wasn't until he'd watched the sun set that he realized what was happening. Thessalon had not yet fallen because he had not yet wanted it to. Immediately he wondered why his desires would matter in such a thing, for he was just a man in this cosmic battle between good and evil.

A man, just as Jesus was a man.

So simple a concept, yet so profound in import. Jesus was man, but Jesus was also God. And God had promised His son would return. And so He had.

As Arlington Poore.

And, as a god, as *the* God, Poore's wishes were a command for reality. So, reluctantly, as God had let Jesus pass into death, so he, too, would allow his beloved Thessalon die.

Die, so I can raise it again as the capital of My kingdom. It all made perfect sense to him. Everything fit together. His upbringing. His fall from grace. His return. His betrayal by Oltmann. It was all perfect. Cites and scriptures to back and justify everything danced through his head. He'd gone immediately to his office to set down his thoughts for the benefit of future generations.

No one should have disturbed him there, but Sarah Thorndyke entered unbidden after timidly knocking on the door. She clutched a sheaf of papers. Her face had gone ashen, and clearly out of more than just fear of him. The other wives had sent her, knowing she would bare the brunt of his ire, but that they deemed things important enough to disturb him trickled worry through his middle.

Her eyes never rose to meet his. "For you, my Lord."

He came around from his desk and snatched the papers from her. Typescripts of messages from Thessalon. The Kell Hounds had attacked and done limited damage. They'd offered a truce, asking only that the Thessalonians do nothing to reinforce their positions while they consulted with him about their next step.

He glanced at the timestamp. The message had been sent at 3:10, but hadn't reached him until 6:15. It shouldn't have taken more than three minutes, much less three hours. He'd have cabled back immediately, shredding the truce and demanding an all-out assault on the mercenaries.

But what are the rest of these papers?

His mouth went dry as he read.

My Thessalonian Brethren,

The gift God hath given us today is great, all praise to His name. Patriarch Oltmann is my designated surrogate for the time I must spend away from thee. God is calling me to a very special mission. I am yours, as always, in fellowship and brotherhood.

Bishop Arlington Poore

Poore read the message again, then slapped Thorndyke with the papers. She spun down into a cringing, sobbing heap. Papers went flying, to drift down gently over her.

"What manner of trick is this? What have you done?"

"I did nothing. I did nothing." The woman hugged her knees to her chest.

Poore went to kick her, but motion at the door stopped him. A man appeared there, dressed in black with only his eyes visible.

Cold, lifeless eyes. He held a silenced pistol in his right hand, the barrel pointed unwaveringly at Poore.

Poore laughed. "Deluded fool. Do you think you can kill me? I *am* God." The bishop held a hand up and out before him. "Submit now, and I may let you live.

The first bullet blew through his hand. It struck Poore that the wound looked rather like stigmata. It seemed appropriate and he thought he would lift the other hand to get a similar wound, but the world began to dim. That's when he realized that his hand had not stopped the bullet, and that the piece of metal had punctured his chest. It opened his aorta, gushing hot blood into his thoracic cavity, and causing a traumatic crashing of his blood pressure.

That first wound would have been enough to kill him, but Frost sent another bullet through his skull. Brains and blood splashed over the stained glass window.

As Poore fell to the floor, Jesus shed red tears.

CHAPTER 15

Morgan smiled as Father Donnelly finished reading Frost's report. The priest looked from one Kell brother to the other, then set the report on the table in front of his chair.

The priest interlaced his fingers. "Rather spare, but lurid in some details."

Patrick nodded. "Almost a footnote his relating how he pulled Colonel Thorndyke out of there."

Donnelly arched an eyebrow. "No doubt then that Bishop Poore has been called home."

Morgan shook his head. "And with Patriarch Oltmann traveling to Paradise Mountains to take possession of the stronghold, there will be no evidence to the contrary, either."

"That would be good." The priest frowned. "When you called me here, I was under the impression there was a theological question you had in mind. Then you hand me Frost's report."

"There is, Father." Morgan stood and stretched, feeling cramped in the offices which had been given over to house the Kell Hounds. "It has to do with going to Hell."

The priest tapped a finger against the report. "Poore, I shall assume, is burning already. Mr. Frost, I'm afraid, has long since been lost. If you wonder about Poore's demise accruing to your souls because you gave the order to kill, then perhaps the sacrament of reconciliation would be in order."

Morgan glanced at his little brother, then shook his head. "If you deem that worthy of a confession, I'll consider it, but that wasn't what we were wondering. It was the Saints, and what we asked them to do."

Donnelly brushed a hand over his unshaven jawline. "That is an interesting question."

While the 'Mechs had drawn Thessalon's defenders to the southeast, a squad of O'Cieran's soldiers led thirty of the Saints up the embankment on Thessalon's north side. When the attack began, they slipped into the city and took up hiding places. Since they looked like every other one of the Majii, hiding wasn't too difficult. They quickly spread out and shortly after dawn started pointing to the sky. Each described the same vision of Bishop Poore being bodily lifted into Heaven and being embraced by Jesus.

At the same time, the counterfeit message the Kell Hounds had sent into Thessalon from Bishop Poore started to leak. Rumors met and merged, then ran rampant. The story became embellished to the point where Poore already had wings and a halo and welcomed by the Archangels on bended knee. Had the Majii been a more boisterous people Morgan would have expected visions of Poore being paraded around on the shoulders of the Apostles.

Donnelly opened his hands. "Well, boys, you did go and uses a people's faith against them. Now, back in the day, various saints did that to convert the pagans. St. Patrick picked a shamrock not just because it was three leaves but one plant. The pagan Irish were used to triune gods, so the example worked for them. Heavens, even a couple of the pantheon made it into Christianity as saints—and we'll not be arguing if the gods themselves converted, or it was a merging of tales."

Patrick frowned. "But in that case, Father, you had their beliefs being used to save their souls. We did nothing of the kind. We might have saved their lives, but we also saved ours."

"Let's not be too harsh, Patrick." Donnelly smiled impishly. "Not to make light of what you did, but the people of Thessalon had strayed into idolatry. You facilitated their returning to a Christian path. But I'd go a bit further. There always has been a recurring thread within Christianity that suggests that without saving the body, you can't save the soul. People dying while apostate would be bound to Hell; so in saving their lives, you saved their souls as well. That you also saved your friends from dying is laudable."

The priest turned to face Morgan. "I'd be betting you're wondering if putting pressure on the Patriarch to accept all this is a sin, then?"

Morgan shook his head slowly, folding his arms over his chest. "It's a bet you'd lose."

"Tell me, then."

"When we first met, you mentioned an old bromide: there's no atheists in a foxhole." Morgan's eyes narrowed. "I'm thinking there should be nothing but. The pilot of that *Victor* is wandering around giving God praise for his delivery from certain death, somehow forgetting it was God that put him in that position to get shot at."

"But it wasn't, Morgan." Patrick waved away his argument. "It was Poore."

"But Poore was God's agent." Morgan pointed a finger at the priest. "And don't try to tell me that Poore appointed himself, and that God had nothing to do with it. If you go down that road you end up with either God being an unfeeling sociopath that's willing to let those who believe in him go to horrible deaths simply because He won't rid Himself of a false prophet. If He'd done to Poore what He did to Sodom and Gomorrah, a lot more of His believers would be alive today."

The priest nodded solemnly. "You had an *either* there. The 'or' is that there's no God at all?"

"You see another alternative?"

"I see a God who takes very seriously the gift of free will. He allows us to make mistakes."

"Even if those mistakes will doom people to Hell?"

Donnelly shrugged. "I'll not be presuming to know God's mind, Morgan, but I am always mindful of His ability to forgive. We know we will be judged, but He can forgive us when we make a mistake. If one of Poore's followers truly believed he was doing God's work, believed it with every fiber of his being, then God might well forgive him. If he had doubt, even the tiniest shred, and still followed Poore, then the story might be different."

"I hear what you're saying, Father, but..." Morgan shook his head. "What was done at Ephaseus, what they were willing to do here, and what the terrorists did in Galaport, none of that was right. And the bitch of it is that even our actions were coerced by a false prophet that God could have eliminated."

The priest stood and laid a hand on Morgan's shoulder. "You're human, Morgan. You're not the first man to have a crisis of faith or wonder why he couldn't understand the workings of the Divine mind. Don't try. God doesn't need you to try. What He wants is for you to just be a man, so try that. Have a drink. Have two. Go do anything else you need to do to remind yourself that you're human. It's okay. You may not understand God, but He understands you. And he'll forgive."

"I hope you're right, Father." Morgan sighed far too wearily for a man of his age. "We'll be sending a lot more people on to judgment, I think, and if He's not in a forgiving mood, I'll spend eternity staring eyeball to eyeball with Arlington Poore. And if that's not your idea of Hell, I can't imagine what would be."

A CLEVER BIT OF FICTION

CHAPTER 1

THE NAGELRING
DISTRICT OF DONEGAL, THARKAD
LYRAN COMMONWEALTH
15 NOVEMBER 3010

Morgan Kell stood on the outer wall of the Nagelring, staring off at the mountains. Winds whipped snow into tattered sheets, letting black rock peek through. Exposed stone glittered with sharp glassy edges as if it had been flaked into a spear point, then another blanket of white would hide it.

He smiled. *Has it been six years?* "My mates and I used to come to this very spot, Veronica, and stare up at those mountains. We'd vow we were going to climb to the very top, no matter the conditions. That a dozen people a year die in such attempts didn't put us off in the least."

As he spoke, the wind whipped breath vapor away and nipped at his cheeks. "Isn't it beautiful?"

"Mmmmphf."

He turned and smiled more broadly, despite the numbness in his face. Veronica Matova shivered beside him. The fur-edged hood had been pulled tight, and a scarf enveloped her face, leaving only her blue eyes visible. The down parka bulked her out, but still could not conceal the tremors shaking her slender body. Her hands hid in a furred muff, and the cast on her left foot had been swathed in a quilted boot.

"I'm sorry, darling. You come from Galatea. You must be freezing."

Her eyes bobbed up and down.

Morgan laughed, and with an arm around her shoulder, steered her to the nearest tower. He preceded her down the iron staircase and had to admit the frigidity of the railing *was* bleeding up through his gloves.

At the tower's base, he ushered her into the main building, and slid her hood back. She shook her head once, freeing a cascade of golden hair, but still said nothing.

He slipped the blue scarf down. "Your tongue can't be frozen." His smile returned. "But, you know, if it is...I can think of a way to warm it up."

Veronica pulled her scarf back up over her nose. "If it was frozen, Morgan Kell, it would be entirely your fault. Rewarding you with a kiss is not something I would do."

"Reward? I sought no reward." Morgan shook his head solemnly. "I merely was thinking of the medicinal value of a kiss..."

"Nice try, soldier-boy. But look, in the future, when I say, 'No, I really don't want to go outside,' take me at my word, okay?" She pulled her hands out of the muff, let oversized mittens fall off, and revealed gloved hands beneath. "I am in, count them, *four* layers, and I'm still cold."

"I'd love to count the layers, one by one..."

Veronica rolled her eyes. "You are so hot-blooded..."

"That's why you love me?"

"Do I?"

"Don't you?"

"Should I? 'Come with me, Veronica, see the Commonwealth and *freeze.*'"

Morgan slipped his arms around her and pulled her close. "I believe I offered other inducements."

"This is not a time for logic, Morgan."

"Oh, right, it's all about you."

"Exactly." Her eyes flashed warmly and a finger tugged the scarf down to her chin. "I'm cold, and I can't help it unless, you know, I load up on potato pancakes and become a heifer like—"

Morgan pressed a finger to her lips. "Ahem, let's not speak ill of our hosts."

Veronica had observed, as they came in system and watched holovision broadcasts, that the image of feminine beauty suggested by the programs was of someone on the stouter side. When Morgan had come to the Nagelring, that had taken a bit of getting used to, but the female cadets in the Lyran Commonwealth's state military academy were athletic. Other women tended to be softer and curvier, which— according to popular legend and song—made those long winter nights just that much warmer.

"You're right, of course. It is cold here. I don't notice it because..."

"Because you're a man, and you wouldn't allow yourself to admit it under threat of torture?"

He raised an eyebrow. "That not withstanding, I spent a lot of time here in school. We'd march along those walls keeping watch.

We'd drill in those mountains. I mentioned people getting lost up there—we'd help find them."

"I understand that." She squeezed his arm. "And I understand that people love the snow. They love skiing and ski-trekking. *I* like the idea of *having* skied; and sitting down with a hot toddy in front of a blazing fire."

He shook his head.

"And don't get me wrong, Morgan, I love that you want to show me the Nagelring. That it was such a big part of your life makes it important to me as well." She smiled softly and looked down the long hallways festooned with portraits and plaques, with rooms named after battles, famed 'Mechs and legendary warriors. "I can feel the history here; and you know I appreciate it. Even on Galatea, the Nagelring is a name that conjures wonder. If you're betting on a fight, you'd feel more confident if the fighter was a Nagelring graduate. If a mercenary company comes recruiting, the N-grads always went first, and you'd expect to see the company again if it was run by N-grads. Grads like you and your brother."

Morgan took her by the elbow and led her down one hallway. Twenty meters along, a break in the wall opened into a large atrium. Eight meters below them, Steiner Hall's lobby glowed with the light of the setting sun.

He led her down a set of stairs and to a big trophy cases. "Look there."

"Class of '04, first in your class." She gave him a small kiss on his cheek, helping warm it considerably.

"And my cumulative cadet score there, 905.3. Check them all before that. No one had ever hit that high on the CCS."

She glanced at the name. "Nor since."

"Yeah, but look at '09."

"Patrick Kell, 905.291." Veronica raised an eyebrow. "Well matched, the Kell brothers."

Morgan shook his head. "You look at all the scores that went into that number, and Patrick smoked me fair and square."

"But how...?"

"He took an elective his last year. Music. Classical Guitar. Scored a 1.8 in it. Brought him down to 905.291."

Veronica's eyes narrowed. "He did it deliberately."

"He's played the guitar since he was four. He won a planetary competition on Arc-Royal when he was ten. His ability to play was noted as a positive for selection to the Nagelring." Morgan took her hand in his and squeezed. "I know you had brothers and sisters, but I only had my brother. I knew he looked up to me when we were grow-ing up, but he was my kid brother. You expect that; but when I heard about this, well...I mean, I'm proud of what I accomplished here but..."

Veronica smiled at him. "You're very lucky your brother loves you so much. And he's lucky you love him so much. Shhhhh, no macho posturing. I was there when you heard he was hurt in the Majii raid. Nothing will erase the memory of the abject horror on your face."

Morgan kissed the finger she'd pressed to his lips. "You know that same look appeared on my face when I heard you'd been injured."

"Thank you." She squeezed his hand. "What else, my dear, did you wish to show me?"

"We could look at my dorm room."

"Oh, I bet *that* line warmed the heart of many a lass during your time here."

Morgan laughed. "Easy way to get tossed. Not to say some didn't risk it, but the honor system didn't reward it."

"You weren't allowed to have fun?"

"We were, but only certain kinds of fun." They strolled from the lobby to a ramp leading down to the network of tunnels that criss-crossed the campus. "Everyone here was training to be an officer and, yes—no wisecracks—a gentleman. Basically everything was about trust. To be a good officer you have to follow orders, and others have to trust that you'll keep your word. No army can function if each commander decides to go his own way. And I have to trust that when someone says his unit is covering my flank, it actually is. If cadets can't foster that sort of trust, if they're going to put themselves ahead of everyone else for a little huffing-and-puffing, they can't be trusted when beams flash and shells fly."

"I can understand that. This honor code, it prohibited you from lying?"

"Oh yeah, seriously."

She stopped, tugging on his hand. "So then, Cadet Kell, answer me this question. Truthfully."

"Yes?"

"Do you want to kiss me?"

Morgan smiled. "I think you know the answer to that."

He very much wanted to kiss her. He'd known her less than a month and had wanted to do much more than just kiss her, but kisses had sufficed while on Galatea. On the flight to Tharkad, with multiple jumps taking place rather quickly, Veronica discovered she did not handle hyperspace jumps at all well. While they had spent a great deal of time together on the journey in, passion had taken a backseat to practicality.

Curiously enough, while part of him found the situation utterly frustrating, he was glad for it. Morgan had, in his time at the Nagelring and since, enjoyed the carnal pleasures. His longest relationship had been for six months and ended only because of circumstances beyond his control. He didn't know if that had been love or not. He'd thought so, he'd hoped, but it all seemed so dreamlike now that he couldn't be certain if it was, or if he had just wanted it to be.

With Veronica, things had been different. The attraction had been there from the first moment he'd met her. He couldn't hide it, and neither could she. Veronica fought it, however, and the problems on Galatea had separated them right at the point when they would have consummated their relationship.

Consummated it prematurely. That judgment surprised Morgan, but it was as important as it was accurate. Veronica might allow him access to her body, but he wanted more. While she was beautiful— even though the parka hid her physical charms completely—it was her nature, her spirit, that drew him to her. He didn't think he wanted to save her; he just wanted to know her.

She reached out and hooked a gloved hand behind his neck. "Then I think you should kiss me."

Morgan resisted for a heartbeat, then let her pull him to her. He slipped his arms past her sides, then pressed her back against the wall with his body. He trapped her with his chest and hips, then kissed her fiercely and hard. His tongue flicked, her lips parted, and the kiss deepened.

Her arms closed behind his neck and her hips ground against his.

Morgan pulled back, gasping.

Her eyes smoldered as she wiped her mouth on the back of a glove. "Did you learn that here?"

"That was my point-three."

She smiled and, darting her head forward, kissed him quickly. "I'm glad you studied hard. Now you'll show me where?"

"Yes." Morgan slipped a hand into hers again. They passed through the labyrinth and emerged in the basement of a dorm. Climbing the stairs to the third floor, then turned right and came to room 317.

Veronica arched a perfect eyebrow. "Rather rustic."

Morgan laughed. The room wasn't much to speak of. A simple square with two built-in hutches, a table and two cots, it was to a luxury hotel room what a potted plant was to a forest. The mattresses had been rolled up, revealing a spring and wire frame, the mere appearance of which made Morgan's back ache.

"It's not exactly the Nova Royale, but all we did in here was study and sleep. Too much of one, not enough of the other. You can see, given the accommodations, why smuggling a girl in would have been less than thrilling."

"I don't know. Table, bed, floor, wall, hutch...I *know* you have an imagination, Morgan." She glanced at the door. "All you'd have to do is to slip inside, close the door and..."

"And wait for holovid reporters to swarm the place." Morgan shook his head. "My brother and I may only be cousins of the Archon's late husband, but Allessandro Steiner would have used any misdeed on our parts to pillory Katrina. Lucky for her, her daughter Melissa is a truly beautiful child. Whenever there is trouble, some reporter gets a chance to holo the child in action, and the news cycle is knocked off-kilter."

"The Archon is a smart woman." Veronica nodded. "I remember fearing she'd been killed back in '05 when she disappeared."

"Yeah, we all were." Morgan waved a hand at the room. "But there it is, my dear. I spent my last year at The Nagelring in here. My roommate smuggled a girl in once. I stayed at the library."

"Co-conspirator or guarding against disaster?"

"The latter. Chauncy Wittenberg and I were not friends, and roomed together only because no one else would have him as a roommate."

"How'd you draw the short straw?"

Morgan shrugged. "He had great potential. A natural with a 'Mech, but a horror with people. Plebes get hazed in their first year here, and Chauncy was a true terror. Lots of reasons for it, I guess. I'm not a shrink, but I figured he was grossly insecure, and picked on anyone showing flaws he figured he had himself."

She smiled. "You realized that 'acting out to compensate for and cover gross insecurities' is probably the most common diagnosis around?"

"Yeah, true. But I thought he could be turned around."

"And?"

Morgan shook his head. "I tried. I tried to get him to ease off. I tried to get him to feel good about himself, but he never dared change. He was comfortable with himself—or, at least, more comfortable being an ass than he would have been making a change. But he knew he was broken. The pressure, especially as he began to get poor marks on leadership evaluations, got to him."

He pointed to a round plaster patch near the light fixture. "Two weeks after he'd had the girl in, he told me she was coming back. She wasn't. He sunk an eye-hook into the ceiling and hung himself. Probably would have died, too, if I'd not come back to tell him how bad he was screwing up."

Veronica hugged him tightly.

"I cut him down, revived him. Medics took him away, but he glared at me. Hated me."

"Oh, Morgan, I'm so sorry." She kissed his ear. "What happened to him?"

"Don't know. He didn't graduate with us. Honorable discharge from the service—it was all hushed up, since you can't have folks trying to off themselves here."

Veronica pulled back and took his cheeks in both her hands. "No matter where he is today, it's better off than in the ground."

"I'm sure you're right." Morgan gave her a quick kiss. "But that was a long time ago and, to be frank, I've not thought of Chauncy since I left here."

"Nor should you think of him now." She smiled and took his hands in hers. "And if you finish this tour without my dying of hypothermia, I think we can shape some new memories that will smother the old."

CHAPTER 2

Gasping for air, Patrick Kell flopped over onto his back. Sweat stung his eyes and the sheets sought to entangle his legs. "Oh my God."

Tisha Hamilton rolled up on her side and draped an arm over his chest. "Me, too."

Patrick kissed her on the forehead. "You are fantastic."

"You're not half-bad yourself." She nipped his shoulder. "How's your leg?"

"It's fine. Not even a twinge." He stared up at the ceiling and shivered. He'd seen the mural up there before, all cherubs and fawns—classical stuff on the fables of Terra—but until that second he hadn't attached any significance to where he was. "Oh my God."

Tisha's eyes narrowed. "That sounded different."

"It just hit me. We're in the Archon's Palace."

"Uh-huh." She nodded. "Walking past the guards kind of tipped me off to that, Patrick. Were you afraid we were too loud, would wake the baby?"

"Melissa? No." Patrick reached down behind Tisha and pulled the sheet up. "I just didn't think, you know..."

"I'm sure people have made love here before, you know. Melissa being prime proof of that."

"It's not that."

She shifted, coming up on her elbows. "Patrick Kell, you are *intimidated!*"

"I am not."

"*Yes*, you *are*." She laughed, her black hair slipping down to veil her face. "You spend your life in the cockpit of a ten-meter tall war machine, but staying in your cousin's home scares you. I mean, you're acting as if someone's going to break into this room, find us, and we're going to get into trouble."

"Don't you feel like that?"

Blue eyes flashed behind the veil. "Well...okay, *yes*. Not that the prospect doesn't add some spice to things." She plucked at the sheets. "I do like seeing my taxes well spent."

Patrick pulled himself up against the padded headboard. In keeping with the mural, ornate furnishings filled the suite, with lots of gold leaf and Steiner blue. There didn't seem to be a straight edge anywhere. Had things not been so brightly decorated, the very weight of the items would have been depressing.

"I know, I mean, I've known the Archon is my cousin—by marriage, not by blood—but Morgan knows her so much better than I do. He and Arthur were closer, I was always just the kid brother. Not that that was a bad thing, but sometimes it hits me. *The Archon*! I mean, they don't come any bigger. And for the Lyran Commonwealth to have hired us for our first mission as a mercenary unit, well, some folks might put it down to our ties with Katrina, but it's still a big deal."

"No doubt about that. But, then again, that die was cast on Galatea." Tisha swept her hair out of her face. "She had to reward your effort."

Patrick nodded. "You're right, darling. I guess part of me expected it, but a bigger part is just awestruck."

Tisha slowly gathered a sheet around herself. "And how do you think I feel? I'm a grease-monkey from a desert planet that couldn't have picked Tharkad out of a constellation. Here I am, in the palace, tucked into bed with the most handsome mercenary in the Inner Sphere. Now, a month ago if someone told me I'd be here..."

"That's two of us." Patrick kissed her again, fully on the lips, letting the kiss linger. "Thank you for coming with us."

Tisha pulled back and stared into Patrick's brown eyes. "Understand something, Colonel Kell. A month ago I met a man who shares my passions, who saved my life, and who has entrusted his life to my talents. That would be you. In case you hadn't noticed, I care a great deal for you. I've no intention of turning down any opportunity to spend time with you. Long distance relationships—especially when that distance is measured in light-years—just don't work."

He started to lean in to kiss her again, but she stopped him with a hand to the middle of his chest. "When you got wounded and I heard about it, my heart flip-flopped. I wanted to run to you, and I wanted to run away from you. But caring for someone means being vulnerable, and I accept that. It's a risk I'm willing to run, because having you in my life is worth it."

She raised an eyebrow. "*Now* you can kiss me."

He laughed, and did as she suggested.

She encouraged him to continue.
He did.

Patrick somehow kept from blushing as Tisha and he met Morgan and Veronica in line for the State Banquet. "Had a fun day?"

Morgan smiled, but let Veronica answer. "The Nagelring is a fascinating historical site, both for the Commonwealth, and the Kells. I saw as many awards there with your name on them as I did your brother's."

"You must have missed a couple, then." Patrick smiled and gave Tisha's hand a squeeze. Both Kell brothers wore dress uniforms marking them as Nagelring graduates. Dark blue, trimmed in grey, the only concessions they made to commanding a mercenary company were their rank insignia and silver gorgets emblazoned with the unit's hound-head crest.

Tisha had opted for a simple sleeveless black gown with a high neck and plunging backline. Platinum earrings matched a necklace which ended with an oval similarly emblazoned with the Kell Hound crest. She looked utterly stunning in it, but her hand communicated her nervousness. She'd never worn so elegant a gown, and would never had worn one so daring, save that Veronica suggested it.

The suggestion had worked, but not because the women had become fast friends. Veronica intimidated Tisha—*heck, she intimidates me*—but Tisha wasn't one to back down in the face of her fears. She accepted the suggestion as a challenge, and solicited Veronica's further advice as they came in-system to have the gown made up.

Though she had last-second misgivings, she'd pulled it on and sighed, "No one will notice me anyway."

That comment wasn't wholly true, for Patrick only had eyes for her. Still, he had to acknowledge that Veronica had pretty much every other pair of eyes in the place locked on her. Tall and gorgeous, she'd chosen a light, Steiner-blue gown with a backline that dipped below her waist, and a neckline that reached her navel. Her hair had been pulled up and was held in place by two platinum sticks, each set with a sapphire. Sapphire earrings and a large sapphire ring completed her raiment, making her an icy vision of beauty.

It didn't hurt that she looked even more beautiful on his brother's arm. Some men—most men—seem oddly ill at ease with a beautiful woman as their companion. In unguarded moments their expressions pass between gloating over the fact that they have her and other's don't; and timid acknowledgement that she is so far out of their league that they expect her to bolt at the first opportunity. That hedge against hurt always undercut the image they sought to project, increasing the chances that she would run.

Morgan showed none of that. His smile remained as wide as always, and though some might read it as a challenge, they also had to see it was genuine. Veronica wasn't a possession. She wasn't a prize to be won or lost, but a friend and companion. By choosing to see her that way, he abandoned fear, exuding only confidence.

The same confidence that fuels him in combat.

Together, tall, handsome, and confident, Morgan and Veronica commanded attention.

Veronica smiled at Patrick's comment. "If I missed any, it was because your brother hid them from me. And he was trying to show me everything."

Morgan winked. "Trying to keep her moving so she'd not freeze."

Patrick raised an eyebrow. "If you're cold, how can you wear..."

"...this gown?" She laughed throatily. "As Tisha can tell you, having to be dressed like this, in heels, never is comfortable. Enduring cold is nothing compared to an evening in these shoes."

Tisha nodded. "Are you going to be okay? Your ankle."

Morgan frowned. "Shot with painkillers, taped, and she will be leaning heavily on my arm all night, then back into the cast."

Veronica kissed him on the cheek as they shuffled closer to the Grand Ballroom. "He even threatened to carry me back to our rooms."

"No dancing." Morgan gave her a stern look, which Veronica returned quickly and coldly.

"That's too bad." Tisha raised Patrick's hand and kissed the back of it. "I was going to offer you Patrick's services. He's light on my feet."

"Hey!" Patrick had already caught strains of a string quartet. "I doubt they're going to be playing our kind of music anyway."

"I am more versatile, Patrick Kell." Tisha smiled playfully. "We'll see how many steps you know after dinner."

Morgan laughed. "I knew there was a reason I liked you, Ms. Hamilton. Aside from how you wield a spanner."

Functionaries of the Ministry of Protocol approached them. One smiled unctuously. "Welcome to the Commonwealth Palace. We will be announcing you this evening. Full ranks and honors..."

Tisha stiffened.

Morgan shook his head. "That won't be necessary."

The official's smile soured. "I'm afraid you don't understand, Colonel."

"No, I understand perfectly." Morgan slipped a hand inside his jacket and produced a folded slip of paper. "It's unnecessary."

The clerk took the paper, unfolded it, and his jaw dropped. "I see, sir."

Morgan recovered the paper, folded it up again and put it away. "I am Morgan Kell, this is Veronica Matova. My brother, Patrick Kell, is escorting Leticia Hamilton."

The man made hasty notes. "You do understand, sir, that everyone else—"

"—is dying of boredom as people are announced, yes."

"Very good, sir. Thank you, sir." The man bowed and withdrew, scurrying off to the head of the line.

"Morgan, what's on that paper?"

The elder Kell smiled at his brother. "It's a little keepsake, courtesy of the Archon. She's under the impression she owes me a favor."

He looked at the two women. "I hope you don't mind our foregoing titles and ranks. I know warriors who've gotten promotions while waiting to get from here to there, it takes so long."

Tisha shook her head. "I don't mind. I'm nobody."

Veronica reached out and caught Tisha's jaw in a hand. "Don't *ever* say that. You look around at all these people. You listen to their titles. You ask yourself, which one of them would be worth a bucket of warm spit on a battlefield. Most of them don't bathe themselves. They can't feed themselves and can barely dress themselves. They may have inherited power, wealth and position, but what have they done, what *could* they do, to make life better for others? Little or nothing, and those who might are seldom inclined to even try."

Tisha nodded, her bright eyes narrowing. "Thank you, Veronica."

"One more thing, Tisha. There will be people in there who are going to judge the both of us. *All* of us. And they only win if you let their judgment get to you. But, you know, they aren't aware we exist before we get announced, and they won't remember us two minutes after we are. Their judgment means nothing."

"I'll remember that."

"You can do more." Veronica smiled at Morgan. "They've got no right to judge you, so don't let them. Let them know they're being rude. Meet artificiality with sincerity. Dance up a storm and laugh, the way they would never let themselves in a million years. Live. Have fun. It will bug the hell out of them for a good long time."

Tisha sighed loudly. "Is challenging me going to be a continual thing with you?"

Veronica's feline smile sufficed as an answer.

The quartet reached the door. The senior protocol official looked at the card he'd been handed, then nodded. *Is he hiding a smile?* He waved them forward to the edge of a broad staircase leading down to a floor filled with the Archon's guests. A receiving line stretched from the base of the stairs around to where the string quartet was playing. A dozen chandeliers, all dripping with cut-crystals, gaily illuminated the party. Light glinted from jewelry, sequins and medals of the few people on the dance floor.

The Ministry official banged a staff on the floor. "I present Morgan Kell and Veronica Matova; Patrick Kell and Leticia Hamilton."

Oh, I get it now. The introduction had its intended effect. Its brevity caught attention. People turned to watch them descend, wondering who they were. They might be nobodies, but then, how would they have been invited? And if they weren't...A couple people mouthed the name "Kell," as if by repeating it to themselves they could jog their memories. Then a few of them got it, and leaned over to tell friends who these guests were.

Patrick smiled. His brother wanted people to work at remembering them. And he wanted to challenge them. Rank meant so much that to eschew it caused people to wonder why you were confident enough to do that. They had to wonder why it meant nothing to them. Being free enough not to care about rank could even strike fear into some hearts, because it meant the brothers were not going to be controlled by offers of rank, or threats to whatever rank they already held.

He looked over at Morgan. "How long did it take you to figure all that out?"

Morgan smiled, despite the question having no context and less meaning. "Less time than you'd think. We can discuss it later."

The brothers led their guests to the receiving line and began to work their way through it. Limp handshakes and lukewarm "Pleased to meet yous" were repeated ritually. Many of the honored guests made an attempt to be sincere, but these were mostly people like scientists and artists who felt even less at home than Patrick did amid the crush of royalty. Nobles, even those who ranked below Patrick, treated him with disdain. Mercenaries, like the General leading the Dry River Devils, paid him little mind.

The Archon's reception made up for all of it.

Katrina Steiner's very nature made her striking. Tall and slender, with silver-grey eyes that blazed with more life than could be found on even the most populous world, she met Patrick's hand with a strong grip. "Patrick, so good to see you. I apologize for not having been able..."

Patrick smiled. "I understand. You've been working."

The Archon laughed. "You've always been too forgiving, Patrick. That is your only fault. And this must be the charming Ms. Hamilton, of whom I have had good reports."

Tisha blinked and shook the Archon's hand. "You exaggerate, Highness."

"Actually, I don't. My security people prepared a full dossier. Even your enemies say good things about you. You're a rare quantity, especially in this room."

Patrick rested his hand on the small of Tisha's back. "More rare than you can imagine, Katrina."

"I'm sure." Katrina released Tisha's hand, then opened her arms wide. "Morgan Kell!"

Morgan swept the Archon up in a hug which started a hissing round of *tsking*, but which neither of them evidently noticed. "Katrina, you're looking wonderful, as always. The picture of health."

"You're a good enough liar, I almost believe you." Katrina brushed a wisp of blonde hair from her face. "More white there than blonde, if I didn't deal with it. That's a state secret, by the way."

Morgan released her, then drew Veronica forward. "Katrina, this is Veronica Matova. Veronica, this is the Archon."

Veronica offered her hand. "This is an honor."

Katrina gave the other woman a quick once-over, then took her hand and shook it. "The pleasure is all mine. I trust you are finding your accommodations suitable?"

"Opulent, Highness."

Before Patrick could figure out if Katrina was actually acting cold toward Veronica, a voice boomed from the end of the receiving line. "So this is the Morgan Kell you've been going on about?"

A large man, with a long nose and longer face, shouldered Patrick aside. "I don't believe, Katrina, he's nearly as tough as you think he is."

"You would be mistaken." Katrina smiled at the interloper. "But then, Prince Davion, that would hardly be a first for you, would it?"

CHAPTER 3

THE TRIAL
DISTRICT OF DONEGAL, THARKAD
LYRAN COMMONWEALTH
15 NOVEMBER 3010

Morgan Kell smiled easily. "The judgment of the man who won the third Battle of Harrow's Sun shouldn't be easily dismissed."

Patrick, annoyance flashing on his face, added, "Even if that was *eight* years ago.

The Prince eyed Patrick. "And that would have been years before you entered the Nagelring, wouldn't it, pup?"

"Meaning I've had the chance to learn from your experience, *Highness.*"

The Davion leader studied the younger Kell for a moment, his eyes tightening. Then an eyebrow arched up, and the prince snorted before facing Morgan. "Younger brothers are so alike, don't you think?"

"For your sake, Highness, I hope not." Morgan rested a hand on Patrick's shoulder. His brother fairly vibrated with anger. "If your younger brother—Hanse, isn't it?—pushes you as much as Patrick does me, you have a rough life. It's difficult when they're better than you are."

Patrick frowned. "Morgan, don't—"

"No, pup, let him continue." Ian Davion nodded. "Your brother is a wise man, if he recognizes what you won't allow yourself to see. You have fire, no doubt, and I would imagine some steel to your spine. Lord knows, the two of you have stones the size—"

Katrina cleared her voice. "I do believe we ought to avoid vulgarities this evening."

Morgan nodded. "And hostilities."

The Prince raised his hands in mock surrender. "I'm just pleased to see that the flower of Steiner youth continues the proud martial tradition of the Lyran Commonwealth. Frankly, it's the threat of your might which reduces Capellan adventurism."

Patrick smiled curtly. "We live to serve."

The Prince laughed. "So like my brother. You and I, Patrick Kell, will never get along. That's good. Leaders seldom do."

"Morgan leads the Hounds, Highness."

"So I've been told. We shall have to speak more on that." The prince lowered his voice. "When we will not make such a spectacle of our speaking."

"I look forward to it, Highness." Morgan offered the man his hand. They shook, then the Kells moved off so the receiving line could continue. In no time at all they sank into anonymity, swallowed by a crowd of people who forgot them as soon as they passed.

Patrick rubbed at his forehead. "I'm sorry, Morgan. I don't know what got into me."

"You know better than that, Patrick." Morgan looped a hand around the back of Patrick's neck and pulled him into a hug. "It's that family pride. *And* your upset at being shouldered aside."

Tisha snorted. "The oaf."

Morgan shook his head. "He was playing at that. No doubt he's prickly and arrogant—who among the Davions is not? He chose to ignore Patrick to see how the both of us would react. He's constantly testing, pushing. He's not a diplomat, just a warrior. That can make him fierce in combat, but means a throne will chafe his butt."

"I'd be happy to kick it."

Morgan laughed, and the women joined him. "I'm sure you would, but that means you missed the high compliment he paid you. He likened you to his brother. Hanse Davion is no slouch, and for the man who knows him best to make that connection shouldn't be taken lightly."

"Does that mean I can't kick his butt?"

The elder Kell sighed. "If the Davions ever invade the Commonwealth—or another client state we're working for—you'll have that chance. Succeeding, on the other hand..."

Patrick nodded. "I know. I *did* study the third battle of Harrow's Sun. The Prince should have died about forty-seven times there."

"More lives than a sackful of cats."

Veronica stroked Morgan's arm. "Luck has a nasty way of running out the moment you depend on it."

"Which is why we Kells believe, my dear, that you make your own luck."

Patrick nodded. "It's the residue of hard work."

Tisha hooked her hand through the crook of Patrick's arm. "I've been working hard. Am I lucky enough to get a dance before dinner?"

"My pleasure." Patrick's expression brightened. "If you'll excuse us."

"Have fun." Morgan took Veronica's hand in his. "You're being quiet."

"Just observing."

"Care to share?"

She smiled and pulled closer to him, kissing his cheek. "Your read of the prince is accurate, save for perhaps one thing."

"Yes?"

"He already knows he's not the right man for the throne. He took over out of obligation when his father died, but he's more content to be a warlord than a ruling Prince. He knows enough to realize this, but working around it isn't something he's able to do."

"He could abdicate in favor of his brother."

"Would you?"

Morgan gave her hand a squeeze. "At the drop of a hat. I trust my brother."

"I don't think Prince Ian is at that point with Hanse yet. That's why he keeps him out there fighting, too, to make sure Hanse can handle everything Ian does."

Morgan nodded solemnly. Veronica's impression struck a chord with him. More than once he'd seen family dynamics play out as she described. Older brothers were too protective or dismissive. Younger brothers were too grasping or worshipful. While acknowledging someone as your equal was easy to do in words, having that sense take root in your head and heart wasn't simple at all.

Morgan had been lucky. Patrick had always been a quiet child, but a studious one. Time and again Patrick would watch, would research, would ask a question and then do something as if it were the most natural thing in the world. Whereas Morgan would have to work at things over and over to get them right, Patrick truly could learn from someone else's experience. He'd do the prep work in his head, and then just leap into action.

On top of that, Patrick had always had good instincts. True, he could get his temper lit up, but mostly he avoided such confrontations. He was one to act quickly, but not rashly. Most folks couldn't see the difference, but Morgan knew his brother well. In the same amount of time plenty of people could act without thought, Patrick could reason his way through dozens of scenarios and choose the right path effortlessly

Which is but one reason why I never play chess with him.

Morgan's eyes narrowed as the Archon and Prince Davion retired through a side door. "If you had a crystal ball, what would be your prediction for the prince?"

She cocked her head to the side. "If he's lucky, he lives for another ten years. No more."

His eyes widened. "That dire?"

"You're the MechWarrior. You tell me. What's the life expectancy for a MechWarrior? The man's all of thirty years old by the calendar, but would you guess that by looking at him?"

"No. Time in the cockpit has put the years on him. He looks at least ten years older."

"And yet, given what you and your brother said about his exploits, he goes charging into battle like someone who just graduated from an academy. It's all well and good that he has more lives than a sackful of cats, but how many of those is he spending needlessly?"

There it is. "Will he find his solution soon enough?"

"No telling, but the affirmative is not the way to bet." Veronica's brows arrowed together for a moment. "Now don't go thinking you're headed down the same path. Not at all. You're smarter than he is, more capable. You're a warrior, but you've the ability to see beyond combat."

"You're very kind."

"Colonel Kell, sorry to interrupt." A Hauptmann and a Leutnant in Steiner uniforms approached the two of them. "If you would indulge the Archon, she would speak with you before dinner. Leutnant Mahler here will escort your companion."

Mahler nodded and offered his arm. "Miss."

Veronica gave Morgan another kiss on the cheek and whispered in his ear, "You *will* make this up to me later."

"Thank you." Morgan nodded to the Hauptmann. "Lead on."

They threaded through the crowd to the side door. Down a small corridor they reached the Archon's personal office. Morgan's escort stopped at the doorway and retreated.

Morgan walked through the door and smiled broadly. "There it is."

Katrina nodded. "I knew you'd recognize it."

The office had been decorated in a thoroughly modern manner, with chrome and shiny, colored metal panels making up the walls. It had no warmth and little personality—clearly a remnant of Alesandro Steiner's rule. But countering all that was Katrina's desk, a huge piece of furniture. Fashioned of oak and stained a rich chocolate brown, it radiated the sort of good feeling that the room itself lacked.

"Recognize it?" Morgan held a finger up. "I still have splinters."

Katrina shook her head. "From what Arthur said, the splinters would have to be in another part of your body."

"Supervising is hard work."

They laughed, and Prince Ian joined in. "It's a lovely piece. Your husband was talented."

"In many things." Katrina swallowed hard, and a sympathetic lump rose in Morgan's throat. "His best work was our collaboration. Melissa."

The prince raised the drink in his hand. "To the success of all collaborations."

"Indeed." Katrina moved to a small sideboard. "A drink, Morgan? I'm afraid I only have Scotch, if you're still drinking whisky."

Morgan recognized the bottle as being the brand Arthur Luvon had favored. He smiled, remembering the long discussions they'd had on the virtues of Scotch versus Irish—and the happy times spent doing the research to bolster their respective arguments. "I'd be honored."

The Davion prince clinked ice cubes around in his glass. "Time is short, so I'll get to the point. The Federated Suns and Lyran Commonwealth have one big common enemy: the Draconis Combine. If they weren't forced to garrison both borders, they could seriously hurt either one of us. I've also got the Capellans making trouble. The Free Worlds League, if it could ever pull itself together, will be trouble for you."

Morgan accepted his drink—taken neat—and nodded.

Ian frowned. "This isn't really my idea, but something Hanse suggested. He thought if our two nations could form an alliance, we would put pressure on the Combine. The Capellans would react, too, assuming our purpose was to eliminate them. They'd try to work an alliance with the Free Worlds League, or the Combine, or both."

The mercenary nodded. "That would be a lethal combination."

Katrina smiled. "How did you mean it, Morgan? One that could overwhelm either of us, or one that would tear itself apart because of treachery?"

"Both, I guess." Morgan sipped the smoky drink. "More the latter, but only after they'd done damage as the former."

The prince nodded. "You've got a good head on your shoulders, Kell. My thinking runs more to the former, but we have to do something. *I* have to do something. I'm not a *vision* person. I don't always get the big picture. I do, however, see enough to know that if I continue in this direction, the Federated Suns are just going to bleed themselves white. If the Combine and CapCon were ever to unite, I would lose serious ground. The Davions would be overthrown, and I don't see anyone coming up to handle the situation."

Morgan raised an eyebrow. "The Haseks or the Sandovals?"

Ian drank, then shrugged. "Sandovals maybe. George Hasek is solid, but his son, Michael, there's a viper. Never catch him at anything, however."

Katrina shook her head. "The gall of calling himself Michael Hasek-*Davion* just because he married your half-sister."

"Hanse says that shows how much he's not good at political thinking. Hanse is, thank God." Ian finished his whisky. "I have to do something, so I came here to ask the Archon if we could have some sort of a joint military exercise. Dress it up as an all-star game. My best against yours. We tear up some turf, we have observers, we learn from each other, and we send a message to our enemies that we don't want them causing trouble."

Morgan chewed his lower lip. "And, presumably, our enemies would hold their own war games just to show what they can do. It would show how seriously they take the threat of an alliance. And buy time for planning."

"Yes, a distraction, if nothing else. In this Prince Ian and I agree."

"Sounds like a good plan, Katrina." Morgan smiled. "Not that you needed to hear that from me, either of you."

The Archon refilled Ian's glass. "Actually, I did. You handled the situation on Galatea discretely, and I have another mission for you of equal discretion."

"Yes?"

She returned the cork to the bottle. "What do you know about the world Zavijava?"

"Just that it fills out a crossword puzzle now and again." Morgan thought hard, but came up a blank, even though the name seemed familiar. "Close to Terra, isn't it?"

"Off near Thorin, on the League border. This week it's ours. Next week that could change. We only have local militia there. It's an agricultural wonder, with temperate zones that produce wonderful wines, and vast oceans with floating algae farms and pearl colonies."

"Does coffee, too, doesn't it?"

"And tobacco. Arthur's father used to import cigars from there."

Morgan nodded. "That's it. Uncle Alister's cigars stank horribly—though they *did* keep the fishflies away in the spring."

"That's the place. Not enough metal deposits or industry to make it worth fighting over, though there have been wine raids. Shouldn't be this year, though. Bad crop three years ago, so the wine isn't going to be worth stealing."

The prince set his glass down. "Anyway, we're thinking Zavijava is where we could hold our exercises. The agrocombines have fields they're leaving fallow for a bit. We can tear them up, maybe go north and scare some penguins—or their local equivalent."

Morgan looked to the Archon. "What's the Kell Hounds' part in this?"

"Right now, it would just be you and few of your officers. I'll keep Patrick here since the Hounds are going to be incoming from Galatea. You'll go with the Prince and scout things out, all very quiet. No one will know you're there."

"Ah, the Prince is going to be hard to disguise."

Ian shook his head. "One nice thing about this face is that with a bit of beard it changes. Besides, I have a double who will be taking a tour of the Combine border. All eyes will be there."

Katrina clasped her hands together. "This will be a working vacation, Morgan. You can even bring your friend with you."

"My friend?" Morgan caught a look passing over the Archon's face. Of course she knew who Veronica was, and what she did. *Is that disappointment on your face, Katrina, or something else?* "She would be something of a distraction—and can change her appearance almost at will."

"It's settled, then." The Archon raised her glass. "To a posture of strength, which leads to a future of peace."

CHAPTER 4

THE TRIAL
DISTRICT OF DONEGAL, THARKAD
LYRAN COMMONWEALTH
15 NOVEMBER 3010

Dancing with Trisha, even though the dance was a more sedate and stately step than what they usually enjoyed, helped calm Patrick down. He wasn't sure what he found more annoying: Prince Ian's deliberate attempt to get him angry, or his rising to the bait. There'd really been no provocation. Patrick had listened to countless people denigrate his brother—always to their regret—and he'd not reacted that badly.

Part of it was their location. The dinner was a social event where everyone was supposed to be on his best behavior. Sure, veiled barbs might fly. Gossip certainly would, and would likely leave more scars than a firefight. But the Prince had been deliberated rude in a place where that was against the rules, and because of Patrick's relationship to the Archon, he felt even more tightly bound by the rules.

I was ambushed and didn't take it well. He'd never have allowed himself to fall into such a trap in combat. He'd have scouts out. He'd have figured the angles, would have air-cover, would know what to expect, and would be formulating a plan of action in case things went awry.

Diplomacy and business, which were now two of the three legs of his career, really demanded that he develop the same level of skills that he had as a warrior. Once he'd realized that need, he started looking around again. It was as if he had new eyes that could see in colors that had never been present before.

As the music ended, he and Trisha returned to find Veronica on the arm of a young Leutnant. Veronica had been engaged in conversation with him, but had been looking around. *She sees the way I will learn to see.* Without a doubt Veronica was reading currents and power flows in the crowd.

Morgan joined them very quickly, then the brothers were split up and sent to different round tables for dinner. Each table seated ten and had a guest host. Patrick and Tisha located their names at the table and were seated across from each other. Tisha sat between their host, a scientist known for his work on myomer fibers, and an aged MechWarrior who looked as if he'd fought in the First Succession War. He certainly had enough stories to suggest he'd been involved in every battle since then, anyway.

Patrick found himself trapped between the MechWarrior's long suffering and equally insufferable wife, and a handsome woman of middle age who wore her brown hair long and dressed fashionably, if somewhat sedately. Being mindful of the admonition that "Neither a gentleman or those seated next to him are in the company of a boor," Patrick politely introduced himself to each woman in turn.

The MechWarrior's wife took one look at his left hand, inspecting it for a wedding ring, then gave him a long once-over. Apparently she didn't find what she was looking for because she dismissed him, so he turned his attention to the other woman, Hippolyta Marik.

She set her salad fork down after having eaten a block or two of cheese, an olive, and rearranged lettuce leaves. "I am an attaché to the embassy here."

"Yes? Area of expertise?"

"Cultural relations." She smiled, the amusement on her face carrying up into her eyes. "Of course, you know that means I'm a spy."

"Really."

"Absolutely." Hippolyta smiled. "They seated me here so I could be bored to death by the General and dazzled by your brilliance."

"Good luck with the bored thing, then." Patrick dug into the salad, spearing lettuce, an anchovy and some cheese without making it a lump too unsightly to consume. "I mean, I appreciate the idea that I'm brilliant, but I talked with an associate of yours on Galatea. He didn't seem to value that attribute too highly."

The attaché sighed. "Yes, Hector Damisceau. Ambitious beyond his abilities, and prone to pretending that spy and secret agent are synonymous."

"They're not?"

"A spy gathers information. Secret agents act on that information. What Hector did, or tried to do, was regrettable on many levels. His view of the universe and the way things work is woefully small." The phrase "woefully small" attracted some attention, as any potentially salacious uttering will in those moments when conversation lapses, but without follow up, the other diners returned to their conversations.

"If you say so. I wasn't inclined to discuss things with him after that day in the hotel."

"If it is any consolation, he has been disciplined. I'm authorized to tell you that. In fact, I was directed to."

"And the reason being?"

She smiled in a way that attracted Tisha's attention from across the table. "Assuming that what he reported as your half of the conversation was accurate, you're absolutely correct. It is true, of course, that your ties to the Archon do concern us; but on Atreus we understand the difference between mercenaries and loyal House troops. We have no doubt that you love the Commonwealth, but we are also aware that you and your brother have other plans for your unit. The cessation of war is different than the conquest of many worlds, and this pleases us.

"But the Free Worlds League is a complicated place. No doubt you've heard it said that where there are two Mariks gathered, there are three conspiracies. A powerful mercenary unit could tip the balance in an internal struggle as easily as an external one. The Captain-General and others would just as soon see the possibility of a civil war eliminated."

Patrick leaned back as wait staff cleared away his salad plate. "Isn't that always a risk, not only in the League, but everywhere? The Succession Wars are, in essence, new episodes in the old Star League civil war."

"An astute observation, Lieutenant Colonel. The difference is this: perhaps only the League is in a position where a civil war could weaken it enough for its enemies to tear it apart. The Capellan Confederation might be easier to conquer, but it's in little danger of a civil war at the moment. Rebel slices of any other nation would be strong enough in and of themselves to hold off attackers from outside."

Patrick nodded. Her analysis wasn't far from that of other experts. While at the Nagelring, Patrick had played in countless simulations—for fun mostly, but grades sometimes—that posited civil wars in the other of the Successor States. By far the Free Worlds League was the most vulnerable because once Atreus' central authority was challenged, many of the administrative districts could pull out. They'd form economically viable units. While they might not be able to field and maintain a military, quickly turning and allying with the Lyran Commonwealth could bind them to a strong economy *and* get the Commonwealth to defend them. The Commonwealth would suddenly have a buffer state that guaranteed any war would be fought on someone else's soil while revving up the economy. That would be a political bonanza for any leader.

Katrina would be all over it in a heartbeat.

He looked at Hippolyta. "What would you have mercenaries do?"

"We wondered if mercenary units might favor auxiliary contracts that would bind them to only working for the legitimate government."

Patrick studied his plate for a second, letting the steam from the rosemary chicken and mushrooms florentine fill his nostrils. "It would depend upon two things, I would imagine. There would have to be an option in which the legitimate government would have to increase what they're paying for that option in the face of a valid offer from another party."

"Some might consider that extortion, Colonel."

"I'm sure, but if you're willing to pay to prevent disaster, you pay to prevent disaster. I'm sure formulae could be worked out that would be reasonable."

"And the second thing?"

"How do you define 'legitimate government?'"

"A worthy question. Ideally, the government in power at the time the contract is signed."

"And in the event the Captain-General is forced out by a coup? Does the contract go with him, or stay with Atreus? Do the mercenaries then hire on with him to toss the rascals back out, or are they bound by an agreement that hurts the previous government?"

She smiled at him again. "Estimations of your intelligence were woefully inadequate."

And if you think I'm blinded by flattery, you need to bring those estimates up a lot higher.

Her comment hadn't blinded him. Her candor, her flattery, her mildly flirtatious manner were all designed to inspire trust. She was setting him up to learn from him. She certainly was learning *about* him. He had no doubt that a report of their entire conversation and evening would be in ComStar's hands before dawn, and on Atreus as fast as possible.

The General had only caught a piece of what Hippolyta had said, but felt compelled to comment nonetheless. "Intelligence estimates, you can never trust them. Need a warrior to see what's going on. No damn good to have a spy talk to a farmer about what came marching by. Farmer could tell you to the feather how many crows land on his fields, but does he give a fig about enemy 'Mechs? No sir, not at all."

Patrick wiped his mouth. "Begging your pardon, General, but to completely discount reports by anyone who isn't a soldier is to make yourself completely blind. Moreover, soldiers can be wrong, too."

"A 'Mech's sensors do not lie, sir."

"But don't they?" Patrick smoothed his napkin in his lap. "I've run through countless simulations where the sensors are fed data that makes a tower of girders look like a 'Mech. A Warrior using mag-res at night could easily be fooled, or one relying on infrared could be taken by a 'Mech that's been buried in snow."

The general, his jowls twitching as color rose to his face, pointed a fork at Patrick. "You might think so, sir, today; but you know nothing of the glory days of war. Now all you have are the bastard children of grand and storied 'Mechs. You piece them together so each is a Frankenstein's Monster of disparate parts. The grand traditions have been sullied, when warriors would venture forth to honorably defend Lord and Nation. The great families of the Star League would scarcely recognize the MechWarrior of today; and likely not lament his slow descent into oblivion."

The man had a point. The Succession Wars, and the raiding that took place between them, continually ground down the technology. Vast robotic factories could turn out JumpShips and the Kearny-Fuchida drives that let them travel between stars in an eye-blink, but exactly *how* that worked, no one quite knew. What had been common and plentiful technology in the days of the Star League had become exotic and scarce. One of the reasons the Kells had so easily pulled in good MechWarriors was because of their access to spare parts from a factory on Arc-Royal. With Techs like Tisha, they could bring a 'Mech back up to being battleworthy. That still didn't mean it would be up to Star League standards.

A long time ago Morgan had coined the phrase "collateral entropy." The wars destroyed factories and smashed irreplaceable technology. A bid to capture scientists or steal prototypes could easily wipe out decades or centuries of knowledge. Not since the burning of the library at Alexandria had such an informational holocaust taken place. It couldn't continue, and reversing collateral entropy was yet another reason Morgan and Patrick had created the Hounds.

Patrick opened his hands. "You lament the passing of an age, General. What would your advice be to the warriors of this age, so we can reclaim what has been lost?"

The old man scowled. "You are a mercenary, are you not, sir?"

"With the Kell Hounds. We're being posted here, to Tharkad."

His expression soured. "You, sir, *are* the problem. Your loyalty is to the Kroner or the C-bill. You fight solely to enrich yourself. You profit from other warriors by salvaging their 'Mechs; and you fight at the direction of whatever unscrupulous person has enough money to procure your services. You, sir, are a whore."

Patrick shook his head, preventing Tisha from stabbing the man with a fork. "You suggest, sir, that only the unscrupulous will hire a mercenary, but the Archon herself hired us. Would you suggest that she is unscrupulous?"

"Well, no, of course—"

"And further, sir, would you posit that all unit commanders and all planetary governors are wholly scrupulous and would never issue orders to a unit in service to them that would be of benefit that commander or governor?"

"That would be silliness."

And I know of a dozen or more cases to point that out if you want to argue about it. Patrick slowly smiled. "Therefore, sir, your suggestion of virtue for service to a government is rejected, as is the suggestion that a mercenary's service cannot be virtuous."

"You are twisting my words."

"No sir, I am just pointing out that you have a selective memory, and view the world through a lens that is warped by that memory." Patrick looked around the table. "None of us here wants war—none of us who think about what war means. Would taking a world from the League or Combine or the Confederation enrich us? It might. But at what cost? How do I look at myself if, for the promotion of personal gain, I consign my comrades to an unnecessary battle? How do I sleep when I think about the children killed in a school destroyed by missiles that miss their intended target? On a map, a town is an objective. It is a hard point that has to be reduced. But those hard points are churches and community centers. Around them lay houses and businesses. To secure a flank I could wipe a town off that map, and even if every single person was evacuated from that town, their lives are still destroyed. All they owned, all they held sacred, heirlooms as valued by them as any 'Mech is by us, are all gone."

Hippolyta rested her elbows on the table. "Is there not a time when combat is justified, Colonel?"

"Of course. In the defense of freedom. In the defense of people. One could even suggest a pre-emptive strike against a military force is justified, but all of those things are a far cry from a unilateral attack with the intent of material gain. That's just piracy under the guise of governmental policy; and that really can't be justified."

The general snorted. "You, sir, have no understanding of the realities of war."

"No, sir, I have no *desire* to validate *your* understandings of war." Patrick gave the man a hard stare. "You have your traditions, and are welcome to them. They have shaped the world I've inherited but, by all that is holy, they will *not* determine the world I pass on to the next generation. And insuring the future is yet one more reason to fight, and one I gladly embrace."

CHAPTER 5

"She's resting. I'm sure she'll be fine." Morgan shook hands with Quintus Allard, Prince Ian's intelligence liaison. "Good to see someone else who doesn't suffer ill effects from burning into a system."

"Had to train myself out of it." Quintus smiled, his brown hair only just having begun to turn white. Affable, with plenty of character in his face, the man often appeared to be distracted, but Morgan suspected that was an affectation. In the discussions on the DropShip from Tharkad to Zavijava, Quintus hadn't missed a thing.

"You were a MechWarrior?"

"No." He tapped a finger against his skull. "Too thick-headed for good neurohelmet connections. My boys are headed that way, though. Justin, my eldest, got embarrassed when he heard I'd vomited during a rough entry. Imagine having your twelve-year-old sitting down to have a serious discussion with you about such a thing."

"I'm sure it was an enlightening talk."

"You don't have any kids, do you?"

Morgan shook his head.

"And Veronica's sickness, that's just space sickness?"

"To the best of my knowledge." Morgan glanced back at the ranch-style resort and the window to the room he shared with Veronica. It had taken some convincing to get her to come along. Morgan figured it wouldn't work, save that the Archon herself had requested Veronica go with them. Veronica recognized the amount of trust the Archon was putting in her and accepted the assignment, despite the resulting misery.

Quintus nodded. "Children are a joy. At least, mine have been. Riva will be a little scientist. Justin's off at the Sakhara Academy, and it looks like Dan may get an appointment to the New Avalon Military Academy in a couple years. He'll be fourteen if he keeps on his accelerated academic track. My wife hates the idea, thinks he needs time to be a kid. Dan's pretty sensible, though, so I'm inclined to give him his head."

Morgan half-smiled. "Besides, he becomes a MechWarrior, and he still has time to be a kid."

"Painfully true. I'll remember you said that, and send him in your direction when he graduates."

"Do that." Morgan opened his arms and breathed in deeply. "All the reports, all the holo, none of it communicates how clean this place feels. Have you tried the water yet? Straight out of the tap it's sweet."

"Shall I make a note that we exempt this area from exercises, or will this be a command post?"

"This will be a command post. Did you see the restaurant's menu? Generals will be getting fat while MechWarriors are eating leftover Star League rations." Morgan walked further from the sprawling resort building toward the herb garden and the gazebo beside it.

"Isn't that always the way?"

"Too often." Morgan ascended the gazebo steps and stretched his hands up to brush fingers over a rafter. "I've done a lot of reading about history, especially military history. So often the disconnect between what the soldiers in the field see and what their commanders and politicians believe is happening goes ahead and determines the outcome of the battle. Troops can be ordered to take hills that don't exist; rumors are reported as fact, which leads to all sorts of disasters—and, somehow, no matter how good the communication, these errors still proliferate."

"I think that's why a leader like Prince Ian prefers to lead from the front."

"That's hardly a realistic solution to the problem." Morgan regarded the smaller man carefully. "Or does that painfully true remark pertain to him as well? Is he still being a kid?"

Quintus remained quiet for a moment, then nodded. "He knows he has to grow up, that he can't be a kid anymore, but he doesn't know how. To be frank, Colonel, I was hoping his dealings with the Archon might give him some benchmarks in that regard. I even have hopes his association with you might do that."

"So my being tapped to be his host wasn't just a happy circumstance?"

"Not wholly." Quintus smiled. "The Archon would have hired the Kell Hounds regardless, but you and your staff wouldn't have come ahead as quickly were this mission not in the offing."

"I'm flattered, but I also think you've got the wrong man here. The prince is older than me, and has much more combat experience. I doubt he'll be inclined to listen to me."

"You'd be surprised. He has taken to you. I think he admires the freedom of your situation. He's also aware that you can do more than shoot." Quintus held a hand up. "We've seen the report on the Majistan affair. You handled that adroitly. The prince was impressed."

"Let's hope he still is a year from now when this operation kicks off."

The intelligence man laughed lightly. "The operation has already begun."

"I'm not sure I follow."

"The whole idea is to make sure *all* of our people are up to snuff. We already have a team here creating the files and documentary evidence of a variety of activities on the planet. We want our intel teams to ferret things out which are then used to formulate plans. If you were able to hack into the planet's computers, you'd find a whole layer of information about economic matters that's entirely false, and we will be keeping it current. When the military end of the operation begins, keywords will be replaced, so projections of wine production can become biological weapon production, warehouses and their contents become ammo dumps."

Morgan frowned. "Then my being here is just a charade. Decisions on locations have already been made."

"No, that's all variable, too. The prince, your entourage, and you will actually choose where the exercises will take place, and information will be adjusted accordingly."

Morgan scrubbed both hands over his face. "What you're telling me is that this is all a phase of the operation, too. It's where the Prince gets to decompress, to learn to work with others, and to renew himself."

"An added benefit."

"Does Prince Hanse know Ian is here?"

"Hanse knows his brother is *not* the person appearing in public. That's all he needs to know." Quintus shook his head. "Hanse has ambitions, and vision; but unlike many Inner Sphere leaders, he actually loves his brother. He would never murder him."

"That's reassuring." Morgan turned and looked to the north, where a verdant valley slowly rose toward the sky. Snow-capped peaks serrated the horizon. Tobacco leaves waved in the light breeze, and rows of grapevines traced their way across hillsides. The sun warmed him and he raised his face toward it.

It may be an impossible mission, but it's hardly difficult duty. He smiled. *And much better than being shot at.*

Veronica moaned softly as Morgan sat on the edge of the bed. He'd set the tea tray on the bedside table and poured. A thick, fragrant, and mildly musky aroma filled the air. He reached over and tugged the coverlet away from Veronica's head.

"The resort better be on fire." She barely opened an eye, then let the lid slide up halfway. "Overcast or dusk?"

"Smoke from the burning resort is hiding the sun. It only *appears* to be dusk."

She let a moan drift into a groan as she stretched. Though the thick quilt muted the outline of her body, Morgan couldn't help but grin. He had other memories of her taut muscles and how that body could writhe in bed. *Very happy memories.*

She caught the look on his face. "Too late for a good morning kiss?"

"Never."

He leaned down, kissing her fully on the mouth. Her scent enveloped him, prompting another smile against her lips. Her fingers sank into his hair, keeping him close, so he kissed her again on the lips, then the ear. "It *is* a little past morning."

Veronica stretched again, then pulled herself up against the headboard. The sheets fell to her waist, but she seemed utterly unconcerned about her nakedness. That was one aspect about her that Morgan greatly admired. She could be shy and coy at times; but she was also confident in her sexuality and comfortable with her body.

"What did you bring me?"

"*Pu-ehr* tea. It's supposed to be good for your stomach."

She took the teacup in both hands and breathed the steam in. "Mmmmm, very nice. This I will like. The little finger sandwiches, however..."

"They're good."

"They're all yours." She raised an eyebrow. "You knew I'd say that, which is why you didn't protest their being put on the tray."

"You're reading me very well."

Veronica sipped tea. "And what did you do today?"

"Allard and I took Cat and Frost to scout out some likely areas. It was a long hike. Ian slept most of the day away, too, so we'll cover the same ground tomorrow with him in tow. Two days from now we'll head north, to the mountains. Don't give me that look. There's a very nice resort up there at the *base* of the mountain. You'll be plenty warm."

"I better be, Morgan, or you'll be cold, too." The smile on her face said one thing, but the slight edge to her voice said another.

"And I'm thinking after that we can head south. Magma Park has volcanoes. You'll have no complaints there."

Her smile shifted, then she sighed.

"What's the matter?"

"I'm not certain." Her blue eyes locked with his. "Part of it not being the center of attention. I'm actually rather used to that. In the past I learned to fade into the background, but it's a habit I'm out of."

"You've got my attention."

"Not when you're dealing with the prince." She stroked Morgan's cheek. "It's not like it's my being jealous of a man-crush. If that were the issue, I'd ignore it or go off to another resort and meet you when your work was done. I think it's something more. The distraction is because you're actually working."

Morgan raised an eyebrow. "It's never been a secret what I do."

"No, darling, but I've never seen you do it before." She smiled at him over the teacup. "You and I are not normal people, but this problem is actually something normal people run into all the time. How often does one partner see the other in action? A man's an as-tech working on 'Mechs. How often does his partner see him with a cutting torch?"

Morgan shrugged. "I don't really know."

"Nor do I. And don't get me wrong. Watching you work is fascinating. You've not noticed, but the men you work with hang on your every word. It's more than just drawing a paycheck. My God, your friend Cat endured a beating on Galatea to fool General Volmer. That's more than friendship."

"Cat and I have shared a number of experiences."

"Yes, you've bonded. I got that." She glanced down into her tea as if trying to read the future in it. "Will we ever bond that way, Morgan?"

"I don't honestly know." He frowned. "Don't take this wrong, but I hope not. I don't want anyone to have to share in the experiences we did."

"Fair enough answer." Veronica set the tea down, brought one of Morgan's hands to her mouth, and kissed it. "And I hope we don't have to share those experiences. I'm not sure I'd like you in combat."

"Hey, I don't want to be shot up, even if you are there to kiss things and make them better."

"That's not what I said."

"What then?"

She sank back against the pillows, crossing her arms. "You have great passion, Morgan. I love that. I see it in how you work, in how you relate to your brother and your men. I feel it when we're together. But I also know you keep it in check, so you don't get out of control. In a battle, however, I think that control might go away. And that would scare me."

Morgan nodded. "That would be two of us."

"I just want you to know that."

"Got it. Anything else wrong?"

Veronica shrugged. "Just a vague sense of unease. Probably nothing. I'll keep you posted. Oh, and then there's the other thing."

"Yes?"

She nodded. "I'm going to have to shower before dinner, and I loathe the idea of leaving my back unwashed."

"I could probably help you with that."

"You're so selfless."

"I do my best."

She came up on her knees and took his face in both hands. "That you do, Morgan Kell, that you do."

Then she kissed him and, sometime later, they both arrived for dinner; clean, glowing, and only slightly late.

About the time the sorbet arrived between the fish course and beef, a JumpShip appeared at a pirate jump point in the Zavijavan system. As the company dined on the resort veranda, it materialized in the shadow of a ringed gas-giant which sparkled in the sky just above and beyond Prince Ian's head. It detached three DropShips, a pair of *Leopards* and an *Overlord*, each fully loaded with 'Mechs and supporting infantry. They'd even jammed trucks and haulers in the holds.

The JumpShip unfurled its sails to recharge the Kearny-Fuchida drive. It would take a long time, the radiation coming from the gas-giant being a fraction of that being pumped out by the sun, but the job would be done by the time the DropShips returned.

The DropShips moved away from their transport and above the plane of the asteroid disk. Though astronomers on Zavijava did have telescopes trained in that general direction, most of their time was spent giving tours, or pointing out the stars from whence visitors had arrived. While radio-telescopes collected data and computers analyzed it, nothing about the ships would be discovered until well after they'd landed on the planet. The asteroid disk camouflaged them very well, leaving the world ignorant of their presence.

And from all the way out there, intelligence specialists started harvesting data. Broadcast mostly, which they were able to display on holovision screens. They would have liked to pick off ComStar HPG communications, but those planning this operation had decided interfering with ComStar would be too dangerous.

Mostly what they watched for were any reports of military operations on Zavijava. Aside from personal-interest stories about militiamen from one region or another, everything appeared quiet. Rather fortunately, the militia's leader welcomed every holovid crew that wanted to come by, allowing them to pan over a phalanx of 'Mechs. The intel crew could break them down and have a complete table of organization and equipment before they had to commence any operations.

And even out there, the intelligence operative picked up glimmers of something else, something secret, buried within economic data. They wouldn't be able to punch all the way into the world's data network until they drew closer, but they learned enough to plan a complete assault.

Zavijava was a treasure trove, and by the time they were burning into atmosphere, they'd know exactly where all the treasure was kept.

CHAPTER 6

KELL HOUNDS PROVISIONAL HEADQUARTERS
DISTRICT OF DONEGAL, THARKAD
LYRAN COMMONWEALTH
12 DECEMBER 3010

Patrick Kell pushed himself back from his desk and ground the heels of his hands against his eyes. Blinking, he hit the enter key, then swung his chair around to face the other man in the office. "Really, Father, you don't need to keep reading through these files."

David Donelly smiled easily. "I'm not minding it, Patrick, not one bit. I like a chance to get to know my flock before I actually meet them."

"You think you can size them up by their files?"

The older man rose from his chair and stretched. His thin, black hair had been cut short. Burn scars marked the left side of his neck and his left hand, leaving Patrick to imagine they likewise covered his arm and neck. If the twisted flesh gave him any pain, the unit's Catholic chaplain gave no sign.

"No document is ever going to tell you the whole story, of course, but you can posit some things. Major Guinn and Mr. Franck are pulling very good warriors. They're sorting fair from foul, and Guinn is negotiating contracts as if he's spending *his* money, not yours. Still and all, there are folks who have quirks."

"Like?"

"This Damon Crowley, Second battalion, Second Company, in the Fire Lance. Graduated highly out of Albion, then went into the Capellan Dragoons. Looks as if he had some discipline problems there."

Patrick swung back to his screen and called up the file. "Drunk and disorderly, AWOL, Insubordination. That's the kind of record I'd expect from some conscript fresh from home, not an Albion graduate."

MICHAEL A. STACKPOLE   **239**

"Exactly. So he resigns there, then beats it over to the Lexington Combat Group. He joins the Golden Hammers, fights well with them, but..."

Patrick slowly nodded. "Another bout of problems. They bounce him and he ends up with Waco's Rangers. His record is horrible with them. Why in hell did Guinn tap him?"

Donelly came over and perched himself on the corner of Patrick's desk. "I was asking myself that, then I looked at the leadership of those specific units, especially when the commanding officers changed. Turns out that the officers in charge when Crowley has his little episodes are congenital morons."

"Fits Waco, certainly." Patrick sighed. "So Guinn thinks we can handle this guy?"

"Not a hair of doubt there, Patrick." The man's dark eyes twinkled. "But you're knowing the whole of the unit is thinking that, right?"

"You're kidding me."

The priest solemnly shook his head. "No, lad, I've heard enough from the troops to know what they're thinking. The way you two faced down Blizzard got a lot of MechWarriors back in their 'Mechs. And then those who went west, they saw a lot. They saw how the two of you operated and reacted. Your saving that child counted for a lot—not just your getting wounded, but that you *acted* without hesitation. And the op to take Thessalon, boldly done, and without splashing warriors as if they were toy soldiers. The men know you're not just going to spend their lives."

"How could any leader do that?"

"There's plenty of them who've found the rationale to let it happen. You think General Vollmer wouldn't have done it?"

"Bishop Poore certainly didn't have any qualms." Patrick stood and arched his back, listening to his spine pop all the way up. "It's good we have our people's trust. Lord knows we'll need their patience."

"You'll straighten things out soon, son." Donelly held his hands up. "And I won't be prying. Need to know, and all that."

Patrick smiled. Originally the plan had been to take the Kell Hounds from Galatea and move them to Tharkad, using commercial shipping on a space available basis. Since the Hounds were moving to Tharkad for garrison duty—the equivalent of being lap dogs for the Archon—there wasn't a lot of urgency to the move. As Guinn got people, he'd send them on.

The planning for the Zavijava exercises changed everything, both because of the need for secrecy and logistics. It was easier to collect everyone at Galatea and move them toward Zavijava than to have them hit Tharkad—even though supplies and some 'Mechs would be heading to Zavijava from the capital.

The biggest difficulty in travel between stars wasn't actually jumping between them. Yes, the JumpShips did take time to recharge their engines, but even more time was taken to move a DropShip from an apex or nadir recharge point to a target world. With the Archon getting assets moved into position, the Kell Hounds would have a command circuit to get them most of the way to their target. The DropShips would arrive in one system, shift to a charged JumpShip, and move to the next star. By switching ships like that, they could cross a lot of space in a very short time. Setting up the command circuit would take time, however, which meant the Hounds had to wait on Galatea.

The command circuit *did* make the unit a lot more flexible if it came to a real problem. Ryde and Skye were but two worlds the Draconis Combine had designs upon, and they were far closer to Galatea than Zavijava or Tharkad. Keeping the Hounds on Galatea until it was time to move them meant they were a mobile reserve that could discourage Kurita adventurism.

"You're not prying, Father, and it's nothing you've likely not seen before. Just a lot of math. Rations for a 'Mech company, not including water, is approximately twelve kilos a day. Our roster, including support personnel is gives us roughly twelve companies. That's a hundred-forty-four kilos of rations per day. A month's rations takes up as much volume as a light 'Mech; and I need machines to distribute it. Add in ammunition, housing, fuel, spare parts, and medical equipment, and our problems are less tactical than they are logistical. And I can figure all this stuff out, put in the requisitions, get all the orders made and paid for, and that's still no guarantee that things will arrive on time, if at all. And even if they do, we might not be able to use them."

"I know, lad." Donelly chuckled. "I've been a party to scavenging armor in the dead of the night to be welding it to a 'Mech. And I've been short rations before, too."

"Well, every new hire means I have to suit parts and ammo to her 'Mech. I also have to estimate time for repairs. Tisha's a big help there, of course, but when I try to sleep, numbers just float through my brain."

"Ever be thinking you might need a vacation, lad?"

Patrick laughed. "No time, Father."

The priest laid his hand on Patrick's shoulder. "I worded that wrong, Patrick. You *need* a vacation."

"Father—"

"Furthermore, lad, you need to be taking your Tisha with you to somewhere it's just the two of you. No, now don't be preparing to lie to me. I may be a priest, but I'm also aware of what goes on between two healthy young people. If you're feeling guilty, you come see me in the confessional. If you're not, shame on you; but you owe it to that young lady to take good care of her."

"But, Father—"

Donelly shook his head. "Think about it this way, Patrick. You've swept her off her feet. You've taken her from the only world she's ever known, and brought her to one where you're at home. You're also famous here. You were living in the palace for Lord's sake. And now she's here, with no 'Mechs to play with. She's not the sort of girl who'd be letting you know how she's feeling. She'll be supportive to the end of time, but you owe it to her to make sure she knows she's still on your radar."

"But we..." Patrick hesitated.

"You sleep in the same bed every night, yes, Patrick, I'm aware of that. But do you get a chance to connect with her, or is it all a recitation of what you did that day, then snoring?"

The younger man frowned. "Okay, maybe you have a point."

The priest came around and typed something into Patrick's computer. The planetary directory came up with a map. "Conrad's."

"Yes, Father."

"They have dancing there. And food." The priest smiled. "And if you get your arse moving, you can be taking Miss Tisha out for a night you both need and will remember for a long time."

The music ended as Patrick spun Tisha down into a dip. He caught her against his thighs, his right hand at the small of her back. She smiled up at him, breathless, her forehead moist, but her eyes aglow.

"I do believe, Patrick Kell, that you like dancing with me."

"I do, very much." He pulled her back up and held her in his arms, brushing a lock of dark hair away from her face. "I don't want you to think...I mean, I want you to *know* how much you mean to me. Without you and your support, I don't know what I'd be doing right now."

She kissed him quickly, then took his hand in hers and led him back to their table. "You would be doing exactly what you always do: you'd work hard and amaze everyone with your brilliance."

"I'm being serious here, Tisha."

"So am I." She smiled carefully. "It's true, I was feeling a little homesick and lonely, but here, on the dance floor, in your arms, I'm at home. Home's where the heart is, and mine's in your hands."

"I'll keep it safe, I promise." Patrick enfolded her in a hug and held on tightly. "Thank you."

"For what?"

"For understanding when I'm being dense." He stepped back, his hands on her shoulders. "And, look, promise me that if you start feeling this way again, you'll tell me. Lonely, overwhelmed, homesick, anything, okay? The stuff I'm doing for the unit is important, but it's not more important than you are. I mean that."

"Not just because I'm the best tech around?"

"And the cutest, too; but that's not it. None of what we're trying to do will be worth anything if we lose ourselves and our families. Morgan and I may have lofty plans, but neither of us wants to be a messiah."

"Okay, I'll tell you what's going on inside if you'll do the same. Deal?"

"Deal."

Tisha smiled. "Okay, I'm going to go powder my nose, then there's a little old man over there I'm going to ask to dance."

Patrick smiled. The man had to be older than God, and was swaying in time with the music. He had a walking cane standing beside him and clearly wanted to dance, but didn't dare. *She'll get him up and moving.* His smile broadened as he imagined being that age and dancing with her.

Tisha had been gone barely five seconds when a woman approached him. "Care to dance, Colonel Kell?"

It took Patrick a moment to recognize her. "Recreation or work?"

"Both?" Hippolyta Marik had dressed down from what she had worn to the state dinner. Oversized blouse, her hair worn up, checked trousers that ended early enough to reveal white socks over two-tone shoes, she looked like a throwback to the music's original era. "I actually dance very well."

"Okay, let's go."

Patrick pulled her out onto the hardwood floor and put her through a couple basic moves. She moved easily and stayed in rhythm with the music. She smiled at him whenever she came out of a turn. Her eyes flashed with just a hint of arrogance and challenge.

Okay, let's see what you can really do.

The mercenary threw the spy through a complicated series of moves that had her spinning one way and then another. He bound her up, released her, pulled her in tightly again, then spun her out in an even more complex maneuver. In the space of three beats she'd turn left, then right, then spin around left again. As she came out of that last spin, Patrick hesitated, declining to lead her into the next step. She moved into it regardless, then a shiver ran through the hand he held.

Patrick shook his head as the music died. "You may dance well, but you don't know how to do this. You've got, what, twelve hours in? Ten?"

The spy glanced down at the floor. "Ten. Private lessons. The instructor said I was doing well."

"You're not bad, but I'm not stupid. Recent lessons. Should I be flattered that you're making me a project?"

"Did you want it to be personal, Colonel? Does my working offend you?"

Patrick held his hands up. "Let's recap here. I have someone from your government try to kidnap me and threaten to murder me. Now you set yourself up to become my buddy, going to great lengths to be able to casually bump into me socially on the only night I'm out? I actually have enough brain cells to form a synapse. What is it you want?"

Hippolyta's expression hardened. "Your brother has vanished."

"Vacation."

"In secrecy?"

"Honeymoon. He doesn't want to be disturbed."

Her eyebrow rose. "He married Matova?"

"You have a problem with that?"

The woman shook her head. "Just surprises me."

"What does? That she can be honest about what she does, and you just wrap yourself in deceit?"

Hippolyta paused then smiled. "Very good, Colonel, but you know there's more than enough deception in the world. Plots, plans, even self-delusion. Histories are written by the victors; all advertising is pure deception, promising undue rewards for purchasing a product; and even religion is subject to political and societal revision. I merely flow with the natural order."

"That means there's a problem."

"Yes?"

Patrick folded his arms across his chest. "If you wheedled my brother's location out of me, you'd probably believe the information I gave you. You'd believe it because you'd have deceived me, and because of that deception, I'd have no reason to lie to you. But you couldn't fully discount the possibility that I spotted your deception, and I deceived you in return."

"And your point?"

"If you'd just asked me, I'd have told you where he is." Patrick kept his face impassive.

The spy's eyes narrowed. "Would you?"

"Yes, sure. Tell you what..." Patrick jerked a thumb toward the people whirling on the floor. "We'll reset. I'll forget you tried to hoodwink me. I'll tell you where my brother is, and then you'll do me the favor of dancing with that old man that Tisha is entertaining."

Hippolyta pulled back slightly, clearly suspicious. "You know I can't believe you just like that."

"You'd have to check things anyway. This gives you a place to start." Patrick shrugged. "My brother is on his way to Arc-Royal. He wants to marry Veronica, but he wants my parents' blessing first. She insists they know what she does, and approve of her. You can appreciate the delicacy of the situation, and the attendant secrecy."

"Yes, yes, I see."

Of course you do. When your stock in trade is deception, you believe others have reasons to deceive. Good luck finding them.

Hippolyta nodded her thanks and withdrew as Tisha came up and rested a hand on Patrick's shoulder. "Wasn't that . . ?"

"Yeah." Patrick turned and kissed Tisha. "May I have this dance?"

"Henry will be tough competition."

"It's okay, darling. I don't mind." Patrick laughed. "There's dancing and there's dancing. And all I want to do right now is dance."

CHAPTER 7

Prince Ian Davion rode a horse well. He'd had lessons, that much Morgan could see, but they certainly weren't *dressage* lessons. The prince sat a horse like a knight in armor, coiled, ready for a fight.

It really didn't matter that the five of them were so far from a battlefield it was hard for Morgan to remember what fighting was like. After three days of scouting through the North Redlands district and picking out several good areas for operations, they'd decided to take a day off. Veronica had arranged for them to get horses from the resort in Alberville and they'd headed into a mountain preserve with special permits that allowed them to do a little hunting. That hadn't been their intent, but everyone rode armed, even Veronica.

Cat Wilson, a large, black MechWarrior, looked the least comfortable on his horse, a big grey mare. He dealt with his discomfort quietly, letting his concerns over security get him past feeling awkward. He wore a needler at the small of his back and had a shotgun in a saddle scabbard.

Frost, the Kell Hounds' sniper, sported more concealed weapons than Morgan had any chance of counting. He relied, however, on a hunting rifle with a scope which he wore slung over his back. Slender and white, the man had cleaned up a bit for the operation. His restless eyes studied everything and, no doubt, he saw more than Morgan ever would.

The prince and Morgan each sported shotguns and slug-throwing pistols. They'd made their choices independently, but ended up with the same models. The prince had smiled and given Morgan a nod, then bought extra ammunition for both. Morgan had thought at the time that there'd be a marksmanship contest proffered, but so far the Prince had just seemed to enjoy the ride.

Veronica had not wanted to carry a weapon, but settled for a small laser pistol. Morgan had asked if she'd shot before, and she nodded. "In my line of work, one learns to be competent at all manner of things. Something about a woman with a gun that excites certain men. Are you one of them?"

"If it's *you*, yes. If it's not, she'd have to be pointing the gun at me."

Frost trailed behind on his brown horse, and Cat rode point. Veronica rode in front of both the Prince and Morgan, who had ended up side by side as they climbed through a narrow valley meadow.

Ian looked around, then faced Morgan. "Tell me, Kell, what do you see when you look at this valley?"

Morgan looked around. Long green grasses flashed silver as a gentle breeze teased them. Insects buzzed and fluttered from one wild flower patch to another. Grasses had been trampled in a few places, suggesting game trails. The same grasses hid a stream, but the melodic sound of water flowing through it reached them easily. At the valley edges sharp hilltops narrowed the sky, and beyond them the tops of distant mountains hid beneath snowcaps.

"Beauty. A place I'm glad is preserved. A place I could remain in for a long time. You?"

"An ambush waiting to happen. You lead a company of 'Mechs in here and you could be trapped. Can't fight your way up with any speed, and you'll careen out of control trying to retreat. In the spring the ground would be so marshy you couldn't really go anywhere."

Morgan gave the Prince a hard look. "Is that truly what you see?"

The long-faced warrior nodded. "You think I'm lying?"

"From the first moment we met, Highness, you've been testing me. You tested my brother. You're measuring us as if we're enemies."

"You could be, couldn't you?"

"If you think that, isn't being out here with us like this rather silly?"

Ian's expression slackened for a moment, then he laughed. "That's a very good point. And you're right, I have been testing you. I *did* test your brother. Not really with intent, however. It is my nature."

Morgan took off his hat and wiped his forehead on his sleeve. "What were you expecting me to answer when you asked that question?"

The Davion leader half-smiled. "I expected the answer you gave me. And I'm actually glad of it. There's hope for you, Kell."

"You suggest there is none for you."

Ian reined back, then opened his arms. "I can see what you see here. The fresh air, the color, the intensity of nature. I do get it, but I have to *work* at it. I have to look past visions of ruin to get there. I wish it was otherwise, but it never has been for me."

"Never?"

"I can't turn it off." The prince's face softened. "It's not paranoia, though with my family's history, that could easily be explained. And it's not a burden. I'm used to it. It is, however, a curse. Even today, relaxing, riding, enjoying myself, I feel as if disaster is waiting to strike—especially because I am not being vigilant."

"Highness, I don't know how to say this, but..."

"I need to get over myself?" The man laughed heartily, but with a tinge of sorrow. "You're probably right. I'll resolve to do that here."

"Colonel."

Morgan reined around. "What is it, Frost?"

The man lowered a pair of binoculars and pointed to the sky. A bright dot moved through the heavens. "DropShips, two *Leopards*, burning fast. Alberville maybe, more likely Sathory."

Ian shaded his eyes with a hand. "Neither one of them has a spaceport."

Morgan fished in a pocket for a communicator. "No signal. Maybe from a top of the valley. It *could* be nothing."

The prince shook his head. "Fate punishing me for relaxing."

"It's not always about you, Highness."

"I'll accept that, but I accept something else, too." Ian exhaled slowly. "If those ships are carrying 'Mechs, before too long, I'll make it all about me."

LEOPARD-CLASS DROPSHIP *DEDALUS*
DISTRICT OF NORTH REDLANDS, ZAVIJAVA

Constantine Fisk chafed at being strapped into a jumpseat on the *Dedalus* bridge. He wanted to be *standing* there, feet spread, hands at the small of his back. He wanted to present a commanding presence, to inspire the confidence of his men. He knew he could project invincibility—he'd done it so often before, in countless holodramas—and knew this was the time to do it again.

He was not, however, an impractical man. The DropShip's bridge was too small for him to stand fully erect without bumping his head. And though he wished to inspire, hitting turbulence would send him careening around in the cockpit. That would be less than efficacious in affecting a landing.

But I do have work to do here.

Seated opposite him, Count Markham Somokis nervously patted his brow with a handkerchief. Somokis appeared more of a mouse than a man, and one with thinning fur at that. He did wear luxurious moustaches, which curled up more broadly than his face, and could have made him look ridiculous. In fact, had he first appeared on screen sweating away like he was, the audience would have dismissed him as a mere foil who would die by page ten in the script.

The actor patted his patron on the knee. "You must have confidence, my lord."

The smaller man snarled. "What I must have is solid ground under my feet."

"Ha, it won't be solid for long. We'll be pounding it hard."

"That I expect." Somokis' eyes hardened. "This is always the point where one wonders if the opposition will blink."

And I wonder that of you.

Constantine had met his patron on Bordon—a planet the holovid crew had quickly dubbed 'Boredom.' They'd chosen to holo the drama *I, MechWarrior* there because of favorable tax policies and a generous offer of financing from Count Somokis. As so often happened, Somokis became an Executive Producer on the holovid; and Constantine was required to treat him as a peer.

Initially it had begun as another acting job. But Constantine quickly realized Somokis was different than other people who invested money just so they could see their name splashed on a theatre screen. Somokis, who had made his fortune by building his father's appliance business into a mercantile empire dealing with everything from electronics to furniture, bulk-sales warehouse stores and luxury items, never got dazzled by the holovid business.

He even took the job of Executive Producer seriously, studying budgets and watching the production. He quickly tightened the reins on financing, making the production more efficient. The man had a talent for logistics and an ability—completely unexpected if one saw him sweating through the flight—to charm cooperation out of even the most hostile of individuals. As a result, *I, MechWarrior* came in under budget. The savings got thrown into publicity, and the holo spawned a franchise.

One late night, after a holo-reviewer had savaged *VII, MechWarrior*, Constantine and several of the other actors and stunt drivers had been grousing. The reviewer had suggested the tactics used in the holo were utterly unrealistic, and that the heroes could have been stopped by the most raw of militia recruits. Constantine and the others, all of whom had had some 'Mech training before moving into the entertainment industry, bristled and drunkenly outlined a plan to stage a raid just to prove the reviewer wrong.

It had been a lark, and everyone knew it, save for Somokis. He'd listened, saying nothing, then summoned Constantine to his office two days later. The huge steel and glass desk had physically dwarfed Somokis, yet he moved with the languid power of a tiger pacing in a cage.

"It could work, your plan. With some refinements." Somokis had hit buttons on his computer, and a holoprojector flashed numbers in the air. "I've run some comparisons, and your crew is good. You *could* stage a raid and pull it off. The simulations suggest you'll come off very well."

"That's nice to know. It's an idea we can develop into a screenplay. Broken down MechWarrior pulls his buddies together to stage a raid. His mother is dying, and he needs money for an operation..."

Somokis had snorted. "I'm not talking make-believe, Mr. Fisk; I'm talking a serious operation. One that would produce a solid return on investment, with minimal risk. Yes, we will gather things under the guise of shooting another holo, but we will actually stage the raid."

"A reality program? It's been done, but not on that sort of scale."

Somokis had slapped a hand against the desk. "Assess your situation, Mr. Fisk. You're forty-five years old. You get no more leading man roles offered to you. The buddy-holo contracts pair you with some young up-and-comer, and you know that one of them will be tapped to 'revive' the *MechWarrior* series."

"They could never do another *MechWarrior* holo without me."

"One's already in development."

"No one told me."

"Because I asked them not to."

Constantine had looked at the smaller man mouth agape. "You did *what*?"

"I effectively ended your career." Somokis looked up through the numbers. "Your career was already dying. It will completely fail, or you will take the opportunity I will offer you. If you do that, you will be bigger than ever before, and rich enough to finance epics from pocket change."

"Is that possible?"

The smaller man's eyes glittered with avarice. "It is. I've found us a target."

Zavijava. Constantine had never heard of it before, and now he was hurtling toward it with two lances of 'Mechs split between two *Leopard* Class DropShips. The *Overlord* Class DropShip, with its two companies of 'Mechs, two companies of infantry and vehicles would land further south, at the lower end of the wine country. That would put it where it could block the local militia coming up from Ellington, the planetary capital.

"They will blink, my lord, of this I am certain."

The smaller man's head came up. "You are, aren't you? Good. So much of this counts on you."

The plan, as Somokis had conceived it, had been simple. He'd presented it in very basic terms because, like many people, he supposed Constantine to be an empty head with a facility for projecting emotion. Granted, Constantine had flunked out of the Sakhara Academy, but that had been due more to the distraction of a dalliance with the Commandant's wife than any lack of brains. Once

Constantine showed Somokis he wasn't a complete idiot, planning accelerated.

What Somokis suggested was a raid that would hit high-end luxury goods—the sort of thing that could appreciate in value. Wine was an obvious example, but cigars were another. The exotic nature of the produce, the distance from the market and any perceived danger or notoriety attached to it, would hike the price. Constantine, having led the raid and endorsing the products, would immediately become a publicity magnet. Not only would it push his career into a higher orbit, but his endorsements wouldn't be seen as hollow. After all, he'd put his life on the line to procure the products, so strongly did he like them.

Constantine had especially liked *that* part of the plan. More than once he'd seen some star accidentally endorsing a product and put that product on the map. With the distribution of holovids through-out the Free Worlds League and even into the Lyran Commonwealth and Capellan Confederation, the publicity would expand the market. While they'd not be able to stage another raid, Somokis already had plans for repackaging domestic products, using Constantine to en-dorse them, and piggyback sales into the future.

The little man *had* thought out many of the details. He'd created the *Ion Knights*—the force Constantine would be leading. They had uniforms, paint schemes, nicknames for all the pilots; and back on Bordon, factories were already churning out action figures, biographi-cal holovids, lunch-pails, clothing and anything else that could carry an *Ion Knights'* logo. The projected income from everything, even when measured conservatively, promised that none of the raiders, nor their children in perpetuity, would ever have to work again.

Constantine had made suggestions, and Somokis graciously ac-cepted them. Many he ignored, save for one which he considered a stroke of genius. Constantine, ever mindful of image, framed the raid around an old myth. Like Robin Hood, the *Ion Knights* were robbing from the rich and would give to the poor. No small part of the intel work being done as they came into the system had been to pinpoint worthy causes that the *Ion Knights* could assist while looting the wine estates.

The pilot glanced back over his shoulder. "ETA two minutes. Deployment in three."

Constantine nodded, infusing confidence into his voice. "Very good. This is all according to plan. Don't worry, Count Somokis. Nothing could possibly go wrong."

CHAPTER 8

Constantine Fisk's *Enforcer* strode from the *Dedalus* with an economy of motion that suggested world-weariness. He had worked hard to impart that sort of body language to a 'Mech. While critics dismissed it—many thinking it was some sort of a special effect—he actually thought it was the highest form of his art. Any half-competent actor—and most politicians—could infuse emotion into their presentations, but to project it out through the skin of a ten-meter tall, humanoid war machine?

That takes talent.

Closed up in the fastness of the *Enforcer's* cockpit, he chuckled. Primary, secondary, and auxiliary monitors reported everything was clear. His armor all showed up as green and healthy. Interior diagnostics and weapons-systems displays were perfect. His holographic display showed the world in a golden-hued version of what he could see out of his cockpit viewscreen, and the pair of crosshairs tracked effortlessly across the landscape.

He laughed because he remembered his first holo. It was a buddy picture where he and an aging star were supposed to be enemies who later joined forces. His co-star was long past it, and Constantine was just learning his art. The holo was supposed to be a special effects extravaganza, and the actors were piloting 'Mechs only so that fact could be noted in the publicity. The director had even gone so far as to tell him, "You're just talent, the machines are the stars. Forget that, and you'll never amount to anything."

But after principle holography, the studio had slashed the effects budget, so the film got released using unadjusted holo. Critics had hailed the film as being "raw and gritty," which started a new trend, and had jump-started Constantine's career.

He turned his *Enforcer* to face the winery. The ranch-style building fronting the operation looked perfect for the setting. All natural wood and tans, it harkened back to Tudoresque constructions. A porch ran along the front and some of the rocking chairs still rocked, though the folks who had been sitting in them had long since vanished.

Beyond it, the fermentation barns and warehouses spread out. They shared the general style of construction, but were larger and more industrial. The warehouse had doors tall and wide enough to let a 'Mech have free access. Two of Constantine's companions—piloting a *Vulcan* and a *Hermes II* respectively—trotted off toward the warehouse. The other member of his lance, in a *Clint*, came up on his right.

A scrawny dog emerged from beneath the porch and ran at them, snarling and barking.

The *Clint* brought the autocannon in its right arm to bear.

Constantine keyed his radio. "Don't shoot the dog."

"That ain't a dog!"

Constantine looked up. Behind the fermentation barn he caught a shadow splashed back over a small hill. He flicked his sensors over to mag-res. The barn had plenty of metal in it, but he still caught the ghostly outline of a 'Mech.

Before he could warn the others, the local 'Mech cut loose. Two salvos of missiles twisted through the air trailing smoke. Half of them missed cleanly, but other blasted armor from the *Vulcan*'s right side and left arm. Scarlet beams from medium lasers lanced out, burning armor off the left flank, leg and arm. Ferro-ceramic sheets sloughed to the ground, exposing the arm. The metal bones glowed a dull red, but the coherent light did no more damage.

Pip Saunders, the pilot, managed to keep his 'Mech upright, but the assault had half spun him around. His *Vulcan* tottered as if the pilot was drunk. Even though the attack had disoriented him, Pip did pull his 'Mech back around so the enemy wouldn't have a shot at his aft armor.

Constantine flipped his radio over to a widebeam transmission. "Unknown 'Mech, don't make us hurt you."

The line, which had become one of Constantine's signature lines, did have an effect on the enemy. Just not the desired one. The pilot answered him in a squeaky voice tightened by nerves.

"This is Leutnant Eric Rosen of the Zavijava Militia. I advise you to surrender now."

A computer screen flashed in the cockpit. Voiceprint identification matched to data they'd pulled from the Militia database. Eric Rosen was a member of the militia, and drove a *Catapult* that had been in his family for two generations. But he wasn't supposed to be at the winery. He was supposed to be south, on maneuvers with the rest of the militia.

Constantine's voice became cold. "Leutnant, you really don't want us to shoot this place up, do you?"

The *Catapult* emerged from behind the fermentation barn. The shroud that had been covering it trailed behind the cylindrical 'Mech, well clear of the bird-like legs. More missiles arced up from the shoulder firing pods, and the medium lasers blazed.

This time the 'Mech targeted Andy Stark, in the *Clint*. Missiles crushed armor on the left arm and both flanks. Lasers scored armor on the left leg and right arm, then burrowed in the right flank. Stripped of armor, the right flank's support structures burned, but nothing collapsed.

Somehow Andy kept the *Clint* upright and returned fire. One laser missed, but the other sliced armor from the *Catapult's* right hip. The *Clint's* autocannon tracked shells across the target's right side. Shards of armor glittered and flashed as it fell to the ground.

Pip brought two of the *Vulcan's* weapons to bear, but missed with both the medium laser and autocannon. Rory Parker's *Hermes II* lit the *Catapult* up with a fiery red beam that slashed a black scar in the armor over the 'Mech's left thigh. The autocannon ground more armor off the *Catapult's* right flank, but that barely reduced the protection to fifty percent.

Constantine glanced at his secondary monitor. The *Catapult's* armor diagram indicated only marginal weakness, but the heat profile had him glowing. *The 'Mech is close to shutting down.* The pilot had been pumping out too much energy without the necessary result. Had he taken Pip or Andy out with one shot, the battle would have been different.

The *Enforcer* brought its weapons to bear. Constantine drifted both crosshairs over the enemy. When the red dot in the center flashed, he tightened up on his triggers. The heavy autocannon in the right arm spat a lethal cargo of depleted uranium shells. They ripped into the already weakened right flank, shredding the remaining armor. A shell punched on through, ricocheting off ferro-titanium bones. It blew through a medium laser. Sparks cascaded down as the *Enforcer's* large laser swept its beam over the 'Mech's heart. More armor melted, setting the grass below afire.

Constantine snapped orders with authority. "Pip, Andy, jet to his six. Rory, move in."

The orders hadn't been so much for his lancemates as they had for the *Catapult* pilot. Overheating, outnumbered, now with smoke billowing from his torso, Leutnant Rosen found himself in a very dicey position. The battle was lost. He had to see that.

To emphasize that point, Constantine pushed his 'Mech forward, swapping weariness for an attitude of predatory anticipation. *That's right, we're coming for you. Eagerly.*

The *Catapult* withdrew behind the barn and yet further. Using his jump jets, he pulled back into the low hills. Constantine admired how the pilot maneuvered to keep Pip and Andy back. *If* the retreat had begun in panic, it didn't finish that way.

Constantine ordered Pip and Andy to remain alert and keep the 'Mech at bay. He set Rory on guard outside the warehouse, then took his *Enforcer* in. He strode toward the heart of the building and pushed through heavy plastic curtains. Moisture frosted the corners of his viewscreen, but he could still see well enough to find his objective.

The Glacial Rift Winery was not a big operation, nor a particularly wealthy one. Their vintages made for good table wine—which was to say not much of it got off Zavijava. A couple restaurant chains would buy blended whites and reds from Glacial Rift and bottle them under their own house labels, but no one mistook those products for fine wine.

Being so far north, however, did afford Glacial Rift a chance to produce a rare vintage. Growing very sweet grapes—a variety once known on Terra as Muscat—they left the grapes on the vine until they froze. They were subsequently harvested and pressed, producing a thick, sweet dessert wine known as ice wine. What all their other vintages lacked, their Rime Nectar brand of ice wine made up for. It commanded a hefty price in the larger cities, and bottles that did make it off Zavijava cost a fortune. Rumors abounded about outrageous prices being paid—including a story that a single bottle had once been swapped straight across for a 'Mech.

Constantine thrust his 'Mech's arms into pallet-jacks, then bent and picked up a pallet stacked tall with cases of the 3010 Rime Nectar. He carried it to the DropShip and returned for two more. At Count Somokis' urging he also took the last remaining pallet of the 3009, though no one thought it nearly as good as the 3010.

A problem of perception, the good count suggested, that could be altered during the relabeling process.

Once the loot had been loaded, Constantine recalled his men. Buttoned up in the *Dedalus,* they took off just as the sun was setting. The *Catapult* pilot vented his impotent fury with a couple laser beams, but even a direct hit wouldn't have been able to dampen the crew's spirit as the DropShip flew south.

Morgan and his companions drew rein in front of the winery on the spot where the *Dedalus* had waited to be loaded. Repair crews were working beneath spotlights and eyed the riders with suspicion. A couple of them went for rifles, which prompted Frost to draw his. Tension thickened until a young man in a uniform came forward.

"Can we help you?" The Leutnant wore a pistol, but didn't even rest a hand on the holster. "You lost?"

Prince Ian started to ride forward, but Morgan restrained him with a hand. "We're guests over in Alberville. We saw DropShips burning in this direction and were curious. Looks like there was fighting."

The young man blushed. "Bandits, four of them in a *Leopard*. I tried to stop them, but couldn't."

Ian rose in the saddle. "What were they using?"

"*Clint, Hermes II, Vulcan,* and *Enforcer*." The young man jerked a thumb back toward a warehouse. "I have a *Catapult—*"

"I don't see any wreckage." Ian's voice boomed with disapproval.

The *Catapult* pilot's head came up, and a few more of the workers started to pay attention. "I don't know if you would have done better or worse than me, mister, but I did what I could."

Morgan held his hands up and glared at the prince. "No offense intended. You were clearly acting responsibly. What did they come for?"

"Looted the warehouse. Took about ten million c-bills worth of wine. That's estimated and probably low. Off planet, there's no telling what they'll get for it."

One of the workers shouted, "And they'll need it to repair the damage you did, sir."

"Thanks, Pete." The young man waved back at them. "I'm Eric Rosen. My family owns the winery. It was lucky I was here, otherwise they'd have gotten away without a shot being fired."

Morgan dismounted. "I'm Dennis O'Brien, this is my wife, Sarah." He completed the introductions using all of their aliases. "We're here looking around, thinking of investing in a resort."

Eric smiled. "Normally we'd offer you a tour of the winery and, well, we're kind of in disarray."

"Understandable."

"It's not the raid. My wife's over in Alberville, at the district medical center. She's just had twins. Wasn't due for a month, then went into labor. That's why I'm still here, not off on maneuvers with the rest of the Militia."

"Congratulations." Morgan smiled. "I'm afraid our horses are exhausted, and we're not much better off. Would you mind if we got some water and rested up a bit?"

"Please, I insist." Eric nodded. "Look, tell you what, I'll call over to the resort, tell them you're here. We've got some stables, and spare rooms. We'll put you up, but you have to promise me that you'll never tell my wife what a mess the place is when I'm batching it."

"Done, thank you."

Eric returned to the work parties. Two of the men came and took care of their horses. Another led them to the main building, pointing them to bathrooms and the kitchen. An array of sandwiches had already been set out for the workers—many of whom, it turned out, were neighbors who'd come to see what they could do to help.

After eating, Frost and Cat joined the workers and pitched in outside filling in missile craters, while Veronica took it upon herself to get the guest rooms ready.

Morgan and Prince Ian wandered the battlefield. The various 'Mechs had left trails of footprints, jet-burn marks, and armor fragments. The way Morgan read the field, Eric Rosen hadn't done that badly. The raiders, by landing instead of doing a combat drop, had given him enough time to get into his *Catapult* and get it ready. He'd used cover well, had targeted the weakest of the 'Mechs first, and had he shot better, he likely would have put both of them down.

Ian rose from the edge of a crater. "He was too close to miss."

"I don't think he's a bad pilot. That's a vintage *Catapult*, and finding parts for those Hollis launchers isn't easy. I'm willing to bet wear on the attitude adjustment gears is what messed him up." Morgan shrugged. "That can be fixed. I'm more interested in his enemies."

The Prince grunted. "Sloppy. They came on like a gang of thugs. No military precision. The *Vulcan* got ahead of his support. The *Clint* pilot just thinks he's the hero in some holovid. Both should have been splashed."

"But they didn't go down. They have some skill." Morgan turned and smiled. "Leutnant Rosen, I hope you don't mind us wandering around."

Eric shook his head, then tossed a disk in a plastic case to Morgan. "I think you'll be wanting to look at that."

"This is?"

"Gun camera footage. The holo of the entire fight. I spliced in the footage from our surveillance cameras, too."

"Thank you, but..."

The young man shook his head. "Hey, tourists don't ride to the sound of guns. I've been watching you two. I bet you can tell me exactly how everything went down here before you even take a look at that."

Ian clasped his hands at the small of his back. "Who do you think we are?"

"I don't know, but I know you've spent time in a cockpit." Eric sighed. "The Militia here is voluntary. Due to this afternoon, I'm now the guy who's fourth in terms of combat experience. Another fifteen minutes, I'd have been second. I don't think the raiders had you come here to do an after-the-battle report, so I'm supposing you might be favorably disposed to helping out."

Ian smiled. "You're perceptive, Leutnant, but I doubt the raiders will be coming back."

"I know they won't." Eric pointed in a southerly direction. "They've landed two 'Mech companies down near Ravensburg, in the Capital District. The militia is two hundred kilometers to the southeast, and coming in fast. Problem is, if the rest of the raiders are only half as good as the guys I faced, they'll go through the militia like water through a screen."

The prince nodded. "Your CO must realize that. A straight up fight would be idiocy. He should go guerrilla."

"He never will—matter of pride with him. Zavijava is his adopted world. He's young, he's game, and is treating this like an invasion." Eric shook his head. "Colonel Wittenberg is..."

A chill ran down Morgan's spine. "Chauncy Wittenberg?"

"You know him?"

"Once upon a time." Morgan nodded. "We better move, or this world's going to lose a lot more than wine."

CHAPTER 9

"Chauncy, it's been a long time." Morgan stopped halfway into the meeting room of the Sugar Plum Inn. The militia had pushed several tables together and covered them with maps. Dominoes and playing cards had been scattered over them, presumably representing 'Mechs and other units.

Colonel Chauncy Wittenburg's head came up slowly, as if he didn't want to look, but felt compelled to do so. His flesh became a bit more grey, and weariness softened his shoulders just a touch more. Never a huge man, he showed the effects of lack of sleep. His hair had thinned since Morgan last saw him, and a turtleneck hid whatever scarring the noose had left around his neck.

"Morgan Kell, as I live and breathe." The rasped words were tinged with hatred. "Come to play the savior again?"

Morgan caught the tightening of Leutnant Rosen's expression, but shook his head. "I'm just here to help."

"I don't need your help."

Chauncey's attitude had been apparent from even before Morgan and Prince Ian had been allowed to see him. The group had traveled with Eric Rosen to Alberville, and then had taken a high-speed maglev train through Ravensburg. Cat, Frost, and Veronica had disembarked there. Quintus Allard had already gone to the second largest city. He and the others would provide intelligence reports, the first of which had come in while the train continued southeast to Ellington.

That report had been favorable, though confusing. The raiders had landed a large force, but instead of occupying the city, had moved off about an hour away, taking over one of the larger tobacco plantations. There two *Leopards* had joined them, and the raiders had brought ice wine and cigars to Ravensburg. They distributed delicacies and established the *Ion Knights* as a force that would take what it wanted, but would share with the common folks. This played well and meant if they retreated into Ravensburg, they'd face little opposition.

Moreover, they might find allies in those who would used their predation to cover a little looting and smuggling of their own. Because the *Ion Knights* made it clear that they didn't want civilian casualties, a lot of people were inclined to ignore them and wait for them to go away.

Chauncy, by the way things were arrayed on the map, seemed inclined to drive them away.

Morgan approached the table, with Prince Ian trailing silently. Chauncy—using suits of cards from ace to Queen— had his militia's three 'Mech battalions neatly organized. The fourth battalion, covering infantry and support personnel, occupied the heart of Ellington. The 'Mech battalions covered the city in an arc from north to west, but did so beyond the ox-bow of Dorsey River, which snaked between them and the city.

Morgan studied the set-up. "What am I missing?"

Wittenberg snorted. "Years of experience with my militia?"

"Having a river at your back isn't good."

"You are suggesting my people will run." The militia commander looked up at his eager young officers. They all smiled, save for Leutnant Rosen. "This is their world, Kell. I don't have them in the city because we don't want it to be crushed. They won't run because this *is* their world."

"But, if I read this map right, you're looking at a broad flood plain with a slight upslope to the north. You should at least be on that ridgeline."

Wittenburg's eyes sharpened. "Don't tell me how to fight my troops. I know these men and women better than you ever will. And for your information, these troops are positioned here only provisionally. Tonight we'll march on Ravensburg and drive the raiders from Zavijava."

Prince Ian couldn't contain himself. He laughed. "You're a fool, if you think that."

"And who do you think you are?"

"I'm—"

Morgan stopped the Prince with a hand. "It doesn't matter, he's right. We came down through the Capital. We were up north and saw the aftermath of a raid. These guys may have been unorganized when they weren't expecting trouble, but they fought. Leutnant Rosen can tell you that they got over their shock fast and operated as a unit."

Eric nodded. "It's true, sir."

Morgan pointed vaguely off toward Ravensburg. "We know what they hit Glacial Rift with. We're working on finding out what they've got outside the capital."

"We?"

"I have some people—good people—in the capital checking things out." Morgan pulled his communicator from a pocket. "I'm expecting another report soon, but it looks like they're not here to take anything over. They want to loot the place and, presumably, go away."

Wittenberg pulled back from the table and crossed his arms. "You have *people* in the capital? You're a mercenary, aren't you? I know I heard that. How do I know the raiders are not *your people*?"

Eric stepped forward. "Sir—"

"No, Leutnant, that's enough. I know Kell. I know how he can put a good face on things. How he can act like a friend, but betray you nonetheless. I have a long memory."

"Then you should remember something else, Chauncy, something from our days at the Nagelring." Morgan stabbed a finger against Ellington. "Defenders have an edge. All you have to do is figure out what these guys want and defend it. Set yourselves up to make them pay for their loot. It's obvious what they're doing."

"What do you suggest? Split my command and put each battalion out to defend warehouses and wineries? Perhaps you'd like to command one for me, is that it?" The man's face soured. "Perhaps you have a copy of their shopping list, so we know where they're going next. And then when I deploy my men to those sites, they hit other ones. Is that what you want?"

"I want you to be sensible."

"I am." Wittenburg's eyes blazed. "This is my world. These are my troops. I am entrusted with the duty of defending this world, and I will acquit that duty. I will do everything I have to in order to save Zavijava."

Prince Ian leaned forward. "Are you just too prideful to see what you're saying, or so congenitally stupid that you don't realized how absurd you're being?"

Wittenburg's chin came up. "If you knew anything about being in a command position—"

"Don't you *dare* take that tone with me!" Ian's face hardened and he seemed to grow yet larger. Morgan knew he should stop him, but he couldn't. Something in Ian's posture and voice said that was impossible.

Ian picked up the Ace of Clubs. "These are *your people*? Are you the lord of this world? Do they owe you fealty beyond gratitude for your volunteering to lead them? Have you the Archon's permission to spend them? No, no, of course you don't. And there is just *part* of your problem. You claim authority *you don't have*."

The Prince tore the card in half. "And worse, you make them into nothing more than objects. Pawns in a game, perhaps, or something even more trivial. I can hear you telling of the fights here when you're older. 'Then my men moved out and gave it their all.' You'll use that line to describe a slaughter where metal and flesh are twisted together and people scream. Do you want to hear them begging to die? Do you want them weeping and calling for their mothers? That's what you're going to get if you go forward."

Ian looked at the officers, all of whom had blanched. "No disrespect intended. All of you have volunteered, and you're to be honored for your service. I'm sure you're all brave and have exercised hard; but how many of you have ever been fired upon? How many of you have been rattled around in a cockpit? How many of you have had to make the decision Leutnant Rosen did—to fight and risk having your 'Mech shut down, or pull back to fight again later?"

The officers all shied from his stare.

Wittenberg stepped in to shield his people. "I don't care who you are. You have no standing here. I have ample evidence to suggest you are working for the enemy."

"*What*?!"

Even Morgan looked at Wittenberg, his jaw agape. "You're insane."

"Am I? You come here, you spread disinformation and try to demoralize my troops? I already know you're for hire, Kell. Who is to say your brother isn't leading the raiders?"

Morgan, stunned, could say nothing.

Ian, stepping forward effortlessly, caught Wittenberg with an uppercut that deposited him on the map table.

Two of the junior officers drew pistols and leveled them at Morgan and Ian.

Wittenberg struggled back to his feet, rubbing his jaw. "That clinches it. You're under arrest. Put them in jail. Once we've taken care of their compatriots in Ravensburg, we will try them, and then hang them by the neck until dead."

Morgan rested on the cell's cot. Across a small corridor, Ian leaned against the front of his cage. He rested his forearms on crossbars, his knuckles still red. The two of them had been strip-searched and given orange jumpsuits to wear.

The Prince sighed. "I would have told them who I was, but I suspect then they'd just have sent me for a psych evaluation."

Morgan found himself laughing. "It wasn't your punch that landed us in here. Chauncy was angling that way once he decided he could claim we were with the enemy. It was more about using his power against me than anything else."

"But he's being willfully blind."

"True." Morgan sat up. "You've heard it said that the worst generals are the ones who are fighting the *last* war, right?"

Ian nodded. "Hanse is fairly vocal on that point."

"Yeah, well, the *worst* general isn't the one fighting the last war. He's the one fighting the *ideal* war. He's a guy who can't or won't take into account variables that don't weigh in his favor. He thinks his troops will always rise above, or the enemy will make a mistake. I'm sure he's taken Eric's fight and spun that into a story about how things will go at Ravensburg. He'll catch them out, hammer them, drive them away. That's the way it has to be for him, so that's the way it will be."

Ian butted his head against an iron bar. "But that can't be the way it is. Eric gave us a very good picture of the militia on the way down. The battalion commanders have seen some combat. The rest of the militia is made up of kids looking for glory or old men trying to recapture it. Asking them to attack is so much more dangerous than asking them to repel attackers. Wittenberg has to see that."

"He doesn't." Morgan shook his head. "You think about the famous generals down through history. We laud the conquerors. We celebrate the warriors who are the spear point, we don't praise those who are the anvil upon which the others are broken. Name a general who mounted a great defense. I can't. I can recall the names of battles where conquerors were defeated, but the leaders who inflicted that defeat, not a chance.

"And that's what Chauncy is looking for. A victory is a chance for him to redeem his life."

"And if his command is slaughtered?"

"They failed him, not the other way around."

The lock on the far end of the corridor buzzed and the steel door swung open. Leutnant Rosen, his expression grave, stepped through. He looked at both men, then glanced down. "I don't know what to think here."

Morgan came to the front of his cell. "Think what you need to, Leutnant. I couldn't let you know who my companions or I were. Operational necessity. Our presence has nothing to do with the raiders. That's just bad luck on our parts."

"The colonel is convinced you're with the raiders. I don't think the whole hanging thing will go through, but..."

"Not something to concern yourself with." Morgan half-closed his eyes. "What happens to you when the units move out?"

Rosen shrugged. "No 'Mech, so I'm attached to the Headquarters company. I'll move north with them and coordinate things. I just don't know..."

Ian arched an eyebrow. "Know what?"

"What you said, it made sense. Look, I love my troops. I have confidence in them, but we've been more about parades than maneuvers; dispersing supplies in secret caches, than burning them with target practice. We're mostly light 'Mechs, and we don't have enough transport to bring our supplies up fast, so any long fight is going to work against us." He glanced down. "And then there's how I felt in the fight. All giddy at first, and then..."

Ian nodded. "Then reality sank in. All of a sudden armor was chipping off and shots were banging around inside your 'Mech."

Eric nodded, but said nothing.

"Doesn't happen much during parades, does it?"

"No, sir." Eric's face came up. "If there's a disaster, what do I do?"

"You give your boys hope." Ian straightened up, his eyes tight. "You, Leutnant Rosen, are the bulwark against disaster. Before people go out, you give them rendezvous points. Pick them out carefully. Make sure you can get supplies to those points. You know this world better than your enemy, so choose places he won't think about. Get them close to those supply caches. Give your people a place to get themselves together. And it's not 'here's where you end up after your run away,' it's 'this is our rendezvous point for the next phase of the operation.' You give them radio frequencies and passwords. You can do that in your new job. That's going to save lives, Leutnant and, in the event of a disaster, it may save your world."

Morgan listened to Ian and slowly smiled. The Prince's reaction to Chauncy—especially the punch—had almost solidified his view of the man as someone who was a great fighter, but not much of a leader. Ian reacted and reacted strongly, which can be enough to turn the tide of a battle, but in those times when it doesn't, salvaging the result is all but impossible.

But here, listening to his advice to the militiaman, Morgan found a new reason to respect Ian. He wasn't unthinking. He could be inspiring. Regardless of what happened outside Ravensburg, Ian's speech would make Eric that much better of an officer. Where the man had seen little hope, he now had both a plan and a purpose. He was the bulwark against disaster.

If lives were going to be saved, Eric's adhering to Ian's advice would be the means through which they were saved.

Eric nodded solemnly. "Thank you."

"Give 'em hell."

The militia Leutnant smiled. "We will. And I'll work on the Colonel. After all this dies down..."

"First things first, Leutnant." Morgan extended a hand through the bars. "Good luck."

Eric shook hands with both of them, then retreated.

As the door clicked shut, Ian looked over at Morgan. "How bad do you think it will be?"

Morgan sighed, hanging his head. "If I remember the map, there's an ocean four hundred kilometers south of here, right?"

"Four-fifty."

"Then the militia—what's left of it—will stop running at four-fifty-one."

CHAPTER 10

Constantine Fisk really wasn't a 'Mech commander, but he'd played one in many holos. His military philosophy could be, and had been, summed up in pithy one-liners he growled onscreen.

Hit 'em where they ain't.

Hit and move.

Give no quarter.

Luckily for the *Ion Knights*, the militia commander was playing things exactly as if reading off a script. He'd failed to quarantine 'refugees' heading south on the maglev, so infiltrating a few scouts had been child's play. Operational security for the militia had been non-existent, and the maglev passed just east of the militia's lines, so the first scouting report confirmed what his intel hackers were pulling from the worldnet.

And that information built itself into a battle plan. Constantine assumed only two things. The first is that the militia plan would go off late simply because these plans always did. Second was that he could guarantee the cooperation of the press, and thereby guarantee his own operational security.

That latter piece had been terribly simple to arrange. News organizations need information. Constantine and Somokis granted interviews, which were broadcast throughout the world. They allowed themselves to come off as slightly disorganized, and made sure the media got plenty of holo of 'Mechs that had taken damage. Lots of them looked as if they had, which was more theatrical magic than reality, making the *Ion Knights* less threatening than they might be. Sharing the wealth of their raids with ordinary folks upped their image and created the Robin Hood mystique, which guaranteed viewer interest.

The *Ion Knights* then offered the local media a chance to embed reporters with the units. They'd get exclusive content and the network managers saw that as a spike in revenues. This made the raids quite lucrative and, for Constantine, would provide a source of publicity that would drive off-world interest in the loot.

The trick of it was, however, that the reporters could only send their material back for broadcast when authorized. Any violation of that plan would sever access, and make a network into a loser in the ratings race. Motivated by profit, reporters used their 'objectivity' to trump their nationality. By withholding information from broadcast, they effectively rendered the *Ion Knights* invisible except when the raiders wanted to be seen.

Colonel Wittenberg, on the other hand, alienated the press from the start, creating an adversarial relationship. Whereas the media had previously loved the militia and reported favorably on them; now they found themselves shut out. Reporters took great delight in ferreting out facts and broadcasting them, as if that would teach the militia a lesson. Again, personal self-interest trumped national pride, making every move the militia made into a news story that kept Constantine and his people wholly up to date on a minute-by-minute basis.

Citing militia activity, Constantine had two lances move back to Ravensburg and begin searching out defensive positions to the southeastern side of the city. That gave the media plenty of holo to keep it occupied. Having learned that the militia was going to come north in the night, Constantine then sent his remaining trio of companies south. One battalion, with his infantry battalion as support, traveled down the western side of the Dorsey River. The other 'Mech battalion forded the river seventy-five kilometers north of Ellington and proceeded down the eastern shore.

The first battalion took up a position twelve kilometers north of the city, on the western side of the maglev roadbed. The infantry crossed over and swung around to the west, positioning itself beyond the militia's western flank. If the militia marched north in a line, they'd bypass the infantry.

The second battalion continued south to the point where the river cut west, and drew off to the east. Using light 'Mechs as pickets, they set up a screening line between them and Ellington, but no one—not even teenagers out off-roading—came near them. The reporters with all the units prepared reports, but weren't allowed to send anything out yet.

The militia had planned to head out at ten in the evening, but it was eleven fifteen before its third company formed up in column and moved toward the east. The first company headed north, and the second came on in good order, leaving only a small gap between the units. The third company reached the launching point for the first company and executed a ninety-degree turn to the north.

And almost completed it.

The *Ion Knights'* second company, consisting largely of medium 'Mechs with long-range missile capabilities, moved west and launched on the militia third from across the river. They concentrated their fire on the middle of the formation, right where the pilots were making their turn. The enfilading fire hit hard, taking 'Mechs in the flank. The first salvo of over two hundred fifty missiles washed fire over the militia. Golden flames burned their azure colors black.

One *Commando* caught the full brunt of two *Trebuchets'* fire on its right side. The missiles slammed into the arm and leg, reducing the armor to glittering dust. More explosions shredded myomer muscles, leaving twitching bundles of artificial flesh on the ground. Bones bent and broke. The arm whirled away to slam into the *Spider* behind him, then the *Commando* toppled back, almost upsetting another 'Mech.

The devastation halted the orderly maneuver. Troops that had already completed the turn sprinted forward. The third lance, led by the *Spider*, stopped its advance and spread out, drawing back from the ruin of the second lance. Only one 'Mech from it survived, a ruined *Panther* that limped away, only to be caught in a second firestorm of missiles.

It vanished from sight.

The panicked first lance ran straight into the second company, disrupting it. Second company had stopped and turned toward the river, but their discipline held for only as long as it took for missile fire to arc in toward them. Having just turned east, now the warriors tried to retreat west, backing into their own rear ranks.

Only the first company, commanded by Colonel Wittenberg, reacted professionally. They stopped, with the third lance immediately withdrawing to the west. Second and first lances turned toward the southeast and drove straight toward the river. Wittenberg anchored his left flank against the maglev bed. His troops pushed forward, launching their own missiles. The third lance ranged further west and south, doing its best to rally second company.

Constantine, safe in his *Enforcer's* cockpit, dropped his crosshairs on the bulky outline of a *Hunchback*. The news media had made it very apparent that Colonel Wittenberg drove that 'Mech, though the markings on it confirmed the pilot's identity. The *Hunchback* had just turned to the right, and a *Jenner* ran past to the south, giving Constantine a clean shot.

He hit the triggers on his two main weapons. The heavy autocannon spat a stream of metal and fire. It traced a path up the stocky mech's right leg, shattering half the armor. The large laser did more. The hellish green beam stabbed into the *Hunchback's* spine, evaporating what little armor existed there, and triggered a secondary explosion. The *Hunchback* wavered as if drunk, suggesting the gyro keeping it upright had been knocked out of phase.

The *Ion Knights'* first company came up over the maglev bed in a wave, beams firing, missiles flying. The militia, caught as it was between two forces, began to crumble. Constantine crested the road-bed, then remained there, his *Enforcer* tall and proud, surveying the mayhem below.

Though he would have thought it impossible, somehow the *Hunchback* managed to pirouette to face him. The boxy, shoulder-mounted autocannon vomited fire. A stream of depleted-uranium shells shot out, striking the *Enforcer* square in the chest.

The impact rocked the 'Mech back, shaking Constantine in the cockpit. Armor sheeted off, grossly shifting the *Enforcer*'s center of balance. The actor tried to step backward, but the roadbed sloped off sharply.

Blasted off its feet, the 'Mech crashed backward. It slammed into the ground hard, pulverizing more armor.

The drop smashed Constantine into the command couch and snapped his head back. The heavy neurohelmet and padding stopped his neck from breaking, but he saw stars. After a moment of black-ness, he tasted blood. He sneezed, spraying it over the inside of his neurohelmet's faceplate.

Dazed and disoriented, it took him a minute to assess his posi-tion. Lights flashed and armor diagrams had shifted from green to red, especially on the 'Mech's chest. He'd landed on his back, crush-ing armor there. His heels had scraped down the roadbed, leaving his feet elevated above the cockpit.

Don't panic, don't panic. He pushed off with one arm, then twisted the 'Mech at the waist. Bending the 'Mech's knees, he got it to slide down to level ground. The *Enforcer* rested on its left side, then he le-vered it back up and regained his feet. He waited for a second, letting some dizziness pass, then quickly mounted the roadbed and got over to the other side.

What had been a battle before had become a rout. First company *Ion Knights* stalked through the evening, shooting at anything that moved, and even things that didn't. Fires guttered in hollow cockpits. Constantine didn't know if pilots had punched out, or had just died in the blackened holes, but his men still shot at the 'Mechs, blowing them to pieces too small to salvage.

No, no, that's all wrong!

Constantine keyed his radio. "Remember our image! Stop shoot-ing the dead 'Mechs. It looks bad in gun-camera holo!"

Off to the west things looked more promising. The rest of the militia had fled beyond missile range. Aside from a *Centurion* firing a rear-mounted laser, resistance had completely collapsed. Switching over to mag-res, Constantine counted fewer than a dozen 'Mechs making their escape. There might have been more, but it was tough to see through the bloody faceplate.

"Two-prime to Lead."

Constantine nodded. "Go, Two-prime."

"We're clear to the city. Do we still occupy it?"

"Status on your company."

"All green. Some armor nicked, but we're all operational."

Constantine punched information up on his auxiliary monitor. "Looks like I've got two down. One is a combat problem, the other is a maintenance failure."

He thought for a moment. Originally Two Company was going to occupy Ellington and cut the Militia off if they put up a stronger fight. From there they'd range east to the Verdant Valley region and loot the wineries. That would complete the preliminary sweep of the area.

"Two-prime, push your guys east. Get a jump on tomorrow. We'll take Ellington and do some refitting there. Send me your dents, and I'll replace them with some of my prisses."

"Wilco, Lead. Enjoy the featherbeds."

"We'll all be sleeping in silk soon enough, Two-prime. Just don't drink too much of the cargo."

"Never, Lead."

"Oh, and leave the press with us."

"On their way."

Constantine switched radio frequencies and got a report from the infantry. The militia had already passed through their lines, completely disorganized. Scouts had put together their best estimates of remaining hostile strength, and it matched Constantine's own survey.

He called the infantry in and had them cross the maglev bridge. He set his own two lance up as a screening force there in the west, then pulled one and three across the bridge. Three took up a position on the town's western outskirts while two lance made the crossing. His infantry then wired the bridge to blow and set up roadblocks on the two main roads in and out.

Though he'd never have been caught dead staying in a place called the Sugar Plum Inn under normal circumstances, Constantine picked it since his ill-fated foe had used it before him. He even took over Wittenburg's room. He cleaned himself up, changing from his bloody cooling vest to a purple jumpsuit with silver cuffs and leg-stripes. He'd designed it himself, and thought it gave him a heroic air while still having a comedic touch that reduced his potential threat.

Ready to address the media, he hesitated and studied the room he'd appropriated. It didn't appear that unusual, which made him wonder about Wittenberg. Not that the man would have moved in *per se*, since it had been a temporary headquarters, but he would have expected to find some sense of the man.

He found very little. Two changes of clothes hung in the closet. One had come back from the laundry and had been heavily starched. That didn't come as much of a surprise. Wittenberg had to have been a man of discipline for him to execute the spin shot that had knocked Constantine flat.

The actor looked for a Bible. In his holodramas, leaders like that always had a Bible, well-thumbed, nearby. It was both their inspiration and solace. He'd imagined Wittenberg had probably read a psalm to his troops as they headed out. *The one about the valley of death, no doubt.*

But no Bible. He did find a diary, but the man's pinched handwriting sent a shiver through Constantine. *Perhaps later.*

Constantine instead turned to a well-worn two book set: *Maxims of Napoleon* and Sun-Tzu's *The Art of War*. The thin pages showed soiled signs of having been read repeatedly, yet none of the pages had been dog-eared nor any passages underlined.

Constantine dropped both books on the bed. *The Art of War* fell open to the fifth chapter. A verse caught his eye. "Know the enemy, know yourself, and victory is never in doubt, not in a hundred battles."

The actor smiled. He read the line over silently, then spoke it aloud, pausing dramatically at each comma. Again, this time emphasizing *enemy, yourself,* and *never*.

Never *is it!*

"Know the enemy, know yourself, and victory is *never* in doubt." He cut the last part. It was too long and drained the line of its full potential. He practiced it one more time, then opened his door and headed off to the conference room, where he'd get to entertain the press.

"As Sun-Tzu said in his classic treatise *The Art of War...*" Constantine smiled. "Perfect. Victory in a hundred battles, starting now with the press."

CHAPTER 11

Even though they'd seen no one since Eric Rosen left, Morgan and Prince Ian had no doubt of the outcome of the battle. To begin with, they'd heard the sound of guns. If Wittenburg's plan had gone as projected, the fight would have happened up at Ravensburg. The Militia had been taken unawares, and that did not bode well for them.

Shooting came closer, but that was mostly small-arms fire. It sounded more like celebratory bursts than anything tactical. After a couple hours, that died down almost entirely. Aside from a shot or two in the wee hours, the night became quiet.

Morgan slept fitfully. He had no idea who the raiders truly were. It was entirely possible they were pirates out to loot the world, but their operation was already so expensive that it almost had to have governmental sanctions. Given Zavijava's location, either the Capellans or House Marik was behind it.

And if they find out who Prince Ian really is...

The Capellans would drag him back to Sian, put him on trial, and ransom him for concessions. *Max might even execute him.* The Free Worlds League would likely ransom him as well, but not publicly, allowing the Archon and Prince Hanse to give them *more*. And the whole ransom scenario didn't go away if the *Ion Knights* were pirates. Ian would be a high-value prize.

This was *not* the sort of situation the Nagelring trained an officer to handle. Morgan had been in tight squeezes before, and he understood the piratical mind fairly well. If the raiders were just raiders, they had a shot at getting out.

If not...Saint Jude's the one deals with lost hope, right?

Before he got a chance to get deeply into prayer, the detention area's lock clicked. The door opened and the dawn's light silhouetted a man. He looked back over his shoulder and shouted, "Got a couple in here."

He stepped into the cell area. The purple and silver uniform reflected enough light to make Morgan shade his eyes. The guy's hair was unkempt and face unshaven, giving Morgan some hope on the pirate front.

He looked the two of them over. "What are you in for?"

Morgan grunted. "Grand theft 'Mech. Seemed like a good idea on the other side of this hangover."

The *Ion Knight* laughed. "Your lucky day, the both of you. You got work-release. Do some work for us, I release you. And you get paid."

Morgan nodded, and Ian aped him. They exchanged covert glances. Ian knew the score. They'd bide their time, get a measure of what was going on, then escape then the opportunity presented itself.

The raider opened their cells and led them out. Five more men in orange jumpsuits joined them. They all marched from the detention center and hopped into the back of a truck painted with the *Ion Knights* logo. It took them to the warehouse district where they went to work loading cases and casks of Scotch whisky onto pallets which 'Mechs came and hauled away.

The operation didn't impress Morgan very much. A quarter of the stuff they were moving just walked away. The raiders were allowing looters who queued up politely to load up with bottles. The looters seemed appreciative of their largess.

Ian wiped his forehead on his sleeve. "This isn't right. Those people shouldn't be sanctioning this kind of action. This is their world, for Heaven's sake."

"But it's not their livelihood."

"They *must* realize that the taxes a business like this pays, as well as the wages that go to the workers, are the underpinnings of the local economy." He waved a hand deeper into the warehouse. "The raiders are cherry-picking the good stuff. You know they'll leave the rest of it to the looters. The Claymore Distillery will lose product extending years into the future. It could collapse, and Ellington would be hurt along with it."

Morgan nodded as they pulled cases of eighteen year old Scotch off a shelf. "No argument from me, but I've also never been in the circumstances many folks are: one payday away from living on the street. Your vision narrows a bunch when that happens. Face it, we're hauling cases of liquor better than anything they can even imagine drinking. This is their chance to get a taste of the rich life. Very tempting."

The commander of the *Ion Knights*' crew came over to them. "What are you two palavering about?"

"Just thinking, boss, that you gotta be having a plan to make something on the side." Morgan loaded the case on the pallet. "You're setting some of this aside, right? Get someone to ship it later. You can't carry it all, 'cepting maybe you leave a 'Mech or two behind."

"Or fill a cockpit." Ian added that with a squint, eyeballing the pallet for how well it would fit. "Empty missile bay would take about four of these, I think."

Morgan laughed. "Lot more than an empty holster."

The *Ion Knight*'s eyes narrowed. "So I give you stuff to ship to me later? Sure. Like that would work."

"It would, boss." Morgan took a step back and lowered his voice. "See, me and Pete here would stash the stuff and send it to you, or an agent you designate, right? ComStar tells you it's arrived. You send us 10% of the value in C-bills, we send you the clearance code. ComStar handles the exchange, it's all good."

The raider scratched his chin. "Tempting."

"Of course, this is high freight to value." Morgan smiled. "Maybe you'd be thinking of looting a museum or one of the art galleries. You could even carry a sample with you, then you broker the rest same way, right?"

"Yeah, maybe. You guys get back to work." The raider pointed them back into line, but wandered off and entered a quiet conversation with his second in command.

Morgan shook his head. "I don't know. Look like pirates, smell like pirates."

"Taking bait like pirates." Ian sighed. "I don't know what appalls me more: the fact that someone could make a raid like this so easily; or that there are people of a criminal bent who could organize this kind of operation."

"It isn't that different from the resource raiding we do."

"But those raids are necessary for sustaining security." Ian opened his arms. "This is a lark."

"Not for the Militia it wasn't." Morgan handed the prince another case of scotch.

"True."

They lugged their cargo to the pallet, but before they could leave it there, the raider commander pulled them aside. "Let's go."

They deposited the liquor in a car's trunk, then joined their boss and another raider. They cruised away from the warehouse district. Small knots of people had gathered in the streets—many drinking from recently liberated bottles—but they thinned as the vehicle moved into the commercial district. There life seemed almost normal, with cafes and restaurants open for business. In fact, things almost had a holiday feel to them—a sense reinforced by banks, galleries, museums and high-end stores being closed up tight.

The Commander turned around in the front passenger seat. "So we did a quick check. There's a museum, got some art, got an exhibit of high-end jewelry. It's on display in some kind of safe."

Morgan shook his head. "Don't know anything 'bout blowing a safe."

Ian smiled. "I do. You got the putty, I'll crack it."

The raider smiled. "I got that covered. I just need you for hauling and storage, got it?"

"We're good, boss."

The vehicle swung around to the back of the Sinclair Foundation Museum of Art. The rectangular building had a simple elegance to it. A narrow side fronted the street, and two large marble lions flanked the main entrance. In the back a loading dock opened into a warehouse with doors large enough for a 'Mech to enter.

As they got out of the vehicle, two night watchmen came out and waved them off. The *Ion Knight* leader went over to talk to them. Shaking heads turned into nods. The raider returned, had Morgan and Ian deposit the cases of Scotch into two other vehicles parked at the back, then all four entered the museum with the night watchmen.

One of the watchmen smiled. "Make it look good, will you, but don't break nothing."

The raiders complied, cracking both men in the back of the head with pistols. Morgan and Ian tied them up, then hauled them to a far corner of the warehouse. One of them dripped blood from a scalp laceration. Morgan tore a sleeve off his jumpsuit to bind it up.

They rejoined the raiders in the main gallery. A huge safe with a glass wall housed jewelry. The various pieces lay on circular shelves that slowly spun, allowing all of them to pass beneath bright lamps that scattered pinpoint rainbows as the gems refracted the light. Diamonds mostly, but a fair number of emeralds and rubies made the whole display absolutely dazzling.

Morgan frowned. "There are grooved tracks inside the windows there. Disturb things and steel panels are going to slide up."

The lead raider smiled. "I know. I've seen the design before. There is a way to crack it."

"Yeah?"

The man nodded, then smiled. "Right on time."

Morgan felt the vibration through the ground. They drifted back through the warehouse and onto the loading dock.

Ian whistled. "I guess you *do* have it covered."

A *Centurion*, ten meters tall, waited for them. Aside from some blackening around the muzzle of the autocannon that ended at the 'Mech's right wrist, it showed no sign of the previous night's battling.

The raider pointed to the laser mounted in the 'Mech's chest. "Hot knife through butter."

"Hot knife that'll melt the jewelry."

"Not this guy. He's good." Leader beckoned the pilot down to join them. "You guys just find crates for all the art and start boxing it up. You got an hour, because that's all it will take to handle that safe."

THE TRIAL
DISTRICT OF DONEGAL, THARKAD
LYRAN COMMONWEALTH

Patrick Kell ran fingers through his hair one last time before stepping into the Archon's office. He'd gotten the call just a half-hour before, and his heart had been in this throat the whole time. Something had happened to Morgan. He knew it, and felt as helpless has he'd been when Morgan disappeared with the Archon before.

Katrina's appearance did little to reassure him. A general weariness weighed her down, and dark circles appeared under her eyes. "Thank you for coming so quickly."

"What's happened?"

Katrina pointed him to a chair and handed him a tumbler half-full of whisky. "You'll want this."

"Katrina...is Morgan . . ?"

The Archon perched herself on the edge of the desk. "I don't know. I don't think so. I can't believe it's possible that he is."

Patrick nodded. The conviction in her voice dispelled the worst of his fears. "What happened?"

"Reports are sketchy. ComStar claims there's some routing problem, which probably is a lie, but who knows with them. The long and short of it is this: the world I sent Morgan to with Prince Ian has been hit by raiders, roughly a battalion in strength. The latest reports indicate that the raiders have squared off against the local militia. My analysts don't give the militia much of a chance."

"Where are the raiders from?"

"No clue. They call themselves the *Ion Knights*." Katrina sipped her Scotch. "I've never heard of them."

"Nor have I." Patrick contemplated his Scotch, then set it on the desk. "No word from Morgan, obviously."

"I was hoping that the two of you had arranged some sort of signals—completely breaching security, of course—in the case of an emergency."

"Well, Archon, *if* we did that, given what ComStar charges, any message from two days ago wouldn't arrive until noon today."

"You'll let me know." Katrina's scowl deepened. "You can appreciate my situation here, yes? If this is just a raid, then I have to treat it as a raid. Aside from being unable to deliver assets there inside ten days, if I overreact, the raiders might figure there is something of extreme value on Zavijava. If Prince Ian were smart, he'd go to ground, stay out of trouble, and thereby stay safe."

Patrick snorted. "You wouldn't do that."

"It's not his world."

"Do you honestly think that would matter to him?"

"Perhaps not." She shrugged. "Your brother will act, won't he?"

"Offer to lend a hand, of course. And..." Patrick sighed. "Prince Ian wouldn't stand for being left behind. Okay, so they're both in the thick of it. Maybe they're bolstering the militia. This could all turn out well."

"I can hope, but I have to plan against disaster." Katrina got up and walked around her desk, taking her place in the big leather chair. "I've just told you that Morgan is on Zavijava. I'll pretend you didn't already know that."

"I actually didn't. Morgan gave me a coded message, but I've not cracked it."

"I've got to get troops there, and quickly. Your Hounds are headed in this direction. How difficult will it be to divert to Zavijava?"

"As long as the JumpShip assets are in place, it should be fast. They're not due to hit the Galatean JumpPoint for another day, so I can divert them. I'll have to plot the course, but there's plenty of worlds there. Two jumps, maybe three. Hit a pirate point around Zavijava. I could have them there inside ten days, maybe eight." He frowned. "I won't be able to be there, but our troops are solid."

"I'll get you those JumpShip assets. They'll be where you need them and fully charged."

He nodded, then looked up. "Archon, you've not mentioned the idea that these raiders are state sponsored. It's not like you to make an oversight like that. Intelligence assets on Atreus and Sian are reporting no sign of this, right? If it had been in the offing, a trip to Zavijava would have been off the table."

Her head came up slowly. "Are you suggesting that I intended Prince Ian to be given over to the enemy, and used your brother's presence to reassure Ian so he'd go quietly to his demise? You've not been on Tharkad so long for such paranoia to sink in."

"That sort of treachery would have suited your predecessor, Archon, so it's hard to avoid it. But, I wasn't thinking ill of you. I was just wondering who would profit by Prince Ian vanishing. Could these raiders be Davion troops in disguise?"

The Archon blinked. "I shouldn't think...Hanse, no. Michael Hasek-Davion, on the other hand? Maybe. Oh God, if that's what's going on here..."

"It's probably just raiders." Patrick stood. "I'll get the course for the Hounds changed. I'll let you know what Morgan says. It will all work out. You know Morgan. You know it will."

Katrina nodded. "Yes, I know Morgan. I hope for the best. And if anyone harms him, they'll learn that angering the Archon of the Lyran Commonwealth is not a way to guarantee longevity."

CHAPTER 12

The nice thing about greed was that it made the raiders less than observant. While the leader and the pilot—both of whom looked so much alike that they had to be brothers—assessed the vault, Morgan and Ian loaded up with hammers, nails, and a couple crates. The other raider kept an eye on them, with a laser carbine at the ready all the time, but his attention wandered easily.

Soon he'll get close enough and...

Ian and Morgan shared a nod. It would take a while. They'd box up a couple paintings and their guard would get bored. Some mumbling about the gems, and he'd look toward the vault. If they took him then, got the carbine, they could hit the other raider and figure out how to elude the *Centurion*.

That was the most iffy part of the plan, but it could be done. Human beings are at an advantage in an urban setting. Corner fast, using buildings as cover, go where the 'Mech can't, and they could get away. The *Centurion* didn't have any anti-personnel weaponry *per se*. While *any* of its weapons would kill a man easily enough, hitting a tiny target wasn't easy. Even the missiles, which had the most lethal potential in this regard, were not suited to close range combat, and the urban setting made everything close range.

Morgan was content to bide his time up until the drunk stumbled into the museum. Bottle of Scotch in one hand, a ragged, soiled overcoat covering him, the slender man banged against a display case. "Wass goin' on here? Are you s'posta be here?"

The lead Raider and pilot turned from where they were measuring the armored panels. The other raider took a step forward, brandishing the carbine. "Get out of here, you bum."

The drunk sagged to the floor beside the case. The bottle spilled, Scotch gushing out in a succession of *glugs*. "Look what you did now! You're in trouble." He flopped over on his belly and started sucking the liquor off the marble tiles.

The pilot and his brother exchanged glances, then ran over to where the drunk was slithering through the whisky puddle. They each bent to grab an arm. "Not in *our* museum, you bum."

The drunk rolled onto his back, filling his left hand with a small laser pistol. The first shot hit the pilot in the face, exploding his left eye. Boiled brains jetted out through a hole behind his left ear.

The lead raider went for his pistol. Three bolts took him, starting at the groin and working up. Eighteen centimeters separated them, all on the centerline. The last roasted his heart. He crashed back into a display, scattering old coins amid an avalanche of broken glass.

The last raider raised the laser carbine, but before he could stroke the trigger, Morgan cracked him with a hammer in the back of the head. The man went down as if all his bones had melted. He wasn't quite dead. His breath came raggedly, and the dent in his skull suggested he wasn't going to last long.

Frost shoved the pilot's body off and stood, letting glass cascade over the floor. "More shopping to do?"

"I'm good."

Ian nodded, scooping up the laser carbine. "I have everything I need."

Frost bent down and stripped the cooling vest off the pilot's corpse. "Cat asked me to get something for him."

Morgan smiled. "You're kidding."

"He left the engine running." Frost led them back out to loading dock. Cat Wilson had climbed up into the *Centurion's* cockpit, appropriated the pilot's neurohelmet, and had buttoned things up again. The *Centurion* gave them a brief wave.

Prince Ian nodded appreciatively to Morgan. "Your people are impressive. Now if only they could get *us* into 'Mechs."

"Funny thing about that, Highness." Frost smiled, and Morgan didn't find it as warm an expression as he might have hoped. "Cat had some thoughts in that regard."

Simpson 'Mechworks was, quite simply, the finest 'Mech repair facility on Zavijava. That made sense, it being in the capital. Still, aside from repairs to Agroand ServiceMechs, it didn't do much business. The militia's exercises rarely did damage, so the closest they got to handling combat-ready 'Mechs was when some captain of industry decided to import a hulk from Solaris VII and have it refurbed for use in local parades or back on the game world.

Handling the *Ion Knights* repairs really put Harry Simpson in something of a quandary. He really didn't want to be doing the job, but having laser carbines pointed at you does have a way of making some decisions a bit easier. Add the fact that the *Ion Knights* were willing to pay for repairs, and he decided to do the work. Granted, they were paying in loot, and he knew he'd have to give it back to the rightful owners, but his insurance would cover the cost of repairs, and returning the loot would be good for folks.

They'd gotten the *Enforcer* completed first, since all that needed to be done there was putting armor plates back on it. Harry had seen what an extra-heavy autocannon could do before, and figured the pilot of that 'Mech had been very lucky. If it had hit an arm, it would have come clean off. It would have blown through the flank armor and done some internal damage—more than his shop could have fixed.

Harry had just marched the *Enforcer* over to the painting station when the *Centurion* showed up. He didn't spot any obvious problems with it, which usually meant it was a computer glitch that could take forever to track down. Then a motorcycle whizzed in between the *Centurion's* legs and skidded to a stop at the *Enforcer's* broad feet. A tall, dark-haired man got off from behind the driver and jogged over to him.

"Can I help you?"

"I hope so." The young man smiled. "My name is Morgan Kell. I have a mercenary unit. I need to borrow a couple of 'Mechs. This *Enforcer,* I think, and what kind of shape is that *Catapult* in?"

Harry's jaw dropped open. "Are you kidding? This gotta be a joke."

"'Fraid not. You're insured, right?"

"You can't..."

The motorcycle's driver flashed a laser pistol. Harry wouldn't have thought it much of a threat, but the man's flat eyes had no mercy in them at all.

"Do you know what they'll do to me?"

Morgan nodded. "Tell your people to go to ground. Lose yourself, somewhere far away. I guarantee this place will be rebuilt better than it was before."

"Are you mad?"

"Just impatient. What's the override on the maintenance codes?"

"I can't just..."

"Yes, you can. You will." The young man peered at the name embroidered on his cooling vest. "Look, Harry, we intend to send these raiders packing. Either you're going to have collaborated with them, or with us. Your choice, but with us is a much safer bet for the long term."

Harry closed his eyes. "Override is Paragon. Why, I don't know, but that's what the guy picked."

"'The guy?'"

"Their leader, the actor. Constantine Fisk."

"An actor?" The young man's brow furrowed. "Well, let's see how he likes improv."

Morgan took the *Enforcer*. Ian squeezed himself into the *Catapult*. Harry Simpson had given them the correct codes. Morgan brought all systems online and smiled.

He keyed his radio to the frequency he shared with the other two machines. "I've got a full load of ammo and my lasers are green and good.

"*Catapult*'s missile loads are at half."

"Let's do some light work and get out of here." Morgan brought the *Enforcer* over, raising the left arm. He pressed the muzzle to the head of a *Vulcan* and hit the trigger. One shot from the green beam evaporated all the armor. The second melted the cockpit.

Ian used his medium lasers to cripple a *JaegerMech*. The resulting fire started the shop's sprinkler system going, and set off an alarm.

Frost's motorcycle raced out of the shop and quickly lost itself in the city. The trio of BattleMechs headed south, skirting the warehouse district. They made for the outskirts of town, figuring on traveling west, crossing the river, then heading up into the Franklin Mountain Preserve.

Just as they hit the suburbs, a light started blinking on Morgan's communications console. A blocky-chested *Vindicator* had appeared in his six. The missile bay's cover remained closed, but the Particle Projection Cannon that made up the 'Mech's right forearm swung into line with the *Enforcer*. One shot could rip through his 'Mech's back armor, and that would end the escape fast.

Morgan cross-linked the communications channels, then punched the glowing button. He clicked his microphone twice.

"Where you heading in such a rush, boss? Need help?"

Shit. Morgan turned the *Enforcer* to face the *Vindicator*. It massed less than his 'Mech, but had a lot of armor. Now that they were facing each other, the *Enforcer* could easily go toe-to-toe with it, but the last thing Morgan wanted was a fight that alert other raiders and turn into a running firefight.

Morgan sought in vain for a peaceful way out, but Ian precluded the search. The *Catapult*'s launch bay doors snapped open. Thirty missiles arced through the air, well over half finding their target. Armor shattered, whirling shards slashing streetlights in half. One daggerish chunk impaled a car—its alarm screaming. Four red lasers punched through the smoky cloud, liquefying armor all over the 'Mech.

Morgan's auxiliary scan showed severe damage on the right leg and left arm, with moderate damage over the chest and left leg.

Cat Wilson's *Centurion* weighed in. Ten missiles shot from the 'Mech's left breast and all of them slammed into the *Vindicator*. Half of them stripped the last of the left arm's armor off and nibbled away at the myomer fibers controlling that arm. His heavy autocannon zipped a line of shells up the blocky Mech's chest, staggering it. Two more lasers vaporized armor on each flank.

When in Rome...

Morgan dropped his crosshairs on the beleaguered raider's 'Mech. The dot at the center pulsed red. His hands convulsed. The large laser's verdant beam burned off the last vestige of the *Vindicator*'s left arm, leaving a guttering hole. The heavy autocannon spat a stream of shells through that opening, striking sparks as they ricocheted around in the 'Mech's chest. They splashed heat sinks and, more importantly slammed into the 'Mech's missile magazine.

The missiles cooked off in a string of explosions that first jetted fire out through the armhole. Next the chest armor became luminescent, as if it was parchment hiding a candle. Quickly enough, the fire burned through from the inside. The explosions continued lifting the shoulder and head from the 'Mech. As the cockpit tumbled upward, the right arm arced like boomerang and cut through the upper story of a brick apartment building.

One leg remained standing, while the other fell over, scraping the façade from an insurance office.

Morgan keyed his radio. "Anyone see him get out?"

"Negative." Ian sounded slightly remorseful.

Cat just remained silent on the subject.

The radio buzzed with excitement. "What happened?"

Morgan replied. "Insurgents. Hit and run with missile launchers. Ammo cook off. They're heading east."

Orders began being shouted. Morgan and the others headed west and disappeared before the bedlam in Ellington had begun to die down.

SUGAR PLUM INN, ELLINGTON
CAPITAL DISTRICT, ZAVIJAVA

Constantine Fisk sat in his room, completely disbelieving what had happened. The search for insurgents had produced no results. The *Ion Knights* had tightened up security as a precaution, and that revealed three missing men, two infantry and one pilot. Then word came that a *Catapult* and his own *Enforcer* had been stolen. All the repair shop workers had vanished.

And the thing which got Fisk is that there was no *way* Chauncy Wittenberg could have planned and executed such an operation. Constantine knew this because he'd spent time in the man's room. He'd read his diary—the pedantic chronicle of an insignificant life spent whining about past failures. Defeats were never Wittenburg's fault, and the victories were described with the sort of mind-numbing exactitude that would only excite future historians with a taste for trivia and banality.

But then, there were the last few entries. Wittenberg had come alive once the raiders had landed. He wrote extensively of his own brilliance in planning the assault on Ravensburg. Constantine was even inclined to imagine that the militia, had the plan unfolded as the Colonel intended, might have done some damage.

As a sidebar Wittenberg had written about a personal victory, a triumph over an old adversary he simply noted as K. Constantine imagined K to be some waiter who had served the man cold soup, but then things unfolded. In backtracking the deaths at the museum, his people found the sleeve of a prisoner's jumpsuit. In returning to the city's detention center, they located two envelopes with personal effects, and a note in one from Wittenberg explaining the charges being leveled against Morgan Kell.

Constantine knew the name. Not well, but he'd been up for the part of Morgan Kell in a docudrama about Archon Katrina Steiner's missing fourteen months. No one had a clue about where she had gone or what she had done, and the holo had some juicy bits with a love triangle between her, Kell, and Arthur Luvon. The project foundered for lack of financing, but not before Constantine had done some research.

He reached for his communicator and punched up a connection to Count Somokis. "It's Constantine."

"What the devil's going on down there? I've had reports."

"Nothing we can't handle."

"Don't be so sure."

Something in Somokis' voice made Constantine sit up. "What's the matter?"

"I've had my intel people sifting computers to ferret out secrets. Our investors want the best, after all."

"And they're getting it."

"They might get more. My people have uncovered files buried deeply that indicate there is a secret weapons development lab on Zavijava. There are projects to extend the range of conventional weapons to roughly double what they are now. Can you imagine how that will revolutionize warfare?"

Constantine raised an eyebrow. "Then it makes sense."

"What does?"

"I have evidence that the Archon's cousin, Morgan Kell, is here, on Zavijava. Who else would she entrust such a project to? She trusts him with her life."

"Wasn't he forming a mercenary group?"

"Presumably. More like her Praetorian Guard, outfitted with advanced weapons. With an army as you describe, there would be no stopping them."

"Agreed." Somokis' voice got cold. "This takes things to a new level. Continue your operations, but be very careful. I have steps to take to secure things here, then we move for the secret lab."

"What if the mercenaries are already here?"

"They would have hit us already. But, their arrival may be imminent." The man laughed, and it came through tinny, yet sinister. "I'll handle that problem. Get me the Archon's cousin. That's a level of insurance I would like very much to hedge against disaster."

CHAPTER 13

Morgan sighed as he closed his communicator. "No signal."

Prince Ian held his communicator aloft and cursed. "None here, either. Just the mountains, or are they jamming things?"

"I doubt it's jamming." Morgan held his hands out over the fire they'd made—using a shot from the *Enforcer's* small laser to kindle it.

Though it hadn't been easy, they'd brought their 'Mechs into a gorge split by a river. While they hadn't seen the raiders use any aerospace assets, the gorge's narrow sky would make a quick-pass scan less likely to find them.

A soft breeze hissed through the pines, and the river's dull roar filled the gorge. Between the scent of the trees and the smoke from the crackling fire, Morgan had a hard time feeling like he was on the run. *When this is over, I want to bring Veronica here.*

He'd not have mentioned it to his compatriots, but he was less concerned about getting tactical data over the communicator than he was in talking to Veronica and letting her know everything was okay. What they'd expected to be a simple getaway had become hopelessly complex. While Veronica was more than capable of taking care of herself, he wasn't sure how she'd handle violence—especially after so nearly dying in a terrorist attack herself.

We're going to need a lot of time.

Cat, squatting by the fire, tossed Morgan a ration packet. "Old, manufactured in Marik space."

Morgan ripped it open. "Instant stroganoff, just add water. At least there's coffee."

The prince accepted a packet from the black MechWarrior. "So, they're from the Free Worlds League. Appears to be a battalion.

They've hit a world with no military or scientific assets, took the capital, but didn't issue any proclamation about the world belonging to the Free Worlds League. If it's an invasion, it's a very poorly run one."

Morgan slit the instant coffee packet open with a thumbnail and put a pinch between his cheek and gum. The bitter taste filled his mouth immediately, so he sipped some water. "Nothing in our dealings with the raiders suggested the *Ion Knights* are anything *but* raiders. That doesn't mean they can't become more, though."

Cat stood, the fire highlighting his face with gold. "Easy hit here, you think the League decides to capitalize on things?"

"If Katrina doesn't react quickly and strongly, yes."

Ian's eyes narrowed. "But she can't, lest she seem to value this world too much."

"Exactly." Morgan glanced up at the night sky. "I don't know the border worlds here. How fast can the League get support troops in position?"

The prince poured dried noodles and water into a steel pot, then nudged it onto coals at fire's edge. "Week, week and a half. We'd picked Zavijava because they don't station troops near here. We didn't want the exercises to trigger an attack."

Cat grunted. "No problem, then."

"Really?" Morgan raised an eyebrow. "Explain."

"You see it, Colonel. It's been easy for them. They're loading up. No one is fighting them. This is an expensive operation. We make it more so. Have a *fine* start."

That was true. Stealing three medium 'Mechs and shooting up three more would crimp their resources. *Even so...*"We have two problem with what you're thinking, Cat. The first is that if we get Ian here killed while fighting League forces, we'll have pissed off three of the larger nation-states. That pretty much means a life of ditch-digging for us."

The prince didn't look up from where he stirred the boiling noodles with a fork. "Ian can take care of himself, thanks. Next problem."

"We have three 'Mechs. Our ammo is limited. We're outnumbered roughly a dozen to one."

"Remember, Frost is out there."

"I counted on him to be taking out the infantry."

"You should have counted on me watching your back-trail, Colonel." Frost slipped out of the shadows, his rifle over his shoulder. "You're clear, by the way. Scout car they sent patrolling west had an accident. Crew drove fast into a bullet."

Ian smiled. "Mr. Frost, if you ever decide to leave the Kell Hounds, I will have ample work for you."

The sniper nodded, but said nothing.

Morgan looked at him. "Anything else to report?"

"Got Allard up in Ravensburg. He's been watching ComStar. The *Ion Knights* have a civilian working communications for them, some League Count. Allard says his name is Somokis; an industrialist with more money than brains. No military types. Allard says he and Veronica are safe. She's sent a couple messages?"

Morgan nodded. "To my brother. A precaution."

"The *Ion Knights* are doing a lot of looting. Was mostly commodities before, but now they're doing art, jewels, other high-value, low-mass stuff. Allard thinks they're looking to hire other DropShip assets to haul things off."

Cat smiled. "Looks like you gave them ideas, Colonel."

"I got that." Morgan's nostrils flared. "We have no choice but to slow them down, even if we are outnumbered."

"Yeah, well, I think I can help you there, too." Frost smiled confidently. "I've done some scouting around and..."

Morgan had hoped, someday, to see Leutnant Rosen again. The surprise on the man's face attested to his innocence, and the fact that it quickly changed into a grim expression marked his maturity. The militia officer had been standing guard near a cavern complex for which the nature preserve was naturally famous.

When Morgan cleared his throat, Rosen had spun, bringing a needler up. Before he could pull the trigger, Frost pressed the muzzle of a laser pistol to his neck. The militiaman stiffened, then let his gun drop to the ground.

"Don't worry, Leutnant, there are no hard feelings about being jailed." Morgan opened his arms easily. "As it is, my companions and I have quit the city. We're in need of munitions and allies. I'm led to believe you might have both here."

Rosen nodded dejectedly. "I have munitions. Colonel Wittenberg was good on hiding ammo stores all over the place. Allies, I'm not so sure."

"How many of your men survived?"

"Physically? Out of a battalion, I have a company and a half of 'Mechs. I've lost six pilots. They've just run away. I have few more men, but none of them are in fighting shape. They're scared." He looked down at the gun. "I think they'd not still be in the cave save that I'm out here with this gun."

Morgan picked up the pistol and handed it back to him. "I think we can do something to help you out. I'll be back in about fifteen minutes. Frost will stand watch out here. You get your boys ready for a show."

When Morgan, Cat and Ian marched their 'Mechs into the cavern, the militiamen stared at them, completely cowed. The war machines did look menacing, and the militia 'Mechs, all parked further back, had a shadowed and docile sense to them. A couple warriors did run toward the 'Mechs—at least Morgan assumed that's where they were going. Leutnant Rosen stopped them with a command, and they turned with resignation.

It was about then that some of them noticed that the 'Mechs, though painted in *Ion Knight* colors, had their faceplates open and weapons-pods closed. The trio of pilots popped out and descended quickly, each wearing a big smile. Morgan greeted them expansively, waving a hand back. "Heard you boys were looking for some fun, and we grabbed some rides to join in."

That got a round of laughs, but it died quickly. There was no missing the fear on their faces. Morgan could smell the fear, too, that acrid, nervous scent. They'd been stewing in it. They'd not bathed since their defeat, and the smoke from the small fires they'd made didn't cover the smell.

Morgan started to say something to rally the troops, but a hand landed on his shoulder. Prince Ian pulled him back, then moved toward the gathering's center. "Gentlemen, ladies, gather 'round. Sit down." His words came low and strong, in a commanding tone that both demanded compliance and built confidence.

The Prince slowly looked from one person to the next, holding their gazes until they shied. Then he began speaking, calmly, matter-of-factly. There was no way to doubt the veracity of his words.

"You're all wondering 'why me?' Why am I under attack? Why did I survive when others didn't? Why am I going to die? Why did they come here to my world? All those questions, natural questions." Ian raised his head. "The questions warriors have asked of themselves since before Troy fell. By asking them, you know you're a warrior.

"I can answer one of them for you. Why did they come to your world? I know." He pressed a hand to his cooling vest. "They came because I'm here. Many of you know my companion is Morgan Kell. This is Cat Wilson, one of his Kell Hounds. That's Frost, another member of the mercenaries. They're here because the Archon—Morgan's *cousin*—asked them to accompany me. So I'm the reason."

Don't do it, Ian...

"Take a good look, all of you. I'm the reason because I'm Prince Ian Davion, ruler of the Federated Suns. No, I truly am. They came here to loot your world, and I'm the biggest prize they could possibly find."

The militiamen stared up at him, half in awe, half disbelieving. Even Morgan stared, and Eric Rosen with him. Ian had started out testing him, but he didn't do that with these warriors. He knew them at a glance, and he knew what had to be done with them. He had them surprised and curious. *Can he bring them back?*

"None of that matters, though, because they don't have me. They're not going to get me, and not because I'm going to run. They won't get me because I won't let them. In fact, there's a lot of things I'm not going to let them do. And one of them, *just one*, is I'm not going to let them loot your world."

His voice began to rise, and echoed deep into the cavern, back amid the militia 'Mechs. "Raids. I've seen raids. I've seen raids by the best the Combine has to offer. I've fought against the Capellan Confederation's Warrior Houses. Now there are some nasty troops. I'll show you scars. Oh, I've fought against the best, and I've lived to tell about it.

"But these guys, the *Ion Knights*? Sloppy. No discipline. Cat just climbed into that *Centurion's* cockpit easy as you please. The pilot treated his 'Mech like a car, leaving the engine running while he went for coffee. Sloppy. Then Morgan and I waltzed into a shop. Simpson Mechworks. You know it. We just walked in, told Simpson and his people to get clear, then took that *Enforcer* and the *Catapult*. Leutnant Rosen left his up north, so we had to bring him a ride. Before we left that shop we melted the heads off two other 'Mechs, then blew up a *Vindicator* that thought it was going to stop us from leaving Ellington. We have gun-camera to show you."

The Prince had begun to pace, his expression earnest. He let outrage build in his words. "Can you imagine anyone being so sloppy?"

One warrior shifted uneasily. "Kicked our asses easily enough."

"So you're just going to let your ass remain kicked?" Ian shook his head. "I've seen reports of what happened. You were ambushed. They deployed, they hit you, panic set in. You broke. You ran. Apparently some of you think that's the end of the world. Why is that? Because in holovids no one ever runs? That wasn't a holovid. Life isn't. Fear's part of it. But a bigger part is getting over fear."

Then Ian smiled, pointing a finger back toward Ellington. "And a *bigger* part, a *better* part, is giving that fear back."

His voice dropped again, and he crouched, his words growled. "I'm offended, *personally* offended. These *Ion Knights*, they come here, they ambush you, drive you off, then start looting the world? They have no honor. I can smell it from here, and I hate it. They're treating your world, your beautiful world, like a store where they can just smash a window and grab whatever they want. That offends me so deeply I can't explain it.

"But I *can* do something about it. And I *am* going to do something about it. But I'm going to need your help." Again his head rose. "They're out there thinking they're the toughest thing since Kerensky left with the SLDF. They're laughing about how they drove you off.

They're making jokes about how many of you had to change your shorts after the first missiles flew."

He laughed. "If I had a C-bill for every soiled pair of shorts I've seen through the years, I could buy the Scotch they're stealing. And, you know what, I *want* a C-bill for every stained set of shorts *they're* going to be changing. And you're going to help me. You know this world better than any of them could. You know the places they're going to hit, like the Leutnant's winery. You know how they're going to get there, and you know how we can nail them coming and going. *They're* thieves. *We're* warriors. And we're going to remind them of the difference."

Ian waved them off toward their 'Mechs. "You go get those beasts ready. I want to know what's operational and what's not. We're going to load up, and we're going to go find us some *Ion Knights* to play with. Morgan, he knows what he's doing, same with Leutnant Rosen. I've been around a few battles myself. We'll form you up into lances, then we're going hunting. As much as you didn't like getting surprised, they're going to hate it even more. Go!"

The pilots scattered to their 'Mechs. Rosen watched them go, then stared at Ian. "Are you really?"

"I am. The *Catapult* is yours. Morgan tells me you have some 'Mechs without pilots. I'll take one of them."

Morgan shook his head. "Nope. You're taking the *Enforcer*. It's the heaviest thing we've got, and its armor is full up. I'll find a ride over there."

The prince nodded. "Thank you."

"Think it was wise?"

"Letting them know who I am?" He smiled. "Human beings are funny. They'll act to protect their families. They'll act to protect their nation, sometimes. But make them feel like they're part of something bigger, make them feel that they've got an emotional connection with something bigger, and they stop thinking about themselves.

"That's the thing about fear. It's all inside. You have to get them out of themselves. Then it doesn't matter anymore."

Ian smiled. "They feel beaten, afraid, dishonored. We're giving them a chance to reverse that. I don't know about you, but I wouldn't be an *Ion Knight* for anything right now. Payback's a bitch, and the *Ion Knights* have got a ton of it coming."

CHAPTER 14

The bullet would have killed Constantine Fisk cleanly, save for a bit of advice a limousine driver had once given him. He was on the way to his first awards show, just to be in the audience and to be seen. He'd not yet had the honor of being nominated for some award he'd never win. He entered on the passenger side and slid all the way over, but when the driver got in, he gently corrected him.

"No, sir, you never sit directly behind the driver." He said it with firm conviction—a conviction Constantine had used later in a holo. He hadn't been certain if there were security concerns, or it was just etiquette, but he'd never again made that mistake.

Which was why when the 12.5-millimeter bullet burst through the car's windscreen and exploded the driver's head, the tumbling slug passed to Constantine's left and shattered the back window. The driver's body slumped right, jerking the wheel. The vehicle swerved right. The truck next in the convoy, traveling too close for speed, caught it in the rear quarter-panel. The car skidded, then spun and tumbled off the two-lane highway.

Time slowed to nothing. Constantine jammed his hands against the seat in front of him. The thought *I'm a leopard!* came unbidden. As the car started to roll, he realized the spots on his hands were blood and brains, maybe bits of bone, too. Then he felt warm wetness on his face and tasted copper on his lips.

His body jackknifed forward as he puked.

That saved his life again.

The careening car spun and flew into a shallow ravine. Traveling rear end first and upside down, the hood hit hard. The car snapped down, flattening the roof. The intact side windows blew out. The vehicle bounced once, rolled again, the crumpled hood flying into the darkness. When it came down again, a large rock ripped the roof off. The car landed heavily, crushing the fuel tank, which immediately gushed its volatile cargo over the hot exhaust system and started a merry little blaze.

His fingers having clawed through the front seat's leather upholstery, Constantine pulled himself up. Something was cooking. *Meat.* It was either him or what was left of the driver, and he really didn't want to stick around to find out. He hit the safety-belt release, then pulled himself clear. He took three steps, then fell.

He wanted to lie there, but he could still smell roasting flesh, so he crawled further from the vehicle. Dragging himself behind a large rock, he rolled onto his back, sucking in lungfuls of cool night air. His chest heaved. A snort cleared blood from his nostrils. The dull ache of a broken nose began making itself known.

He lay there on his back until he remembered something an advisor on a movie told him. The guy was an old infantry officer. "Men who are alive hung the earth face down. Looking at the stars, they've given up."

I can't die like this.

He rolled over, getting his back against the stone. Up on the hillside, deep from within the forest, machine guns flickered, spraying the coastal highway. The *Jenner* and *Firestarter* that had been on point for the convoy, returned fire. The *Jenner* launched short-range missiles that exploded at treetop level. A golden flash lit the forest as a lethal mixture of metal shrapnel and wooden splinters rained down through foliage. The missiles tore divots from the greenery, but other guns opened up from different points.

The *Firestarter*'s chest-mounted machine-guns opened up. Spent shells cascaded down into the ravine, a tinkling river of hot metal. Tracer rounds zipped into the forest, tracked along to muzzle-flashes. No telling if the fire hit anything, but Constantine wasn't willing to bet it had.

Then nothing.

No fire coming in at the convoy. It just stopped. There's been nothing to indicate the counter-fire had been effective. *Why stop?*

Constantine knew the answer was out there, but it wasn't coming to him. Up on the highway vehicle doors opened and closed. Men descended in the dark, stones clacking, branches snapping. He pulled himself to his feet, then called out to his would-be rescuers. "Over here!"

Two men—locals the *Ion Knights* had hired to do some driving—ran over to him. Their expressions said it all. *I have to look like hell.* "The driver's gone."

The larger of the two men looked stricken. "I'm sorry. I couldn't stop soon enough."

"It wasn't the crash that killed him." Constantine blinked, and shook his head. The word 'stop' kept bouncing around in his head. *That's why they stopped!*

Constantine turned and looked up. That's how he spotted the long-range missile salvo as it crested the hill. Slipping into shock as he was, Constantine couldn't count. It was just *many* missiles. They arced up on golden flames, then did a lazy spin and started their descent.

They covered the highway in a torrent of fire that, for a handful of seconds, completely obscuring the *Firestarter* and *Jenner*. The fire's heat washed over Constantine. Blood—his and the driver's—steamed off his jacket. The shockwave battered him back against the stone. He lost his grip and fell.

His companions rolled away like tumbleweeds in a gale.

The firestorm evaporated into a black cloud that lifted slowly like a curtain. Both *Ion Knight* 'Mechs yet stood, but the barrage had devastated them. The *Jenner*'s pilot was fighting to keep the 'Mech upright—clearly the gyro had been damaged. The *Firestarter's* right arm had been entirely stripped of armor and the shoulder joint fused, rendering the flamer and medium laser in that limb all but useless. A pinpoint of light glimmered from within the 'Mech's chest, flashing from a crack in the armor.

Engine hit. The 'Mech would run hot and risk shutting down. Worse yet for both light 'Mechs, another salvo like that and they could both be put out of action permanently.

But no more missiles flew.

As Constantine scrambled back up to the highway, a couple of things made themselves very clear. The missiles had been launched by at least a lance of 'Mechs, and had come down on pre-plotted points. The sniper who killed his driver and the other teams had targeted the vehicles in the convoy to get the convoy to stop. The point 'Mechs had obliged by parking themselves in the open to return the small-arms fire.

Constantine doubted any of the drivers had sold them out, but the same couldn't be said for people in Saint Helene. He'd taken the trucks and a lance down to the coast to hit the pearl farms. They'd made a good haul and loaded it into the trucks. Since there were only two roads in and out of Saint Helene, someone in town merely had to let the enemy know which route they picked.

Very careless of us.

Up on the roadbed, he surveyed the damage. The missiles had reduced the highway to rubble, so there was no going forward in that direction. They'd have to go back to town and up the Intermountain Highway.

And I bet they have something set up there, too.

Constantine flagged down the *Dervish* that had come up from the rearguard. He cupped his hands around his mouth and shouted.

"We're going back to Saint Helene. Round everyone up, and be *damned* careful as we go."

Constantine's caution paid off. The pearls got to Ravensburg and were loaded into the *Dedalus* without further incident. He'd ordered the rest of his first company to come down the highway and clear it before escorting them back home.

Their easy journey was not mirrored elsewhere. In the past two days, patrols had been harassed and incidents against personnel had increased. Constantine studied a glowing holomap with little red stars marking incidents. Half of them could be dismissed as local incidents, like someone resisting the theft of his property, or a drunk taking a dislike to one of the *Knights*.

He looked up at Count Somokis. "There's something going on here. The serious incidents, the ones that are costing us the most, are being run with a high degree of coordination. The local militia wasn't capable of that. The best pilot they had didn't even graduate from the Nagelring. The Saint Helene attack and the raid at Wolverton showed discipline and planning."

The smaller man looked up, smiling, from his noteputer. "Of course it did."

"You seem far too at ease with this, my lord." Constantine shivered, still aching from his broken nose, and still ducking at loud sounds. The count's complacency irritated him no end. *I can't wait until you have another rough ride in a DropShip.*

"I am at ease, my dear Constantine, because I understand the phenomena."

"Do tell."

"I have told. This world has a secret base on it, one with experimental 'Mech technology in the throes of development. What sort of pilots do you imagine they'd use for testing? Raw recruits? Hardly. They've hired the best, which is why we have the rumors of mercenaries like Jamie Wolf and the Archon's cousin being here. Those pilots are the ones staging these raids."

Constantine's eyes narrowed. "And this doesn't concern you?"

"Under normal circumstances, it would." Somokis smiled slowly, then flicked his noteputer off. "Confirmation that they're here is comforting. While we don't have the computing power to decrypt the files that will pinpoint the lab's location, Atreus does. In fact, inside three days they expect to have the file broken, and can send the location to us."

"Really?" Constantine thought for a moment. "And they expect us to crack it open all by ourselves?"

"No, Atreus will be happy to help. They're very desirous of it, in fact." Somokis patted his noteputer. "And as proof of their com-

MICHAEL A. STACKPOLE

mitment, the Sixth Marik Militia Regiment just arrived at the nadir JumpPoint. By the time that file's open, they'll be here to give us all the help we need."

THE TRIAL
DISTRICT OF DONEGAL, THARKAD
LYRAN COMMONWEALTH

The only warning Patrick Kell had for the Archon's imminent arrival at his office was the quick entry and sweep by two very large security agents. One of them nodded at him, the other just ignored him. Patrick quickly saved the file on his computer, then rose and extended his arms out from his sides.

One of them moved to pat him down, but Katrina's voice cut him off. "Don't you dare. If he was ever to be a threat to me, it would be because I was out of control and deserved to die."

Both men bowed their heads and retreated, closing the office door behind them.

Patrick sighed. "How bad is it?"

"Depends upon how you keep score. Morgan is fine, unless you have information to the contrary."

"No. I had another message, sent by Veronica. Upbeat. Apparently they've hurt the raiders, and have slowed them down."

"You'd think the raiders would be wanting to leave, then."

The Archon nodded. "You would, but there's a problem. How soon can the Hounds be there?"

The mercenary glanced at his computer. "We're still four days out, even if we hit a pirate point, and there are none which are terribly convenient at the moment."

"Damn." Katrina clasped her hands behind her neck. "Priority message came in from assets on Atreus. The prep work we've been doing on Zavijava for war games included exercises for intel. The raiders hit the databases and pulled out information that was communicated to Atreus. It suggested we had a research center there that was working on superior targeting systems and advances in myomers—the kind of stuff that would revolutionize 'Mech warfare. Atreus believes it's all true, and have sent the Sixth Marik Militia to secure the site."

Patrick hid his eyes behind a hand. "The Regiment will land, won't want to give the world up, leaving Morgan and Ian down there behind enemy lines. How long until the Militia arrives?"

"They're in-system already."

He looked at her. "How fast can you get me there?"

"Your intervention, Patrick, isn't going to save the day."

"I wasn't planning on traveling alone. The Hounds will already be there. You've got troops here that can tag along with me."

Katrina's eyes hardened. "Realistically, it will take a month to deliver enough troops there to retake the world. I have to move things to threaten Marik, make them shift their forces. I don't want this to break out into a war, but it has that potential."

"Can't you just send a message to Atreus saying 'April Fools?' You know, excepting that it's not April."

"If I thought it would work, I would do it." She shook her head. "If I had the same reports they did, I'd have to act. I'd have no choice. Frankly, the fact that they're only sending *one* regiment points out how precarious the internal political situation is. Atreus is driving this, and Janos Marik is acting outside his political base. If he had this advanced technology, there would be no stopping him consolidating his power. He *has* to go for it."

"This really is a blind, right? There's no such research station?"

The Archon shook her head. "I wish there was. *If* there was, it would be here, or on Arc-Royal; some place I could trust it wouldn't be taken and used against me."

Patrick posted both hands on the desktop and sighed. "Okay, we have to get word to Morgan to let him know what's going on. He and Ian need to get to...What?"

"Here's where it gets bad. The Precentor informed me that there is some problem with the HPG station serving Zavijava. ComStar expects to have it fixed in a week."

He looked up. "Meaning Marik is paying them out the butt to embargo all communications from outside."

"Right. They're not going to see what's coming until too late."

Patrick pounded a fist on the desk. "Dammit."

"You can hit it again for me." Katrina groaned. "A lot of trouble for a clever bit of fiction."

"True enough but, you know..." His eyes widened and a smile blossomed. "That's it!"

"What?"

Patrick grabbed Katrina by the shoulders. "You have to trust me on something, okay? If it works, we're halfway home."

"If what works?"

The mercenary smiled. "You said 'a clever bit of fiction' got us into this problem. I'm going to see if a clever bit of fiction can get us back out again."

CHAPTER 15

The atmosphere in the cavern had changed completely in the last four days. Morgan had served beneath natural leaders before—the Archon being but one of them—but there was something about Ian that made him just that much better. Perhaps it was his lack of distractions in other areas like politics.

Or maybe it's just that he understands war and warriors better than anyone else.

The militia warriors gathered in a semi-circle at his feet. They would have seemed childlike, save for the way they sat. Expectant, yes, but with a wolfish expression. They knew something was coming, and nothing could hide their eagerness.

Ian had played the game very well. As a tactician, he had few equals. His grasp of the effects of terrain on a battle, and willingness to exploit the strengths and weaknesses thereof, was rare in the Inner Sphere. Ian chose missions and assignments to best match his people with circumstance.

Unlike other leaders, he didn't reach for too much. In planning the Saint Helene ambush he'd not split his force and set up on both highways. He picked one and when they got the word that the *Ion Knights* were obliging them, he punished the *Knights*. And while he'd predicted their reaction to the attack, he didn't set up on the Intermountain Highway. That would have been too obvious.

Likewise, he'd not done more than have that one salvo go off. It had done damage. It had delayed the *Ion Knights*. It made them feel vulnerable, and diverted resources to getting their 'Mechs repaired. He hurt them, but not so badly that they retaliated against the civilian population.

His restraint had another effect. The militiamen were hungry for revenge. He'd showed them that the *Ion Knights* were far from invulnerable. He'd put them into positions to strike back at the enemy. He built their confidence and now, he was going to give them the mission that would allow them to redeem their honor.

Ian opened his hands. "Hope you all realize how much we've accomplished so far. We know the places we've hit, and yet stories abound about other places, other raids that are attributed to us. Sure, that's the vaunted 'fog of war' kicking in, but people spreading these stories do so because they are hopeful. That, or they are *Ion Knights* and are afraid. Very afraid."

He turned and pointed to the man standing beside Morgan. "This is a friend of mine, Quintus Allard. He and some of the Commonwealth's finest intelligence operatives have been doing some work here. They were preparing things for an exercise, and discovered that the *Ion Knights* were interested in what they were doing. They fed them a file that suggested some very valuable loot could be found down in the Magma Park District, southwest of here."

A couple of faces brightened.

Ian smiled. "I knew you'd like that, Jensen, and you, Hamish. I'm going to be counting on the two of you to help me work up our plan of attack. We expect them to bring everything they still have. That will put them up on us about one and a half to one, but we'll have the land working for us. But this will be it. This will be the chance to pound them back utterly and completely."

The militiamen cheered, and Ian let them for a few moments, then held up a hand. "But you have to remember, discipline is what's served us well before. Break it, and you'll die. It's as simple as that. Magma Park is merciless. We will be, too."

The prince gave them a solemn nod. "Go, get some sleep. We will have a plan for you in the morning. When they come, we'll be waiting for them."

Laughing and smiling, the militiamen retreated further into the cavern. Ian remained standing there, a smile on his face, nodding at those who turned to look back at him. Once the shadows had swallowed them all, he crossed to Morgan and Quintus.

"What do you think?"

The intelligence operative nodded. "Well done, sire. I do believe they would follow you to the gates of Hell."

The prince grunted. "Magma Park is as close to Hell as I want to get. Steep mountains, heavy rainforest, then broken lava plains that might have active flows beneath them. Hideous place, and yet beautiful, I guess. You were going to take your friend there, weren't you, Morgan?"

"That had been part of the plan. Let's hope there's enough of it left to enjoy." He turned to Quintus. "In positioning this 'facility' inside the dormant crater, you really made it pretty obvious where defenders would be waiting."

"We didn't expect anyone would really be acting on this intel, if you'll recall. As such, however, some details have been fancifully imagined. The place where the crater wall has broken down covers an arc of about a hundred and ten degrees. The lava plains have plenty of breaks for concealment, and the rainforest inside and out around the crater will work for you. As you and the Prince have discussed, the idea is to draw them into the crater, then hammer them as they try to leave."

The mercenary looked over at the prince. "Are we counting on them being too stupid?"

"Too stupid? I don't think any enemy can be *too stupid* for my tastes." Ian shrugged. "They believe there is a force of super-'Mechs in that crater. They're going to have to go in, and in strength. You and I would do an outside sweep. They won't, but they'll still have to use a company to bottle up the opening while they go in. That evens things up for us. We hit and run, and part of their force is still pinned. The only way this whole attack doesn't work is if they refuse to piecemeal their force."

"They *could* do that."

"In which case we use the terrain to break them up, and we shoot them up." Ian clapped the mercenary on the shoulders. "I do appreciate your concern. I don't want to die in that sort of place any more than you do."

Morgan smiled. "I don't want to die *anywhere*."

"Good luck with that." Ian glanced into the shadows where the other warriors were bedding down. "Quintus is right. They'll follow me into Hell. I'm mindful of the responsibility. If it's Hell, it'll be a hell of our making, and one that will roast the *Ion Knights*."

CONRADS
DISTRICT OF DONEGAL, THARKAD
LYRAN COMMONWEALTH

Patrick forced himself to calm down, hoping his heart would stop racing at the pace of the music. He cut through the crowd and across the edge of the dance floor. Pulling back a chair, he seated himself opposite Hippolyta.

"Glad to see you got my message."

She sipped a drink in a sweating glass. "I was intrigued. You said you had a story to tell me. Is it as good as the last one?"

He arched an eyebrow.

"The one about your brother. He's not on Arc-Royal."

"Plans changed."

"Imagine that." Her tone matched her eyes: cold.

"He's on Zavijava." Patrick waited for her to react. *Not even a flicker.* "But you knew that."

"Did I?"

He leaned forward. "I have to assume one of two things. Either you truly don't know, or you think I'm stupid enough to believe you don't know. Either one works here. You have operatives on Zavijava who have uncovered the location of a secret research center. In it, according to seized documents, the Lyran Commonwealth has not only succeeded in rediscovering much of the *lostech* which has been lost down through the years; but we have improved on it. In fact, we've created a class of *uberMech*, stronger, faster, able to hit at extreme range. They can best anything the rest of the Inner Sphere could throw at them; and your agents have already suffered at their hands."

Hippolyta sipped her drink again. "Fascinating."

"Here's the interesting part. Your agents alerted Atreus. Atreus has sent the Sixth Marik Militia to secure the prize. There's one problem."

She nodded. "A big one. Zavijava will be lost."

Patrick snorted. "The problem is that the research facility doesn't exist."

"And I should believe you when you've already lied to me?" She rose. "I think I've heard this story before."

He grabbed her wrist and held on tight. "I've not started telling you the story. Sit down."

She covered her moment of indecision well, then sat.

"Listen carefully. You're going to have a big decision to make." Patrick released her and lowered his voice. "So, here's my story. Once upon a time there was a mercenary who loved his brother very much..."

MAGMA PARK
MAGMA PARK DISTRICT, ZAVIJAVA

The weather had turned nasty. A storm came in off the coast, bringing high winds and torrential rains that moved swiftly from the coast all the way up to Ellington. Despite making travel painful, two days of drenching rain helped the militia. The *Ion Knights* moved very slowly into the area since they did not know it well, whereas the militia was able to get to its positions quickly under cover of horrible weather.

The morning before the *Ion Knights* were supposed to arrive, the weather began tapering off. Even before the sun burned off the clouds, Morgan got a good dose of the park's beauty. The rain gathered into magnificent waterfalls that plunged for hundreds of meters into azure pools. Cataracts flowed, and out toward the ocean steam rose where magma leaked from subsurface vents. Birds took off in brilliantly—colored flocks, flashing green and red plumage.

Fearless, some of them even roosted on his 'Mech.

Morgan had picked up a *Whitworth*. Its long-range missile launchers could pack a punch at range, and the trio of medium lasers would do for a closer fight. While he favored fighting in something heavier, the *Whitworth* had a fair amount of armor. It wouldn't be one of the first 'Mechs down in the fight.

He'd been put in command of a reinforced lance, and had it arrayed in a two-one-two formation. At the far end, but still under the cover of his missiles, he'd positioned a pair of *Javelins*. The squat 'Mech featured two short-range missile launchers built into the chest, and jump jets. The pilots knew their roles well. They'd pop up, fire a salvo, then pull back.

The unit's *UrbanMech* took up the central position. It had a heavy autocannon that packed a punch at close range. Because the terrain didn't encourage long-range engagements, the *UrbanMech* suddenly became formidable. Equipped with jump jets, it had the sort of mobility that would promote longevity.

The last 'Mech had to be the strangest Morgan had ever encountered, or the rarest anyway. The *Thorn* was an antique, dating back to Star League days. Instead of a right arm, it had square long range missile launcher. A pair of medium lasers completed its armament, making it a *Whitworth* in miniature. It remained back with Morgan, positioned to strike at any 'Mech trying to close with their forward element.

His communications monitor lit up. To reduce the chances of discovery, they'd laid wire between the command 'Mechs. All other messages would be tight-beamed with an ultraviolet laser between 'Mechs.

Morgan punched the communications button. "Alpha One."

Ian's voice betrayed no excitement. "Delta reports movement. Infantry screen. It's going right to the entrance."

"No sweep?" A shiver ran down Morgan's spine. "Something doesn't feel right."

"There's a reason greed is a deadly sin."

Morgan punched magnification up on his holographic display. 'Mechs came into view, working south and west toward the crater opening. The militia waited further south, in a perfect position to launch on the *Ion Knights*. "I have visuals on 'Mechs. They're going for it."

"Setting up a screen."

"Only a lance."

Ian chuckled. "Let's doom that lance. Good luck, Morgan. Launch on my signal."

"Same to you, Highness. Alpha One out."

Morgan shifted his shoulders, then beamed an alert to his lance. It included targeting information for the screening lance. He assigned the *Javelins* and *UrbanMech* to hitting the *Jenner* closest to them. He fixed on the *Blackjack* and had the *Thorn* target it as well. Ian's lance would hit the *Clint* and *Hermes II*. Rosen's lance would pick up anything left over.

Ian growled through the radio. "Hit it *now!*"

Having had time to set up gave the militia a great advantage for that first strike. All but two of Morgan's missiles found their target. They pulverized armor over both legs and the left arm. Five of them slammed into the *Blackjack*'s head. Armor shards spun away. Morgan followed the missiles with a single laser shot. The ruby red beam hit the *Blackjack's* head as well, boiling off the last of the armor. Sparks flew.

The *Thorn's* assault pumped five missiles into the left flank, ruining the pristine armor there. Medium lasers slashed more off the *Blackjack's* left arm and right leg, burning through the purple and silver paint.

Cheers spiked through Alpha Lance's tactical frequency. The *UrbanMech's* heavy autocannon sent a stream of shells straight into the *Jenner's* right arm. The projectiles blew entirely through the armor and ripped the stubby-wing clean off. The medium lasers in it exploded as the wing bounced back into the crater.

The *Javelins* followed up with missile barrages that peppered the light 'Mech. Several passed through the smoking hole where the arm had been, exploding inside its right flank. A secondary blast twisted the *Jenner* around, dumping it to the ground. Obsidian shards combined with ferro-ceramic armor as the 'Mech went down.

Victorious yelps filled Alpha lance's tactical frequency.

Morgan keyed his radio. "You cheer when the fight's *over*. That going to be a lot more shooting from now."

Ian's lance drilled the *Hermes II*, shearing the left leg off. The 'Mech pitched back, crashing down on the *Jenner's* legs. The *Clint*, armor in tatters and left arm hanging by myomer fibers alone, staggered back to the crater entrance, leaving the *Blackjack* there as the lone sentinel.

"Push to forward positions." Ian's command boomed through the NeuroHelmet's speakers. "Bottle 'em up."

Moving with precision, the lances advanced. They'd picked their defensive positions, making the best use of cover available. Rosen's lance struck, finishing the *Blackjack*. Morgan splashed missiles over the *Clint*, but it still managed to withdraw by the time Alpha lance reached its assigned position.

Alpha held the right flank. Morgan would have preferred to anchor against the ocean, but the drive to turn his flank would leave the *Ion Knights* open to a pounding before they ever got there. Ian's lance held the middle, and Rosen moved down to the left flank. Ian's position was the most tenuous, but enfilading fire from Rosen's lance would make a direct assault very costly.

Morgan reached his forward position without opposition, and his stomach tightened. *Unless they're going to surrender, there's no way...*

A blip appeared on his auxiliary monitor. Morgan turned his head, focusing on part of the holographic display showing the *Whitworth's* rear arc.

Oh, God. No wonder they don't fear being trapped.

Three *Overlord* Class DropShips, each capable of holding thirty-six BattleMechs, hovered just off the coast. They bore the insignia of the Free Worlds League's Sixth Marik Militia. As they maneuvered into position behind the militia, their drop bay doors opened.

CHAPTER 16

"Beta lead..."

"I see them, Alpha." Ian's voice shrank. "I guess we have no choice but to—"

Whatever Ian Davion had intended to say was cut off as the *Ion Knights* came boiling back out the crater. Two lances of light 'Mechs—apparently operating on intelligence broadcast from the DropShips—sprinted out and wheeled south, driving at Rosen's lance. A third mixed lance broke straight east, using a small cut for cover, securing the northern flank.

That left two lances of medium 'Mechs to hold the crater's entrance. Morgan's heart sank. *Whitworths, Centurions, Trebuchets, and a Dervish—all missile-boats. Outnumbered, outgunned, and trapped, and they're not offering any quarter.*

Morgan keyed his radio. "Give them everything. Move as you can. Take the lights, first."

The Kell Hound shifted his crosshairs onto the outline of a sprinting *Commando.* Missiles arced out, tearing into the armor on the left and right flanks, utterly denuding the left side of the 'Mech's chest. A secondary explosion within the *Commando's* chest marked the destruction of a heat sink. All three of his medium lasers hit as well, ablating armor on both legs and pouring through the hole in the left flank. That beam carved its way through the internal structures. The shoulder joint, lacking any support, collapsed, letting the left arm sail past the stricken 'Mech.

More importantly, the cumulative loss of armor and arm grossly shifted the 'Mech's weight. It began twisting to the left, then a foot hit a small shelf, chipping stone and armor. The *Commando's* pilot lost control. The 'Mech sprawled forward, sparks flying, as the hardened lava ground more armor off.

Heat spiked in the *Whitworth*'s cockpit, rising dangerously. Another full salvo like that and Morgan risked his 'Mech overheating and shutting down. It really didn't matter, given their situation. *Once the Marik Militia drops, we're done.*

He had a moment to wonder why they hadn't dropped yet, and why the DropShips hadn't opened up on them. Before he could come up with a reason, *Ion Knight* missile fire slammed into the *Whitworth*. LRMs blasted armor from the chest and right arm. A flight of five slammed into the 'Mech's head, tearing into the armor there, too.

The blasts rattled Morgan around, jamming his head back against the command couch. Alarms sounded, but he punched buttons, cutting them off. Blood dripped from his nose, but he just licked it away.

The rest of his lance acquitted itself well. The *UrbanMech* tracked autocannon fire up a *Panther*'s right leg. The *Thorn* likewise hit it, driving missiles and a laser into the chest, and used another laser to slash armor from the left flank. Morgan's *Javelins*, despite taking fire themselves, peppered an *Ion Knight Javelin*. They sanded armor and paint off all over the sprinting 'Mech, failing to breach it anywhere, but the concentrated fire—including a missile that dented armor over the cockpit—unsettled the pilot. The *Javelin* went down, skidding to a stop against the *Commando*.

Zavijavan militia fire ripped through the charging light 'Mech lances. What was left of them engaged Rosen's lance in a straight-up fight. Morgan's and Ian's lances turned their attention to the medium-weight 'Mechs emerging from the crater. While the *Ion Knights* sacrificed cover by moving forward, the sheer weight of their 'Mechs and the thickness of their armor made the fight more than even.

A *Centurion* nailed the *Thorn*. One burst from the heavy autocannon tore the small 'Mech's right arm off. The *Ion Knight* pumped kilojoules of energy into the *Thorn*'s chest, melting over half the armor protecting the engine. The *Thorn* shot back, hitting the *Centurion* dead center in return; but the damage didn't even slow the larger 'Mech down.

Missiles battered the *Javelins*. Armor flew from their chests and legs. One barrage caught Alpha Three in the head. The 'Mech staggered and stayed upright. When they returned fire, they targeted the *Centurion*, scattering missiles all over it. Fire blossomed from twenty different points, filling the air with ferro-ceramic armor dust.

The *UrbanMech* directed its fire onto the *Centurion*. The autocannon's shells chewed into the armor over its left arm, savaging it, but failing to breach it.

Another *Ion Knight Centurion* targeted the *UrbanMech*. Missiles corkscrewed in, pockmarking armor over both legs. Its heavy autocannon gnawed every scrap of armor from the smaller 'Mech's left arm. The medium laser raked over the cockpit, sending half the armor oozing down in a molten mass. The punishing assault sent the 'Mech reeling back, where it crashed down into the cut that had failed to protect it.

Morgan fired back at the first *Centurion*. His long-range missiles rippled fire over the 'Mech's chest and left leg. The explosions sliced the last bit of armor off the 'Mech's chest. Shrapnel ricocheted within, damaging the magnetic containment bubble on the fusion reaction. It held, but heat blossomed on Morgan's secondary monitor. The laser trio likewise hit, melting armor on the chest, right leg and left arm. Part of the unspent energy cooked some of the myomer fibers in that arm, but left it functional.

Still, the battering that 'Mech had taken proved too much for the pilot. The *Centurion* pitched forward, hitting on its knees before smashing face down on the ground. Armor snapped, pieces of it dancing across the hardened lava.

A torrent of heat rippled up through Morgan's cockpit, and warning alarms pulsed in his ears. The raiders scattered missiles over his 'Mech, giving him no time to take any joy in dropping the *Centurion*. The 'Mech was hardly out of the fight, and the other medium 'Mechs had taken virtually no damage. His lance would be a memory after the next exchange, leaving him, Prince Ian, and what was left Rosen's lance.

And that won't be for long. Morgan glanced at the hovering DropShips. *They're not deploying because they don't need to.*

As Morgan shifted his aim-point and waited for heat to drain, he began to mumble a prayer to St. Jude. *If ever there was a lost hope...* People said there were no atheists in fox holes. Morgan didn't know if that was true, but he was certain all soldiers were open to a miracle or two.

He laughed. "No need to be greedy. I'll settle for one."

And he got it.

An *Ion Knight Trebuchet* moved out from the crater mouth. The humanoid 'Mech had two fifteen-pack missile launchers—one in its right breast and the second on its right forearm. A trio of medium lasers completed its armament, with two replacing the right forearm, and the last grafted onto the left-arm missile pod. It outmassed the *Whitworth*, and all the extra tonnage had gone into weaponry. Battle hadn't touched it yet, save where missile salvoes had blackened the launch-tubes.

As it turned to face south, fire lanced into it from the jungle to the north. A steady stream of shells from an extra-heavy autocannon zipped through the armor on its right flank. Shells careened around, shredding internal structures. What few remained intact evaporated seconds later as one of two medium lasers beams vented its scarlet fury. The right side of the 'Mech's body collapsed. The right arm dropped off, bounced once, then flopped over. The *Trebuchet*, spun around by the force of the assault, tripped over its own severed limb and went down.

A couple of missile salvos reached out from the same verdant depths, pounding the light lance securing that northern flank. A *Panther* went down while the other 'Mechs spun. They returned fire, scattering it all over the jungle with no discernable effect.

One of the *Ion Knight's* medium lances—the one the doomed *Trebuchet* had belonged to—turned north to cover that flank, leaving a trio of *Whitworths* and the downed *Centurion* to handle the Zavijavan militia.

Eric Rosen's *Catapult* pummeled one of the *Whitworths*. Missiles worried its virgin armor, all but stripping the right arm and scouring armor over the legs and chest. The militiaman only used three of his four lasers, lancing the ruby beams into the blocky *Ion Knight* 'Mech. They vaporized armor over its left arm, right leg, and heart. Despite the pounding, however, the pilot kept his 'Mech upright.

Prince Ian's *Enforcer* hit the second *Whitworth*. The autocannon's fire shattered armor, all but denuding the 'Mech's left thigh. The large laser's green beam burned a black scar the length of the 'Mech's left arm. Though neither assault breached armor, they left those limbs vulnerable, so the *Whitworth* pilot turned to hide the damage.

Morgan, his 'Mech running very hot, just launched two missile flights at the third *Whitworth*. His missiles scraped armor from both flanks and the left shoulder. Morgan braced himself for a return strike, but the *Whitworth* pilot—either thinking tactically or greedily seeking kills—targeted the *UrbanMech*, which had just come upright again.

The *Whitworth's* missiles scoured more armor off the smaller 'Mech. One of the two lasers toasted armor on the *Urban's* right leg, but the other did the most damage. The coruscating beam pierced the 'Mech's left breast, bursting both heat sinks.

Somehow the *UrbanMech's* pilot kept his machine upright and even returned fire. The autocannon tracked fire up the larger 'Mech's right arm, nearly stripping it of armor.

The *Thorn* also hit the *Whitworth*. Its twin lasers burned armor off the 'Mech legs before the rising *Centurion* hit it dead center with an autocannon blast that opened a huge hole and snuffed the fusion engine. The *Thorn* pitched back, its chest a smoking ruin, and lay still.

The *Javelins* targeted the *Centurion* and, in doing so, won Morgan's respect for the 'Mechs and their pilots. The cloud of short-range missiles struck all over, chipping armor in some places and penetrating deep into the 'Mech in others. The *Centurion* had already been running hot because of damage to the fusion reactor's containment shield. Two more missiles completed the job.

The *Centurion*, upright and recoiling slightly from having destroyed the *Thorn*, suddenly danced back as fire vomited from its chest. The fusion reactor shut down after the nova-like burst of light, then the 'Mech just flopped back. It hit the ground hard enough that the shoulders and head snapped off and skidded away from the rest of the smoking body.

Prince Ian growled through the radio. "If the damned Marik Militia is going to come, they're going to come now."

"Give me two more lances of *Javelins* and we'll take them." Morgan glanced at his holographic display. "Wait a minute. Beta Lead, look at the DropShips."

"What? Oh my God. I don't believe it."

Neither could Morgan.

The DropShips had closed their drop bay doors.

Ian's hearty laugh echoed through the NeuroHelmet. "One last push. Hit them hard!"

The third *Whitworth* pounded the *UrbanMech* again, finally severing the right leg. The smaller 'Mech went down for good, but not before drilling the *Whitworth* with one more shot from the autocannon. The depleted uranium shells devoured the last of the armor over its left arm, then mangled the elbow joint, fusing it.

Morgan slipped his crosshairs over the *Whitworth* and launched two missile salvoes. They hit each arm, blowing the left one clean off. The missiles scoured the right, finishing the last of the armor, then crushed the shoulder and elbow, leaving the limb twisted and useless.

Ian again targeted the second *Whitworth*. The heavy autocannon sawed into the armor on the right flank, but it was the large laser's green beam that did the worst damage. The remaining shreds of armor disappeared beneath its hellish touch, then the 'Mech's forearm came off at the elbow.

Over on the far side, a blocky *Hunchback* silhouette moved within the jungle. The extra-heavy autocannon mounted on its shoulder fired, stabbing a lethal cluster of shells into a *Centurion*'s left flank. The metal storm blew through the armor and hit the long-range missile launcher's magazine.

In the blink of an eye, the humanoid 'Mech disintegrated. Fire flashed out hot and red, bisecting it at the waist. The explosion expanded up and out, devouring the warm machine, spitting out bits and pieces. Shrapnel—none of the fragments recognizable—bounded over the landscape. Those that reached the ocean made the water boil.

"Poor bastard."

That blast, which rocked the nearby *Ion Knights*, completed the raiders' demoralization. In the course of a half hour they'd been ambushed, rescued, ambushed again, abandoned, and then the *Centurion* vanished in a ball of fire.

The communications console lit up immediately. Morgan punched up an emergency frequency. "—surrender, we surrender. We give up."

Morgan smiled. "Your call, Beta Lead."

Another voice cut in on the frequency. "I believe it is *my* call."

Across the way, the *Hunchback* stepped clear of cover, with two *Javelins* trailing behind it. "In the name of the Zavijavan Militia I, Colonel Wittenberg, accept your surrender. Power down your weapons, or you will be destroyed."

CHAPTER 17

Morgan wasn't sure which surprised him more: the departure of the Sixth Marik Militia, or the timely arrival of Chauncy Wittenberg. He was certainly more thankful that the Marik Militia had taken off, but not by as large a margin as he might have expected. The fighting had been close, and without Wittenberg's intervention, the *Ion Knights* would have swept them from the battlefield.

When Morgan commented on that to Prince Ian, the older man disagreed. He sat back on the foot of his *Enforcer,* his cooling vest open. "You forget, Morgan, that we only held our positions here because we *couldn't* run from the Sixth. They became an anvil, and the *Ion Knights* the hammer. Had the Sixth not been here, the *Knights* wouldn't have been so bold, and we would have maneuvered ourselves out of trouble."

"But they *were* here." Morgan shook his head. "I've heard it said that the best warriors are those who never have to fire a shot."

"That's not the lesson to take from here." The Prince's expression became earnest. "We both fought one way because we perceived ourselves as trapped. We should have fought in the wise way. If the Sixth had deployed, we would have been trapped no matter what. We denied ourselves options, and that's not a mistake I want ever to make again."

"Agreed." Morgan glanced over at where Cat and the surviving militia members had the *Ion Knights* rounded up and sitting on the ground. Of the fifteen people in the local force, over half had been shot out of their 'Mechs, and three had died. The *Ion Knights* 'Mechs— those captured and the salvage for the rest of them—would allow the militia to come back up to strength fairly quickly. *And provide lots of work for Simpson.*

Ian nodded at Wittenberg, who was standing deep in conversation with Leutnant Rosen. "Your friend and his lance must have been responsible for some of the stories of our activities in those places where we weren't."

"Most likely." Morgan rubbed a hand over his unshaven chin. "I wonder if he came down here knowing we were here, or if it was some sort of suicidal mission that changed when he heard the fighting?"

"Does it matter?"

"I guess not." Morgan straightened up as Chauncy came walking over. "Thank you, again, Colonel, for rescuing us."

The man nodded hesitantly. "And I must thank you for saving all of us."

Morgan frowned. "How?"

Wittenberg held up a communicator. "It seems your Kell Hounds arrived in system an hour and a half ago. They broadcast wide-spectrum messages making veiled threats. The Militia took them seriously and pulled out."

Ian's head came up. "It sounds as if you resent the Kell Hounds saving you."

"I don't need Morgan Kell's help. I never have."

The prince stood, towering over the militia officer. "You have a choice, Colonel. One is to realize that we were all very close to dying out here. Your intervention bought us time, but it was running out fast. A peculiar set of circumstances let us win. Accept that and be happy. Otherwise, your choice is to deny yourself a piece of this victory. The Kell Hounds being out there might have scared the Marik Militia off, but we weren't fighting them. If they *had* landed, a dozen mercenary regiments couldn't have saved us. So, don't be bitter about not having to fight a battle we couldn't have won, whatever the reason."

"With all due respect—" Chauncy began, his nose wrinkling as if Ian was lower than gutter mud, "—you really have no idea what you're talking about."

Ian stared at him, then laughed. "You think that, do you?"

Chauncy snorted. "Oh, I've been told who you *said* you are, but I don't believe it. I'm glad it worked as a trick to bring troops together, but I'm not some farmboy to be bedazzled by a title, legitimate or fraudulent."

Morgan shook his head. "'Better to reign in Hell than to serve a day in Heaven?'"

Chauncey's eyes tightened. "Death before dishonor."

"Then how lucky it is for you, Chauncy, that I gave you this chance at honor." Morgan pointed at the surviving militiamen. "They're going to remember that you saved us. Do yourself a favor. Don't spoil it. "

Chauncy glared at him, then spun on his heel and walked away.

The prince shook his head. "Hatred like that will kill him."

"It's not me he hates. It's himself." Morgan shrugged. "Let us just hope that hatred doesn't get anyone else killed."

ARCHON'S PARK, THARKAD CITY
DISTRICT OF DONEGAL, THARKAD
LYRAN COMMONWEALTH

Patrick Kell nodded as Hippolyta Marik cut across a snowy field toward him. She had the hood of her purple quilted parka up, and the tan fur framed her face perfectly. She hid her hands in a matching muff. The cold had given her some color in her cheeks.

"Thank you, and thank you."

She raised an eyebrow. "For?"

"Agreeing to meet, and doing what you did."

"Ah. So you know."

He nodded. "ComStar managed to repair their HyperPulse generator. I got a message from the Hounds that suggested they'd be passing the Sixth Marik Militia coming out as they were going in."

"The Sixth didn't mention your unit in their message."

"Not a surprise."

She pulled a hand from the muff and flipped him a small op-dat disk. "Holo of the battle against the *Ion Knights*. We think your brother is in a *Whitworth*. They fought very well."

Patrick tucked the disk away. "Thanks. Seems the cover story is that the *Ion Knights* were a bunch of actors looking to steal commodities and make a killing in the League with them. Am I expected to believe that, or is Atreus just disavowing all knowledge of the operation?"

"Think of them as self-funding mercenaries."

"You mean pirates."

"That's so harsh." She smiled. "They did have one DropShip get off-world with loot. It will come back with the Sixth. Their agents will be arrested and returned to Zavijava."

"The loot?"

Hippolyta smile broadened. "I suspect they'll dump it to avoid prosecution."

"Uh huh." Patrick shook his head, but thought it was a good dodge. *I'll have to remember that.* "I'm sure anything that is recovered will be enjoyed."

"Well above my pay grade."

"Mine as well." He smiled. "Thank you for your help in all this. Perhaps I'll see you out dancing some night."

"Perhaps. If you answer two questions for me."

"If I can."

"You weren't lying. That research base doesn't exist, correct?"

"God as my witness."

"Good. If it ever was revealed, they'd kill me, you know."

"And your other question?"

Her voice became tiny. "Would you really have done what you threatened to do?"

"Absolutely." Patrick sighed a cloud of steam. "Atreus would have killed my brother. You already told me Atreus is afraid mercenaries could tip the balance in the League. The Hounds never would have landed on Zavijava. We'd just have jumped straight into League space and picked a world, *any* world. We would have hit it, hit it hard, and moved on. Dissident League forces would have fed us and armed us, given us intel, and we would have used it all. I'd have even hired more mercenaries to follow in our wake, wreaking more havoc."

She looked at him, her eyes widened. "But you've claimed you're against war."

"We are. If your forces had decided to fight despite knowing the truth, it would have been because your leadership was willing to gamble with lives. Anyone in that position needs to be removed." He nodded solemnly. "We would have done that."

"But billions could have died." She shook her head. "That would have been insane."

"Maybe Morgan is the brake on my insanity." He gave her a smile he hoped would chill her more than the winter wind. "Let's resolve, in the future, not to test that proposition."

TYROL HOUSE HOTEL, RAVENSBURG
CENTRAL RIVER DISTRICT, ZAVIJAVA
CHRISTMAS EVE, 3010

Morgan Kell came through the hotel's door and strode straight across to the reception desk. His boots clicked on the white marble.

A small woman looked up and smiled. "May I help you, sir?"

"I'm Colonel Kell."

The woman's eyes brightened. "Oh, yes, sir." She handed him a card key, then held up a hand. She retreated to the office, then returned with a shopping bag containing three gaily wrapped packages. "These got here just an hour ago, and Mrs. Kell just had dinner delivered to the room, the Archon's suite. Lifts are right over there."

Morgan took the bag, and saluted her with the card. He couldn't help but smile, and caught a glimpse of himself in the lobby's mirror wall. He looked happy, and felt happy.

He'd called Veronica as quickly as he could to let her know he had survived. The relief in her voice had gushed through the communicator. Then she matter-of-factly reported the messages she'd sent to Patrick. He'd let her talk, let her show him she'd been doing things, too; not because he needed to hear that, but because she needed to say it.

The maglev took four hours from the Magma Park terminal to Ravensburg. Morgan had used his communicator to speak with a shopper for a large department store and had purchased the presents in the bag. He knew, in general, what they were, but would be as surprised as she was. Then he called her from the station, to let her know he was on his way.

While on campaign, he'd purposely tried to put Veronica out of his mind, but had not been wholly successful. She invaded his dreams in most delicious ways. Even while he was waiting in Magma Park he looked at the birds and orchids nestled in trees, then thought of what she would make of them. More importantly, he *needed* to know what she thought of them. He wanted to share experiences like that with her.

I want to share everything with her.

The simplicity of that statement, and the complexity of its implications, struck him. He had started his career with one plan, and that had gotten him through the Nagelring. Then the time with Katrina and Arthur had changed all that. He'd tried to return to it, but it didn't fit. Arthur's unfortunate death had provided him the means to pursue a different course.

Never before had he considered taking a wife and having a family. He had, of course, thought of it some when younger. And when dating, he'd always wondered if she was *the one*. While he had searched, no one ever was, and he had come to doubt that there was a *one*.

But now...

The lift whisked him to the penthouse. It opened onto a small lobby with ornate double-doors, all blond wood and gold-leaf trim. The lock clicked and he stepped into the foyer, pausing at the top of three steps that led down into the suite. There, to the left, the table had been set. Candles burned, steam rose from dinners, and bubbles gently rose in flutes of champagne. And then to the right, a large box, wrapped with bright paper and bound with a big bow, sat on the couch.

But of Veronica Matova, there was no trace.

LOOKING FOR MORE HARD HITTING BATTLETECH FICTION?

WE'LL GET YOU RIGHT BACK INTO THE BATTLE!

Catalyst Game Labs brings you the very best in *BattleTech* fiction, available at most ebook retailers, including Amazon, Apple Books, Kobo, Barnes & Noble, and more!

NOVELS

1. *Decision at Thunder Rift* by William H. Keith Jr.
2. *Mercenary's Star* by William H. Keith Jr.
3. *The Price of Glory* by William H. Keith, Jr.
4. *Warrior: En Garde* by Michael A. Stackpole ✓
5. *Warrior: Riposte* by Michael A. Stackpole ✓
6. *Warrior: Coupé* by Michael A. Stackpole ✓
7. Wolves on the Border by Robert N. Charrette
8. *Heir to the Dragon* by Robert N. Charrette
9. *Lethal Heritage* (The Blood of Kerensky, Volume 1) by Michael A. Stackpole
10. *Blood Legacy* (The Blood of Kerensky, Volume 2) by Michael A. Stackpole
11. *Lost Destiny* (The Blood of Kerensky, Volume 3) by Michael A. Stackpole
12. *Way of the Clans* (Legend of the Jade Phoenix, Volume 1) by Robert Thurston
13. *Bloodname* (Legend of the Jade Phoenix, Volume 2) by Robert Thurston
14. *Falcon Guard* (Legend of the Jade Phoenix, Volume 3) by Robert Thurston
15. *Wolf Pack* by Robert N. Charrette
16. *Main Event* by James D. Long
17. *Natural Selection* by Michael A. Stackpole
18. *Assumption of Risk* by Michael A. Stackpole
19. *Blood of Heroes* by Andrew Keith
20. *Close Quarters* by Victor Milán
21. *Far Country* by Peter L. Rice
22. *D.R.T.* by James D. Long
23. *Tactics of Duty* by William H. Keith
24. *Bred for War* by Michael A. Stackpole
25. *I Am Jade Falcon* by Robert Thurston
26. *Highlander Gambit* by Blaine Lee Pardoe
27. *Hearts of Chaos* by Victor Milán
28. *Operation Excalibur* by William H. Keith

NOVELLAS

1. *A Splinter of Hope* by Philip A. Lee
2. *The Anvil* by Blaine Lee Pardoe
3. *Not the Way the Smart Money Bets* (Kell Hounds Ascendant 1)
   by Michael A. Stackpole
4. *A Tiny Spot of Rebellion* (Kell Hounds Ascendant 2) by Michael A. Stackpole
5. *A Clever Bit of Fiction* (Kell Hounds Ascendant 3) by Michael A. Stackpole

ANTHOLOGIES

1. *Shrapnel: Fragments from the Inner Sphere*
2. *Onslaught: Tales from the Clan Invasion!*
3. *The Corps* (BattleCorps Anthology vol. 1)
4. *First Strike* (BattleCorps Anthology vol. 2)
5. *Weapons Free* (BattleCorps Anthology vol. 3)
6. *Fire for Effect* (BattleCorps Anthology vol. 4)
7. *Counterattack* (BattleCorps Anthology vol. 5)
8. *Front Lines* (BattleCorps Anthology vol. 6)
9. *BattleTech: Legacy*

BattleTech fiction is back. 50 titles available now in popular ePub formats. Immerse yourself in exciting action, intrigue, and drama. Visit the Catalyst Game Labs store to download your next adventure!

STORE.CATALYSTGAMELABS.COM

Made in United States
Orlando, FL
14 November 2022

24519305R00176